# THE LAST TIME I SAW HER

*a novel*

## ALEXANDRA HARRINGTON

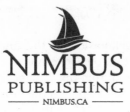

### NIMBUS
PUBLISHING
— NIMBUS.CA —

Nimbus Publishing Limited
3660 Strawberry Hill St, Halifax, NS, B3K 5A9
(902) 455-4286 nimbus.ca

Printed and bound in Canada

NB1476

*This story is a work of fiction. Names characters, incidents, and places, including organizations and institutions, either are the product of the author's imagination or are used fictitiously.*

Cover Design: Heather Bryan
Interior Design: Jenn Embree
Editor: Emily MacKinnon

Library and Archives Canada Cataloguing in Publication

Title: The last time I saw her : a novel / Alexandra Harrington.
Names: Harrington, Alexandra, 1995- author.
Identifiers: Canadiana (print) 20200386654 | Canadiana (ebook) 20200386700 | ISBN 9781771089364 (softcover) | ISBN 9781771089876 (EPUB)
Classification: LCC PS8615.A74715 L37 2021 | DDC jC813/.6—dc23

Nimbus Publishing acknowledges the financial support for its publishing activities from the Government of Canada, the Canada Council for the Arts, and from the Province of Nova Scotia. We are pleased to work in partnership with the Province of Nova Scotia to develop and promote our creative industries for the benefit of all Nova Scotians.

# one

IT WAS HOT FOR JUNE. *Well, July,* Charlotte corrected herself, the word rolling out of her head slow and thick. June had burned itself out quietly, almost like smoke slipping away, and she'd been occupied with things other than the days of the week. Charlotte went mostly by the numbers. Prom was six days ago; graduation, four. Everyone had to be completely moved out of housing as of one day ago.

Charlotte pressed the heel of her hand to the top of her cheekbone, trying to wipe away a streak of sweat without smudging whatever pitiful bits were left of her makeup. Here, the summer air usually pulled back and forth the same way the tide did. Living beside the sea usually meant a crisp, salty breeze that shimmered between layers of sunshine. But tonight it was humid and the air was heavy—honey instead of salt. *Fitting,* Charlotte thought. Today was Sophie Thompson's eighteenth birthday.

It was hot for July. She was home, but Charlotte Romer was scared. She figured her fear leaned more toward dread, probably, if she were thinking straight and had the time to sort her feelings into boxes. Dread usually popped up when you were waiting for it. Dread was when you knew you deserved it.

She pulled herself up the narrow walkway of the Thompsons' bungalow for what was probably the millionth time in her life. Mornings before school, sunny Saturday afternoons, sneaking back under blooming darkness three minutes short of curfew: it was a familiar path. But this was the first time Charlotte felt like she shouldn't be there.

Charlotte stopped at the steps of the porch, her suitcase bumping her behind the knees like it was trying to be encouraging. *Pull yourself together.* Charlotte looked at the house and prayed Sophie wasn't home.

Charlotte knew, though, that this was highly unlikely, considering she'd been able to hear the party sounds from halfway down the road. She flicked her phone awake. It was late. She'd missed the earlier bus, and the only other one to the North Shore had been running late. So not only was Charlotte Romer crashing Sophie Thompson's birthday party, she was also way more than fashionably behind schedule.

River John buzzed around her, like it always did. A combination of lazy summer bugs, the easy swell of an ocean that was never too far, and the worn-out power lines overhead. It was a familiar heartbeat, and she had missed it. Looking back down the road, she saw the tail lights from the bus had long since disappeared.

No retreat. Surrender only.

Charlotte steadied herself and pulled her suitcase up the steps behind her. *Get it over with.* She tucked her luggage in a corner of the porch beside a dilapidated green swing and smoothed down the front of her wrinkled dress. Her frenzied quick-change in the tiny bus bathroom had left her looking a bit dishevelled. She had forced herself into the bathroom and into her dress, knowing if she went home first to change, she'd never gather the courage to leave again. Ever.

*Deep breaths.*

Like an omen—she wasn't sure whether good or bad—the window to the right of the front door flew open. Charlotte's knowledge of the bungalow's floor plan told her it was the bathroom window. Robert Ross, of North Colchester High basketball fame, stuck his head out of the opening and promptly vomited into the flowerbed. There was a chorus of groans from the bathroom and Robert was dragged back inside.

If Charlotte had been waiting for a sign, she figured this was probably it. She pushed open the unlocked door and stepped inside, feeling the familiar surroundings shudder into place. A year ago she would have been one of the vital, working parts of Sophie's birthday party, but she'd been there for thirty seconds and already felt like she'd triggered a burglar alarm. Charlotte immediately decided that showing up here uninvited was probably one of her worst ideas this year. Certainly in the top three. Unexpectedly leaving town without a word to anyone was definitely up there, too. Followed closely by turning up again now, a year later.

Dave Mackenzie, from her eleventh grade history class, was the first to spot her. Charlotte could feel the heat creeping up her neck. Without taking his eyes off her, Dave Mackenzie inched sideways and jabbed at Mitchell MacKenzie (no relation: capital K MacKenzie), who was playing DJ. All the kids in River John pretty much grew up together, because families didn't really move to the North Shore of Nova Scotia from anywhere else; they just grew there from the start. (The tiny town was generational and the longer your last name had been kicking around, the better.) Mitchell MacKenzie yanked the AUX cord out of his iPhone and looked around.

The party came to a crashing halt as the music stopped. The two teams playing beer pong out back on the patio stopped mid-chug. A group of girls in the kitchen looked annoyed at being disrupted; their heads swivelled like tiny owls, trying to source the interruption. A cluster of guys near the back door exchanged uneasy looks, checking their phones for the time. In River John, parties were only ever interrupted by the sheriff's department when they raged too late into the night. But then people started looking at Charlotte and the feeling in the room shifted to something else completely.

Theories came tumbling out right away—that Charlotte was pregnant; she'd killed a man; she'd run off for a shotgun wedding down south and only just returned. Some were a combination of all three. Charlotte didn't care, not really. Searching the sea of surprised and uneasy faces, she finally found the one she had come home for.

It was like the realization of who exactly was crashing her party set in Sophie's jaw first, then worked its way up to her eyes. Charlotte watched Sophie's eyes narrow from across the room, lids sliding down until there were just little slits of the grey-blue underneath. Charlotte was vaguely aware of everyone looking between her and Sophie, wondering who would make the first move. Odds typically would have been on Sophie, but Charlotte could tell Sophie wasn't going to make it that easy.

In the time they'd known each other—Charlotte startled herself a bit, realizing that meant almost ten years now—the two had become experts at knowing what the other was thinking. When they were younger, when Sophie's skin was tanned from summer and Charlotte's hair wasn't so long and wild, people often thought they were sisters. Not because they looked particularly alike, but because they were always together and had a sort of synchronized look to them. Connected, like the moon and tide.

Charlotte could tell by Sophie's perfectly straight face that she was uncomfortable, surprised even, but not flustered—she was calculating. Working out her next ten, fifty moves. If Sophie was angry or upset, she was very good at hiding it. Charlotte was convinced at least a year had passed since she first opened the door.

Someone had to go first.

"Hi," Charlotte let out finally. As the moment struck, it was the best she could come up with. A less triumphant return speech than she'd planned on the bus.

By the look on Sophie's face, Charlotte may as well have just smacked her. Honestly, that might have gone over better. Without any sort of reply, Sophie twisted back from the table and turned toward the kitchen. Charlotte sighed, pushed her way through the crowd, and followed Sophie out of the living room. No one said anything or tried to stop her. Too drunk or too stunned. Charlotte slipped into the kitchen behind Sophie and slid the door closed behind them. She heard the party gather itself up in their absence—the music returned, but Charlotte wasn't sure anyone was really speaking yet.

Charlotte leaned back against the door once it was shut and they were sealed away from the other side. The kitchen was exactly the same as she remembered it—faded green walls and cupboards, and a black-and-white tile backsplash. At the far side of the room, Sophie's German shepherd, Denzel, was curled up disinterestedly on the mat near the back door. At first he didn't seem phased by Charlotte's arrival—she certainly wasn't a stranger—but then he stood up with his back tensed straight, like he could sense trouble.

Sophie was facing away from her, trying to get herself a drink. She was struggling to reach the plastic cups.

"Do you need—" Charlotte lurched forward but knew she'd just made it worse when Sophie immediately froze. It was exactly the way Sophie had reacted a year ago. Like she'd been caught in the act.

"No, I don't," Sophie snapped once time had resumed. "I got it."

Charlotte checked herself; Sophie had been getting along without her for months now. Sophie closed a shaking hand around one of the cups, almost crushing it. She grabbed a nearby bottle of clear liquid and dumped the rest of it into the cup. No mix.

Charlotte waited what felt like hours for Sophie to face her. She watched Sophie as she sipped her drink. After many years of silent contests, Charlotte knew all too well how long this standoff could go on.

"Sophie...," Charlotte said eventually.

"*What?*" Sophie spat back almost before her name had left Charlotte's mouth. Like she had been waiting for it—like she knew Charlotte would break first. Sophie's voice was high and clear. Not the way she used to speak to her, never so cold. Charlotte steadied herself. Okay. This was it.

Sophie looked so different, Charlotte reflected, now that they were finally facing each other. She was still tall and her eyes were still light and her face still had that way of looking uniquely *Sophie* but completely familiar. Sophie had always carried herself like she knew she was being looked at, because she always was.

Sophie looked older, duller—tired. Not the warm, colourful, sparkling Sophie Charlotte had grown up beside. It was like someone had been hired to make a robot to replace Sophie without ever having met her. It looked like Sophie, but it wasn't. Charlotte knew she didn't know this Sophie.

"Are you going to say anything else?" Sophie hissed, her line of white, even teeth flashing beneath her perfectly painted lips.

"Happy birthday," Charlotte blurted lamely. She decided to just keep talking, because the alternative was smacking herself with the empty Jack Daniel's bottle on the counter. "I mailed you a card a few days ago. There was a letter with it. I don't know if it got here—"

"I threw it out. And the letter."

*Awesome.* Charlotte wasn't sure how to answer that.

"If you came back here just to let me know that you're capable of mailing a Dollar Store card, then you've wasted your time. And your dollar. What could you have possibly written that you'd think I would want to read?"

"Sophie, I'm so sorry," Charlotte said, and god, it was the truth, "I missed you so much—"

"Yeah, and I missed homecoming. Life's a bitch." Sophie was smiling but it didn't reach her eyes. "What do you even want, at this point? It's been a *year*, Charlotte."

"I just...I want to apologize for leaving—"

Sophie interrupted her with a high little laugh aimed into her drink. Charlotte recognized it as the Impending Social Demise Laugh™, one of Sophie's trademarks. Following an unfortunate incident in tenth grade involving Jamie Berwick, raspberry vodka, and an ill-fated attempt on Jamie's part to hook up with Sophie's then-boyfriend, Brad Sutherland, a rumour circulated that anyone who faced Sophie's wrath would never be heard from again. In reality, Jamie's family had just moved to Halifax, but still.

"Are you sorry for leaving, or sorry for yourself?" Sophie demanded. "Because there's a big difference."

Charlotte sighed and traced a watermark on the faded green countertop as Sophie took another long sip from her drink. Ten-second time out. For some reason Charlotte was picturing an old battle-fighter video game and her health metre kept going down every time Sophie said anything. Denzel had settled a bit, laying back down on the mat with his paws crossed under his chin. Charlotte could tell he was keeping an eye on her, ready to come to Sophie's defense.

"I know that it seems like...like I just ran away," Charlotte said, trying very hard to keep her voice even, "and it's because I did. Really. There's no excuse for it, but I left because I had to."

"Yeah, and that's exactly what the shitty letter you left with Sean said. It didn't mean anything then, and it definitely doesn't mean anything a whole year later. What was it, half a page?"

"I would have said more but I..." Charlotte paused. Would she have, really? Why didn't she write more? Was it because she knew Sophie deserved better than a messy note, written in the half-light of the passenger seat while Charlotte cried? Anyway, she knew Sophie was right—whatever she said, it wouldn't have mattered.

"So you left. Fine." Sophie shrugged, but the action was slower now than it had been before. Like Sophie had to force her body through it. "It's not that. It's that you couldn't even tell me why. Or talk to me *once*."

Like a pulse, Charlotte felt the vague throbbing of everything she wasn't telling Sophie. The feeling was just enough in the background that she could push it away. She knew why the letter didn't say more, and why she had never called. Charlotte knew, but Sophie never could. "It's complicated," she said.

"Yeah, and the timing couldn't have been better!" Sophie trilled. "A month into senior year, and after everything that happened to us, you just left. It hadn't even been, what, three weeks?"

Charlotte couldn't look at her. It had been three weeks. Twenty-one days, almost to the hour. No getting around it, and no excuse for up and leaving her entire life. For leaving Sophie. Sophie cleared her throat, but Charlotte didn't have to look up to know she was crying.

"How could you not say goodbye to me?"

Charlotte felt like she couldn't drag her eyes away from her shoes, lining them up against the scuffed linoleum where the dark tiles met the light ones. "I knew if I came to say goodbye I never would have been able to go," she tried, like she was struggling to set up a house of cards that kept buckling. "I just did what I thought was best."

"Well, fine then. But I didn't think we were living in the Dark Ages, Charlotte. You could have called, or texted, or anything. Given me a tiny sign that you still gave a damn about what was happening in River John. About me."

Charlotte's chest clenched. "Of course I did. I do."

Sophie wiped hastily under her eyes. "My parents split up this year. Dad moved down to Toney River. Just far enough away, I guess. And Max and I broke up. Right after you left."

That made Charlotte look up. This wouldn't have been much of a surprise a year ago. It seemed like Sophie and Max used to break up and get back together at least once a week. But since last September, everything that happened seemed final, like a last word. Like everything from before that night didn't matter. Sophie Thompson and Maxwell Hale were at the top of North Colchester High's (and if you asked a few tenth graders, possibly the entire world's) power-couple hierarchy. Max was nice enough—smart, charming—but he was also one of those guys who grew, like, eighteen inches in one summer and then was suddenly on every girl's radar, including Sophie's. And then became a bit of a dick. Charlotte had known Max since they were kids, kept in proximity by parent-organized playdates, but as they grew up they grew apart. Max and Sophie were the opposite—one day they would act like complete strangers, and the next they were totally in love. As a couple, they were explosive. They were part of the same friend group at school, but once they started dating it was like someone had cranked the volume up and busted the speakers. They fought more than they didn't. But now Sophie wasn't talking about fighting, she was talking about being done.

"I'm sorry, about your parents," Charlotte said truthfully. "And Max."

"It didn't matter after you left. And after...," Sophie gestured vaguely.

Charlotte figured almost everyone had a moment in their life that they could point to and say, this is where everything changed. Everything divided into Before This or After This. In River John, the whole town, almost everyone Charlotte knew, had the same moment to point to. Charlotte just stood there stupidly; she knew there wasn't anything she could say that would make Sophie hate her any less. Aside from maybe throwing herself in front of an oncoming bus.

"Now." Sophie pressed her pinky finger into the corner of her eye, scraping out a smudge of mascara. "I have a party to host. My life can't stop because you've all of a sudden decided to turn up again. And if you're just going to keep looking at me like that, you can leave. I've gotten enough pity this year. But if not, feel free to stay. I'm sure there's some guy here who'll buy your sob story in exchange for a hookup in the guest room."

Charlotte resisted the urge to roll her eyes as Sophie moved to leave the kitchen, but Charlotte realized then that she was in Sophie's way. Even though the kitchen door was double wide, Sophie's wheelchair couldn't fit through with Charlotte standing there. Charlotte slid the door open and stepped aside as Sophie downed the rest of her drink and tossed the empty cup onto the counter. Her chair clattered loudly against the door frame.

Charlotte couldn't think of anything to say, and took Sophie's dismissal as her cue to leave, heading directly for the front door. Embarrassment curled around the edges of her face as she felt people's eyes following her retreat.

"Charlotte," Sophie called lightly, in a voice that Charlotte would have taken to be kind if she didn't know Sophie better. Anyone listening might even have thought everything was fine and that the two best friends had made up. Charlotte looked over her shoulder. "Welcome home."

Sophie had positioned herself back where she had been when Charlotte first came in, as if there had been no interruption. Charlotte left the house, grabbed her suitcase from its hiding spot, and shuffled down the narrow walkway to the road. Mist twisted in the air, like rain was finally coming after all this heat. Inside, the party carried on without her, as they all had for the last year. If Charlotte was going to stop running, she would have to be ready for when things caught up to her.

Because they would. And quickly.

# two

NARROW STREETS WOUND IN WIDE turns around River John, all
the way out to where they would eventually meet the highway into
Halifax. The small village was rooted unceremoniously on the
opposite edge of Nova Scotia. The opposite edge from anything,
really. A cluster of homes, summer cottages, and a few stores were
lined up along the stretch of water that separated Nova Scotia
from Prince Edward Island. It was a peninsula, surrounded by
water on all sides but one. Charlotte had lived surrounded by the
sea her entire life, and she had missed it while she was tucked
away inland.

It was so humid now that it was teetering on the edge between
raining and not. *Please don't downpour*, Charlotte prayed. In a
town where there was nothing to do, rain just left you with even
fewer options. After Sophie's frigid reception, a post-party rain-
storm was the last thing Charlotte needed. She wasn't sure, but
she had a pretty good feeling that the dress she'd picked out on
sale at the mall in Halifax two days after Christmas was not water-
proof. She shivered. Dying of pneumonia was not on her list of
things to accomplish.

Charlotte made her way down the uneven pavement of the
main road, dragging her suitcase behind her. On the other hand,

maybe dying of exposure would speed up the healing process with Sophie. That would teach her. Charlotte sidestepped a large pothole on the edge of the road. The only reason she could imagine Sophie mourning her death would be because Sophie hadn't had the pleasure of bringing it on herself. *Kind of dark*, she told herself.

Anyway.

She continued. It wasn't that long of a walk, but something was slowing her down. Gravity, destiny, existential dread, etc. Charlotte knew that once she got home, there was no going back. She'd be home for good. She was trying to calculate how much farther she had to go when she realized the last sounds from the party had finally faded.

Focused on the pavement before her, she looked up just in time to see headlights illuminating her path from ahead, twisting around the bend. She paused and waited for a car to appear. A pickup truck, actually. Charlotte stepped off the asphalt, pressing herself along the treeline and out of the pickup's way. A tiny thought tugged at her brain. The one someone she hadn't seen at the party—and had expected to—popped into her mind. That one someone drove a truck just like this, and it looked like he could be on his way to the party now. He always did run late. Charlotte stepped farther back into the brush.

The lights of the truck caught her face for half a second as it rolled past. She held her breath. It didn't stop. Charlotte pushed out a sigh of relief and dragged her suitcase out of a bit of mud and leaves. She started back on the pavement just in time to hear the faintest squeal of tires; out of the corner of her eye she could see the glow of red brake lights against the trees. *Shit.*

She looked over her shoulder. The truck had creaked to a stop. *Please let me be wrong. Please be someone else. Anyone else.*

In a town as small as River John, people stopped to pick you up. It was just a thing that happened. Anyone walking anywhere on the side of the road was almost definitely someone you went to school with, or a family friend, or your regular server at the

Chinese food place. Maybe the driver hadn't recognized her, and was just being nice. She stuck her head back straight, sucking in a bit of the cool night air. *Please don't be him.*

The driver cut the engine. Charlotte heard the thud of feet against pavement as they jumped out to help. They didn't say anything—no greeting, no confirmation that they weren't a murderer. More air. She muttered something in the direction of the sky, a prayer that she was wrong, and looked over her shoulder again.

She was right.

When she saw his face, she felt a familiar discomfort—the same feeling you get when someone brought up something from years ago you still felt guilty about. She pulled her suitcase closer, as if it could hide her from his view.

He was tall—way taller than her, and even taller than Sophie—all long limbs and messy hair that he was always pushing back from his face. She placed a smile on his features from memory, one that was easy and happy, and one she had known since they were kids. Charlotte tried to pinpoint the last time they had seen each other. Those three weeks had been hazy and disjointed; the two of them had sort of co-existed, orbiting Sophie carefully and avoiding collisions with each other, like satellites around their home planet. She remembered nights they spent together in Sophie's living room after the accident, tucked together on the sofa, waiting, while Sophie slept. It was a small rekindling of their friendship, contained to their tiny cosmos, which came out of the worst thing that had ever happened to them. She figured the last time they had seen each other would have been on Sophie's back porch, just as the sun was starting to dip behind the horizon, the air rosy and the bugs out in full force. That was where they usually saw each other, when they were swapping out. Charlotte would go home and sleep and he would stay with Sophie until Charlotte came back.

Maxwell Hale blinked at her a few times in the semi-darkness, his silhouette outlined by the truck lights glowing behind him. Like Sophie, he looked a lot older now.

"Hi," Charlotte said. She thought she saw a tiny smile flicker at the corner of his lips, but it could have been a trick of the light.

"It's like...seeing a ghost," Max said.

"I haven't been gone that long," scoffed Charlotte. "And didn't think I looked that bad."

"I knew you'd turn up here again one day. Didn't picture it being on the side of the road." He paused. "And you look good."

She guessed that by *good* he meant *healthier*, because they weren't spending all their time crying and not eating and barely sleeping.

"Uh, yeah, so do you," she offered.

He looked at her for a second and she couldn't tell if he was angry at her for leaving, or surprised that she was back, or what. Max reached out, closing the space between them, and he touched her arm like he wasn't entirely sure she was even there. He sighed. Relief or exasperation, or a mix of the two. But he moved and pulled her toward him quickly, arms coiling around her waist and holding her tight and she didn't think that he was angry.

"Hi, Charlie."

She smiled without even realizing it. No one had called her that in almost a year; it was a nickname bestowed lovingly by her brother when he was three and would fumble over the extra syllable. For her dad and her friends, it had stuck.

"Where've you been?" he asked into her shoulder.

She pulled away from him. This, of course, was the simpler half of the question. The why was the tricky part.

"Uh, I've actually just been hiding out in the woods. Social experiment. Watched too much *Survivorman*. You found me." As the sarcastic words left her mouth Charlotte realized just how hard explaining anything about her absence was going to be.

He raised his eyebrows but didn't push it as he stepped away from her. "You sound like the same old Charlie."

"It would be a shame if I didn't."

Max chuckled and looked at the ground. His face twisted like he was nervous. "Does Sophie know you're here?"

Charlotte swallowed. "Yes."

"How did she take it?"

Ah. "I think...better than she should have."

Max scratched his head and looked at her again. "I don't know what's crazier: you being home or Sophie leaving you in one piece."

"Gee, thanks."

He grinned. "Come on. Throw your bag in the back, I'll give you a lift."

She hesitated, but he was already grabbing her suitcase and heaving it into the bed of the pickup. Charlotte circled around the truck as he returned to the driver's side and slid into the seat. She caught him staring at her through the open passenger window before she got in.

"What?" she asked.

"You finally come back and the first place you go is Sophie's birthday? Did you really think you were going to get out of that unscathed?"

She folded her arms. "No, I didn't. And how do you know I even went to the party? Maybe I just called her."

Max laughed, nodding to her dress. "You're dressed for a party. And besides: it's River John. Still only twenty kids in our graduating class. Only so many parties you could be going to. And it's not like anyone else is going to have a party the same night as Sophie's birthday."

Charlotte rolled her eyes as he unlocked the door and she climbed inside.

"Seat belt," he said.

"Got it."

"Charlotte Tabitha Romer crashing Sophie Jane Thompson's birthday." He chuckled and shook his head. "That is something I am sorry to have missed." He put a mostly disintegrated cigarette from the ashtray into his mouth and swung the truck around into a U-turn, in the direction she'd been walking.

"My middle name is *not* Tabitha. Were you heading there? Sophie told me you broke up."

Max nodded slightly as the truck gathered speed, winding through dark trees and grey dirt roads, flying past the Chinese food restaurant and adjoining gas station. "You heard right," he said.

Charlotte couldn't help herself. "What happened?"

"Uh, it was just hard, after..." he trailed off, rolling his fingers against the steering wheel to fill the empty space. "And fixing it wasn't important compared to everything else, so we just didn't, and...I dunno, we both stopped bothering." He glanced at her. "One day she just told me to leave her alone and I did."

"That's...shitty." *Very articulate, Charlotte.*

Max shrugged. "I guess so."

In an effort to look at anything but him, Charlotte kept her eyes trained straight ahead. "So you weren't going to the party, then?"

"No, I figured I'd leave Sophie in peace on her birthday. Plus, it would have been rude to show up uninvited and without a gift." He paused and looked at her pointedly. "One party-crasher is enough, I think."

Charlotte balanced her elbow on the window ledge and cradled her chin. "Sorry I beat you to it."

"Are you going to tell me how it went?"

She glanced at him. "How what went?"

"You turn up after being missing in action for a year and go straight to Sophie. Well, you always go straight to her, I'll give you that."

"She chewed me out for all of ten minutes and then I left."

"I don't know what else you were expecting. You should consider yourself lucky to be alive. I'm pretty sure Sophie has trained assassins at her beck and call."

Charlotte pressed her tongue to the back of her teeth and sighed. "I wouldn't rule it out yet. She hates me."

"I think...." Max paused. "Yeah, probably. But she hates that you left. She doesn't hate *you*. And now you're back. After a while she just missed you. I was there. She slept and cried and waited for her best friend to come back."

Charlotte dragged a hand through her hair, not really in the mood for any more conversation about her fight with Sophie. But as reality began to set in, she found herself reconsidering her decision to come home. She hated herself for being a coward, for not being able to face Sophie and properly explain herself. But maybe it was a mistake to come back. To disrupt any bit of normal that Sophie had managed to scrape together since the accident. Maybe Charlotte had lost the right to try and make peace with her a year later.

The dark yellow line waved in and out of view on the fractured pavement as the truck sped along. Charlotte's vision blurred around the edges for a moment and she blinked away the burning that threatened tears. She'd die before she let herself get worked up in front of Max.

"I'm scared I'm too late," Charlotte admitted to the windshield.

Out of the corner of her eye she could see Max shift his shoulders. "I guess there's only one person who gets to decide that."

"Yeah, well, Sophie was never much into changing her mind."

A silence rolled between them. She realized they were stopped at a red light. They hadn't seen another car the entire drive.

"Hey, uh." She felt Max's hand on her back, between her shoulder blades. "It's okay. It takes a lot...to show up to what you knew was waiting for you at Sophie's."

Charlotte twisted to face him. "I'm fine. I probably deserved it. Er, I definitely did."

"Well." Max gave a tiny shrug, the red light shining on his face switching to green. "It's not like any of us are going anywhere. Sophie's either going to forgive you or she's not, so. Go figure it out. You won't know until you know. And you guys have always worked things out before."

"Things aren't really like before."

He didn't answer, so he was either ignoring what she'd said or using the silence to acknowledge that she was right.

It wasn't a long drive from Sophie's to Charlotte's, but tonight the road seemed to stretch on for ages. Eventually they reached the gravel driveway that led to her house. The truck bumped its way down the lane, until Max turned the bend into the clearing where her home stood. It was small and grey, and looked exactly the same as she remembered. The faded wood siding broke the darkness along the treeline behind it, like a splash of bright in the woods. There were no lights on. Dark and quiet. She found her eyes raking the perimeter, looking for anything or anyone out of place. She was happy to be home, she told herself. She wasn't scared. She couldn't be, now.

"Does anyone else know you're back?" Max asked, snapping her out of it and leaning forward to look out his windshield toward the porch.

"Sean should...theoretically. If he's been paying his phone bill and bothers to read my messages." She sighed. "I called him about a million times because he was actually supposed to come pick me up from school, but you know Sean."

Max cut the ignition and looked at her. "I would've come to get you. You could have called me."

Charlotte raised her eyebrows. Max's blatant kindness towards her was something she wasn't familiar with. "No, it's fine. I made friends on the bus. The lady next to me offered me Doritos for two hours." She looked at him pointedly. "From an empty Tupperware container. I'm writing a memoir."

Max laughed.

"Other than Sean, no one else knows—" she stopped herself. "Well, no one *did*. I forgot that all my friends were at Sophie's party."

He turned his head to look at her. "Not all of them."

She smiled a bit at that.

"Listen, it's been a long year, Charlie," Max told her. "But we've got way more years to go. We're all still getting used to everything being...different."

Different was a nice way of saying worse, Charlotte thought, but Max was right, and she knew it. He wasn't the same, just like Sophie wasn't. It was the same difference she knew she would probably see if she could bear to examine herself.

"I should go. Thanks for everything," she said honestly.

He looked away, suddenly awkward, throwing a hand through his hair and pushing it back from his face. "No problem-o." He flashed a finger gun toward the windshield and then looked away, embarrassed.

Charlotte swung open the door and hopped out, slamming it shut behind her. After a few tries, she managed to wrestle her suitcase out of the back of the truck. She caught Max looking at her again through passenger door window.

"What?"

"Are you gonna tell me—or anyone—why you left?" he asked quietly. *Fair question*, Charlotte thought. It should have been easy to answer.

"Ah." She nudged the gravel nervously with the toe of her shoe. "It's a really long story, Max."

He shook his head. "I didn't ask for the story. I asked if you were ever going to tell anyone the reason."

Charlotte bit her lip. That was an even simpler question. "No," she said.

She wasn't sure what the expression was that crossed his face, but she thought that maybe he didn't quite believe her.

"All right," he said with a shrug.

She gave him an uncomfortable smile before turning and heading for the steps.

"Charlie!"

She froze but didn't turn around.

"I'm glad you're back."

Charlotte turned to face Max a final time and tried to believe what she said next. "So am I."

# three

CHARLOTTE WATCHED THE RED TAIL lights of the truck disappear between the trees before climbing the steps of the porch, the dull glow of the overhead lamp leaking down her path. The lamp swayed a bit in the breeze. As Max and his truck creaked away, she was completely alone again and everything was quiet.

Propping the screen door open with her hip, Charlotte tried the doorknob. Locked. Of all the nights. *When did Sean start bothering to lock the door?* Charlotte slapped her palm against the heavy wood a few times.

"Sean!" she barked at the door. The sound pressed against the little grooves in the wood but didn't seem to make it any farther. There was no answer. Not that she really expected one. Sean wasn't home much. She pounded a few more times just to be sure. No heavy, blustery footsteps. No grumbling over the inconvenience. No Sean.

She cursed under her breath and dug around in the outside pocket of her suitcase for the house key. It was tangled with her headphones and lip chap. She looped her finger through the key chain. The car, the workshop, dad's truck, Sophie's. Charlotte traced the cool, floral-patterned metal. Sophie and Charlotte had gotten keys of each other's houses made back in the sixth grade in case of emergencies. Charlotte's key to Sophie's had tiny pink roses, while Sophie's to Charlotte's was baby blue with white, fluffy clouds. She wondered if Sophie still had hers.

Trying not to linger on the fact that Sophie may have access to the place where Charlotte slept, Charlotte flipped past the pink key to the plain one that unlocked her house. As she straightened up, her back to the front yard and the trees, Charlotte wondered if someone could be watching her. She hated that she felt that way. *Don't be paranoid.* She jammed the key in the lock and threw her weight against the door. It stuck, like it always did in the heat and humidity of summer, and after a few more tries she finally stumbled inside.

The front door opened right into the main room—into everything. The Romer home looked about the same as when she'd left it. At least something did. It had been a dark, rainy morning when she'd left town, so a grey and half-remembered version of the place she grew up was all she'd left with. The house wasn't much—small and rustic and cluttered, with pale wooden walls and thick rafters overhead. Memories hung on the walls and lined shelves. The whole thing sort of reminded her of a museum now, filled with artifacts from a different era. Maybe that's why it looked exactly the same as when she'd left—Sean hadn't touched anything. She probably wouldn't have either, were she in his place. It was as if they were preserving something that didn't exist anymore.

A beat-up leather sofa and mismatched loveseat were arranged in front of the rabbit-ear TV (the TV worked but the rabbit ears weren't even hooked up; she knew Sean just kept them around for decorative purposes, like their dad had). At the far side of the room was the uneven dining room table, only kept upright and even by Sean's high school yearbook under one foot. A memory of legs swinging under the drapey tablecloth, pumping back and forth, as she struggled through her homework every afternoon. Her dad over her shoulder, all whispered hints and gentle corrections. The galley kitchen beside the table was just as tiny as she remembered. Beside the kitchen, a narrow hallway led off to

Charlotte's bedroom, the bedroom her parents used to share, the bathroom, and Sean's bedroom tucked in the back.

She was home.

Charlotte lined up her suitcase against the wall by the door. It was quiet, just her and the dust and the sea, somewhere nearby. For a startling second, she felt calm. Home.

"Sean?" she heard herself call out. More silence. "It's me!"

Charlotte chucked her keys on the coffee table and headed for the kitchen. She was hungry, but then suddenly not. Dishes caked with old food were piled high in the sink. Glasses and empty beer cans covered the counter like some kind of shrine. A big paper liquor store bag stained with dark spots from the food inside sat on the floor beside the fridge. At least it looked like Sean was making an effort to compost.

"Jesus, Sean," she muttered to herself. Whatever. She'd make him clean it up tomorrow. Right now she was too tired to deal with anything. When she turned to leave she almost wiped out on a stray beer bottle rolling on the floor. Kicking it aside, she left the war zone of a kitchen and headed to the back of the house. She made a detour to Sean's bedroom. Charlotte disobeyed the handmade *Keep Out* sign Sean had plastered on the door when he was twelve, and stuck her head inside.

"Hello?" The bedroom was about as tidy as the kitchen, but it was empty. Her brother was not home. He was probably god knows where, doing god knows what, even though really, she knew what. She loved her brother. A lot. But he had a tendency toward trouble. Busted selling weed, and before their dad died, underage drinking. Vandalism, disorderly conduct, you name it. Charlotte blamed his friends. They were way worse than Sean—a lot less petty and a lot more criminal. Sean never did anything that bad. Charlotte knew that. Sean would never hurt anyone, except himself.

Closing Sean's door behind her, she stood facing the back exit, a crappy, clattering metal screen door that looked out on the backyard. Pulling aside the faded blue curtains at the window, she could just make out the small building that stood beside the house beyond the back porch.

Another memory, a newer one, came to her—her dad out in the workshop, tinkering and fixing and blowing through a pack and a half of cigarettes every summer afternoon. He'd taught Charlotte to use a hammer and Sean how to put things together. Fittingly, Sean would fix what she broke. As they got older, their roles had switched.

It had been just her and Sean for a while now. Almost two whole years before she left. Boarding school had been Sean's idea. A relative, their mom's sister, came up with the tuition money. Aunt Heather, whom Charlotte had never met or even heard of before then. Sean had insisted it was the best solution. After all this time, Charlotte still didn't think he was right. He had just wanted her out of River John. She should have wanted out, too, but it wasn't that simple.

Charlotte snapped herself back to reality and turned away from the window, letting the blue curtain fall back down, covering up the view of the darkened backyard. She found herself at the last part of the house she'd yet to face. She took a deep breath and told herself she was being stupid.

Her North Colchester High School banner was still taped above the dresser in her bedroom; half-full binders of scribbled notes were peeking out from under her bed. A bulletin board beside the window was covered in photos: her and Sean as babies; old photos of her dad; young, awkward versions of her and Sophie. There were so many of her and Sophie. Max appeared in a few. They got older and less awkward-looking—though Charlotte thought Sophie never really looked awkward. Sophie always looked completely comfortable with herself. There was a small dry-erase board next to the photos. In hot pink, curly writing: *Sophie was here.*

Memories were shapes: round and soft, or square and sharp. Hard angles and steep drop-offs. Thinking of her dad was hazier; blurry lines that she couldn't place on a timeline other than somewhere from childhood. Thinking about Sophie, about last year, was all sharp edges—gaps for missing moments or things that tripped her up. She didn't know what she'd expected. Did she think some magical Ghost of Christmas Past would have swept in while she was away and cleared out all the evidence of Before? Everything here was a reminder that things used to be better. Easier.

Charlotte sat down on the lumpy grey bedspread, a cloud of dust rising like blown snow. She couldn't take her eyes off the photos hanging right in front of her. It was like she was seeing them for the first time. They were all from before the accident.

Every September, the senior class of their high school hosted a car rally after the first week back to school. The entire class divided into teams to partake in a town-wide, free-for-all scavenger hunt. Performing wild and borderline-illegal activities earned you points. These ranged from kidnapping a freshman (who was in on it, of course; it was considered an honour to be chosen), which was thirty points, to convincing someone from the sheriff's department to let you and another teammate make out in the back of a squad car (one hundred and fifty points). You could also earn points by solving clues, written by the host, that led you to different spots around town. Each team paid a one-hundred-dollar entry fee, which covered the winner's prize money (or their posted bail, depending on how the night went).

Max was the host last year. He had been meticulous. Down to every last detail, Max had spent most of the previous summer making sure everything would work, coming up with clues, shortcuts, and hints within hints. The rally had been all anyone talked about for the weeks leading up to the return to school. Teams had matching outfits, people decorated their cars, and teachers were wary of assigning too much homework that weekend.

Originally, Charlotte, Max, and Sophie had been a team. They were the three-person-exception team, because Max had insisted on being with Sophie, and Sophie had insisted on being with Charlotte. Everyone else was in pairs. It didn't really matter, though, because Max wasn't technically allowed to play since he'd made up the questions and knew the answers. The clue-solving had to be up to Sophie and Charlotte.

But a week before, Sean had informed Charlotte—abruptly, and maybe strategically, just as she was going out the door—that she would have to miss the car rally for a babysitting job he'd set up. They'd fought about it for days. But Charlotte did end up missing the scavenger hunt and instead spent her evening with an eight-year-old boy who was obsessed with *Star Wars*. Sophie made Charlotte swear to show up at the afterparty. In her purse she'd packed makeup and something less family-friendly than what she'd worn babysitting to change into afterward.

But Charlotte never made it to the afterparty.

As it turned out, no one did.

Charlotte had just finished babysitting, and was heading for her car when her phone rang. The first words that had come flying out of Max's mouth when Charlotte had answered were, "It's Sophie." At the hospital she found Sophie's family, and eventually Max's, and a few kids from school who'd heard what happened and followed the ambulance.

Charlotte learned later, through the police and what little Sophie and Max remembered, that there had been a collision. Direct impact on the passenger side. Max had been driving. Technically, the police said, Max wasn't at fault, but Charlotte had seen how the guilt warped him in the weeks that followed. His truck had flipped, and Max was the one who had woken up and managed to call 911. They never found the other driver, and no one ever came forward. If it had been someone just passing through River John, they were gone forever.

Sophie refused to speak to anyone for a long time. Everyone else just spent a lot of time not knowing what to say. Charlotte had tried to string together words but nothing seemed to line up right. Looking back, she knew she was a lot quieter than she should have been. It was like all those years of friendship didn't mean much when everything came falling down.

Max became closed-off, a different person. He was a kind of dark that Charlotte had never seen in him. She remembered him during those terrible days at school after the accident, if he did show up at all. Max wouldn't talk to anyone, and if he did it was only to her or his buddy Leo. Leo was the only one who seemed to be able to cheer him up a bit, but if Max ever cracked a smile he just went back to looking completely miserable two seconds later.

Max, like Sophie, had been the type of person who could talk to anyone, good-natured and charming. Charlotte didn't know a single person who seriously disliked him. Except her, maybe, but that was on purpose—because he wanted her to, and because he liked antagonizing his girlfriend's best friend. Harmless. Charlotte never thought she would miss Max's smug attitude and biting sarcasm. He used to be friends with everyone, but after the accident it was like he didn't know how to move when every single person in town knew about the worst thing that had ever happened to him.

And then, within a few weeks of the accident, Charlotte left for boarding school. Sean had said there wasn't time for her to offer any explanations to her friends and that it would only make everything harder. That sounded like the right answer for the first few days, but after that Charlotte knew it had only sounded right because it was easier. She was a coward for not saying goodbye to Sophie. For not explaining.

There hadn't been a day since that night last September that Charlotte hadn't thought about what would have happened had she been in the car, too. *Selfish*, she thought. But she figured maybe with three of them, they wouldn't have been in that exact spot at that exact time. Maybe they would have solved another clue first and wouldn't have driven that way at all. Maybe Charlotte would have taken a few extra seconds at one stop and held them up. Maybe if she'd been there it wouldn't have happened at all. Or maybe it would have been worse.

Charlotte let out a deep breath, throwing herself backward onto her bed. She turned her head sideways, looking to the message scrawled on the whiteboard.

● ● ●

Charlotte groaned against her pillow as she rolled over in bed, the sunlight peeking through the floral curtains across the room. She reached out blindly for her phone on the night stand, checking the time. The display read 12:24 P.M.

She twisted onto her back, staring up at the discoloured ceiling. Squeezing her eyes shut, Charlotte tried to remember what time it had been when she had fallen asleep. It must have been after 4 A.M. Her brain just wouldn't shut down last night. Lots to think about.

She had made a cup of tea (which turned out to be difficult, as she didn't know where Sean had hidden their kettle) and spent the evening—which eventually deteriorated into early morning—organizing and reorganizing her old school binders. It was pointless, because the notes were more than a year old, but it helped. Organize what she could. Put some order to this chaos.

Charlotte sat up, swinging her legs over the side of the bed. Lots of housekeeping to do today. She padded out toward the main room, where she found the only other Romer child draped majestically over the worn leather sofa, hugging a half-eaten bag of barbecue chips. She had been up until nearly daylight and hadn't heard him come home, which she found vaguely concerning.

"Sean?" she called, only drawing a low murmur from her brother. "Hey, Sean!" Charlotte said more sharply, the sound snapping through the empty house. Sean flew upright, the bag of chips drifting to the floor.

"What the fu—" he muttered, disoriented. He looked around, peering down at his spilt breakfast before he looked up at her. They looked alike. Dark hair and tanned skin and the same dark eyes. They both resembled their mom, or at least the mom Charlotte knew from the faded photographs their dad used to keep in his bedside table. They both looked different from the other people in River John—like they'd been transplanted in at the last second. They looked alike, but the Sean in front of her looked exhausted, as if he hadn't had a decent night's sleep in a year. His eyes were rimmed with dark, unforgiving circles and Charlotte couldn't stop herself from noticing the way his loose clothing hung off a slimmer frame.

"Morning, sunshine," Charlotte said.

Sean checked his wrist for a watch that wasn't there. "Was that today?"

"Last night, actually." She sat down in front of him on the oversized chest that they used as a makeshift coffee table. "I only called you, like, a thousand times."

Sean put his face into his hands, pulling down on his cheeks. "Shit. School. The car. Driving. Right."

"Yup."

Sean sighed and grabbed his watch from beside her leg. "I'm sorry. I just...lost track of the days, I guess."

"And the rest of the house too, apparently," she noted.

"Sorry, Mom." Sean fastened the strap around his wrist. "I'm sorry I forgot to come get you, all right?" He softened. "Next time for sure."

"Right. The next time I'm returning from a mysterious long-term absence?"

He smirked, and looked a bit more like the Sean she remembered. "Precisely."

Charlotte picked her way to the kitchen and found half a pot of cold coffee in the maker. She inspected it and wondered about its age. Whatever. She wasn't the one drinking it. She dumped it in a mug and threw it in the microwave. (The plate didn't spin anymore. Excellent.)

Charlotte poked her head back into the main room. "You were out late last night," she commented before retrieving the mug. Turning back to the microwave, she could practically see the look Sean was giving her through the wall. She brought him the coffee as a peace offering.

"Sorry that I haven't really been in touch," he said, ignoring the previous remark.

"That's fine, you only sent me off to boarding school away from all my friends and then ignored me while I was there. I'm really only upset that you haven't been answering my Snapchats."

"You ignored me, too," Sean reminded her, as if he didn't deserve it.

"I was mad at you," Charlotte said honestly.

"Are you still?"

"A bit."

Sean laughed into his drink.

"So...what have you been doing?" she asked. A loaded question.

Sean returned to eating chips out of the bag. He avoided her gaze. "Oh, you know me. Same old, same old."

Charlotte raised her eyebrows. She did know him. *Same old* was not good news.

"You know what I mean," he added coolly, catching her look. "Nothing exciting."

The implication hung in the air for a few seconds, and his look pressed her to challenge him. Sean had only been eighteen, and legally an adult for about a month, when their dad died. Since Charlotte had been only sixteen, there'd been talk of moving her. The question of their financial stability and Sean's criminal record threatened to separate them. But in the end, it was decided that they had been through enough already and Charlotte stayed where she'd always been. Sean just had to stay out of trouble.

"The house is a mess though, really." Charlotte veered the conversation, letting him win, for now.

"You're right. I know." Sean nodded a few times, taking advantage of the change in subject. "Yeah. We can work on it later."

Charlotte smirked. "There's no 'we' in that one."

"Oh, come on."

"Not my mess," she told him, shaking her head.

"*Charlie*," he whined. "I don't know why we even pretend like I'm gonna clean up." Sean leaned back against the sofa and dug at a bit of lint on his T-shirt. "You can't just come back here and start bossing me around."

"Why not? I bossed you around before I left."

"Yeah, well, things are different than before you left." He said it lightly, and she knew he wasn't implying anything, but the choice of words hit her weirdly. She knew Sean saw it in her face. "I didn't mean—" he started.

"No, it's..." she trailed off, pulling herself up to her feet, "true."

Sean looked at her. There were only two years between them but sometimes it felt like either a lot more or a lot less. "I'm still not...." He stopped, waited. "I'm still worried. I'm not sure you should be back here."

Charlotte stiffened, curling her fingers around the cuffs of her sleeves and adjusting her shoulders like she was ready for a fight. "School's over, Sean. This is what we agreed on, and—"

"I know," Sean cut her off. "I guess I'm just not ready to...deal with everything."

Sean had gone back to not looking at her and Charlotte sucked in a deep breath. She felt like it wasn't the last time they were going to have this conversation.

"Glad you're back," Sean said after a few seconds, pressing the scuffed mug to his mouth. He looked like their dad when he was thinking.

Charlotte nodded and disappeared down the hall to her room.

# four

august
eleven months earlier

"RISE AND SHINE! WE HAVE to leave *now* if we want to beat the crowds!"

Charlotte yanked her comforter over her head, trying to block out both the early morning sun and the shrill intruder in her bedroom. She peeked out from beneath the blanket, eyeing the clock on her bedside table. 7:26 A.M. taunted her in blue-green letters.

"Charlie, get up! We have a two-hour drive ahead of us!" Sophie had pulled back the curtains, summer sunlight spilling into the small room. Sophie propped a hand on her hip and looked down at her with a displeased expression. "CBR, up!"

It was one of Sophie's less-creative nicknames for her (full name: Charlotte Beth Romer) and Sophie always said it with the letters blurred together like it was a word (SeeBurr). It reminded Charlotte of that three-headed dog from Greek mythology who guarded the gates to hell or whatever. Cerberus? Anyway, the further Sophie strayed from the traditional "Charlie," the more trouble Charlotte was in.

Charlotte buried her face in the mattress, wondering how long she'd have to stay unmoving for Sophie to believe she had spontaneously died. She had completely forgotten about the plans she'd made last week to drive to the city with Sophie and Max.

She pulled the blanket back over her head.

Charlotte felt a sudden crushing weight, which could only be all one hundred and twenty-five pounds of Sophie. With an aggravated sigh, Charlotte threw back the blankets and sat up as best she could. Sophie was sprawled over her on her back, arms spread like she'd been shot. Sophie flipped over onto her stomach so they were face to face, one squished-together creature, two-headed. Sophie was grinning and planted a tiny kiss on the tip of Charlotte's nose.

"Oh, hey Soph, didn't hear you knock," Charlotte said, "by all means, come on in."

"I told you pickup was seven sharp." Sophie dragged herself back to her feet and crossed her arms, back to being angry. "We're already behind schedule, because *someone* couldn't tear themselves away from some stupid documentary."

"How come we never do what I want to do?" Max was standing in the doorway, leaning against the frame looking halfway between confused and amused. The third head.

"It was about zombies, Max," Sophie said. "*Zombies*, Charlotte."

"It was very informative," Max explained. "Cute jammies, Charlie."

Charlotte squeezed her eyes shut and tilted her head. "Oh, good morning, Max, that makes so much more sense, I thought I could smell something." She pushed some hair from her face, not even bothering to try and puzzle out what Max was doing watching documentaries about the undead before dawn. She stood up and stretched. Max was usually around if Sophie was around. Most of the time Charlotte and Max just tolerated each other. She was sure Max would much rather be alone with Sophie and Charlotte felt the same.

"C'mon, Charlie, you *promised*," Sophie whined, grabbing a purse from the hook on the back of Charlotte's door and throwing what seemed like random items inside. Charlotte wasn't sure why Sophie thought she'd need an extra bottle of nail polish. "Let's go."

"Yeah, yeah, I know." Charlotte sighed. "Just give me a few minutes. We're still going to *Halifax*, right? It's not like they only let a certain number of people in every day." She tried to leave the room, but Max blocked her path.

"Good morning to you, too." He smirked, his eyes sweeping over her wild mass of bedhead. "Your hair looks nice."

"Shut up," she barked, colour flushing her cheeks as she pushed past him.

"A pleasure as always, Charlie," Max called over his shoulder before she slammed the door to the bathroom.

• • •

"Next. Next. Next. Back. No, back. *Back*. Jesus Christ, just let me do it!" Sophie made a grab for Charlotte's phone.

"Sophie!" Charlotte shrieked, holding the music out of her reach. "Hands on the wheel, please!"

Max poked his head into the front seat from the back. "Cripes, Soph. You're going to get us all killed. Anyone up to date on their praying?"

"You, shut up." Sophie stuck her tongue out at her boyfriend in the rear-view mirror. "I *will* come back there."

"I like the sound of that." Max leaned back, sprawling out in the seat. "Why don't you come back here and shut me up? Charlotte can drive for a bit."

Charlotte pinched the bridge of her nose between her thumb and forefinger. "Yeah, no. I'm not playing chauffeur so you two can have a make-out session in the backseat."

"Well, hey Charlotte, you're welcome to come back here and make out with us, too," he suggested, wiggling his eyebrows at her.

Charlotte swivelled around to look at him. "Perfect. I'll be able to cross 'threesome from hell' off my bucket list. You're so gross, Max." Oh, what she wouldn't give to dump Max roadside halfway to Truro and never return.

Sophie laughed. "Charlie, you always let him wind you up for no reason. Just ignore him, that's what I do."

"It's her Sagittarius energy," Max said sagely. "She can't help it. And there's no room back here anyway," he said, shifting around in the tiny backseat of Sophie's Volkswagen, wedged between their bags, clothes, gym stuff, and other miscellany Sophie was hoarding.

"Right," Charlotte said, rolling her eyes. "*That's* why we're voting no on the threesome."

"See how she doesn't even try to hide her love for me, Soph? Honestly, it's so embarrassing. I can't balance two relationships."

"As if," Charlotte snapped. "The only relationship balancing you're doing is the one with Sophie and the one with your right hand."

"I'm left-handed, thank you very much, so—"

"Kids, would you give it a rest? I'm not listening to this for the next hour." Sophie grabbed the phone from Charlotte. "And I've had enough of your emo shit."

"It's...Lorde."

"What*ever*. Did you bring your fake?" Sophie settled on a Beach Boys song and tossed the phone back in Charlotte's lap.

"ID? No."

"Charlie!"

"That laminated piece of crap barely gets us beer at the liquor store in Tatamagouche. I don't think we're going to be getting into any bars in Halifax," Charlotte said.

"Wait, your fake works?" Max sat up.

Sophie smiled sweetly at him in the mirror. "You don't look like us," she told him. Charlotte snorted; the only time her fake ever worked was if she went to the liquor store with Sophie, peeking over her shoulder and not saying a word while Sophie was all confidence. Sophie would question the clerk about Argentinian wine varietals as a diversion before settling on a case of vodka sodas.

Thirty minutes or so later, Charlotte nodded to a passing sign on the highway.

"Bridge is coming up, somebody get money out."

"Since you brought it up, I vote you," Max said dryly, laying across the backseat with an issue of *Cosmo* open on his face.

"No way. I paid for ice cream, since Sophie conveniently left her wallet in the car." She shot Sophie a look. "You guys have five and a half kilometres to decide."

"Maxie." Sophie craned around in her seat to look at him.

He lifted the magazine from his face. "Don't call me that."

"Um, eyes on the road please!" Charlotte cried in alarm. "It's literally a dollar."

"My Maximus Prime," Sophie giggled, still turned to look at him.

"Please stop."

"Sophie, we are going to die!" said Charlotte.

"Fine, I'll pay if you stop." Max grinned.

Sophie turned back to the road, satisfied. "Ye of little faith," she said to Charlotte.

• • •

The Halifax waterfront was crowded with people, tourists or otherwise, in search of fried foods and various knickknacks. The harbour shimmered under the sun in a pleasant way, but it wasn't the same as the ocean in River John. It didn't smell the same for one thing, and you didn't get the same vibration in the air from the waves. Charlotte looked across the water to Georges Island before ducking into a souvenir tent. It was completely the opposite side of the sea from River John.

Charlotte picked up a silver ring. "Buy me this."

"No," Sophie said.

"Please?"

"*Stop.*"

Charlotte sighed and slid the ring back into its faux-velvet place on the table.

"Don't give me that." Sophie rolled her eyes. "I don't have any more money to spend than you do."

"Not true. I saw your new MacBook. Jeeze. I don't know how you can even use it. It cost more than my car."

At the beginning of the summer, Sophie got the receptionist's job at the bank in town while the regular girl was on maternity leave. Charlotte didn't know exactly what it was Sophie did, but she thought Sophie just liked having a desk. It must pay extraordinarily well.

"I needed it for school," Sophie said.

They made their way through the small marketplace along the boardwalk. Max was a little ways down, examining the display outside the Maritime Museum of the Atlantic. Sophie picked up a bobblehead clad in a kilt and fur hat.

"Now *this* I need." Sophie held the tiny man up to her face.

"Oh, really? You *need* a bagpiping bobblehead?"

Sophie looked at her blankly. "This speaks to me."

Charlotte laughed. "He can go in your dorm next year."

"Ah." Sophie set the figurine back on the shelf as if it had lost its appeal. "It's too soon for that."

Charlotte slipped a wooden bangle around her wrist. "Sooner than you think."

Sophie's life goal had been to become a lawyer ever since they'd watched *Legally Blonde* together when they were nine. Dalhousie University in Halifax offered a respected law program, once you had your undergrad. Way more years of school than Charlotte could ever afford.

"That's terrifying." Sophie sighed and looked at Charlotte out of the corner of her eye. "I don't suppose you've changed your mind at all?"

Charlotte removed the bracelet and put it back on the table. "No. I think it's best if I take the year off to work."

Sophie looked sad. "That's why I'm so scared."

"Sophie, we're still gonna see each other all the time."

"It'll be the first time we've been apart since the third grade."

"You went to Florida in grade seven. We survived that."

"That was for a week."

"I'll probably be in the city all the time. Nothing is going to change."

Sophie seemed unsure, reaching for the bagpiper again. "I just don't know if college is the right choice, right now. I don't know how I'm gonna feel in a year. It's ridiculous that we're supposed to choose the rest of our lives. Not just at eighteen, but at any point, really."

"Listen." Charlotte raised a finger to Sophie's face. "One of us has gotta go to university. There's twelve dollars in my bank account. So guess who's going? You."

Sophie smacked Charlotte's hand away playfully. "Or we could both blow it off, get an apartment, and pay for rent and food by becoming women of the night!"

"You mean like vigilante crime fighters?"

Sophie laughed. "Sure, let's go with that."

*"Damn."*

"What?"

"Forgot to tell Max no mayo."

Charlotte glanced through the windshield into the sandwich shop, where she could see Max waiting in line behind a cluster of middle-school girls. She skimmed her finger the length of the rubber runner along the bottom of the passenger side window. "But you love mayo."

Sophie eyed her. "I'm off it."

They'd spent the majority of the day down by the water, doing touristy things and taking touristy pictures even though they weren't really tourists at all. The day winding to a close left them headed back to River John, stopping for food right before the on-ramp for the highway.

"I was using his laptop when I was at his place," Sophie said quietly. "He had all these tabs open for Queen's University in Ontario."

Charlotte frowned and propped her feet up on the dashboard. "That might not mean anything."

"He would've said something if it didn't. The reason he hasn't mentioned it is because he's seriously considering it." Sophie pushed her hair back from her face, and Charlotte could see her eyes following Max through the window.

"Grade twelve hasn't even started yet," Charlotte reminded her. "He's going to change his mind a million times. You both will."

"Is it bad I don't care?" Sophie blurted out. Then she paused. "That sounds bad. I just mean...we can barely do no-distance, I can't exactly see us dating from different provinces."

"Maybe it would be good for you two," Charlotte joked.

Sophie laughed. "Maybe. But, I mean...sometimes I think we got together just out of habit. Or familiarity? We were already good friends, but dating is, like, too much more work or something. It's not sustainable."

"Then just end it. If you're so miserable."

"The thing is, I'm not miserable—I'm comfortable. It's fine...if I were brave enough, things would be very different."

Charlotte shifted and tucked her legs back underneath her. "You'll figure it out. You always do. And you have me."

Sophie bit her lip and looked at Charlotte, a cross between melancholy and a million miles away. "There's something else I need to tell you."

"Ugh. Sophie, please, I really don't want to know what else you found on Max's computer."

"Good call. We absolutely cannot let Charlotte find my blog about her." Max had appeared at Sophie's window, carrying three foot-long sandwiches. "Daily accounts of your life, Charlie, and my readers are so moved. I'm very close to getting you a movie deal."

"It probably won't be the kind of movie you're interested in, Max. Scarce nudity," Charlotte commented.

Max threw her sandwich onto her lap and handed Sophie hers. "You girls ready to go, then?"

"Yeah," Sophie said. "I'll drive."

The two hours passed in comfortable silence. Charlotte knew from experience that long car rides at night had more therapeutic value than almost anything else. The radio played quietly in the background, and Charlotte let her eyes flutter closed when she tilted her head against the window. Before she drifted off, something reminded her of her unfinished conversation with Sophie. Charlotte made a mental note to ask her about it the next time they were alone.

However, the next week was back to school, and the weekend after that was the car rally...and the following weeks made everything else seem unimportant, and the conversation dropped from her mind entirely.

# five

UNPACKING DIDN'T TAKE CHARLOTTE very long. There wasn't much to slide back into drawers or hang in closets or tuck away under her bed. When she left a year ago, she left most of her stuff behind. That way, she figured she'd have to come back for it. Her clothes were mostly second-hand—she and Sophie used to nag Sean to take them to the Frenchys in Truro where they'd spend hours rifling through the bins. Charlotte had her favourite things: a chunky Roots sweater she'd saved her birthday money for, and a pair of dark-wash Levi's that were fading at the edges from so much wear. Some of her nicer pieces were from Sophie, actually, who'd pass them down to her without ever making Charlotte feel like it was charity. "It just looks better on you. Keep it." She would shrug it off like it was nothing. Sophie had the extraordinary ability to only make you feel bad if she wanted to. Charlotte kept a few of her dad's big T-shirts with Alexander Keith's and other Canadian beer logos in her top drawer. She only wore them to sleep in, but it was nice to have them there.

Charlotte finished up and decided she should rediscover the town she had only glimpsed in the dark the night before. *Better get it over with quick.*

Charlotte sighed at herself in the mirror. She looked exhausted. Her skin was uneven and her eyebrows needed work. Sophie used to shape them for her when she was bored. "Sisters, not twins," Sophie would always say. Frowning, Charlotte picked at an impending zit on her chin. *Damnit.*

Sean had turned the TV on by the time she was back in the living room.

"I'm going out," she announced.

Sean managed to tear his eyes away from the *Today Show*, which was trying to teach him the mechanics of tiramisu. "You taking the car?"

"No, I'll walk."

Sean turned back to the screen. "Can you make tiramisu?"

"No, Sean. I can barely make Kraft Dinner."

"Damn." He sat up. "Hey, can you pick me up some smokes?"

"I thought you quit?" Sean quit smoking every couple of weeks.

He shot her a look and fished a crumpled twenty-dollar bill out of his pocket. "Just when I thought I missed you."

She took the money and jammed it in her pocket.

"Bring back the change," he told her as she slipped on her shoes.

Charlotte let the screen door slam closed behind her, pretending she hadn't heard him. The change would make up for her bus money last night.

The walk to the Quik Mart convenience store was exactly seven and a half minutes. The Quik Mart, a.k.a. the only social establishment in walking distance, served as the halfway point between Sophie's and Charlotte's.

Living in a small town wasn't all that different from boarding school, as it turned out. But at least at boarding school, people didn't know—and often didn't care—where you came from, or who your brother was, or how long your aunt and uncle had lived on the same plot of land. In River John, everyone knew everyone. Everyone was someone's ex, someone's little sister, or someone's best friend. Everyone's parents grew up together. There are no secrets in a small town.

At least, nothing stayed secret.

Charlotte was sixteen and Sean was eighteen when their dad had gotten sick. Everyone had acted like Charlotte was too young to understand, but that didn't stop her from hearing things around town. It was like she was the last person to know, for real. But she knew something was wrong when she realized that Mr. Anderson, the guy who owned the Quik Mart, had been under-charging her for everything out of pity.

Charlotte crossed the Quik Mart parking lot. The building looked the same as she remembered: faded white bricks and garbage bins lined up out back, and the same old men smoking outside beside their trucks. She could picture Sean here, in the field behind the store, drinking with his friends. She realized then how fast her heart was beating. Things looked completely different in the daylight—things *were* different, she told herself—but all she could see was that night in the dark and the heat.

Someone came out of the store then. The person nodded to her in the River John way as they passed. Charlotte jumped a bit but didn't think they noticed and pushed her way into the store, the air conditioning a sharp relief from the afternoon heat and her mind. The faint smell of egg rolls and honey garlic chicken wafted over from the Chinese restaurant next door. The door closed behind her and the little bell hanging above it announced her. The guy working the counter looked up and gave her a warm smile and a wave. He was Leo Hudson, a boy in her year who looked a bit like he had escaped from a boy band. Max's best friend. The two were almost never apart. Kind of like her and Sophie. Used to be.

"Charlotte! Max told me you were back," Leo said brightly as she approached the counter and he put down his phone. "What a text to wake up to. It's been a while. I heard one rumour that you ran off for a shotgun wedding."

"Close," she said, "you should try and get your info from a more credible source next time."

"Give me something."

"Windsor. Boarding school," Charlotte clarified.

"No wedding? Delilah Cooke owes me five bucks."

Delilah Cooke was the girl in their grade who knew everything about everyone. And a whole lot more about people that wasn't anywhere near true. If any gossip reached her, it would be out to the entire school within the hour.

"It wouldn't be the first time she was wrong." Charlotte smiled. "I'm just here for cigarettes for Sean."

Leo rang them up as Charlotte dug around her pockets for her brother's money.

"Her truth-to-bullshit ratio has gotten a lot better, though, to be fair. She's gotten way into fact checking. I'm starting to think she might be a tiny bit prophetic. And that's twelve bucks," Leo told her.

Charlotte sighed and passed over the twenty. "What a waste of money."

Leo handed back her change and the box of cigarettes. "I'm working here all summer, so please visit. I'll let you help yourself to the slushies in exchange for the company."

She smiled. "Might be illegal but still sounds like something I could get behind." She waved goodbye and made her way to the back of the store, seeing if there was anything that struck her fancy in the hardware section that she could buy with the rest of Sean's money.

"What are you doing?"

Charlotte didn't need to look up to recognize the voice. She motioned to an electric drill that was on display beside the nails. "Just looking to save some money on dental work."

Max was standing at the ancient pinball machine in the back of the store, looking at her over his shoulder. He had a cigarette tucked behind one ear and was wearing dark jeans with a black T-shirt, his hair all tossed back from his face. He didn't look all that surprised to see her, and for half a second she felt like she hadn't been gone at all. Max was back to being completely indifferent to her presence and it put her at ease.

"What are *you* doing?" she asked.

"Wasting my inheritance," he muttered bitterly, turning back to the game, which was dinging and chiming frantically.

She moved past him and leaned her shoulder against the top half of the machine that displayed Max's apparently unsatisfactory score.

"Thanks again for the ride home last night," she said.

"No problem. Happy to be of ser—*shit!*" Max slammed his hands against the sides of the machine. He looked at her. "You're distracting me."

"I can't help how unfairly beautiful I am," she said, batting her eyelashes at him sarcastically with her hands posed under her chin. "But I'll try and be less disruptive next time I'm minding my own business in a convenience store."

"If you came all this way to thank me for a lift, you could've sprung for a muffin basket."

"Allow me to jot that down."

"I've never received a muffin basket," Max explained with a shrug. "I think it's a nice idea."

She rolled her eyes.

"So I stopped by Sophie's this morning, to wish her a happy birthday," he continued.

"Oh? How'd that go?"

"Well, the good news is everyone at that party was far too wasted to really care one way or the other that you showed up. I *did* receive a text message from Delilah last night, which just had your name and a bunch of smiley faces and exclamation points, so we can assume she saw your grand entrance. I think she likes you." He looked up and caught her eye. "Not a bad alliance to have."

Charlotte laughed. She had to give Delilah credit for her dedication to spreading gossip. "So, what's the bad news?"

"I went to see Sophie."

"Yes, I got that. Did she say anything about me?"

"Not until I brought it up."

Charlotte pursed her lips. "So, shit disturber is just your job description, then?"

Max fiddled aggressively with the buttons on the sides of the machine. "I'm entitled to antagonize my ex-girlfriend. It's in the rules."

"Whatever. What did she say?"

Max cleared his throat and squared his shoulders in what Charlotte took to be an imitation of Sophie. *"I don't care if you saw her begging for change outside the Quik Mart, you're blocking my light!* Something like that. Then she started talking to Amy Chamberlain about whatever and I left." He jammed a button. "I didn't remind her that *I am,* in fact, her light."

"Well, that's not so bad—"

He cut her off with a sympathetic look. "I was paraphrasing. She really wanted me to promise to never speak to you again. I said, 'Sophie, how am I supposed to seduce and spy on her if we can't even *talk*?' She didn't like that."

"So we shouldn't be having this conversation right now?"

Max scoffed and pushed hair back from his face. "I'll talk to whoever I want. I don't care what Sophie thinks."

"How've you guys been? Since you ended things?"

"I didn't end anything," Max said, hip-checking the machine.

Huh. Charlotte had figured the breakup had been mutual—that's how Max made it sound last night. And if it hadn't been mutual, at least pushed for from his end.

"I wasn't really in a rush to break up with my girlfriend after a car accident put her in a wheelchair for the rest of her life. Jeeze." Like he had read her mind. Max must have been ready for people to think he'd dumped her.

Charlotte shifted her weight and looked at the floor, not used to being honest and serious with him. "Right. I'm sorry."

Max shrugged. "You didn't do it."

Charlotte didn't know why she assumed Sophie wouldn't have done the dumping. She thought Sophie might have needed Max, after everything. It's not like Charlotte had been around. That meant Sophie had lost the two people she'd been closest with in a matter of months, and that was on top of all the damage the accident had done. If she were on better terms with Sophie, Charlotte knew she would have known every single detail about the breakup in advance—they would have role-played and practiced how Sophie was going to do it and Charlotte would have been standing by, waiting for it to be over. A well orchestrated operation that they'd pull off together. It was strange, being so cut off from Sophie's life.

Charlotte folded her arms. Change the subject, Charlie. "So... don't you have anything better to do than hang out in the back of a convenience store?"

"Not that it's any of your business," Max's voice shot up several octaves as he struggled to maintain control of the pinball, "but if I had another option, that's where I'd be. One that is less emotionally grating on my poor nerves—"

"Max! Would you SHUT UP?" Leo's voice shot back from the front of the store.

"Anyway," Max continued, "if you must know, I'm here because the air conditioning at my house is busted. My dad has people there fixing it and I don't feel like socializing. And thirty degrees is too much for my weak constitution."

"What about your truck? It's summer vacation, wouldn't cruising around with the AC and a Michael Bublé CD be right up your alley?"

"We both know you never returned that CD the last time you borrowed it," he shot back. "And, I, uh...." Max apparently had no more quarters. She felt strangely like she had caught him off guard. "I don't really—the truck is.... Even after they cleaned it and everything." He scratched the back of his neck and avoided her eye. "I don't even know why I bothered getting them to fix it up, it was so mangled after.... I kind of hate driving now."

Charlotte's stomach lurched. Of course Max wouldn't enjoy hanging out in the steel death trap that had hurled him and his girlfriend into a ditch.

"I'm sorry," she said quickly. "I'm an idiot, I wasn't thinking—"

He held up a hand to stop her. "Don't worry about it."

"Max—"

"Charlotte. Honestly. It's just a...thing. It's for driving places that I can't walk to and that's it. I'm selling it when I leave for school in the fall. Forget about it," he assured her.

"Right. I, uh, should probably get going, anyway...." she trailed off uncomfortably. *Swing and a miss, Charlotte!* Had she forgotten how to socialize without touching on every sensitive subject possible? Max pulled out the cigarette he had tucked behind his ear and held it between his teeth.

"Want a walk home?" he asked, digging around for his lighter. She shook her head. "I'm okay."

Baby steps. Too much old-life interaction all at once.

Max looked put out. "Oh-*kay*."

She pulled out a quarter from the change in her pocket and placed it on the glass in front of him with two fingers. "Thanks again. I'll see you around, Max."

She marched out of the store, waving goodbye to Leo as she went. As she reached the door, she realized that this was probably one of the more meaningful conversations she and Max had ever shared, and it hinged on a muffin basket and a Michael Bublé CD. Perhaps she would have to reevaluate her passive-aggressive friendship with Max. In recent years, their only link had been Sophie. Sophie was where they overlapped. With Sophie removed from the equation, Charlotte didn't know what they were to each other. Her options in the pool of people who wanted to hang out with her were scarce. They'd been friends before, right? Maybe they could be friends again.

She heard Max swear loudly from the back of the store, and in the reflection of the door caught Leo shaking his head at his phone.

# six

THE SCREEN DOOR BANGED SHUT behind her.

"Got your cigarettes!" Charlotte called as she waltzed into the main room. After the Quik Mart, Charlotte had ducked into the Chinese restaurant to say hello to the owners and then trekked home along the beach. The water was warm and she had scooped up a few pieces of beach glass for her collection. Sean, somewhat surprisingly, had moved off his place on the sofa. His face emerged from the kitchen doorway. She wandered over and placed the pack of cigarettes on the counter. He was eating pizza out of a cardboard box.

"Thank you, kindly." Sean flicked a chunk of pineapple off his slice. He apparently had more faith in their ancient refrigerator than she did. He pulled out a cigarette and lifted it to his lips. Charlotte watched him dig a lighter out of his pocket; it was covered in yellow smiley faces.

"How cute," she said.

"It was a gift. To me. From me. Ah, *romance*."

"Don't smoke in the house." Charlotte rolled her eyes as she passed him, knowing it was one hundred percent likely Sean would smoke in the house anyway.

Next item on her list of things to conquer was her bedroom. She shut the door behind her, though the open-rafter layout of the house cancelled out any kind of privacy. She could hear Sean singing a Taylor Swift song from the other room.

Charlotte got down on her hands and knees, inspecting under her bed.

*Max + Sophie* was scrawled in Sophie's curly handwriting in the top corner of the English binder she dragged out. She contemplated this for a few moments before promptly tossing the binder over her shoulder. It hit the door and clattered to the ground with a crash. She heard Sean give a yelp of surprise from the kitchen.

That would be the garbage pile. She Frisbee-d the rest of her binders in the same direction as the first. A few minutes and several prayers of *please don't let that be a mouse* later, she had withdrawn two unmatched socks, a balled-up T-shirt that belonged to Sophie, a shot glass Max had gotten her in Cuba, half a pint of vodka that Sean had given her for her birthday, and five dollars and eleven cents. She left the liquor where it was and placed the money and shot glass on her dresser. She unfolded the T-shirt.

It was hot pink and sequins embellished the front. She caught a whiff of Sophie's familiar perfume. Flowery, but subtle. Charlotte threw the shirt in the corner; Sophie would never wear something that loud nowadays. They weren't fourteen anymore, no matter how much a part of Charlotte wished they were.

By mid-afternoon, she was sitting on her bed, facing the products of her purge. In front of the door was a large pile of things she had decided to throw out. Beside that was the cardboard box she had finally relented and filled with Sophie's belongings. Maybe she could convince Max to deliver it to the Thompsons' house for her. Or she could hold it hostage until Sophie vowed to be her friend again.

The cleaning made her feel a lot better. Sophie always told her that clutter promoted stress, and she was certainly clutter-free for the time being. Not exactly stress-free, but perhaps on the right track.

Charlotte turned her attention to the bed beneath her. The sheets had felt old and musty last night, because they hadn't been slept in for ages. With a fresh start came fresh linens, she supposed. She pulled herself to her feet and wandered back out to the hallway. Standing in the small space at the end of the hall, she reached up on her tip-toes and pulled down on the hatch. The wooden ladder unfolded before her, and she climbed the stairs to the attic.

The heat was thick and heavy at the top of the house, and the slanted ceiling was so low she had to stoop to move around. She peered over a couple old cardboard boxes. She and Sean had gone on a major cleaning spree after their dad died, and moved a ton of stuff into the attic. She'd told herself to label her own stuff that she packed away so she could find it later. If there was ever a time Charlotte wished she could go back and kick herself in the teeth for being so goddamn lazy, it was now.

She nudged one of the nearest boxes with her foot. Too heavy to be sheets. She knelt down and tore open the one beside it. Charlotte dug her hand through a box of china wrapped in old newspaper. Really, they should sell this stuff. Not like they'd be having a formal dinner party any time soon. She looked up and a dark object a couple feet farther back caught her eye.

A large, flat book. A photo album. Charlotte pulled it to her and took a seat on the dusty attic floor. On the inside cover, someone had written—in handwriting eerily similar to her own—the name *Eliza Montgomery*. Charlotte felt a weird sort of nostalgia. She didn't remember her.

Her dad used to call her mom Lizzie; apparently everyone had. Charlotte never got the chance to call her much of anything; she was gone before Charlotte had really started forming solid memories. Charlotte turned the plastic-lined pages slowly. They were filled with old photos of her mom in high school, concert tickets, and scraps of handwritten notes. Her dad was in a few of the photos. They had been high school sweethearts. They never married. Her dad hadn't really talked about her. Sean, especially not. There was a piece of her that didn't envy her brother, who had gotten to know and love their mom before she left. He missed her more.

Her mom had left when Charlotte was about three years old. A classic case of River John Syndrome. Charlotte thought it might have been better, romantic even, if her mom had fallen in love with someone else and left to be with them—at least there would have been a reason. Sean told Charlotte later that their mom just got sick of living in a town that was smaller than most high schools and simply took off one day. Sean had barely started school when it happened—came home one day and she was gone. She'd sent birthday cards until Charlotte turned nine, and that was the last contact she'd ever had with her. Sean had a picture of a three-year-old version of himself holding hands with a baby Charlotte, their mom laughing in the background because Charlotte had a grumpy baby face. It was the only picture Charlotte knew of with the three of them.

Charlotte closed the album with a loud thud, columns of dust swirling at the edges. A faded piece of newspaper peeked out of the top. Pulling it free of the pages, she saw it was an obituary for an Owen Montgomery, whom Charlotte guessed to be Eliza Montgomery's father—her grandfather.

Owen Montgomery had apparently been a loving husband and father, worked as an accountant, lived in Halifax for a while, and then moved to River John. He died of heart problems at age fifty-four. The date put her mom at not much older than Charlotte when her own father had died. It seemed like a pretty basic, tragic-yet-ordinary obituary. Charlotte wondered for half a second if her own eventual write-up would be the same twenty lines about how she lived and died in the same tiny town. To have your whole life summed up like that was kind of an unfair final evaluation.

Charlotte scanned the last line: *Survived by his wife, Catherine, and only child, Eliza.* Charlotte frowned. She didn't know very much about her mom, but she knew she had a sister. Heather. She was the one who had paid the tuition for Charlotte's boarding school last year. So the obituary was wrong about the number of kids he had.

Or...what?

If the missing-from-this-obituary Aunt Heather wasn't real, who had paid the thousands of dollars to enroll her at boarding school? Their dad's parents had passed away before Charlotte was born, and she didn't know her mother's family. There wasn't much in the way of extended family. That left Sean. How would he have come up with the money? Their dad had left them with some, but not nearly enough to cover school. She doubted there was some secret family bank account. Not when they'd spent the months after he died worrying how they would pay the bills and cover funeral costs.

Maybe "aunt" was being used lightly. Maybe Aunt Heather was more of a friend of their mom's who had stepped in to save the day. Maybe Sean had asked her. But the more Charlotte thought about it, the more unlikely it sounded. An essentially random person had footed a twenty-thousand-dollar bill to send her to boarding school at the last minute? Even if Sean had explained the whole situation to this theoretical Heather, it still seemed like too large a favour.

Charlotte had met very few people who she only connected to her mom. Most of the people in town knew her dad because he had grown up here—her mom hadn't moved to River John until high school. Charlotte didn't think she'd be able to convince the person who loved her most in the entire world to fork over twenty grand, let alone someone she had never met. Let alone someone who might not even exist.

Sean and Charlotte never heard from their mom, not even after their dad had died. They had enough money to stay afloat for a while, but Sean had had to give up college. He'd made it into the program he'd wanted at Saint Mary's University in Halifax. He originally planned on deferring a year after high school, to work and save money so he could eventually afford to live on campus. But their dad died just before Sean's high school graduation, and then Sean didn't have much of a choice. He had a little sister who couldn't live by herself while he went off to university. She still felt guilty. Sean started taking full-time hours at Home Depot,

Charlotte became the town's most frequent babysitter, and together they managed to scrape up enough money at the end of every month to pay the bills.

Sitting back on her heels, Charlotte pulled out her phone. She scrolled through her contacts, reading the names she hadn't looked at in a year. When she found who she was looking for, she took a deep breath before hitting *Call.* It rang several times before he answered.

"That didn't take long." She could hear Max smiling on his end. It was a stretch, maybe, but Max might be able to help her. Simon Hale, Max's father, ran the only bank in River John. Simon was the one who gave Sophie the job at the bank last summer—after Max asked him, after Sophie had begged Max for a month. Maybe with some convincing, Max could get her in to see Sean's bank account.

"Don't start," Charlotte snapped, tucking the photo album with the obituary under her arm and clambering toward the exit. "I need your help."


Charlotte pushed the ladder back into place and shut the attic hatch.

Sean was in his bedroom, shuffling around boxes and god knows what else under his bed, just like she had been doing earlier.

"What are you looking for?" she asked.

"Uh." Sean pulled his head out from the clearance. You couldn't pay her to even look under there. "Nothing. Just reorganizing. What can I say, you've inspired me. Who were you just talking to?"

Certainly not anyone who would help her figure out where Sean had found twenty thousand dollars. "Max."

"Hale?"

"No, from Fury Road."

"Max Hale?"

"Am I speaking English?"

"What are you talking to Max Hale for?" Sean asked.

"Nothing," she said, "it's not your business." She narrowed her eyes. "What do you care?" Charlotte didn't understand his hostility. She'd been friends with Max since they were young. Sean had too, really. That was just what happened in a small town.

Sean sat back on his heels with a sigh. "Whatever. What are we doing for lunch?"

Charlotte traced a pattern on the door frame. "Based on what's in the cupboard, probably Scooby-Doo gummies."

Sean angled his head like he wasn't all that opposed to the idea.

"If you leave me twenty bucks I can get food later," she said. "Hang in there until dinner."

"What are you doing today?"

She shifted her weight away from the door frame. "Baking muffins."

"For me?"

"No." Charlotte turned to leave him, but the nagging from the photo album under her arm kept her there. "Do you ever think about mom?" she asked before she could stop herself.

Sean, who was pulling himself to his feet, staggered slightly. "What?"

She tilted the album toward him a bit while still holding onto it protectively. She watched his eyes settle on the album for the first time. "Do you miss her?"

"I, uh." He shifted uncomfortably. "I don't really think about her."

Charlotte hadn't expected his bluntness. "Oh."

"Do you?" Sean returned without looking at her, like he felt it was his brotherly duty to ask.

She shrugged. "I don't know. I didn't really know her. Did you ever know any of her family?" Charlotte pressed the words out carefully.

"No," Sean said, his gaze focused back under his bed.

Charlotte took the lull in conversation as an opportunity to slip back to her room. So much for philanthropic Aunt Heather.

# seven

SHE WOKE UP THE NEXT morning to a text from Max: *Come over.* Either he was propositioning her, or he had found what she wanted.

The closest thing she could find to a basket for her muffins was a popcorn bowl from the movie theatre that had characters from *Shrek 2* on it. Martha Stewart would be so proud. Hopefully Max wouldn't notice that the muffins inside were a day old.

Max's house was large, sprawling, and flat. Floor-to-ceiling bay windows lined the walls. Charlotte remembered driving the getaway car last year when Sophie egged those very windows after he had dumped her four days before the winter formal. They reconciled a few days later, the morning of the dance.

Charlotte had met Max in grade primary. Sophie's family moved to River John in the third grade, and Sophie made them a trio. As she and Sophie grew closer, Max branched off toward the other guys at school, like Leo. In what Charlotte saw as a diplomatic arranged marriage of two friend groups, Sophie and Max started dating around Christmas of grade eleven. They broke up for a while in the spring, but got back together in time for the end of school.

She knocked a few times on the glass sliding door until Max appeared on the other side. He pulled the door open and she pushed the ogre-covered bucket into his hands.

Max looked down at it for several seconds, before his eyes flicked to hers. Smirking, he said: "Is this...a muffin basket?"

"It was the best I could come up with on short notice. They're oatmeal. I didn't have any chocolate chips."

Max laughed and stepped aside, motioning for her to come in. "Mental note to do you favours more often."

Max's house had the same cottage-type layout as most of the houses in River John. His was similar to hers, only with nicer furniture that actually matched. Doors lined the walls of the main room and led off to a couple bedrooms, bathroom, and an office. The kitchen was off to the side.

"So, what did you find out?" she asked as Max peeled the plastic wrap off the top of the bucket and inspected the inside carefully.

"Oh, right. It's in my room, one sec."

He disappeared into a room at the back corner of the house, taking the muffins with him.

Charlotte looked around. She hadn't been here in ages. On the coffee table was a photo of Max's stepmother, Deirdre. Max's mom and dad had gotten divorced back when Max and Charlotte were in junior high. His mom lived in Halifax now, and Max visited semi-frequently. Charlotte wandered over to look at the wall above an armoire, decorated with photos from town events and local newspaper clippings about Simon's various business endeavours.

Simon Hale looked like he had taken a wrong turn two hours back and decided to stay for the hell of it. With the exception of maybe some sentimental entrepreneurs and lottery winners who had retired here, Simon was arguably the richest man in town. He was successful, handsome, well groomed. He was young, too. Charlotte guessed him to be early forties. She knew Max and his father were not very close.

"Ta-da." Max re-emerged holding a file folder. He was still carrying the bucket of muffins. "I'm amazing, don't worry. Blood, sweat, and, like, four tears. Sean's transaction records, courtesy of my father. Not that he, uh, knows about it. So don't bring it up." Together, they walked to the dining room. "We're lucky he can access the bank server from this computer here and that I know his password is the same for everything. It's *I Love My Son 123*."

Charlotte grinned. "Really?"

"No."

"Thank you," she said sincerely as he laid the folder on the dining room table. "I owe you."

Max shrugged and popped a bite of muffin in his mouth. "It gave me something to do. Very thrilling," he said, his words distorted by the muffin chunk. "Oops. Sorry." He swallowed. "It's been a while since I had this much fun."

"Yeah," Charlotte said, reaching for the folder. "It hasn't exactly been a fun year."

She could feel Max's eyes on her as she flipped through the papers.

"Well," he said, "you missed most of the fun when you were gallivanting across the province."

Offhanded, like always, but Charlotte caught his meaning. *What would you know about it, Charlotte? You weren't here.*

"Thanks for reminding me," she said coolly, pivoting between him and the door, her fight or flight response warning her to leave.

"I didn't mean it like—"

"No, you're right. I wasn't here. I can't...change that." That was a weak answer and she knew it, but she didn't feel like explaining herself to Max. What she'd done was between her and Sophie.

"I don't know if that's how apologies work," Max observed. Sophie may have been Charlotte's best friend but Max knew her too. Could see right through her.

"What's it to you?" she hissed. "You didn't care about me before I left. I didn't do anything to *you.*"

So much for flight.

Max looked at her like he couldn't believe what he was hearing. "Are you kidding me? I didn't say you did anything to *me.*

I watched Sophie go through hell without her best friend. My girlfriend. The worst year of her life. Our lives."

Charlotte knew it was hard to excuse what she did, especially when it seemed that there was no reason. She could scream the truth at him, fling it right back in his face, and maybe he'd understand. He might even pity her. But was it worth it? Probably not. She didn't need pity, anyway.

"This," Charlotte said slowly, "is about me and Sophie. Not you. You don't *get* to take what I broke and make it about you. And Sophie doesn't need you to defend her."

"I know that. Sophie and I may have sometimes been shitty to each other, but we protected each other. We always did. We still do."

Charlotte pressed her fingers to her temple like she had a headache. "Why now, then?" She looked him in the eye. "Why not have this fight yesterday? You were fine with me twenty-four hours ago."

"Because what's your plan, Charlie?" Max threw his hands out, gesturing at nothing. "You're more preoccupied with what drugs your brother might be doing and what he may or may not have in his bank account than Sophie. I thought you would at least be making an effort, I thought...." He sighed. "You came back here expecting everything to go back to how it was."

Charlotte grimaced. "I've been back for two days, Max. I'm giving Sophie space. Time."

"Right. I'm sure she didn't get enough of that while you were gone," he shot back. "There's a difference between remorse and guilt, Charlotte." Max's cheeks were flushed, and Charlotte wondered how long he'd wanted to say of all this to her. He'd had the year to think about it. She shook her head and turned to leave, but he grabbed her arm and spun her back around.

"Sophie wrote to you, you know. Dozens of letters."

"Let go of me."

Max released her arm. "And she never sent them. Do you know how much she cried over you?"

Charlotte froze. She didn't like thinking about the interim days between when Sophie found out Charlotte had left and when she realized she wasn't coming back. If it had been the other way around, Charlotte wouldn't have believed it. She would have waited for Sophie to reappear, saying it had all been a joke.

Charlotte stepped closer to him. "Don't act like my being there would have magically made everything better—"

"Well it damn sure would have helped! Sophie isn't the only person you left behind, Charlotte!" Max yelled. They were suddenly so close that Charlotte found herself backed against the sliding glass door. "I had a paralyzed girlfriend who refused to speak to me, and I couldn't do anything to help. You weren't there; you didn't see what I did. You don't spend every single second terrified that the accident could have gone differently. You didn't have to—you were gone. All she wanted was you, and I was the consolation prize and I hate that you left us here like we were nothing."

The pause hung in the air. There it was. Even Max looked surprised by the statement. There was the truth: he hated her because he had to piece his life—the life the three of them used to share—back together. No, Charlotte corrected herself. He didn't hate her because of that. Max was a good person, whether Charlotte wanted to admit it or not. He resented her because she didn't have to do that same piecing back together. She had naively thought that the only person who got to hate her was Sophie. But that wasn't how grief worked, really. It was more like water, seeping into everything. And you couldn't help what it touched, where it flowed. Max was allowed to hate her not just because he loved Sophie, but because she'd left him behind, too.

And they both couldn't ignore the fact that a simple slip, or a split-second difference in timing, and things could have ended differently.

"Sometimes it doesn't matter how much you love someone," Max said quietly, focused on the patterned tablecloth on the dining room table. "Sometimes it doesn't fix shit."

"I'm sorry," Charlotte said feebly.

"No, you aren't." He shook his head. "God. Not for anyone but yourself. By the way—there was nothing. Sean has all of ninety-six dollars in his bank account. As far as I'm concerned, this is the last thing we have in common."

"What, because we had so much in common before?" she asked bitterly.

"Yeah, at least Sophie could tolerate us both before."

"Well, as far as I'm concerned, you can go to hell," Charlotte snapped. She grabbed the folder from the table and slid the door open with more force than necessary, sending it rattling down the tracks. She stormed out of the house, and Max made no move to stop her.

# eight

june
two years earlier

ALL CHARLOTTE REMEMBERED ABOUT THE funeral service was
shoulders. Shoulders in neat lines in each of the pews, and people
gently touching her on the shoulder with quiet, uneasy smiles.
Max and Sophie on either side of her, their shoulders pressed
together because they never left her on her own. Charlotte always
making an effort to keep her shoulders back. Straight. *Don't cry.*
Halfway through the service when she felt her shoulders sliding
down, buckling a bit as she tried to keep a sob inside, Charlotte
felt Sophie slip a hand inside hers, felt her press her shoulders into
hers, and Charlotte felt a bit stronger.

"What's wrong?"

Charlotte stared down at the scuffed porcelain mug in her
hand. The service had just finished. "Nothing," she said.

Max raised his eyebrows, watching her from where he was
standing. "Something's wrong."

"My dad just died."

Sophie gave a tiny, bitter laugh and Max sighed. "Something
other than that," he said.

Charlotte twisted up her mouth. Whatever. If anyone at this funeral got to be dramatic it was her. And Sean, but she didn't know where he was.

"Too much cream," Charlotte admitted finally, holding the mug out to him. Max took it back and looked inside.

"It's not too bad," he said.

Sophie stretched up on to her tiptoes to look at the coffee. "Bleh," she said.

Max tried to give the mug to Sophie. "Do you want this?" Sophie shook her head. "Do you want me to get another one?" Max asked Charlotte.

"No, I'm fine."

"Go," Sophie said to Max, who turned away and took the coffee with him.

Charlotte pushed herself back a bit farther onto the stage, sticking her legs straight out. The reception was at the Legion hall, just down the road from the old elementary school, where they always held the community lobster suppers. People were milling around the hall in the quiet, funereal sort of way, clutching coffees and teas and little pieces of shortbread. As Charlotte watched them she realized it actually didn't look that different from when tables were laid out with goods and wares for the Sunday flea market. People kind of had the same demeanour. Her dad had loved the Sunday market.

Charlotte tilted her head back and looked straight up at the speckled ceiling. *Don't cry.* She didn't know why she was so fixated on not crying. It was her dad's funeral. Her dad, who was a fisherman and a chronic smoker and exceptionally good at *Jeopardy*. Who had been young and healthy until last year. Well, maybe not super healthy, hence the chain-smoking, but strong. Indestructible and constant. They buried him at the small cemetery down the Cape John Road and Charlotte couldn't decide if she was happy or sad she'd have to drive by it every day. She thought, for a while at least, that she just might not look.

She pictured the misty mornings when she was little, when he'd head off to work early and she'd get out of bed to say goodbye to him. "Be back at high tide," he used to say to her. She would say something like, "Dad, I'm seven, I don't know when high tide is," and he'd explain he'd be back just before supper. Sean was in charge until then, he'd tell her. Usually her dad left so early that they were supposed to be asleep for almost half the time he was gone, but as soon as their dad left the house Charlotte was always awake. Mrs. Duncan, a tiny old lady from down the lane, would come check in on them and stay with them when she had time. Thinking about it later, Charlotte couldn't believe she and her brother hadn't burned the house down or stuck a fork in an electrical outlet or something. Even once Charlotte was old enough to understand how tides worked, and how they were usually at different times every week or so, her dad would still tell her he'd be back at high tide.

Really, Charlotte knew the reason she so badly wanted not to cry was because if she started, she had no idea when she would be able to stop.

"How're you doing, CBR?" Sophie reached across and squeezed Charlotte's knee.

"I'm okay," Charlotte lied, because it was the easiest thing to say. "I'm tired. And I don't know where Sean is."

"Do you wanna go look for him?" Sophie asked.

"Nah. He'll turn up."

Someone had come to stand in front of them and cleared their throat.

Simon Hale, Max's father, looked down his very straight nose at them like he didn't know what he should say.

"Charlotte," he began, sounding very much like the young kids from town whose parents had forced them to come up and tell Charlotte they were sorry her dad died, "Max and I are very sorry about your father. He was a good man."

*Duh*, Charlotte thought. It's not like anyone turned up at a funeral to say the person sucked. Saying he was good was about as obvious as saying he was dead.

"Uh, thanks," Charlotte said, looking up to meet Simon's eye, which was more than she could say for him.

Simon Hale was tall, quiet, and serious. Half the people Charlotte and Sophie went to school with were in love with him. The other half were in love with Max. Simon had dark hair like his son and the same kind of floppy curls and wide shoulders. Charlotte had never seen a dad smile as rarely as Simon Hale.

"I don't know if he and I ever had a conversation that wasn't about you or your brother," Simon told her quietly.

"Oh. Thanks," Charlotte realized she was repeating herself. "I guess? Uh. Sorry. I know. I know he loved us."

Max appeared beside his father and held a new cup of coffee out to her. "This okay?" he asked.

Charlotte took the mug and inspected it. The coffee was a sort of almond colour. Good. There was a commotion at the far end of the hall and Charlotte looked up to see Sean coming back through the doors, his top button undone and his hair messy. Charlotte didn't know where he would have gotten booze but hey, it was their father's funeral. The siblings made eye contact from across the old wooden floor and it was almost like they didn't know each other. Charlotte felt like they were estranged parents at a kid's recital but with less to celebrate. Charlotte realized her whole little group had turned around to look at Sean.

"How's that coffee?" Sophie asked, turning back to her. Max swivelled back around to hear her answer. Simon stalked off, his duty done.

Charlotte raised the mug in a tiny toast and silently called out to her dad. "Peachy," she said.

Charlotte could feel something close to her face. She weighed her options, keeping her eyes shut. It was either a ghost-slash-murderer (both?), a member of the family of squirrels that her dad said he'd gotten rid of last summer, or it was Sophie Thompson looking for attention. Charlotte took her chances and opened her eyes.

Sophie was beside her, her face on Charlotte's pillow and their noses almost touching. Sophie looked wide awake and expectant.

"You promised that if you slept over you would actually sleep," Charlotte mumbled, closing her eyes again.

She could picture the glint Sophie got in her eyes when she was about to ask Charlotte to do something. Charlotte would protest, and then Sophie would get her way. It was a familiar routine.

"Wanna go for a swim?" Sophie asked.

"No, it's like one A.M."

"Yes. High tide."

"It's too dark." Charlotte sniffed and snuggled her face down farther into the pillow.

"There's a full moon."

"Isn't that a bad omen?"

"Well, it's not like today can get any worse," Sophie reasoned.

Charlotte opened her eyes again and looked at Sophie.

"What?"

Charlotte rolled over and faced the wall. Sophie made some grumbling noises and sat up.

"What's the temperature?" Charlotte asked the wall.

There was a pause while Sophie checked her phone. "It's sixteen."

"That's not warm."

Sophie shrugged, sensing victory. "It's not cold. Come on," she said. "Max is with Leo and they really want to go. Max suggested it. Spend quality time together, you know."

"Don't I get a one-time veto against your crazy ideas on today of all days?"

"No. Today is why we need to do this."

"Ah, shit. Christ." Sophie was swearing as the four of them tried a hopeless stumble down the rocky bank to the beach.

"It's almost like," Max started, his hands shooting out in both directions for balance, "rock climbing in the dark is a bad idea."

"Wasn't this your idea?" Charlotte asked as she stuck her foot out and tapped her flip-flop on a suspicious patch of tiny flat rocks to test her weight.

"Hell, no. I'm doing this for you. Sophie told me you wanted to swim."

Charlotte sighed, hopping over a downed driftwood log and onto the beach. "I can't believe she Parent Trapped us again."

"I wasn't even given a choice," Leo complained from behind Max as the boys clambered down onto the rocky shore. "Max was all: 'we gotta go, *Leo*, Charlotte's dad died, *Leo*, I know you signed up for a night of *Twin Peaks, Leo.*' I mean, no offence, Charlie, but it's like ten degrees out here."

"That's what I said," Charlotte agreed.

"It's sixteen," Sophie called testily from ahead of them.

Sophie was right; the tide was high and the waterline had come to eat up most of the rock and sand. Charlotte watched Sophie slip out of her flip-flops and dip a foot into the water. Even if Sophie was cold, she would never let them see. Never admit defeat. Charlotte stepped forward and joined her, the water swirling around their ankles. It was cold. It was only June, after all, and the Northumberland Strait was never warm until at least July. Still, it felt refreshing. Charlotte took a deep breath and couldn't really remember the last time she'd done so. The white moon shimmered against the surface of the water like a silver lake on the ocean and Charlotte couldn't help but think there were reflections of some things in everything else.

Even though the water was freezing, they were able to splash around for about twenty minutes before Charlotte thought she could feel ice clinging to her eyelashes. She knew that wasn't possible for June, but still. It felt like it. Max was the most chicken of all of them and only really came in to his hips. Sophie dunked her hair. It was invigorating to feel cold and clean and awake. To be in the same water she'd been in so many times with her dad, who'd help her jump waves and then carry her home. The ocean felt like a tribute to him, and it felt like he was everywhere.

"Let's go home," Sophie finally said. Charlotte had been watching the waves move against the shore while Max and Leo sat back out of the water on a couple flat rocks, towels pulled tightly around their shoulders. "Warm up."

They all trooped behind Sophie as she led them back up the bank and over the hill to Charlotte's house, dripping and shivering. The sky was so clear, all stars and far-off galaxies. That was one of Charlotte's favourite things about River John—no city meant no light pollution to dim everything out there in space.

They bumped their way back inside, trying to be quiet because Sean might be sleeping. Sophie was scrubbing her towel into her wet hair while Max pulled chairs up to the wood stove for the four of them. Charlotte was looking through one of the drawers by the fridge for a lighter when a gloomy-looking Sean appeared at the other end of the kitchen.

"What're you guys doing?" he grumbled. The moonlight through the window made him look like he was made of stone.

"Sorry, we didn't mean to wake you," Charlotte said, pulling a lighter free from under a few pairs of tongs. "We went swimming."

"S'okay."

"Charlie?" She heard Max's voice in the other room.

Charlotte poked her head out of the kitchen doorway so she could see him. He was holding a white envelope.

"It was on top of the fireplace," Max said. "It's for you."

Charlotte felt Sean step forward behind her. On the back of the envelope, *Charlotte & Sean* was written in straight letters. Charlotte recognized the handwriting. She crossed the room and grabbed it out of Max's hand and tore the seal open, all in the space of a breath. She could feel Sean reading over her shoulder.

*Dear Sean, Dear Charlotte,*

*This is not an emergency letter, or a sad letter, or a goodbye letter. It would only be an emergency if I knew you two didn't have each other. And it's not goodbye, either, because you know* it's not true. I'll be just where you know to look for me. I'll be around when you need me, somewhere out there in the water. Lord willing, we would have had a lot more time together, the three of us, but I'm sorry that this is how we have to leave things for now. There's more I could say, but you already know it all. There's lots we talked about near the end but I wanted you to have it in writing, too. You two were the biggest part of my life and I want you two to have the biggest life. Wherever you go, I hope you take River John and your family with you.

*Hell or high water,*
*Dad*

# nine

HER FIGHT WITH MAX, at the very least, made Charlotte determined to prove him wrong. She wasn't afraid of Sophie. Charlotte gathered herself out of bed the next morning and stopped at the Quik Mart on the way to grab a few Mars bars (Sophie's favourite).

Okay, maybe she was a little afraid.

When she arrived, the bungalow was quiet. Any evidence of the party the other night was gone. An SUV Charlotte had never seen before sat in the driveway—a new ride that she guessed was wheelchair accessible.

Maybe Sophie wasn't home. She could leave the chocolate in the mailbox and Sophie could riddle out the meaning herself. Max's harsh words—and true words, Charlotte reminded herself as she considered running in the opposite direction—tugged at a guilty part of her brain. She sighed. Didn't exactly qualify as making an effort.

On her right was a ramp she hadn't noticed in the dark the night of the party. Sophie had built a new life. She'd had to. Charlotte knocked on the door to avoid looking at the new wood against the old.

Denzel barked a few times and there was movement from the inside of the house. After a minute, the door was pulled open. Sophie's expression shifted from interested to less.

"I got out of bed for this," Sophie said, sounding like it was aimed more at herself or Denzel than at Charlotte. Sophie pushed herself back from the door, but the fact that she didn't slam it in Charlotte's face made her figure it was safe to come inside. Denzel padded over to her and Charlotte scratched between his ears.

"What, did you leave something here on Friday?" Sophie asked. "Other than your dignity?"

Charlotte mimed a fake laugh at the back of Sophie's head and aimed a kick at Sophie's Hunter boots beside the door. Sophie turned and raised an eyebrow when they smacked to the ground.

The doorway opened into Sophie's living room, which Charlotte had last seen flooded with their classmates. Charlotte folded her arms and leaned her hip against the edge of the sofa. Sophie was at the back of the room near the patio door, where the afternoon sun cast a golden halo around her hair. It was bizarre; Sophie had always towered over Charlotte.

"I brought you chocolate," Charlotte explained, stepping forward to place it on the coffee table between them like some sort of sacrificial offering.

Sophie looked down at the gift for a half second before her eyes flicked away. "Well," she mused sarcastically, "consider yourself forgiven."

Charlotte sighed and a silence fell between them. Thirty seconds in and they already had nothing to say to each other.

"Tell me what I can do," Charlotte finally said. "I need things to be okay between us."

"That doesn't do anything for me," Sophie said, looking out into the yard like she was plotting her escape. "Why would I want to do anything for you?"

"Sophie, please—"

Sophie made an aggravated sort of noise. "You can't do anything. Don't you get it? You've done enough, Charlie."

"We've been friends for ten years, more than that, you're my best friend—"

"*Shut up*," Sophie hissed. It was a tone she reserved for when her lackeys were being needy, or when a guy wouldn't give up flirting with her. An inconvenience, instead of something that was truly bothering her. It wasn't venomous or laced with hate the way Max's words had been. If Sophie hated her, it would be a relief, Charlotte thought. Because Sophie only hated people she loved. "Don't call me that," Sophie continued.

"We're just calling it quits, then?" Charlotte countered.

Sophie frowned. "Let's not even *try* to make me sound like the bad guy here. I didn't flee the town in the dead of night."

"I know, okay?" Charlotte pushed back some hair from her face. "You're right."

"You never called, or even texted."

"I didn't know what to say," Charlotte said honestly. "'Hey Soph, I moved across the province for a bit, mind shipping me my phone charger?'"

"Literally *anything* would have been better than finding out from your brother. You didn't even say goodbye."

"I didn't know when—or if—I was coming back," Charlotte said. "I didn't know how to tell you that."

"This is the same conversation we had on my birthday. We're going in circles." Sophie tossed her hair back off her tanned shoulders, staring blankly out the window for several seconds. Sophie suddenly snapped back to attention. "I'm tired. You should go."

"It's barely noon," Charlotte noted.

"Yes. Well, Charlotte, I've had a very long, hard day already due to my estranged childhood best friend reappearing from nowhere after a year of total silence," Sophie said sweetly.

Charlotte played her last card. "If you make me leave, I'm taking the chocolate with me."

Sophie's head whipped back in her direction—mild panic. Charlotte smirked and for a brief second, Sophie looked less murderous than usual.

Sophie moved over to the coffee table and grabbed one of the bars, tearing open the wrapper. "Fine. You have until I finish this."

Charlotte's first reaction was that maybe she should have prepared a please-forgive-me PowerPoint.

"You don't have to forgive me now, I wouldn't expect you to...I just want you to know I didn't do any of it to hurt you, or—"

Sophie waved a hand through the air, mid-bite. "I don't care that you're sorry. I should friggin' hope you are. I want to know *why*."

Charlotte knew that was coming. Running off to a mysterious boarding school a few counties over was a move that invited people to ask questions. And she couldn't just brush Sophie off like she did everyone else.

"It was...Sean wanted me to go," she told her. Not entirely a lie. Not technically. There was no point making up something more elaborate; they were experts at knowing when the other was lying.

Sophie chewed and looked at Charlotte like she had confessed to leaving because she was secretly Kate Middleton.

"Reeeally?" Sophie stretched about four extra syllables out of the word. "He wanted *you* to go to *boarding school*? Was that so he can focus more on his crappy part-time job and pot money?"

Charlotte ignored the dig at her only remaining family member. "It's a long story. I don't even know where to start—"

Sophie cut her off by rolling her eyes. "*Please*, spare me the dramatics. I'm losing interest and have actual problems to deal with. Now, can I eat this other chocolate bar or do you need to return it to pay the mortgage?"

Charlotte recalled fondly, just moments earlier, when she had missed Sophie.

"Good to know the year I missed hasn't made you any less of a raging bitch," Charlotte said.

Sophie peeled back the wrapper of the second chocolate bar without looking at Charlotte. "It's good to know you're not going to be one of those people who is only nice to me because of my tragic backstory."

Charlotte pushed herself away from the sofa. "I'm trying this new thing where I'm not so pathetic, which you were so kind to point out at your party."

Sophie threw her hands in the air and choked on a laugh. Charlotte noticed she used her hands while she was talking about a million times more than she'd used to.

"Oh, yes, leave it to Charlotte Anne-Hathaway-in-*Les-Mis* Romer to play the victim," Sophie snapped. "The world has really been oh-so-unfair to you, my dear."

"Sophie, please—"

"Stop saying my name," Sophie cried, her voice gaining more of an edge with every word. She didn't sound sad or hurt; she sounded angry. Angry, finally, because Charlotte knew she was sort of pushing her luck. She knew how it looked, reappearing in Sophie's life but completely unable to explain herself. She'd be angry, too.

"I want you to know—" Charlotte tried.

"I don't care!" Sophie screamed at last. "I don't care what you, or anybody else, wants! You want to say you're sorry, you want to help, you want us to be friends—I don't care. Not about anyone. Definitely not about you. I stopped caring after I lost everything. My boyfriend, my parents, my baby, everyone at school, and like— ha, ha—the ability to walk—" Sophie stopped herself like she'd made a mistake.

Charlotte replayed the list in her head. "What did you say?"

Sophie opened and closed her mouth and was eying Charlotte carefully.

"Your...baby?" Charlotte asked.

"Max," Sophie said unevenly, looking intently at the coffee table.

"You already said Max."

Sophie shrunk in her chair. She twisted the ring on her middle finger—a gift from Max for her seventeenth birthday—and wouldn't make eye contact with Charlotte.

"I used to tell you everything," Sophie said quietly. "And then you weren't there. So I didn't tell anyone."

Charlotte swallowed. "What?"

"I lost it...in the hospital, after."

Charlotte crossed the room and sank into a kneeling position. She tentatively reached out and placed a hand on Sophie's cheek. "I don't know you were...."

"You can't tell anyone," Sophie whispered to her knees. "Please."

"I won't, I won't." Charlotte smoothed back a few pieces of Sophie's blonde hair. "Come on, talk to me."

"No one knows."

"Max?"

"*No*," Sophie said quickly. "Especially not. He would hate me for not telling him. You can't tell him. You have to swear."

"Okay, okay," Charlotte said, still trying to process. "I'm sorry."

"Don't." Sophie shook her head. "I'm so sick of pity. People think that when something bad happens to you they have a free pass to just...*commiserate* with you. And tell you about whatever bad thing happened to them. Like it opens you up. I'm tired of people trying to get in."

"I wasn't trying to pry," Charlotte started, having to actively stop herself from apologizing again.

"I wasn't talking about you, really. You've known me for a long time. You're about as in as they get." Charlotte caught Sophie's sort-of smile before she shifted back to reserved. "Whether I like it or not."

Sean wasn't home when Charlotte got back. She made herself a late lunch of peanut butter toast with the last of the bread that wasn't approximately older than she was. The pop-up contraption inside the toaster didn't work properly, so they sort of had to guess when the toast was done and pluck it out with a pair of plastic chopsticks. She always ended up burning hers.

As Charlotte smeared the peanut butter on the dark slab that no longer really resembled bread, her visit with Sophie looped through her mind. Sophie had cried for a while before claiming she needed "alone time" and dismissed her.

So, they had taken what seemed like a step forward, but now somehow everything was a thousand times worse. The thought occurred to Charlotte that, had there been no accident, Sophie would not only be able to walk but she might have had a baby, too. Maybe. She wasn't sure what Sophie would have chosen to do, but she should have had the chance to choose. All the misery the accident had caused was still unfolding. Like little ripples.

There was an uncomfortable clenching in Charlotte's chest. She wondered if Max and Sophie would have stayed together if they had to raise a baby together. Is that why Sophie had broken up with him, for good? Charlotte wiped the remaining peanut butter off the knife and onto the rim of the jar, licking a stray glob off her thumb. She sighed. It had been a long day. Er, morning and early afternoon.

She spent the rest of the day indoors, trying to clean and tidy and trying not to think of much else. Charlotte went to bed early that night, after a dinner of peanut butter right off a spoon and some stale goldfish crackers. All the DVDs they owned had been arranged alphabetically by title. Sean didn't come home.

# ten

CHARLOTTE FIGURED ALL HER ACCUMULATED bad karma must have ripped a hole in the time-space continuum because time refused to pass. Two days trickled by in what felt like a week. She was putting off getting out of bed, watching the sun carve a path across the ceiling as a new day leaked into the house. Mornings were sneaky bastards. For a split second or two she'd be ready to tackle the day, and then she remembered all the shitty things that happened in the previous twenty-four hours and she'd change her mind, deciding that burying her face under the covers was the best option. Then she'd start the vicious cycle of being too anxious to do anything followed by feeling guilty for doing nothing.

So, status report. What Sophie had told her two days ago was... complicated. And Sophie had gone through that alone, on top of everything else. A selfish part of Charlotte was glad Sophie had been able to confide in her, but it wasn't totally fair to treat this as a step forward. Sophie probably still hated her, but at least they had talked. Max, on the other hand, definitely hated her. No real loss there. And last but not least, there was the lingering question of how Sean managed to pull twenty thousand dollars out of his ass. Charlotte groaned, weighing the probability that if she simply never got out of bed again no one would come looking for her.

Sean might. Debatable.

The smell of frying pancakes was what eventually dragged her out of bed that morning. Nothing said keep on keeping on like pancakes. She leaned against the door frame at the far end of the kitchen, watching Sean poke the half-cooked batter in the pan expectantly.

"Morning!" he said cheerily without looking up. The thick liquid sputtered a bit.

"Morning. You got mix?" Charlotte asked, referring to the few groceries she had seen him bring home yesterday morning. She shimmied past him to the coffee machine, flicking the switch at the back and digging for a filter off the shelf above it.

He looked at her as she scooped the last bit of coffee grinds at the bottom of the tin into the machine.

"Mix? Nah, in this house we wing it."

She leaned back against the counter, facing the fridge. Beside the grocery list that was more wishful thinking than anything, a small photograph was held in place by a smiley face magnet. It showed younger versions of their dad and one of his friends in front of the Berlin Wall.

Charlotte wrinkled her nose, peering into the large ceramic bowl containing the rest of the batter. "Winged it to what degree?"

Sean waved the spatula nonchalantly. "You can substitute eggs for extra butter, right?"

"I think I'll just stick to the coffee."

"You drink way too much of that stuff," Sean commented. "It's not good for you."

"Hmm, kind of like smoking?"

"I'm just saying." He flipped a pancake. "It's no wonder you're up all night."

Charlotte filled her mug once the maker was finished gurgling and retrieved the borderline-expired milk from the fridge. She hadn't been sleeping, which was apparently no secret in their house, but it wasn't because of the coffee, she knew that much.

"Well, I'll swear off coffee when you quit smoking."

He bumped her shoulder with his own. "You worry about yourself."

"Maybe you should take your own advice?"

"I'm your brother," he grumbled, flipping another pancake, which was stark white on one side and had visible clumps of flour clinging to it. "And I don't like your attitude. Don't act all holier-than-thou just because of your fancy boarding school book-learning."

Charlotte and Sean had spoken once, maybe twice, while she was in Windsor. Normally, they were very close. They weren't particularly affectionate, didn't wear matching sweaters or anything, and Charlotte had had to miss homecoming to bail Sean out of jail, but they were still close. That's what happened when you were all that was left of your family. But in the month or so leading up to her departure, there'd been an obvious shift. Charlotte knew she had to leave, that she couldn't risk staying in town. But she still would have, if Sean hadn't made her go. And once she was gone, it took a long time before they found things to say to each other again.

"It wasn't that fancy." She shrugged. "It was fine. School is school."

This was her chance.

"I'll have to send Aunt Heather a thank-you note," she tried. "You know, for the tuition."

He didn't meet her eyes as he studied the browned side of his pancake. It was like it took him a second to remember who Aunt Heather was. "Yeah, maybe."

"Actually, that's a great idea," she said, testing her coffee and her luck, "you wouldn't happen to have her home address, would you?"

She watched his face contort into a frown. "No, I don't," he said thinly.

"Phone number? Do you think she has Facebook? Social insurance number? Oh, I could Skype her!" Charlotte knew she was pushing it, but she continued. You couldn't just go around making up distant relatives and expect to get away with it. "I feel like she's the kind of woman with a blog," Charlotte mused.

Sean was glaring at her now. "Something you'd like to say, Charlie?"

She folded her arms and matched his gaze. "Nothing. Just how lucky I am to have such a caring, generous family member like Aunt Heather."

"Whatever it is that you think you know—"

"Look, I know we don't have an Aunt Heather, Sean! Or any aunt, for that matter."

His jaw was hard set. "How do you—"

"It doesn't matter. What matters is where the hell you got all that money."

Sean turned away, staring determinedly at the display on the stove like he could make time move faster through the conversation. "It doesn't make a difference now."

"Doesn't make a difference? Sean, do you not remember how broke we were? We barely had enough money to pay for anything after dad died. Do you not remember how they were gonna take me away?" That had been a scary two weeks.

"Of course I remember," Sean snapped. "Why do you think I got a job? Gave up college? So that I wouldn't lose you. Charlie, *everything* I've done is so I wouldn't lose you."

He wasn't talking about foster care anymore. They were caught up to much more recent events. Caught up to her leaving, and why.

She sighed, and put her coffee cup down. "I know that, all right? But that doesn't mean I can just let you off the hook. We're not talking about dealing a hundred bucks' worth of weed, Sean, we're talking about twenty thousand dollars."

"I know how this sounds," he hissed, "but I'm asking you to trust me."

Charlotte raised a hand and rubbed her forehead absently. "That's kind of asking a lot, Sean. I don't know where that money came from; I don't even really want to think about it. There was no money after dad died—"

"I know that!" Sean roared suddenly. "I did what I needed to—"

"Do you *hear* yourself right now?" Charlotte cried. "You can't just say stuff like that and then expect me to not think the worst! You sound like a goddamn hit man, Sean."

"The money was mine from another account."

"You mean the accounts that were closed after dad died, because we had to drain them all? Come on, I'm not stupid."

Sean had let the second pancake burn, pinching the bridge of his nose between his thumb and forefinger as if he were dealing with an irritating child. "What do you want me to say? It's my work money."

Charlotte threw her hands in the air in exasperation. "Well, good to know you're sticking to your story! What happened to Aunt Heather?"

Sean turned off the burner with a sigh and scooped the rest of the batter into the trash. "Aunt Heather was a lie I made up so my nosy sister would be able to live with herself and not have to wake up every morning thinking that her brother sacrificed everything for her. Next time, I'll spare you and get straight to it: the money for your boarding school was the last shred of hope I had for one day getting out of this shithole town and doing something with my life. Dad's savings. For both of us. You think I didn't want to keep it for you to go to university? But I had to. I had to use it. Feel better?"

He didn't even give her time to respond before he left the kitchen, shooting a last venomous glare over his shoulder.

"Sean, wait!" she called after him. "Where are you going?"

"Nowhere, obviously."

She heard the back door slam. A few seconds later, she saw the car rumble down the lane through the kitchen window. Charlotte sighed, sorting some dishes on the counter into the sink. That had gone about as well as her previous encounters over the last few days. *Congrats, Charlie. There's officially not a person in town who'll speak to you.*

Running a hand through her hair, she followed Sean's path out the back door and hopped off the porch. She was heading for the shed—the old workshop.

A brief struggle ensued as she attempted to slide open the heavy wooden door. Inside felt more like a museum than a workshop. Nothing looked like it had been touched since her dad passed away. Beneath a giant drop cloth sat the old truck their dad had used to teach Sean to drive standard. Charlotte flicked the switch for the solitary overhead light bulb, and was surprised when a hum of strained electricity filled the room.

Nearest to the door was the old work desk. Every inch of it was covered in a thick layer of sawdust and regular dust. The wall above the desktop was covered entirely with faded photographs off an old disposable camera, discoloured and curling at the edges from a lifetime in a shed that was less than weatherproof. The photos were all combinations of her family with Max and Sophie's families. There was one of her (princess), Sophie (Raggedy Ann), Max (pirate), and Sean (zombie) on Halloween approximately a million years ago. Sean teaching her to ride a bike when she was seven and he was nine. Sophie's parents and Charlotte's dad at a barbecue in their backyard, not far from where Charlotte stood now. Sean and Max, twelve and ten, hanging upside down backwards off a sofa and watching TV. Sophie taking a one-handed selfie with Sean in the background. Sophie had always loved to take pictures, would force you to line up and pose for any minor event or celebration until she got one that was perfect. Charlotte stared at the photo, frowning. Sophie was an only child but spent so much time over at their place it sometimes seemed like there were three Romer siblings.

Sean was lying. But why? Charlotte knew there was no secret money from their dad. There couldn't be.

Toward the bottom of the wall, almost hidden from view by a soup can filled with screwdrivers, was a picture of her mom and dad. They weren't much older than Sean was now. They were standing on the beach, a huge smile on her mom's face. Charlotte reflected that she really did look like her mom. Must be the hair. Her dad looked younger, scruffier, and healthier than she had ever seen him, particularly in the last months of his life.

Beside their dad, a two-year-old Sean clutched his father's hand and waved to the camera. Charlotte's mother had both hands resting on her protruding belly, and Charlotte knew that it wouldn't be long before she was added to the family.

She also realized that it wouldn't be long before her mom left them for good.

People often said that Charlotte reminded them of her mother. She knew that they looked alike, that they talked in the same cadence, and curled cursive letters the same way. But Charlotte didn't like cherries and her dad ate them like candy so Charlotte had always wondered where she got that from.

Charlotte studied her father's content expression in the beach photograph. She wondered how much he'd hated her mom for leaving. How do you forgive someone you love for completely abandoning you?

Charlotte was gripped with the thought that perhaps she had more in common with her mother than she thought.

No, she steadied herself. No. She, at least, had come back.

# eleven

IT WAS FOUR DAYS LATER and she and Sean had barely spoken. Sean had asked her to pass the Wheat Thins once (a nutritious dinner) but she'd tossed them with a little more force than necessary and dumped the entire box in his lap. That was the end of that conversation. Since they had no more Wheat Thins and she didn't want to ask Sean for money to order pizza, she settled on walking to the Quik Mart. A slushie and chocolate bar would do her. Plus, she could get out of the house for a while and talk to Leo. She'd texted Sophie, but didn't get a response. Charlotte didn't really blame her.

It was dark by the time she got to the store. When she stepped inside, the first thing she saw was Max buying cigarettes at the counter. Both he and Leo looked up at her as she entered. With a jolt, she remembered her conversation with Sophie and found herself trying to picture Max as dad to a tiny baby who was a mix of him and Sophie. And Max didn't even know. Her stomach stirred with unease but she wasn't sure if it was because she pitied Max or felt guilty because she knew and he didn't.

"Hey!" Leo smiled brightly and waved.

Scowling, Max snatched his cigarettes and placed one between his teeth. "God. I hate small towns."

Even though Leo frowned at Max's comment, Charlotte was sure he had been filled in on what a shitty person Max thought she was.

"He's just trying to flirt, Charlotte," Leo said loudly. Max shot him a look.

"Hey, Leo." She sent him a polite smile before backing up out of the store, returning the way she'd come. "Sorry, forgot my wallet." She wasn't really up to another fight with Max.

Someone followed her out of the store. "Hey!"

She spun around, intending on telling Max to kindly screw off, thank you very much, but it was not Max who had stumbled out behind her.

"I thought that was you." The boy caught up to her as she rounded the corner of the building. It was considerably darker out of sight from giant, well-lit windows. Nick Sutter—the same age, make, and model as her brother, but lacking Sean's decency.

Charlotte felt her breath catch in her throat but immediately swallowed it.

"Nick," she said quietly. The name tasted bitter in her mouth.

"I heard you were back in town."

"Sean's waiting up for me," was all Charlotte managed.

Nick gave a low chuckle. He reached out and took her chin in his fingers. "Aw, maybe you should tell him you'll be home late—"

"Don't touch me," she spat, shoving his hand away. Her eyes darted around the deserted parking lot. Of course there was nobody around.

"Hey, hey." Nick put his hands up. "You know I'm just playing with you."

"Stay away from me," she said. She had to stop herself from adding "please." Her manners came out in times of sheer panic and desperation. "Don't forget, I was there. I saw what you did."

"I really hope that wasn't supposed to be a threat," Nick hissed, the words sliding out through gritted teeth.

Before she could react, he twisted his hand around her wrist and yanked her towards him. Charlotte cried out in protest, using her free hand as her only protection. He tried to stop her, grabbing her arms roughly and pinning them to her sides, but she squirmed and slipped an arm free. She swung her fist around, aiming blindly for his face. Nick growled when her knuckles connected with his cheekbone and shoved her hard, sending her sprawling on the sidewalk. Pain cracked through her wrists and at her knees where she slammed unevenly against the concrete.

"What the hell are you doing?"

Charlotte's head snapped up. Max, holding a bag of Doritos, glanced between the two of them.

"Nothing," Nick muttered, straightening up. "None of your business."

"Get away from her."

From her place on the ground, Charlotte could see Nick slowly moving his left hand to his back pocket. God knew what he had on him. This could be bad. She felt like she was on fire. Her blood pulsed with the heat of anxiety and adrenaline.

"Max, please," she said, "come on, let's just go."

Max looked like he had forgotten she was there. Nick seemed to have weighed his options and took the momentary distraction to slink around the corner, out of sight. Watching him leave allowed Charlotte to try to breathe for the first time since she'd left the Quik Mart.

Max appeared at her side, kneeling down on the pavement. "Christ, what—are you hurt?"

"Don't, no, stop." She shook her head frantically, squeezing her eyes tightly together. She could still feel Nick's hand around her wrist, could feel him near her. She couldn't catch her breath and the earth was spinning and she thought she was going to be sick.

No. She took a deep breath, forcing air into her lungs. She allowed herself ten seconds. Ten seconds to break and put everything back together again. She thought of her favourite song and the way the sea looked in the sunlight and the mornings when she woke up and everything was dewy and fog hung in the air. Her ten seconds were up.

"Charlie," Max tried again, "you have to tell me if you're hurt."

"I'm okay," she managed to say.

"Can you stand?"

"Yes."

Carefully, he helped her to her feet.

"You have to let me take you to the clinic."

*"No."* Sean would lose it if he found out. "It's okay. I'm okay. It's just a few scrapes."

She let the wall behind her support her weight. Deep breaths. She could feel Max's eyes on her, standing a few steps away.

"You're bleeding."

Charlotte glanced down. He was right. Her palms and knees were cut up from when she'd fallen. "Yeah, I...."

"No." Max took a step toward her. He reached out and gently placed his hand alongside her cheek. "Here. You're bleeding."

Her hand rose to her face, feeling the split skin his hand was nearly covering. She withdrew it. There were smudges of blood on her fingertips. She must have done a face-plant when Nick knocked her down.

Max moved closer. "What...was that," his voice didn't go up at the end. It wasn't a question.

She shook her head. "Nothing."

Max pulled his hand back from her face. "Yes, that would have been my exact thoughts when I read the paper tomorrow under the headline: Local Girl Murdered Outside Convenience Store."

She matched his hard stare. "You've made it perfectly clear that we're not friends," she said coolly. "What do you want me to say?"

"Um, something along the lines of 'gee, thanks for saving my skin, Max.'"

Charlotte glared at him. "You want my gratitude?"

"No, I want an explanation. That guy could have hurt you, Charlotte. Bad. That was not random. That was not nothing."

Charlotte closed her eyes and rubbed at the back of her neck. She wasn't really inclined to admit that Max had probably just saved her from being a lot worse off than she was. Was she ungrateful? No. Was she too proud to admit that? Absolutely.

"Charlie?"

"I just want to go home," she said quietly, her voice even.

"Charlotte—"

"I'm fine," she snapped. She wondered if she'd ever uttered the damn phrase and actually meant it. Charlotte pushed away from the wall. Her right knee shuddered at the movement.

"Shit." Max's hand shot out to hold her side.

Her heartbeat quickened when she was reminded of Nick groping her. She squirmed away. "I'm okay, let go of me—"

He immediately stepped back from her, dropping his hands, probably seeing the panic in her eyes. "I'm sorry. I'm just trying to help."

"I know, I know." Charlotte buried her face in her hands, focusing on breathing. "I'm sorry."

"You don't have to apologize. Just...take a second, all right?" Max said quietly. "It's okay. You're safe."

She nodded. "I know."

He was quiet for a moment, and then: "What can I do?"

"Nothing. I just want to go home."

She wandered away from the deserted parking lot, and knew Max was trailing behind. He caught up to her in a few strides, and they fell into a silent step along the side of the road. She wiped at her eyes and focused on keeping her breathing steady. River John was a town of a few hundred people. Charlotte had always known she would encounter Nick at some point—once school ended and she didn't have anywhere to hide. She just hadn't expected it to be so soon. She hadn't anticipated how quickly the anxiety and fear could come racing back, infecting every inch of her. She didn't want to be scared. If she was scared, then she felt like everything had been for nothing. Then Nick won.

Her feet were moving independently, her mind moving faster than she could. In a matter of moments, in a chance encounter outside a gas station, Nick was back in her life.

Max took her wrist gently and she realized she had walked past her own driveway.

"Right." She shook her head. She faced the narrow lane for a moment before starting down it. He followed all the way to her front door, where she watched him stop himself from stepping across the threshold.

"Are you okay?" he asked for what felt like the millionth time as she stepped inside. "To be alone?"

Charlotte sucked in a breath through her teeth. Sean had gone out earlier; it was unlikely he was home or would be coming back at all. She wasn't sure of the answer to Max's question. "Um...it doesn't matter, I think I'll just go to bed—"

"It does matter. It doesn't have to be me but...." He shrugged. "You should talk to someone. Keeping things to yourself will eat you alive. Believe me."

Charlotte pressed her palms together, making the cuts sting. She stared down at them, tears pricking at the backs of her eyes, but she blinked them away. She hadn't cried about what happened with Nick in a very long time. "I can't," she whispered.

"Tell me. I'll never bring it up again. What did he do to you?"

A light laugh escaped her lips. The answer to that was simple. It was everything that came after that was complicated. She'd spent the last year trying to keep what had happened a secret. To protect Sean. To protect herself. *Tell him!* a part of her was screaming. *Tell him why you left and hurt everyone you loved and ruined your life.* But Charlotte knew if she told him, then it would be real.

"Charlie," he said softly. "You can trust me."

It wasn't that. She trusted Max, she just didn't know if she trusted herself not to drown again.

"You have people who care about you, you know that right?" Max said.

For them, she'd have to swim. She took a shaky breath.

"Nick is...why I left a year ago."

Max's eyebrows shot up his forehead. "*What?*"

Charlotte sighed. "Come in, it's kind of a long story."

She turned and headed down the hallway and almost regretted her decision when she heard the front door shut behind him.

She slid into the tiny bathroom and waited for him to appear behind her.

*Lay down some ground rules. Set some boundaries. Retain something close to control.*

"I'll tell you everything," she said to his reflection in the mirror above the sink, "but you have to promise not to say anything until I'm completely finished. All right?"

Charlotte took several deep breaths and opened the medicine cabinet. She reached for what she was looking for. The small tube of antibiotic cream slipped through her fingers into the basin of the sink.

"Let me," he said, his hand at her waist, thumb parallel with her spine. Max guided her into sitting on the edge of the tub and knelt down in front of her.

"Okay." Charlotte lined up her feet with the edge of the tile. "Last year, like, two weeks before the accident, I got in a huge fight with Sean. I was so *sick* of him being out all night and never being home and getting into trouble and I just lost it."

It had been like any of their fights. Always the same. When Sean left, he let the screen door slam and the whole house shook behind him. She didn't know how long she had stood at the sink, seething.

Max was using a facecloth to gently clean her knee. His expression was blank.

"One night," Charlotte continued, "it was past three and I went out looking for him. I found him at the Quik Mart, drinking out back with Nick. They were messing around with some guy who was with them. It got rough, the guy was pissed, Nick was drunk."

She could see herself tucked against the wall, peeking around the corner at her brother and two others. The dark helped, kept all four of them shadowed. One shoved the other. She watched Sean jump out of the way. Nick wound his fist back and he and the other boy collided. Charlotte slammed her eyes shut but wasn't quick enough to block out the sound of his head hitting the pavement.

"That was the guy they found dead there last summer," Max finished for her. He swiped some of the antibiotic cream across the mark before peeling the wrapping off of a Band-Aid and pressing it to her knee. "He was only young. Sean knew him?"

She didn't know his name. As she stared at him on the concrete, she didn't realize she had given herself away. When she'd looked up, Nick was staring at her, trying to place who she was. Everything was different after that.

"They had met. I think he ran in the same circles as Nick." She nodded. "And then Nick spotted me. I took off, ran home. When Sean got back he told me he'd tried to convince Nick I hadn't seen anything. But Nick couldn't afford to have witnesses. His record is worse than Sean's." Charlotte sighed. "It was stupid of me. I should have gone straight to the police.

"But Sean told me he would take care of it. And then school started, and then that weekend was the car rally. And what happened with Nick wasn't important anymore. The only thing that mattered was Sophie." Charlotte felt like she was talking about something that had happened to someone else. She was staring at the same spot on the floor, going through the facts in order like they were a grocery list. She didn't feel anything as the words left her. "One night I was walking home from the Quik Mart or whatever, and...well, Nick was waiting for me at the end of the driveway."

Charlotte could still feel Nick's tight grip on her arm, pulling her down. Headphones ripped out of her ears in the struggle and her phone knocked to the ground.

Max had moved up to cleaning her hands, and paused to search her face. "But, I mean, you—you're fine, right? Nothing happened, nothing happened to you—"

Nick had his hood covering his face but she had known exactly who he was. Knew what he wanted. She saw the glint of something silver in the streetlight.

"I'm okay. Sean was home. He heard me scream. But Nick was right there and I tried to get away but...," she trailed off. She had never shown anyone what she was about to show Max. She pulled up the hem of her T-shirt, revealing a jagged scar above her hip. A grim reminder of last year. It had hurt when Nick struck bone, but his carelessness had saved her life.

"I think he just meant to scare me but it got out of hand. Nick stabbed me when I tried to run," she blurted out quicker than she had intended, and realized after that it was the first time she had ever said it aloud. Max immediately released her.

"It wasn't that bad," Charlotte explained, letting her shirt fall back down. She wasn't sure why she felt the need to downplay one of the most traumatic experiences of her life but she felt weirdly embarrassed. Exposed. "I'm lucky Nick's an idiot."

"But you—you never told us...." Max kept reaching toward her but then retracting, like he wanted to comfort her but didn't want to make her uneasy.

"Sean went ballistic," she continued. "He told me to pack my things and I was on my way to school in Windsor. So that's the story. I wasn't...pregnant, and I'm not undercover for the CIA, and I didn't run off with some guy." She laughed bitterly. "I just had to go. And I never said goodbye because I couldn't. The last time I saw Sophie was...us falling asleep in her bed after an episode of *Vampire Diaries*. And that was it."

"You should've told someone," Max insisted quietly. "If you had told someone what you saw, there would've been no way in hell you'd have been walking home alone that night."

"Who was I going to tell, you or Sophie?" Really, she told herself, that was what she'd been the most nervous about. If Nick knew that she was still talking to her friends while she was away, he might think she'd told them what happened, which would put them at risk too. It was better to cultivate a mystery—to disappear in the middle of the night and have no one left with any information. Sophie hating her, in front of everyone, cleared Sophie of any connection to what happened. Charlotte fumbled to explain. "I couldn't let...I wouldn't be able to forgive myself if either of you had gotten hurt."

"Yeah, and how are we supposed to forgive ourselves now that you've gotten hurt?"

She paused for a moment. "It wasn't your responsibility. It was my mess."

"Go to the police," Max said.

Charlotte shook her head. "Nick and Sean were the only ones there. I can't risk it. Nothing is worth Sean ending up in prison."

"Then tell Sophie. She'd understand—"

Charlotte cut him off. "Sophie has enough going on," And Max didn't even know the whole story—not about the baby Sophie lost. For a split second she wanted to tell him, but she checked herself. Not her story to tell. "Besides, whatever the reason I left, it's still not an excuse." She didn't need Max to tell her what he thought would be the best way out of her own misery. Charlotte shook her head. "And the fewer people who know, the better. I didn't want anyone to know about this. I don't want Nick to go after anyone else. If no one else knows...then it's just done."

Max didn't say anything. Charlotte filled the moments by twisting the cap of a shampoo bottle sitting on the arm of the tub next to her. She couldn't believe she'd told him. When she came home, she had sworn she would never tell anyone. Technically she'd never even told Sean. *Oh, so what Charlotte?* she scolded herself. The person she'd ended up confiding her darkest secret in was a sarcastic know-it-all whom she'd spent the majority of last few days planning the best way to have shipped off to Peru.

Max pulled her from those thoughts when he touched a dab of cream to her cheek. "I'm sorry," he said hoarsely, "I didn't know."

Charlotte shivered as the wind picked up outside and rattled through the house. It was dark and it was cold. And it was too late to hate him. "You have nothing to be sorry for."

"No, but I'm sorry about the other day. About what I said."

She didn't say anything.

"I shouldn't have said I hated you."

"Why, because it's true? Or because it isn't?"

His thumb accidentally grazed the mark on her cheek and he avoided answering. "How's your head?"

"Spinning," she admitted, though it wasn't entirely because of being knocked down. She'd been knocked down plenty of times before.

"I'm glad you aren't dead," he said without looking at her.

A laugh burst past Charlotte's lips—a genuine one—and the sensation felt foreign. It had been a while since she'd really laughed. And even longer since she'd felt like someone would lament her death.

The realization knocked her over the back of the head all over again. She was having trouble connecting the Max who was Sophie's boyfriend—who was loud and charming and filled up a room, and whom Sophie had never told what happened—to the Max sitting in front of her. Charlotte wasn't sure Sophie should have kept him in the dark, but looking at him now she saw no other option. It would just be another thing for Max to add to the list of things he blamed himself for. And maybe just another thing that would have driven him and Sophie apart. She wondered then if holding back the truth was ever for the better, if it was to protect the people you loved.

"Thank you for telling me," he said, stretching to his feet. He still wouldn't look at her.

"Thanks for...well, you know." She'd have to check the Quik Mart to see if they had thank-you cards for situations like this ("Roses are red, violets are blue, shout-out to you for saving me from being stabbed again").

"Are you okay to be alone?" Max asked.

She squirmed past him into the hall. "I'm gonna have to be," she said, nodding to Sean's empty bedroom.

Max was watching her carefully. "I can stay until you fall asleep. If you want."

Charlotte paused in the doorway to her bedroom. Her heart twinged a bit at his offer—she knew he meant to comfort her, and deep down that was how he made her feel, but embarrassment flared in her stomach. "You don't have to do that. Really," she said, because she felt like that was the right thing to say. Like she was weak, a burden, if she admitted she needed help. Was that a girl thing?

Max did a weird sort of half-dance a few steps down the hall toward the living room. "I'll just...be on the couch. For a bit. Really. If you need anything...you shouldn't be alone."

"Max—"

"Just until you fall asleep," he said again, and she watched him disappear into the other room.

# twelve

december
nineteen months earlier

"DO YOU LIKE THE silver or gold?"

Charlotte lifted her eyes from the box she was rooting through. "I already told you gold twice. I don't think you care, Soph."

Sophie twisted her face like that offended her. She weighed a loop of garland in either hand, holding them against the pine tree.

"I like the silver," Sophie decided.

"Hallelujah." Charlotte flipped the flaps of the box shut. "Can we put stuff on the tree yet?"

"Yes, jeeze." Sophie rolled her eyes. "You got somewhere else to be?"

Charlotte ignored her and draped the rejected gold tinsel around her shoulders like a boa.

"You and Sean still coming tonight?" Sophie continued as she hoisted a box of ornaments from the floor to rest on her hip.

"Yup." Charlotte nodded. "I'm getting him out of the house. And you know how Sean loves those animated felt Christmas movies. You want a ride over?"

"Yes, please. You know how I love Sean." Sophie winked at Charlotte, because flirting with Sean was one of Sophie's favourite pastimes—and one of her favourite ways to annoy Charlotte. Sophie fished an ornament out of the box that looked like a potato covered with feathers and sequins and held it out to her questioningly.

Charlotte didn't have a chance to respond before a cool breeze blew through the living room when the front door opened.

Max stepped in, a flurry of snowflakes and cold.

"It's freezing," he bit out, sliding his shoulders free of his coat.

"What took so long?" Sophie pranced over and pressed a kiss to his lips.

Max scoffed as he pulled away. "Sorry it took so long to get you two gas station coffee and Doritos. It's blizzarding."

"That's why you're my favourite of all my boyfriends," Sophie sang, sweeter than usual. "Where is it?"

Max blinked a few times, apparently expecting more gratitude. He lifted a plastic bag and coffee tray onto the dining room table. "You're welcome."

Sophie peeked under the coffee lids. "Mine is...?"

Max wandered over to the Christmas tree, where Charlotte stood. "Mine has milk, Charlie's has whipped cream, as per her demands."

Charlotte threaded an ornament hook through a delicate gold ball. Sophie drank her coffee black.

"I appreciate it," Charlotte told him.

"You put whipped cream on everything. Grow up. It cost extra, by the way."

Charlotte rolled her eyes. "I doubt Leo even charged you for any of this."

"Getting coffee for my girlfriend is one thing, Charlie, but I don't even like you."

"Whatever happened to the season of giving?"

"I like your boa," he said with a laugh, tugging at the end of the tinsel near her elbow.

"He's right, Charlie," Sophie said as she handed Charlotte her drink. "It's coffee. It doesn't need whipped cream."

"Keeps me sweet."

Max laughed again, nodding toward the bare tree. "Looks like you two have been working hard."

"We've been *planning*," Sophie explained. "More than half the battle. Not that you'd know."

Max threw himself down in an armchair angled beside the tree. "Christ. How long am I gonna hear about this?"

Charlotte bit her lip and didn't want to see the look on Sophie's face. Max had gotten Sophie a gift card for Christmas. Hadn't gone over well. They'd exchanged early because Max was supposed to be going to Florida with his mom for Christmas.

"Isn't our one-month anniversary enough of a gift?" Max asked.

Charlotte snorted.

"You're lucky it's Christmas and I'm in a forgiving mood," Sophie snapped.

"FYI, I've started charting your progress in a spreadsheet," Charlotte said to Max. "You're not doing too hot."

"I didn't think it was that bad a gift!" Max argued.

Charlotte winced. "It *is* a little impersonal."

"We've only been together for a few weeks," he protested.

"You've known me since I was ten!" Sophie said.

Max shrugged. "So has everyone in River John."

Sophie set her jaw but didn't reply, grabbing the tinsel from Charlotte and nearly strangling her in the process as she forcefully returned it to its box. Charlotte made a circle with her thumb and finger behind Sophie's back and aimed the gesture at Max.

Max replied with a different hand gesture.

• • •

"No, no, a little more to the left. Left. *Sean, left.*"

Sean ignored her instructions and stepped back from the tree, now pushed against the wall in almost the way she wanted.

Charlotte tilted her head and framed the tree, making an L with each hand.

She patted Sean on the shoulder. "Close enough. Good work, bro. Charlie Brown would be proud."

Snow was falling in twisting columns outside, layering the ground in a white blanket. Their not-such-a-bad-little-tree was the last thing on their holiday to-do list. They had a strict no-presents rule. Presents were expensive, and there were very limited shopping options in town anyway. Two years ago she'd gotten Sean a pack of disposable lighters and beef jerky from the Quik Mart, and he'd gotten her a wrench from Home Depot (for what, exactly? So she could fix things? Was it a heavy-handed metaphor? Because it doubled as a weapon?). That'd been the end of the Romer Sibling Christmas Gift Exchange.

"What time's dinner, again?" Sean shook his head vigorously, a couple of pine needles bouncing out of his hair.

"Max said to be at his place for six. Please wear a shirt that doesn't have a Boston sports team logo on it."

Sean shot her a look. "But I ironed one and everything."

She would have believed him, but she knew they didn't own an iron. "Wear the shirt I got you for your birthday," she suggested.

Sean wrinkled his face. "It makes me look twelve."

Charlotte was distracted by the kitchen timer, which was beeping loudly from the stovetop. "It just has a collar, Sean."

She grabbed a pair of oven mitts and checked inside the oven. Shortbread cookies were basically the only thing she was capable of making. School bake sale? Shortbread cookies. Someone's birthday? Shortbread cookies. Someone found your long-term boyfriend on Tinder? Have some shortbread cookies.

Charlotte pulled the trays from the oven and chucked them on top of the stove. A few of the Santas were a bit lopsided and one Rudolph was missing a leg. File those under the abstract category.

"Oh," she started, remembering the conversation from earlier, "and I told Sophie we'd pick her up."

"Sophie Thompson?"

"No, the other Sophie I spend all my time with."

"Oh." He nodded a few times. "All right, that's fine."

Charlotte turned back to her cookies, shaking her head. "Good to know."


"This one looks like an *ogre*."

"Really? It's from my Maxwell Hale cookie cutter set." Charlotte set the tray of cookies down on the coffee table as Max inspected the one he'd snatched during the trip from the kitchen to the living room. He was looking at the cookie as if it were an oversized bug.

"You don't have to eat it, you know," Charlotte said.

"Oh, I'm going to eat it. Will I be happy about it? No."

Charlotte rolled her eyes and returned to the kitchen, where Sean and Sophie were working on dinner.

"PSA: the turkey is now spaghetti," Sophie told her. "Did you know turkey takes, like, six hours to cook? And it's six, so. We'll skip it."

"Ah, yes, we're doing really well on that *planning* thing, eh, Soph?" Charlotte folded her arms and leaned against the counter.

Sean was scooping canned sauce into a pan. "We should just order a pizza."

Sophie smacked him in shoulder. "We should *not*. It's Christmas."

Sean flushed and Charlotte pretended she hadn't noticed. Sophie, on the other hand, smiled to herself and elbowed him gently in the side. Sean would never admit it but Sophie was just about the only person he let boss him around.

Max ducked into the kitchen, shoving Charlotte out of the way. "You guys are missing *A Christmas Story*."

"Charlie can't watch that movie because the kid in it reminds her of Jamie Stevenson," Sophie said matter-of-factly.

Charlotte groaned and covered her face with her hand. Jamie Stevenson had attended North Colchester High for a few months last year. Charlotte met him at one of Sophie's parties, but they never spoke again. "We made out once. Don't remind me."

"You made out with Jamie Stevenson?" Max asked.

"They did a lot more than make out," Sophie said, making a face at the sauce she had taken over stirring.

"Sophie!"

"I don't think I want to be here for this," Sean said.

"Don't worry, Sean, they didn't sleep together," Sophie said reassuringly. "Everyone knows Charlotte was saving herself for Jude Peters. Last Canada Day weekend."

"*Sophie!*"

"Okay, I'm out," Sean dropped the empty sauce can and pushed himself away from the counter.

"She's right," Max said to Charlotte, "everyone does know that. Jude told the whole school."

"Miss him," Charlotte recalled sarcastically. Jude Peters had been Charlotte's beloved boyfriend who moved to Ottawa with his family just before school started. Like most of her interactions with boys, Charlotte and Jude's awkward first sex had been weird and disappointing. But everyone had taken the proper precautions and no one got pregnant or died.

"She beat me by *three weeks*!" Sophie cried, slapping her hand to the counter for emphasis. "Three weeks."

Sean was covering his eyes and looked like he wanted the floor to open beneath him. "Kill me, please."

"I'm going for a smoke, wanna come?" Max offered.

"Yup."

"It's freezing out," Sophie said, scolding.

They shrugged and left anyway.

"Those two are not long for this world." Sophie shook her head as Charlotte began filling a large pot with water for the pasta.

"Thanks for all that, by the way."

Sophie sighed, resting her elbow on Charlotte's shoulder. She ignored Charlotte's comment. "They're so lucky to have us."

"Tell me about it."

• • •

"I didn't say *Die Hard* wasn't a Christmas movie, I just said we weren't watching it." Sophie grabbed the remote from Max as they flicked through the Netflix queue.

"*The Vow* is not a Christmas movie, Sophie."

Sean sat next to Charlotte on the sofa. "Are they always like this?" he asked.

Charlotte was flipping through the December issue of *Cosmo*. She shrugged. Max and Sophie's honeymoon period had barely lasted through its first school lunch hour. "You sort of don't notice after a while."

"I'll make it worth it." Sophie raised an eyebrow at her boyfriend.

"You can't fool me with your empty promises, foul temptress."

"What a touching sentiment at Christmastime."

The front door slid open and Simon Hale blew inside. A few seconds behind him, Deirdre appeared, carrying armfuls of shopping bags. Max stood up quickly.

"You missed dinner," Max said shortly to his father.

Simon swivelled around to look at him before he checked his watch. "Shouldn't you be headed to Halifax? Aren't you going to Florida with your mother?"

"No," Max said, "I told you. She's just going with Michael."

"Oh." Simon fidgeted. "You know Deirdre and I aren't going to be here tonight or tomorrow."

"I know."

Charlotte pushed herself back into the cushions a bit harder. She was waiting for Simon's *Come with us, dear son*, but the silence hung in the air.

"I didn't think you would be with us for Christmas," Simon clarified.

"Well, I won't be, apparently," Max said cooly.

Sophie scurried to his side and slipped her hand inside his. "You can come home with me. My parents love you."

Charlotte watched him smile at Sophie and she was reminded for a second that they were, sometimes, good to each other. Simon frowned at the couple.

Deirdre, thankfully, broke the quiet that followed. "So, what do you kids have planned for this evening?" she asked.

Charlotte guessed that referring to them as kids was supposed to be a joke, because Deirdre was maybe a few years older than Sean.

"Well, Deirdre," Max said, fiddling with the zipper on his sweater, "I was thinking we'd sit around and make friendship bracelets while we sip cocoa and watch *It's A Wonderful Life*. Then we'll be in bed by eight thirty as we await the imminent arrival of Mr. Claus."

Deirdre pressed her lips together in a thin line. "How adorable."

Deirdre Hale was probably one of the most perfect-looking people Charlotte had ever seen in real life. Her glossy blonde hair looked like she had it blown out once a week and her nails were always perfectly manicured, which was impressive in a town with no nail salon. She was almost as tall as Simon when she stood beside him, though that could have been her designer heels. According to Max, Deirdre had been working as a hotel receptionist and met Simon when he'd gone to Halifax for some work thing last summer. They'd been engaged by Christmas and had a spring wedding.

"There's food in the fridge. Hope none of you starve," she said.

Max smiled widely at her and sat down beside Charlotte. "Thanks, Mom."

Deirdre turned away from her stepson and looked toward Sean expectantly. "I don't think we've been introduced."

"This is my brother, Sean," Charlotte said.

"He was at the wedding," Simon put in. Simon and their dad had been friends.

Deirdre's lip curled back to reveal her perfect teeth. "Ah, yes."

"Hey." Sean waved from the sofa.

Simon cleared his throat. "Anyway, Max, we'll see you tomorrow afternoon."

Max saluted.

"Simon's being so romantic," Deirdre told them. "He put so much *planning*—" Max's eyebrows shot up at the word "—into this. We're staying at the hotel where we met." Deirdre wiggled her fingers—and the enormous engagement/wedding ring combo—at them.

"The hotel where she was a receptionist, or the one where my dad hired an escort?" Max asked quietly. Charlotte smacked him in the leg. Deirdre took no notice.

"Well, we can agree the Hale men know what they're doing," Sophie sighed, throwing herself onto Max's lap. Max laughed and kissed Sophie's cheek. Sean looked away.

They all said their polite goodbyes, then Deirdre and Simon left as quickly as they'd come. Max brushed some hair back from Sophie's shoulders as they listened to the sound of the car fade.

"Finally," Max said, straightening up and placing Sophie on her feet. "Time to crack the liquor cabinet."


"Charlie? Charlie, come on."

Her eyes snapped open, her surroundings forming slowly around her. She was curled up in an armchair, the wood stove was still crackling quietly as the end credits of *The Vow* (Sophie won) rolled on the TV. Sean stood over her, holding both their coats.

"Hi," she murmured sleepily.

"The truck's snowed in. You okay to walk home?"

She nodded a few times and pulled herself from the chair. They shouldn't drive, anyway. Max had made good on his promise about the liquor cabinet. Sophie and Max were both asleep on the sofa.

Charlotte pulled on her coat. "Let's go," she whispered.

The night was dark and frigid in an icy, still way, but it had stopped snowing. Weaving their way across the yard, their footprints trailing behind, they eventually found the road. Snow plows weren't common in River John. Charlotte walked a line directly where she guessed the middle to be, white splayed in all directions.

"Do you have the time?" she asked Sean.

Sean was lighting a cigarette. "Uh, one sec." He checked the beat-up old wristwatch that used to belong to their dad. "One-twenty-three A.M."

"Officially Christmas," Charlotte said to no one in particular.

"Oh!" Sean said, pulling away his cigarette. "That reminds me. I have something for you."

"We said no gifts—"

"It's hardly a gift. I found it. Here." Sean reached inside his coat and pulled out a small envelope. In messy handwriting it read, *September 1998.*

She took it, tearing it open with clumsy gloved hands. Inside were two things: a letter and a photo.

*To: Romer baby, now Charlotte,*

*We've found out you're a girl, and you have a name now. We're naming you Charlotte, after my grandmother. Your great-grandmother. Sean's very put-out that he won't be having a little brother. Wants to call you Charlie, like Charlie Brown. I'm sure he'll come around. That's it for this letter, my love. See you in a few months!*

*Hell or high water,*
*Dad*

Charlotte looked up. "Where'd you find this?"

"His room. Bedside table. Actually inside one of those big biographies."

Charlotte smiled at the image spun by Sean's words. She could see their dad, in a crappy plastic lawn chair that they kept for the beach, planted right down in the sand, the water coming in around his ankles as the tide came in. Their dad loved reading about people. Musicians, war generals, world-famous chefs, politicians. He was always reading and rattling off trivia to them about whoever he was learning about.

"Which one?" Charlotte wanted to know.

"Brian Wilson. Turns out, I think I need reading glasses." Sean laughed quietly. "Thought I might find some in his drawer. There must be more letters, like the one Max found after he...but I haven't found any."

Charlotte folded up the letter with a shaky sigh. The photo enclosed with the letter was of her parents, her dad's hand on her mom's stomach. They both flashed a thumbs-up to the camera.

"I know it's hard this time of year without him," Sean said, "but I wanted you to have that so you'd know that, at some point, you had people looking after you who loved you, and knew what they were doing."

Charlotte wiped hastily under her eyes and pulled him toward her. She couldn't even remember the last time she'd hugged him. "I still do."

# thirteen

IT TOOK CHARLOTTE A FEW days after her confrontation with Nick before she felt ready to face the world again. When she finally pulled herself out of bed, she had come to a few conclusions. The first was that they really needed to soundproof the walls between her and Sean's room. When she got home last night, Sean had a girl over who worked at the salon next to the Home Depot—that's how Sean had introduced her—and their bedroom tirades were not an ideal soundtrack for Charlotte to fall asleep to. Sean only ever had one real girlfriend, Abby, whom he dated in high school. Charlotte was in the ninth grade at the time, and she had liked Abby. Long story short: she liked Abby, her dad liked Abby, and Sean liked Abby, but Abby didn't like River John. Abby was a year older and went off to Dalhousie, and Sean didn't.

Anyway, soundproof the walls, or one of the Romers was moving out. And it wasn't gonna be her. The second was that after being home for more than two weeks, she had accomplished next to nothing. She could feel the guilt and dread sloshing around inside of her. It was time for her to stop feeling sorry for herself and get her shit together—if she wasn't going to be mending fences (after violently trashing them with a sledgehammer), then it was time to get a job and help Sean pay the mortgage.

Gathering all the motivation she could, Charlotte dragged herself out of bed. God, she was still sore. She caught her reflection in the mirror. The bruises she'd expected from her run-in with Nick had appeared that first night, but they hadn't gotten better. Now they snaked around her forearm in an angry black-blue and looked worse than ever. Charlotte grabbed her North Colchester High hoodie. The last thing she needed was Sean seeing her injuries. She didn't really want to look at them, either.

She went out to the living room, twisting her hair into a huge bun on the top of her head as she went. Easing down gingerly onto the sofa, she picked the newspaper up off the table, the headline of the *River John Gazette* informing her that residents were angry about the new wind turbines being installed in town. She had asked Sean a million times to cancel their subscription to the local paper. They hardly ever read it and definitely couldn't afford it. It mostly ended up as fuel for the wood stove. She was even fairly sure that Mrs. McGrady, the retired old lady who edited the paper, had somehow figured out how to upload the thing online. Go Mrs. McGrady.

Charlotte lay on her back and flipped to the classifieds.

"Sean!" she yelled. "Are you up?"

"What?" he called back from what sounded like the bathroom.

"I think I'm going to get a job," she called. "Help you out with the money thing."

Sean fired back some retort she couldn't make out, but it sounded mostly like laughter or crying. On the plus side, a job would probably keep her distracted from drowning in anxiety about running into Nick again. She supposed it would be better not to mention the twenty thousand dollars Sean didn't seem to want to talk about.

"Shut up," she said, but didn't think Sean could hear her.

They never really made up after their fight, but they weren't still fighting, either. You could only stay mad at the person you lived with for so long. Like most things in their family that posed an issue, it was simply ignored until it went away.

It couldn't be that hard, it was just a job. The problem was the town. There was nowhere to work. The jobs in the classifieds were things like yardwork or handyman stuff, which she wasn't exactly qualified for. She couldn't really become a barista at a trendy café like she might be able to in Halifax. Her options were pretty narrow. Basically the Chinese place, May's, or the Quik Mart, or the dry cleaners. The Home Depot Sean worked at shared a parking lot with a hair salon. Maybe Sean's mystery woman could help her get a job. She considered this for a second, until she remembered the time she tried to give Sophie auburn highlights from a box kit two summers ago. Sophie had to chop her hair short to hide it. So, probably not.

May's Chinese could work, maybe. She didn't really know anything about food service. Then again, she didn't really know anything about anything in the want ads. How hard could it be to be a waitress? She realized it was probably sentiments like this that she'd regret later, when she was mopping up spaghetti thrown at her by an angry customer dissatisfied with her serving skills. *Silly Charlotte*, she scolded herself. *They don't sell spaghetti at May's.*

But she figured Chinese food would make just as big a mess.

The bell above the door tinkled brightly when Charlotte waltzed into the convenience store later that day.

Leo, as always, was hunched over the front counter, chewing on the straw of a huge blue slushie as he scanned a crossword puzzle.

"Miss Romer, how can I be of assistance today?"

Charlotte braced her hands against the counter. "I was wondering if you guys were hiring."

Leo placed his pen on top of the newspaper. "I'd love to help you out, Charlotte, really. But there's already, like, five guys who work here and there really only needs to be, like, one. Maybe two, to keep up the team-building skills."

She sighed, resting her elbows on the glass. "I understand. I'm just trying to help Sean out with money."

"Well, Charlotte." Leo unfolded his paper. "It's your lucky day. I just so happen to be an employment counsellor."

"Employment counselling and convenience store clerking?" Charlotte raised an eyebrow. "Did you have to go to two separate schools for that?"

"Well, the convenience store was my undergrad. I had to go to grad school for the counselling thing."

Charlotte laughed. "You headed anywhere in the fall?"

"Yep," Leo announced proudly. "Saint Mary's, for business."

"That's awesome! Really," Charlotte said sincerely. "That's what Sean wanted to do."

"He didn't go, though, right? I still see him around."

"Ah." She hesitated. "No. He didn't go. But, um, are you excited?"

"Yeah. But more nervous, really." He nodded. "Mostly about the roommate thing. What if they're, like, a taxidermist or something? Or listen to country music?"

"Well, it will probably be one or the other."

Leo shuddered. "I'd take the stuffed animals. How about you?"

"Probably the country music."

"I mean about school."

"Oh. Not this year. I'm gonna take some time off and try and make some money." She paused. "I mean, maybe. If I find a job." The reality of her zero prospects shook her for a second.

"Right you are. So!" Leo flipped a few pages through the paper. "Here. The classifieds."

"I just went through them this morning," Charlotte said. "It was pretty dire."

"No, no, no," Leo spun the front page toward her. "This is the *Pictou Country Star*. Much larger reach. The possibilities are endless, really. I steal this from the big Irving on my drive in every day. I'm sort of in a blood feud with the clerk who works there, it's this whole thing." He waved his hand. "Anyway. What are your credentials?"

Charlotte thought for a second. "Uh, babysitting? I can also make Kraft Dinner and am somewhat capable of answering the phone," she told him, counting off on her fingers.

"Well, would you look at that. A listing for a childcare receptionist that requires experience in macaroni making."

"Ha ha." Charlotte tried to smile. It wasn't looking good. How did people get jobs? Who applying for a first job had any experience other than mowing lawns or babysitting? *Hi, I'm Charlotte Romer. I live with my brother who's been to jail one and a half times but he's super nice once you get to know him. I'm super nice too! Just don't ask Sophie Thompson or pretty much anyone, just take my word for it. Please hire me.*

A stellar resumé.

"The Shore Club is looking for someone to teach kayaking to kids," Leo offered as he scanned the page.

She shook her head. "Someone would have to teach me to kayak first."

Leo listed off nearly every potential job in the want ads. They all required experience or skills she didn't have. The closest fit was a cashier at Sobeys in Pictou, but that was nearly thirty minutes away.

"You could try next door." Leo motioned with his head to the adjoining building.

She ran a hand through her hair. "That was my plan B. Thanks for all your help."

In the almost non-existent walk between the Quik Mart and May's, Charlotte tried to make herself the most job-interview ready she could. She'd dug out a three-quarter-length-sleeve shirt from the back of her closet this morning to hide the bruises. The shirt was one she'd had since the eighth grade, and she was lucky there was no junior-high–worthy slogan written across it. And at least it was clean.

She tied her hair back in a ponytail. If her hair was a clear reflection of the state of her life, she didn't want the fine people of May's Restaurant to think that her life was an unmanageable walking disaster (which it totally was) with a severe aversion to humidity.

The place was crowded. As basically the only social establishment in River John, the occupants ranged from elderly couples to families to teenagers sitting by themselves and pretending they were at a Starbucks.

At the front counter, Laurie Rossi was fighting a losing battle with a temperamental cash register that looked like it was from the mid-twentieth century. She and her husband had owned the restaurant for as long as Charlotte had known them.

Beside Laurie, a toddler sat on the counter kicking his legs. He noticed Charlotte before his mother did.

"Char, Char!" The tiny boy uncurled one finger from around the bottle he was clutching and pointed at her. Laurie looked up.

"Hi, Sebastian." Charlotte smiled. She had babysat for the Rossis a few times before she'd left for Windsor. The Rossis oldest daughter was older than Charlotte, had finished school and wiggled out of River John. The rest of their kids were younger— Charlotte thought around junior high and elementary age. The Rossi kids were at the restaurant as often as their parents were, either helping out or wreaking havoc, twisting between booths and customers.

"Charlotte! It's been quite a long time since you've been in here." Laurie smiled kindly at her. She was always nice. She had been friends with Charlotte's dad; they went to high school together. Laurie had brought Charlotte and Sean two casseroles after their dad died.

"I know, I miss the egg rolls," Charlotte said.

"Can I get you a table, or...?"

"No, no," Charlotte cut her off, "not right now, thanks. I'm actually here because I'm looking for a job."

"A job?" Laurie looked at her closely. "Here?"

"I have no experience," Charlotte admitted. "But I'd take any and as many hours as you could give me, and I'll make it work, I swear. Washing dishes, or whatever. I have to help Sean out with the money thing." Might as well tell her they were completely broke.

"Oh, Charlotte, bless your heart." Laurie sighed. "We've already got about four girls here to serve...we really don't have room for or need any more."

It had been what Charlotte expected. "Okay. I completely understand. You don't know anywhere else that's hiring?"

"You could try the Quik Mart," Laurie suggested.

Charlotte smiled politely, not bothering to explain the Quik Mart in River John wasn't a haven for job opportunities. "All right. Thanks, though. I'll come by for lunch sometime soon." She fluttered her fingers at Sebastian. "See ya, Seb."

"Mama, Mama, *Char*," the toddler hummed.

Laurie looked at her son. Charlotte saw it in her eyes before she even spoke.

"The money from your dad is really all gone, isn't it?" Laurie brushed back pieces of hair from her son's eyes.

Charlotte's father had smoked his entire life, so looking back it really shouldn't have come as a surprise when he was diagnosed with lung cancer. He passed away six months after his diagnosis. Charlotte remembered spending as much free time as she could at the hospital, but it was hard. He was staying in the QEII hospital in Halifax, a near two-hour drive away. It was three years this past June that he died. Charlotte had been staying with Sophie's family while Sean was spending nights at the hospital. When things had gotten bad, Sean called and Sophie's parents had driven Charlotte to the hospital. They made it in enough time to share a few quiet minutes as a family.

It was hard after that; all of a sudden she and Sean were two kids with nothing but mortgage payments, electric bills, and strangers who didn't know what to do with them.

"Nothing ever lasts as long as you think it will," Charlotte said, smiling sadly.

Laurie pulled Sebastian into her arms, propping him against her hip as she gave up on the cash register. "I'll see what I can do for you, Charlotte. I'll check the schedule and see if any of my wait-resses aren't gonna be around for a bit, does that sound all right?"

Charlotte felt an unfamiliar stirring of optimism in her stom-ach. "Anything you can do, I really really appreciate it." A smile broke on her face. "Thank you so much, Laurie."

"And I'm gonna call you for a babysitting gig, Miss." Laurie pointed at her warningly as Charlotte backed toward the door. "And I expect the supreme care package with a discount."

"I'd do it for free!" Charlotte replied cheerily as she left the restaurant with a final wave, which both Laurie and Sebastian returned.

Well, maybe. Free was a strong word. She'd babysit for free when she and Sean could afford bread again.


"Charlie! You home?"

Charlotte was lying on her back, leafing through a year-old issue of *Cosmo* in her bedroom. She paused, studying a photo of Jennifer Lawrence's hair. "Why?"

A tennis ball came flying over the top of the wall from the living room. Dropping her magazine, she caught it instinctively in one hand. They used to play this game all the time. If she was lying on her bed and Sean was lying on the sofa, it was an easy throw over the top of the wall.

She lobbed the ball back into the living room. "What do you want?"

"I'm bored." She heard him sigh. "Let's go out for lunch."

Charlotte missed the second time, the ball rebounding off her ear. She massaged it. "We literally have no money. I spent what was left of it on groceries yesterday."

Sean groaned. "What day is it?"

It took her a second. Summer Paralysis Syndrome. She tossed the ball back over the wall. "Wednesday?"

"I don't get paid until Friday."

"Well, we've survived on cereal for two days before."

They completed a few more throws without speaking.

"I went job hunting today," she said finally. "I'm gonna get a job as soon as I can."

"Don't worry about it. We'll figure something out. We always do."

She didn't want to argue with him about it. She knew their lack of money was a touchy subject—not including the twenty thousand dollars Sean had acquired out of thin air, Charlotte figured.

She chucked the ball from her side with a little more force than was necessary. The ball didn't come sailing back, and instead she heard Sean's uneven footsteps on the wood floor. He appeared in her doorway.

"Hey, also," he started, kind of nervous, "were you out in the shed?"

She closed her magazine and looked at him. "Dad's workshop?"

"Yeah."

"Yeah, why?"

"Nothing, I just saw...you left the door a bit open. Was worried it was an animal," he grunted.

"Oh." Charlotte tilted her phone toward her to check for messages. None. "No. It was just me."

"Might be unsafe," he said quietly.

"What?" Charlotte was pretty sure there were way more unsafe things in River John than the workshop, but okay.

"Nothing. Nothing."

# fourteen

A BUZZING ON HER BEDSIDE table eventually dragged Charlotte from an uneasy sleep. It was hot for July. Too hot to sleep for long. She peeked around the pillow and slid her alarm clock toward her. It was eight in the morning. She grabbed her vibrating phone from its spot on the side table and pressed it to her ear without checking the display.

"Mm?" she managed.

"Were you sleeping?"

Max.

"Sort of." Charlotte pushed herself up onto an elbow. "What do you want?"

"Don't sound so thrilled, jeeze," Max said. "I need a favour."

Charlotte rolled onto her back and focused on the stained wooden ceiling. "I baked you muffins, Max. My debts are paid."

"Yeah, and then you yelled at me. And those muffins were *bad*. And—*AND* someone at the bank told my dad someone was accessing his server from home."

Charlotte scooped a crusty bit of mascara out of the edge of her eye. "Shit. What'd your dad say?"

"Nothing major. I've been written out of my inheritance, but it's fine. I'm gonna pick you up in an hour."

"Wait, really?"

Her phone beeped. Max was finished with the conversation. About an hour later, she'd rounded up a pair of clean denim shorts and a T-shirt that was clean enough. Her hair couldn't be helped—she'd always been jealous of Sophie's blonde, pin-straight hair, while Charlotte's tangled mane gave her a bride-of-Frankenstein look more often than not. She frowned at the mirror, tying it back into a ponytail. Whatever. It was only Max.

From the bathroom she could hear Max's truck rumbling down the gravel lane. True gentleman that he was, the horn sounded from the driveway a few seconds later. A rudely awakened Sean was swearing in his bedroom by the time Charlotte slipped out the back door. She could tell it was going to be hot today, heat leaking from the ground even this early in the morning. It would be a scorcher once the sun was overhead.

Max wore a pleased smile as she pulled the passenger door open, which she did not return.

"Good morning to you too, sunshine," he remarked.

"Sunshine?" She climbed into the truck. "You should've invited Sean."

"Seat belt," Max said as he swivelled around in his seat to back out of the driveway. Max was wearing a white T-shirt and the same faded Levi's he always wore, with sunglasses pushed up into his dark hair. Charlotte hadn't noticed before how long his hair had gotten, curling down below his ears. He looked so much healthier than when she'd left him last year, his skin all bronzed from the summer sun and his face filled out a bit—not as gaunt. She realized seeing him not completely miserable lifted her spirits a bit. Maybe there was more life, after everything.

"I saw Sean, actually," Max said. "Eating at May's. I waved. He ignored me and ripped open a soy sauce packet."

"Oh, that means he likes you," she said. "Are you going to tell me why you dragged me out of bed?"

"I figured you owed me one." Max looked at her out of the corner of his eye.

It had been nearly a week since Nick 2.0, and she and Max hadn't spoken. There was a pause.

"For Sean's money thing," he clarified.

Charlotte pressed her tongue to the back of her front teeth. "Where are we going?"

"Don't worry about it."

"Can I at least call Sean and tell him there are leftovers in the fridge before you murder me?"

"All right, please relax." Max readjusted his sunglasses. She caught his eyes darting away when she'd shifted in her seat, exposing her banged-up knees.

"Are you...are you okay?" He started slow but blurted out the second half all in one breath.

Max had fallen asleep on her couch that night so she wouldn't be alone. She'd barely heard him sneak out as the sun was coming up. She knew they weren't exactly friends, but she had meant to get in touch with Max since that night outside the store. She kept finding herself purposefully distracted.

"Yes, I'm okay," she said. He didn't ask her about Nick again.

She flicked at a scratch on the door, wondering if it was from the accident, a tiny bit that'd gotten missed when they fixed and repainted the truck. Like a tiny scar. Charlotte snapped her hand away and avoided looking at the mark for the rest of the drive. They streaked down cracked pavement under the bright morning sun, and Charlotte caught glimpses of blue water between the trees. She didn't know why she ever thought she could live away from the ocean.

They stopped at the Quik Mart for gas. Max ended up buying Popsicles for a couple of kids who were counting quarters in the parking lot while Charlotte pointed a lost family crowded around a Subaru vaguely in the direction of Tatamagouche. They'd taken the wrong exit. Charlotte could tell they were tourists because she didn't recognize the kids. There weren't a ton of people under twenty-five in and around River John. The ones who were there were stuck there, and usually left as soon as they got the chance.

She, Max, Sophie, and the other hundred-odd high school students from North Colchester were a dying breed.

Charlotte heard Max smack the fuel door closed and he hopped back inside the truck. He wordlessly handed her a Popsicle. She pressed her thumb into the groove down the middle, splitting it in half, before she pulled the wrapper off. Charlotte handed Max half the frozen purple goodness and he smiled.

"Can I at least have a hint?" Charlotte asked after she had finished her Popsicle and they had been driving in silence for a while.

"Yeah," Max said. "Hint: we're here."

She hadn't realized where they were going. The words were barely out of his mouth before he pulled into the huge gravel lot that she simultaneously recognized and resented.

"*No*," she groaned.

"Welcome home."

North Colchester High School was an out-of-place-looking building tucked behind the main road. It was two storeys of white wood with tall windows, columns by the front doors, and a black roof. It looked more like an old plantation house than a high school. Just seeing the building made Charlotte feel sick, reminding her of a life she didn't have anymore. Charlotte had thrived here. She had friends, and Sophie was her partner in pretty much everything. She could see jewel tones from her art class, and the lights from school dances, and the old creaky bleachers with their pale, peeling paint. And when the memories settled in her chest, she didn't think she'd ever felt her own absence more.

"What are we doing here, Max?" she asked finally. He was already sliding out of the truck, circling around the hood, and pulling her door open.

"Important, official business," he said. "I need to get into my old locker."

She twisted at the waist and kicked her legs out of the truck. "And why do you need to do that?"

He closed the door after her. "I think my physics textbook is in there. I got charged fifty dollars because I never returned it.

If I'm getting charged to keep it, I would like to actually keep it."

"Excellent, let's break into the school, then." Charlotte jammed her hands into her back pockets and joined him at the front of the truck, where he had stopped short.

He turned away from her. "I think all we have to worry about is that janitor who hangs around and just says vaguely sinister things from a safe distance. Unlike my father, who is less vague. And closer." He gave a little shudder.

Max led the way around the building to a side door. The latch on the gym door never caught properly, or at least hadn't a year ago. Unsurprisingly, Max pulled the door open with ease.

"It's like they *want* us to do this," he said.

She followed him across the gym and down the familiar halls, which were lined with lockers on either side, punctuated by the occasional inspirational poster. Charlotte paused to study one poster tacked to a corkboard at the end of the hall. It showed a man in bike shorts with both hands raised in fists above his head. He was at the top of a mountain in front of a rising sun and the words above his head instructed her to *Never Give Up*. Original. Charlotte and Max passed classrooms, the principal's office, the cafeteria. It was quiet.

"This is eerie," Charlotte commented. "The last time I was here was…September twenty-ninth." The date was burned on her brain. The night Nick attacked her had been a school night.

"Ages ago. I missed a lot of school that month," Max admitted as they climbed the stairs. "And the next months. I couldn't…it was too weird, without her. I worked from home a lot; whole units and extra credit essays to make up for stuff." He shrugged. "I'm surprised I even managed to finish the year. I think the teachers just took pity on me, to be honest. On us."

A brightly coloured bulletin board at the top of the stairs caught Charlotte's attention. Photos were stapled to blue tissue paper and wrapped in a shiny cardboard border under the heading *Class of 2017*. In the bottom corner: a photo of Charlotte and Sophie on the first day of grade twelve, arms around each other at one of those back-to-school pep rally things. Sophie was laughing, her cheek pressed to Charlotte's. Charlotte's heart stopped for a second. That was the last photo of the two of them, ever. The accident had been just a few days after it was taken, and Charlotte had left town a few weeks after that. Charlotte had never seen the picture before. She didn't even know who took it. Probably Max.

"God, I almost forgot what her smile was like," Max said, following Charlotte's gaze.

Charlotte stepped forward and pried the staples free with her fingernails. "I'd trade anything to be back there."

"It's hard to remember...I mean, most times it just doesn't even feel real. Like there was anything before this," Max said. Charlotte looked down at the photo for several seconds before she slid it into the back pocket of her shorts.

"You know we talk about her like she's dead, sometimes, right?" Charlotte said.

Max grimaced. Charlotte knew she was dead to Sophie right now, so maybe she wasn't that far off.

"I want to show you something," he said.

Max ducked into the nearest classroom, where the desks were neatly aligned in rows of five.

"Our old English room, you'll remember." He swept his arms around grandly. "And it was our first class of the day, the day Sophie came back to school." Max wandered over to the teacher's desk, taking a seat in the chair behind it. "I was so nervous. Me and Sophie's mom tested the elevator, to see how long it took. I went in early and moved all the desks and chairs so there'd be room for Sophie's chair and, like, made sure there weren't *Fast and Furious* posters on the wall or shit like that." He put his feet up on the desk. "Delilah Cooke helped—yeah, the Delilah Cooke who I've seen reduce a freshman to tears over the last order of cafeteria potato wedges."

Charlotte slid into the desk nearest her. "What happened?"

"She was screaming about the rights of seniors and this other girl was like ninety pounds—"

"With Sophie."

"Oh. Not a thing. Sophie didn't speak. Not to me, not to Delilah. Probably wouldn't have even spoken to you. We went to class. Mr. Ingraham talked about *Pride & Prejudice* like he was...defusing a bomb. Basically just read aloud for an hour straight and I think that was the first time he ever forgot to assign us homework. After first period, Sophie asked me to take her home."

Charlotte didn't know what to say. She could picture Sophie, who was so good at pretending that sometimes it was even hard for Charlotte to tell what she was thinking. Charlotte wondered how it would have gone down had they been together on that first day of school. Usually it was up to Charlotte to detect any tiny cracks in Sophie's mask and go from there. She hated thinking about Sophie, on top of everything, having to pretend that she was fine, for the sake of everyone else's comfort.

"I know I'm not making you feel any better," he said, taking his feet down. "But I'm just saying—it's slow going. It still is. You think Sophie's bitter now?" He gave Charlotte an incredulous look. "Imagine her when they announced the first swim meet of the year. Or at winter formal. Or just every day when the people who used to follow her down the halls couldn't even look her in the face."

Charlotte rubbed at a rude word scribbled on the desk.

Max sighed. "I just mean—no offence—Sophie's been through a lot worse than you leaving. You missed a lot this year. A lot of being late for class because of the shitty elevator. Teaching Sophie to drive her new car. A lot of Sophie at her absolute worst. A lot of me at my worst, too—even after we broke up."

Charlotte cleared her throat. "I'm sorry."

"We already did this once," Max said. "But you're never going to fix things with Sophie until you come to terms with how bad it really was. This is something no one can gloss over."

"I wish I could have been here."

Max shrugged and stood up. "It doesn't matter now. But the quest for my physics book continues."

Down the hall and to the right was the bank of lockers for seniors. It was your twelfth-grade privilege that your locker was upstairs. The novelty was short-lived. Charlotte, Sophie, and Max's lockers were all beside each other, Sophie's in the middle.

"Shit. What is it...." Max was mumbling to himself, spinning the combination dial.

"Alas, foiled by the one thing we knew we needed to get your damn book." Charlotte folded her arms and leaned against the lockers.

"Okay, let's pipe down, please," Max spat, "my memory is coming back. 8-6-99. It's my birthday."

Charlotte rolled her eyes.

"Ta-da!" He flung the door open, nearly hitting her in the face. "Mission accomplished."

Max held the book out to show her; the cover featured a couple of kids who looked far too happy to be learning twelfth-grade physics. He flipped it open. "See, loo—shit."

Charlotte reached onto her tiptoes and looked down at the book over his shoulder. In the top left corner, *Charlotte Romer* was written in her own handwriting. "That's *mine!*"

"Ah yes. I forgot. I lost mine and, ahem, borrowed yours after you left. Damn."

"So did *I* get charged fifty dollars since you stole my textbook?"

"Sean would have gotten the bill." Max shut the book and handed it to her. "And I wouldn't say *charged*, I'd say forcibly donated—"

"You owe me fifty dollars."

"I think, personally, we should call it even, on account of the memories we've made and fun we've had this morning."

A new voice interrupted their squabble. "Memories will not fill the void of a debt unpaid."

Charlotte and Max whipped around. The janitor was standing several paces back, clinging to a mop handle like it was keeping him upright. "The collectors come for us all, in the end," the janitor said ominously.

"Okaaay," Max answered. "Right. Okay. We're just gonna.... Okay. Goodbye."

Max grabbed Charlotte's arm dragged her down the hall before she could stop him.

After their narrow escape, Max dropped Charlotte off at home.

"I'm sorry I stole your book," he said sheepishly.

"It's okay," she said as she climbed out of the truck and hopped down on to the dry grass.

"I would forget that it was yours sometimes, and then see your name up in the corner."

"That's touching."

"You have nice handwriting."

"I know. I'm great."

He smiled. "Bye, Charlie."

Inside, Sean was awake, alternating between a half-eaten bowl of Cheerios and the guitar he'd been trying to teach himself to play for the last twenty years.

"How was your morning?" he asked from the sofa once she'd stepped inside.

"Good. Yours?"

"Laurie Rossi called, from May's."

Charlotte's heart leapt. "What?"

Sean strummed a painfully dissonant chord. "Apparently one of her best servers is gonna be out for the next nine months. They're in a state of crisis." He caught her eye. "Your first shift's tomorrow morning. Nine A.M."

# fifteen

"CHARLOTTE, FATHER SUTHERLAND is going to lose it if he doesn't get that coffee. Table seven."

"I got it," Charlotte answered. The coffee wasn't quite finished brewing, and the last few drops spilled into the base of the machine when she grabbed her pot.

"Coffee?" She raised her pot proudly as she sidestepped her way to the table.

The booth held a middle-aged woman on one side, and two blonde children on the other. Wrong table seven.

"Sorry." Charlotte shook her head quickly.

The restaurant was packed. Serving was hard, and she'd only been a server for approximately fifty minutes. It was almost ten. How did so many people want Chinese food this early? To its credit, however, and since it was the only restaurant in town, May's had expanded its menu beyond the boundaries of strictly Chinese cuisine. You could get everything from onion rings to bacon and eggs to dim sum.

There were four servers on—any more and the fire department would have had to step in. Charlotte eventually got the coffee to the correct table seven. Father Sutherland politely hummed his appreciation. It took her and the rest of the staff almost two hours to clear up the breakfast rush, and by then it was practically time for lunch. Her current first-day-on-the-job score was: two and a half spilled coffees, one very angry eighty-year-old woman who was enraged to discover she couldn't order from the dinner menu at nine in the morning, and one piece of chocolate cake Charlotte had scarfed down during her ten-minute break.

"Charlotte, hey, can you run over and refill coffee for my table two?" One of the other waitresses—Katie Cooke, Delilah's cousin—leaned across the divider from the kitchen. "I've got a takeout order to deal with."

"Sure thing." Charlotte grabbed coffee pot number ten thousand and eleven and headed into the front room. Table two was... near the front! Aha! Numerical order prevailed once again. *Take that, grade twelve math.* Table two was one of the only non-booth tables, nestled below the front window.

There sat Sophie Thompson, sipping coffee by herself while she blew through the novel in her hand.

Sophie looked up at her before Charlotte had a chance to come up with a plan. *Shit. Be cool. Turn and go back to the kitchen. Better yet, run out of the restaurant.*

Sophie laid down her book (*Never Let Me Go* by Kazuo Ishiguro). "Hey."

"Hi." Charlotte gripped the coffee pot tightly, as it was the only battle weapon she had.

"Do you work here or something?" Sophie asked.

"Or something." Charlotte looked down at her apron. "It's my first day."

Sophie nodded a couple of times. "That's...great. The place is always busy."

"Refill?" Charlotte raised the pot.

"Oh, yeah. Sure."

Charlotte carefully filled the mug right to the top. Sophie never used cream or sugar. Sophie stared fixedly at the tabletop while Charlotte watched the black coffee rise against the white porcelain. The last time they'd talked would have been...almost two weeks ago. When Sophie told Charlotte about the baby. Sophie puffed out her cheeks and blew out the air as Charlotte slid her mug back to her.

"So, um, what's new?" Charlotte asked, fiddling with the waist of her apron.

Sophie spun the mug around and shrugged half-heartedly, keeping her eyes down. "Not a whole lot."

Charlotte sighed lightly. *Right.* She shook her head and dismissed the notion that they'd be capable of carrying on a conversation. "Can I get you anything else?"

Sophie shook her head. "No, thanks."

Charlotte nodded, and for a split second, Sophie glanced up at her.

It was like those moments where you looked at your reflection in a mirror for too long and eventually you start to look weird, even to yourself. After a while, you don't really recognize yourself. Did you always have that freckle? Was your hairline always that uneven?

Did Sophie always look at her like that?

No, she reminded herself, a year ago Sophie was her best friend. Now, it was hard to tell who she was looking at, and what they were to each other. If they were going to repair this relationship, Charlotte knew she was going to have to be ready to rebuild from the ground up. They weren't the same people they'd been a year ago, and especially not to each other.

"See you around." Charlotte looked away and turned toward the kitchen.

"Charlie," Sophie called after her. Charlotte looked back over her shoulder. "When do you work again?"

Slightly taken aback, Charlotte recalled her schedule. "Um, Thursday, I think. If I don't get fired by then. Why?"

"I sail most mornings, off the wharf at the Cape. It's usually sunny, but always freezing. Summer in the Maritimes, you know?"

"Oh, Sophie, that's really cool," Charlotte said honestly. She hadn't considered what Sophie got up to in her downtime. Charlotte reflected that the closest thing *she* had to a hobby these days was walking to the Quik Mart to buy Sour Patch Kids.

"Yeah well, we all took sailing when we were young, and it was something I could get back into. I like being on the water. And look how strong my arms are now." If Charlotte didn't know better, she'd have said Sophie smiled a bit as she flexed her tanned arms exaggeratedly. Must've been a trick of the light.

Sophie raised her mug and took a delicate sip. "Anyway, I usually come here for coffee after, and to read. So, I'll see ya around, I guess."

Charlotte smiled in spite of herself, and there was no mistaking Sophie's expression this time.

Freedom came at 4 P.M. She'd survived her first shift. Inhale, exhale, go home and shower. After stopping at the desk to grab her tips (an admirable forty-seven dollars) and thank Laurie another four million times for employing her, she gratefully pushed her way out of the restaurant and into the afternoon heat. The first thing she saw was Max, sitting on the curb between May's and the Quik Mart, turned away from her as he scrolled through Twitter on his phone.

She dropped down onto her butt next to him. "Afternoon."

He jumped. "Hey," he said, pulling the cigarette from between his teeth and quickly snuffing it out on the sidewalk.

"Don't stop on my account."

"Not yours. Your dad's."

"Well, gee. That just might bring him back," Charlotte said dryly.

"God, you're a treat," Max guffawed as he tossed his dead cigarette into the bin outside the restaurant without standing up.

"Is there any particular reason you're hanging out on a sidewalk mid-afternoon?" she asked, pulling her knees in toward her chest.

"A scary birdie told me you were off at four," he explained, pulling his shirt away from his body and shaking it. His shirt clung to his shoulders.

The heat of the afternoon sun crept under Charlotte's dark hair, prickling against her scalp. A kind of sticky heat that made you not want to touch anything or anyone.

"Sean?"

"Correct. I came calling, expecting you to be still asleep at noon as per usual, but your brother informed me that you're now a working woman."

"Hard to believe, isn't it?"

"I'm proud of you, Charlie," Max said, "really. Now you can start paying back all the money you owe me. And I got you these."

From his other side he produced a limp and malnourished-looking bouquet of daisies. Over his shoulder, she could see the planters outside the restaurant were slightly more bare than usual.

She took them with a smirk. "Wow, did you drive all the way to the florist in Tatamagouche for these?"

"Yeah, actually. Paid the big bucks."

"Gorgeous." She twirled the dirty stems between her fingers. "Why are you looking for me anyway?"

"Ah, yes. The plot thickens." From his back pocket he withdrew a slightly crumpled, square white envelope and held it out to her.

"Oh, no." She grinned knowingly and took it from him. She held the envelope to her face, using it to hide her smile. "Please tell me this isn't what I think this is."

Max's birthday was the first week of August, and every year on the following weekend, Max's father hosted a massive get-together that was half Max's birthday party, half mixer for the bank. Max liked to use the infamous party to lure his friends with the promise of an open bar. Paper invitations were always distributed, though when it came down to it, they were mostly just a formality. The whole town always showed up. Each year, alcohol was consumed, shenanigans were carried out, people slept together, and it all occurred under the pretense of a sort-of birthday party.

"It's *exactly* what you think it is. What you've been counting down the days until, I'm sure. Isn't this the reason you came home?" He nudged her shoulder with his. "And the party happens to be on the actual day of my birth this year—so you're required to bring a gift."

"Is Leo going?"

"Obviously."

"Then I'll go. For Leo. Consider this my RSVP." She tucked the envelope into her work bag. "Looking forward to the booze. And the little finger sandwiches. Because I don't get paid for two weeks so I'll take all the free food I can get."

"Good. I wanted to deliver the invite in person."

"Why?"

"Because you're the only person I was worried might not come who I actually want to be there."

"What, you think I'd chicken out?"

"I didn't say that."

"It was heavily implied." Charlotte stood up.

"And maybe I just wanted an excuse to come see you?" He rose with her, brushing dust off the back of his shorts.

She raised her eyebrows. "You saw me yesterday."

"Absence makes the heart grow fonder."

"No, *absinthe*."

He laughed. "Like some company for the walk home?"

She thought about it, her mind returning to the last time he'd offered to walk her home, after she'd run into him playing pinball inside the Quik Mart.

"Yeah, why not."

# sixteen

"WHY ARE WE SO *GODDAMN* POOR?" Charlotte wrenched the dresser drawer open. Okay, that was a bit harsh, because she knew why they were so goddamn poor. (Exhibit one: family breadwinner was a twenty-one-year-old Home Depot cashier; exhibit two: she'd spent the year at a bourgeois boarding school.) And it wasn't very kind of her to scream it while Sean was standing in the doorway.

She peeked over her shoulder at her brother, who was staring absently at the ceiling. She slammed the drawer shut loudly with her hip, snapping his attention back to the very important matter at hand.

"Why don't you call Max," Sean suggested, "and convince him to change the dress code to Romer-attainable casual? I'm sure he'd do it. I'll let you borrow my barbecue wings bib."

"Ha, haha, hahaha." She wasn't laughing. At this rate, she'd be showing up to Max's birthday as the Paper Bag Princess.

"Why don't you wear the dress that was on the line the other day?" Sean asked.

Charlotte tore through the second drawer. The dress she'd worn to Sophie's party on her first night back.

"Nope. Tainted," she said, shaking her head.

Sean rolled his eyes and sighed. "You're an idiot."

Charlotte scrunched up her face and mouthed *genetic* into her T-shirts.

"Some girl I brought home a few weeks ago left a dress here," Sean suggested.

Charlotte made a frustrated noise as she flipped through the hangers in her closet. In Ye Good Olden Days, Charlotte would have just called Sophie and borrowed something from Sophie's personal Forever 21 stash. She probably wouldn't have even had to call; Sophie loved a project.

"Ah, yes, a dress that once belonged to some random girl that you slept with. How could your *little sister* say no to that?" Would a beach cover-up pass as black tie appropriate? Hm.

"Just trying to help," Sean said.

"What did she *leave* in?"

Sean shrugged. "Didn't see her leave."

"Our parents would be so proud."

She pushed past a few more hangers before she saw Sean spasm into a weird sort of jig out of the corner of her eye.

"Our parents. I just thought of something."

Charlotte whirled around, but Sean was gone. She tripped her way past the piles of clothes strewn across the floor and followed him. Sean was halfway up the attic ladder.

"What are you doing?" She craned her neck, trying to see up the gap.

"Do you remember Nick?" Sean's voice floated down from somewhere obscured by boxes and maybe asbestos.

"Um, yeah. He *stabbed me*?"

"No, OTHER Nick, Charlotte, Jesus." Sean re-emerged at the top and backed down the ladder with a box under one arm. "Davidson. He needed a dress for Halloween in grade eleven. It didn't fit. Anyway." Sean pushed the box into her hands. "Open it."

Charlotte rested the box against her stomach and pulled open the flaps. The top of the box revealed a smooth layer of silky baby pink fabric.

"Oh, god," Charlotte groaned.

Sean looked pleased with himself. "Good thing Dad was so sentimental. Mom's prom dress. I think she made it."

Charlotte stood, pulling the dress free of the box. She held it against her, the seam hitting just above her knee. "She did not. There's a Sears tag on it."

"I'm a genius, you don't need to thank me," he said, waving his hands in front of him and stooping over into a deep bow.

Charlotte raised her eyebrows and held the dress at arm's length. It smelled musty, but she was running low on options. With a sigh, she folded it over her arm. "The jury's still out on that one, I think."

She'd done her hair and makeup before she started the great quest to find a dress, so once she'd found one, she was almost ready. It was a good thing she'd spent approximately four hours conditioning her hair last night.

The dress was...eighties. The whole thing was pink with big, off-the-shoulder fringed sleeves. It fit, but she felt like she should be in some fun-less town with Kevin Bacon. Maybe people would think she was being ironic. Vintage stuff was in, right?

Pushing in a pair of earrings, she turned away from the mirror and started down the hall, pulling on her only pair of heels as she went. She found Sean in the living room, sprawled on the sofa. He was focused on the TV with a can of Oland's resting on his chest, balancing against his chin.

Sean sat up with a wicked grin. "No, allow me. Summer loving, had you a blast."

"Wrong decade." Charlotte folded her arms. "I take it you aren't coming? You're invited, you know."

"Yeah...I'm gonna skip it."

"You sure? There's free booze."

"Yes, I'm sure," Sean said in a tone that told her not to ask again.

"Okay. Whatever. I'll be back late, don't wait up. I'm taking the car."

"Have fun. Don't drink and drive."

She didn't bother answering, grabbed Max's poorly wrapped gift off the kitchen table, and headed out the door. For the first time in the history of humanity, the River John weather seemed to be cooperating for an event that was to be held outside. Backing down the lane, she tried very hard not to think about everyone from school she was going to have to face at this party.

She'd half considered bailing, but decided if she showed up she could then bail more politely if things ended up going the way they were going in her head. Plus, her recent encounters with Sophie had been good...ish? Better? She'd seen Sophie a couple more times at the restaurant, always alone, and they hadn't even really talked much but it was better than before. Sophie came early in the morning, when the restaurant was quiet, and she usually just wanted coffee and maybe some toast. Charlotte would top up Sophie's coffee for free and refused to accept tips. She figured it was unfair that Sophie throw an eighteen-percent gratuity on a three-dollar cup of coffee for the person who abandoned her. Still, a weird situation. Sometimes when Charlotte went by the table Sophie would wave her over to show her something funny on Instagram. Charlotte felt her heart bounce happily whenever Sophie caught her eye, but she wasn't sure if things were improving or if Sophie was just treating her like a server at the local restaurant she was friendly with.

Cars lined the side of the road as she got closer to the Hale house. Charlotte parked behind a grey Honda and started walking.

She found the gravel lane that would eventually lead to Max's, looping the strap of her clutch around her wrist. She could hear the party long before it came into view. The party was on the grounds beyond the house, near the cliff overlooking the water. String lights glimmered around several giant white tents. It sort of looked like a wedding. Simon had clearly spared no expense. Max said Simon always used his son's birthday as an elaborate excuse to schmooze and impress his clients while still managing to look like a model father. Max's words, not hers. She didn't really care about the subtle meaning behind the party so long as there were finger sandwiches.

She started down the enormous manicured lawn until she reached a few waist-high round tables at the edge of the tent. Now what? Navigating Social Events 101 was not her favourite class. The crowd was split between kids and adults, but there were at least a couple hundred people there.

"Oh, hey! I owe Leo five bucks."

Charlotte turned. Max had shouldered through the crowd, wearing an expensive-looking suit jacket and clutching a red plastic cup like it was even more expensive.

Charlotte pushed her hair out of her face. "You bet him I wouldn't show up?"

"No, I bet him you wouldn't look nice." Max grinned into his cup, dodging her well-aimed swat with her handbag. "What? I said I lost."

"Well, thanks."

"I'm kidding. I said you wouldn't show up. But you do look really good."

She folded her arms. "And what time did you start drinking?"

"Around two." He held his cup out to her but she shook her head. "I think. If I time it right, I'll be drunk up to, and including, my dad's horrible speech later."

"Wow, that's...," she trailed off, glancing over the crowd, "commitment. Here. This is for you."

His eyes lit up when she handed him the gift. "You didn't *actually* have to."

She watched him tear away the newspaper wrapping. Inside was a book, thick and heavy, and it had seen better days. The spine was cracked and the pages were starting to yellow around the edges. Max turned it over in his hands.

"It was my dad's," Charlotte explained. "I know you like this kind of stuff. He got it after high school, when he went to Europe. He ran into—"

"Dr. Dimitri Leva," Max finished, eyes scanning the plain cover and nodding to the name along the bottom. *The Origin of Gods and Heroes* was written straight down the middle. "I've watched his documentary on Netflix like eight hundred times."

"Oh." That'd worked out better than she'd planned. "Check the inside cover."

Max flipped the cover open before the words had completely left her mouth.

"Joel," Max read aloud. "Thanks for the drinks. And for boosting my ego. Here's to many more long years of travel, and to hoping you'll find something interesting among the gods and a few monsters. Cheers, Dimitri Leva." Max shut the book and looked at her. "Since I know you found this in your attic, like, today, this is great. Thank you."

"First of all," Charlotte retorted, "it wasn't in the attic; I had been using it to balance the wobbly sofa leg. And second, with my luck, it'll probably end up being worth ten thousand dollars someday." She smiled. "But you're welcome. Happy birthday."

He took another sip of his drink. "I should probably do some rounds," he said. "I'll catch up with you later, Charlie."

He held his drink out to her again.

She shook her head. "Still too early for me."

"I just saw Sophie show up with her entourage."

Charlotte took the cup gratefully as Max slipped back into the crowd, tucking his new book under one arm as he went.

There were tiny pink floaties on the surface of her punch. There was a rumour that Thomas Henderson had spiked four of the five bowls already, and she prayed hers was one of them.

So far, she'd managed to fly mostly under the radar. Most people greeted her like she was an estranged cousin no one talked about. Leo, thankfully, had dedicated a solid twenty minutes to her on the dance floor, which was nice. The sun was hanging lower in the sky, just touching the horizon, the edge nearly slipping behind the water.

Charlotte turned to leave the designated punch bowl perimeter and found herself facing two girls from school. They stopped short when they saw her, and Charlotte had the feeling she had been the subject of a very recently dropped conversation.

"Hey, Charlotte." Emma Langille wiggled her fingers at her with a sickeningly sweet smile. "Long time, eh?"

Charlotte raised her eyebrows and weighed her options. She considered giving her the benefit of the doubt. Perhaps Emma and her companion, Amy Chamberlain, had gotten personality transplants during the time Charlotte been away. Perhaps they were no longer the girls who'd once convinced a few freshman girls that vodka had the same alcohol percentage as Bud Light, filmed the strip tease that ensued, and plastered it on Instagram. They both emulated Sophie, followed her around and did stuff for her, even though Sophie never asked. But Sophie never stopped them, either. Lackeys might be the right word.

"Hi, Emma. Amy."

"We're just getting some punch." Amy nodded, her giant earrings dangling in sync with her chin.

"Well, you found the right place." Charlotte motioned to the table and intended to leave them to their business. "Go right ahead."

"Funny, that's exactly what Ian Donovan said you told him at Blake McIntyre's party the other night." Emma smirked.

Charlotte rolled her eyes and didn't even bother explaining that she wasn't even at Blake Mc-whatever's party, because she didn't see the point in defending herself.

"It's been lovely talking to you both," she spat, and elbowed her way past them.

Amy's hand shot forward, catching Charlotte's punch glass and sending it flying to the ground at her feet. The plastic cup held up, but the pink liquid splashed all over her shins and shoes.

"Pull it together, Charlie." Emma tsked. "Are you drunk already?"

Charlotte pressed back against the table, away from them. "Not nearly enough for this conversation."

"Remember that your blood-alcohol level doesn't excuse being a slut," Amy added. Charlotte resisted the urge to drown herself in the punch bowl but instead gave Amy a withering look. "I don't know who the hell you think you are," Amy continued, "but the only reason any of us gave you the time of day before was because of Sophie, so I'd watch it."

"*Any of us?*" Charlotte repeated. "What are you guys, the Avengers? And I wasn't aware of you ever giving me the time of day. I certainly wasn't giving you mine."

Even in heels, Charlotte still stood about a head shorter than both of them. Damn genetics. Made it hard to be intimidating.

"You act like you're so much better than the rest of us," Amy said. "But everyone's talking about it. Even Sophie. We all know you're chasing after Max like some pathetic lost puppy."

Charlotte scoffed. "Right. Do you have any extra T-shirts for your club? I remember when you asked him to spring formal in grade ten and he said no."

Amy balked. "How do you know about that?"

"Sophie," Emma said dryly. Emma's lips pulled an evil smile, and Charlotte watched, half expecting it, as she dumped the contents of her glass down Charlotte's front.

The pink punch stained her pink dress—*Mom's dress*, Charlotte thought vaguely—spreading a dark magenta pool across her chest. It looked a bit like she'd been shot.

"Well." Charlotte sighed, not even sure she had it in her to care anymore. She grabbed her bag off the table. "I'll see you both in hell."

She turned around and stopped in her tracks. Sophie looked stunning in a royal blue sundress with lacy sleeves, her hair tied back in a loose ponytail. The self esteem of every girl at the party was knocked down a few points.

Sophie studied Charlotte for a few seconds, her eyes flickering between her face and the punch that was sticking to her through her second-hand dress. Sophie leaned to the left the slightest bit, her eyes settling on Emma and Amy before a tiny smirk appeared.

Sophie looked back to Charlotte. "Would you excuse me? I'm thirsty."

Charlotte felt the prickling stab of betrayal as she moved aside.

Charlotte stood there for several seconds, sticky and frazzled. She wanted nothing more than for the floor to open up and swallow her, but she knew from experience that she wasn't that lucky. She crossed the dance floor stiffly and intended to disappear under the tents until she got back to her car. Someone caught her around the arm just before she was free of the hell-party.

"Charlie?"

It was Max.

"Are you leaving?" he asked. "What's wrong?"

"Um," she started, looking down at her dress. "Punch bowl casualty. I think it's best that I just go."

"What?" Max looked over her head, and she saw recognition flicker on his face when his eyes fell on Sophie and the girls clustered around punch bowl. "Oh," he said.

"Have a good night, Max. Really."

"No." Max looked back at her. "Stay."

"I feel like an idiot." She gestured at her silly, ruined, eighties dress. "And I look like one."

Max thought about it for several seconds before he turned and headed back toward the punch bowl.

"Max!" Charlotte whisper-yelled, following clumsily behind him in her heels. Was he going to say something? Duel Amy?

"Excuse me, ladies, friends, er, Sophie," Max said as he reached them. "Just getting some punch. You guys look great. You enjoying the party? Great. Glad to hear it. So great."

He poured himself a glass of punch and held it to his lips, catching Charlotte's eye from a few metres away. Max raised his glass to her.

"Cheers." He smiled, before promptly dumping the contents down his crisp white dress shirt.

Charlotte buried her face in her hand while Amy, Emma, and Sophie let out an in-unison gasp.

"Ah, damn, I'm cut off." Max shook his head. "Let's all act like adults, shall we?" he said straight to Sophie. He stepped away from the table and headed back in the direction of the tents.

On his way past Charlotte, he leaned down and muttered, "Don't say I never did anything for you."

# seventeen

"PLEASE DON'T MAKE ME go back," Leo said, half hiding his face along the wall.

Charlotte cupped her hand around the twisting flame, shielding it from the wind as Leo flicked his lighter again underneath the end of his cigarette.

"I'm not making you go anywhere," she said.

Leo took a long drag and leaned back against the siding of the house. They were avoiding the party, tucked away behind the far side of Max's house. Leo was easily the best-dressed person at the party. He paired a silver-grey tie with a perfectly pressed white dress shirt and well-fitting salmon-coloured suit jacket. Velvet loafers tied the look together. Leo was definitely the only person Charlotte knew who could pull that off.

"If Delilah asks me to take her shopping one more time, I'm going to jump into the Atlantic Ocean," he said, blowing smoke over his shoulder.

"She just wants to be your friend."

"Oh, no, I love Delilah," Leo said. "It's not that. Her parents caught her smoking pot, so they took her car away. She literally wants me to drive her to Halifax."

"Oh."

Leo tilted the cigarette toward her as an offer. She shook her head.

"Right. My bad," he said. Leo peeked around the corner of the house; they were just out of sight from the rest of the party. "God, how much longer will this thing go on?"

Charlotte followed his gaze. It was almost dark, creeping past eight o'clock. "Simon still has to give his toast thing, right?"

"Jeeze. We'll have to rein Max in for that one. Keep him from heckling his own father," Leo said, inhaling deeply.

"You seen him lately?"

Leo shook his head, and exhaled. "Last thing he said to me was that you poured punch on him—er, because you're in love with him, or something—and then he poured it on you."

Charlotte rolled her eyes.

"We should go back." Leo snuffed the butt out against the siding. "They fall apart without us. Look what happened when you disappeared for a year."

"Ten months," she corrected, mostly to herself.

Leo looped his arm through hers and guided her back down the lawn towards the tents and more people she would have to refrain from picking a fight with.

"Come dance," he said.

Leo wove her through the crowd to the centre of the dance floor, amid a mix of group dances and couples swaying together with varying levels of interest.

They killed two Ed Sheeran songs trying to guess exactly how many different types of finger sandwiches were available on the circulating silver platters. Leo swore he'd had a caviar one, but Charlotte didn't believe him.

"Can I cut in?" Max slid through the crowd, hovering near Leo's shoulder. His shirt was still all mussed and ruined.

"Of course." Charlotte smiled, pulling away. "I'm gonna go eat some shrimp."

"I've already danced with him." Leo laughed. "He's all yours, C."

Leo sashayed back across the dance floor—in the direction of the shrimp platter, Charlotte noted with a twinge of jealousy.

"Sorry, should've clarified," Max said. "You wanna dance?"

Charlotte considered for a moment and then said, "Ah, it's your birthday. What the hell."

Max slipped his arms around her waist and pulled her against him. "How are you doing?" he asked.

"Sticky," she said, nodding to her dress.

"I'm sorry. That that happened."

Charlotte shrugged, readjusting her hands around his shoulders. "It could have been worse. And I do still kind of deserve it."

"Not from Amy and Emma. Sophie, maybe." Max spun her around under one arm, miscalculating the number of drinks they'd both had. She nearly stumbled in her cheap heels. Charlotte laughed as Max pulled her back upright, his hand finding the low of her back to steady her.

"This is going to really piss her off," Max said quietly.

Charlotte stiffened, her laughter gone. "I didn't...that's not what I want," Charlotte said.

"Sorry." Max dropped his hands away from her. "I just meant... us being friends."

She looked at him. Were they friends? Drunken dance floor giggling with your ex-best friend's ex-boyfriend was certainly not a way to get back in said ex-best friend's good graces. Charlotte took a second to remind herself what was important: Sophie. Always.

Charlotte looked in the direction Leo had disappeared, praying for his return. Her eyes settled on a few boys clustered near the bar. They'd just arrived. For a second she'd thought it was Sean. Then her hand curled around Max's elbow.

"It's Nick," she said. "They're crashing."

Max whipped his head around, seeing what she did.

"Just stay here," he muttered.

It took her a few seconds before she could force herself to follow him. She felt like someone had jammed a stake through the gears in her brain, keeping her from moving. She cut through the crowd in time to see Max pulling Nick back from a three-tiered display of cupcakes.

"Leave. Now," Max said.

Nick twisted around to look at him, the cronies he had dragged along merely glancing at Max like he was an annoying insect. Charlotte recognized them; they used to hang around with Sean. They'd been to her house, drinking and playing video games.

"You gonna drag me out yourself?" Nick challenged.

Leo scuttled along the edge of the table to stand behind Max.

Nick raised his eyebrows. "Ooh, I'm terrified."

"Get out," Max said again, closer to Nick's face.

Nick was looking at him like he couldn't quite figure out where he knew Max from and how invested Max was in throwing him out. When his eyes settled on Charlotte, she saw the recognition flicker on his face.

"Ah." Nick tilted his head. "I get it. You're protecting that bitch."

A few other guests had caught onto the weirdly tense standoff the guest of honour was having at the buffet table with a crew that looked like they'd walked out of West Side Story. Out of the corner of her eye, Charlotte spied Sophie at the edge of the crowd, Delilah in tow. Charlotte could feel her heartbeat in every inch of her.

"Leave or I'll call the cops," Max said, his voice never faltering.

"We both know she's not gonna let you do that." Nick picked up a strawberry from the pile beside a shiny fondue fountain that looked like it cost more than the Romer family car. He dragged the strawberry through the chocolate stream and raised it in Charlotte's direction like a toast before popping it in his mouth. "So feel free to make me leave yourself," he said with his mouth full.

Nick punctuated his muffled sentence with a shove aimed at Max's shoulders. Max bumped the table, and the elaborate pyramids of glassware tinkled in warning.

Boys were stupid about stuff like this. Charlotte knew what was coming.

Max returned the shove and Nick stumbled sideways, not expecting it. His arm flew out toward his friends for assistance but he missed and his elbow took out the chocolate fountain. Both Nick and the fountain crashed to the ground.

Charlotte clapped a hand over her mouth. So much for subtle. Delilah was taking a video with her phone.

Deirdre broke through the crowd, looking horrified. Last Charlotte had seen her, she had been double-fisting white wine spritzers in a circle of Simon's bank colleagues. Simon appeared behind Deirdre, also looking horrified, but it seemed his horror had more to do with the chocolate fountain than his son's wellbeing.

"Max!" Simon roared. Max hadn't really moved since Nick fell, and neither of them seemed to know what to do with themselves.

Simon wrenched Nick to his feet by his arm. "Both of you. Out."

Nick drenched in chocolate would have been funny, Charlotte thought, if he hadn't tried to kill her once, maybe twice. Nick shot the Hales a venomous look and turned to leave, but not before pulling out a wine glass from the bottom of the pyramid. The entire structure collapsed and shattered on the wooden floor.

"Call the police," Nick said evenly, like a dare.

Simon looked like he hadn't heard him, and Charlotte watched Nick and his cronies track back over the hill and out of sight.

"You," Simon said to Max. "Office."

Charlotte didn't like the sound of that.

Charlotte twisted the faucet off. *Jesus. Worst party ever. Even worse than Sophie's birthday.* She straightened her rumpled dress, still spectacularly stained and unfixable. She dabbed at it halfheartedly with a fistful of damp Kleenex before she opened the door to the empty living room. Leo had tried to ask her what happened with Max and Nick and the chocolate, but she dodged his questions. The bathroom was quiet. She took her time. The rest of the house was empty, so she could hear the voices clearly. Simon's office was just across the hall. The voices were even in tone, but one was louder than the other. Both voices got louder, and she saw the doorknob turn. Charlotte quickly stepped back and swung the bathroom door shut quietly.

"...embarrassing!"

"I didn't start anything!" Max said gruffly.

"You knew all my clients were here," Simon retorted. "You were looking for any excuse to cause a scene. You've been drinking since *noon*."

"Yeah, Dad, that's my goal. My life's ambition. Embarrassing you in front of River John's banking community," Max said sarcastically. "All three of them."

"You're to apologize to every one of my clients when you go back out there."

"Please stop saying the word 'clients.' And I'm sorry, but it's not like I asked those guys to show up."

"Honestly, it wouldn't surprise me," Simon said. "It wouldn't be the only trash you invited to this party."

Silence. Charlotte almost laughed at her side of the door. Shit. Who did Simon hate that much?

"Excuse me?" Max asked.

"You know those kids," Simon said. "No money since their father passed. They're trouble. Do what you want but don't be surprised if you get a bill in the mail."

Oh. That's who.

More silence. Charlotte found herself thinking about homemade jam and fish catch her dad used to send the Hales whenever he came back with extra.

"That's funny coming from someone with a twenty-five-year-old second wife."

"We're done here."

"Don't say anything about her, ever," Max said firmly. "And your *clients*"—he dragged the word out—"can piss off."

Her bathroom door opened and she had to step back to avoid Max hitting her in the face. Simon, thankfully, was gone from the hall.

"Hi," she said meekly.

Max looked at her like he had been the one to say all those awful things. "How much did you hear?"

Charlotte puffed her cheeks up and blew the air out slowly. "Enough."

"All of it?"

"Yep." She met his gaze.

"I'm sorry," Max said. He looked it.

"You don't have to apologize for him."

Max stepped into the bathroom and shut the door behind them. "You should have left when you had the chance."

Charlotte half-smiled at his pink shirt. "And miss all this drama? It's like I was never gone."

"It's starting to feel that way." Max leaned back against the door. He crossed the narrow room and pulled back the shower curtain. "I was worried—well, still am—that Sophie was going to go party-game-dictator and make us play seven minutes in Max's bathroom. So I prepared."

Max pulled a forty-ounce bottle of Captain Morgan out of the tub with a few inches missing from the top. He unscrewed it and took a swig.

"Last time I had this party, Sophie was my girlfriend," Max said.

"I know," Charlotte answered. She had been there. Things were a lot more fun, a lot lighter and easier than they were now. And she'd been a lot drunker. Sophie, the dutiful girlfriend, made sure Max introduced her to any family that showed up, and she played the part perfectly. But Sophie made time for Charlotte too; their friendship never suffered because of Max, and Sophie would never choose whatever guy she was dating over Charlotte.

"I didn't think anyone was going to come tonight," Max admitted quietly. "Thought it would be weird...and I think they only came anyway because of Sophie."

"They didn't," Charlotte said gently. "They came for the free liquor."

His face twisted into a lopsided grin and she laughed a tiny bit.

"I didn't come for Sophie," Charlotte clarified, clearing her throat.

"Thank you." Max dragged back another long mouthful from the bottle. "Worst party ever," he said, holding it out to her.

She took it around the neck. "Cheers."

# eighteen

## NEVER. AGAIN.

Charlotte threw her hand out blindly for the cup of water on her bedside table. She crammed two Advil into her mouth. Christ. She dragged her palm over her face and opened her eyes.

The sun from the window hurt her eyes as she sat up. Max had decided she couldn't make the ten-minute journey alone and walked her home—both stumbling messes; it was a miracle they'd even made it—at around four in the morning. And then, she assumed, he had stumbled back to his place. Charlotte pushed her hair out of her face. She'd have to go back for the car.

She checked her phone for—well, nothing. It's not like Sophie texted her anymore. And she didn't have any message notifying her that Max had fallen in a ditch after his latest fit of gallantry. She checked her and Sophie's conversation…she last texted Sophie a week after she had crashed her birthday, after Sophie told her about the baby. *Here if you want to talk*. Sophie never answered.

Max texted her sometimes, but usually about things that were happening on *Antiques Roadshow* that Charlotte didn't understand or care about. She didn't even really text Sean, except for when he sent her the occasional message asking what was for dinner. And he hardly ever used emojis.

She scrolled back. She didn't have to scroll far—a lot shorter than it seemed in real life—and stared at the wall of messages she'd sent him last year on September 9.

*Call me. Call me. Call me.*

He'd called, eventually. Sean had been in Cape Breton with the guys the weekend of the accident. Charlotte had the car so he had hitched a ride back to River John with one of his friends the next day. Or it might have been the day after. They sort of all blurred together the second she heard about Sophie.

Enough. Charlotte flicked her phone screen off. The rumination was making her hangover worse. She pulled herself out of bed and into clean clothes, and filled a water bottle to bring with her on the walk to Max's to get the car.

Charlotte detoured across the Quik Mart parking lot and ducked into the store. A) because it was hotter outside than she'd anticipated, which was not helping her stomach, and B) because she remembered Leo mentioning last night that he was working this morning.

Leo was hunched over with his elbows resting on the counter, plugging his ears with his fingers and drinking steadily from an electric blue slushie.

"Rough night?" Charlotte asked as the bell chimed behind her.

Leo unplugged his ears. "This cures hangovers."

Charlotte frowned. "I think that's for hiccups."

Leo straightened up and looked at her blankly. "I've drunk three of these this morning."

Charlotte laughed as he pushed the slushie toward her and rubbed a bit of sleep out of his eyes.

"How was last night?" he asked her. "You know, aside from the guys fighting over you."

"They were not fighting over me," she said. She took a sip; it tasted slightly radioactive. "And it was...fine. How was your night?"

"Honestly, excellent. Unparalleled drama. Delilah's Twitter? New heights, Charlie. River John missed you. Did you see Sophie tell off those townies?"

A townie was Sophie's affectionate nickname for someone from Halifax, or anywhere, really, that wasn't River John. She often went on long rants about city folk appropriating their country lifestyle over summer vacations, living like parasites who fed off beach glass and the unsuspecting farm boys. Sophie's words.

Had the townie tell-off been before or after Sophie let Amy and Emma ruin Charlotte's dress?

"Must've missed it," Charlotte said.

"I sometimes forget how terrifying Sophie was. Is," Leo corrected. "I kind of miss having her around. She doesn't really make many appearances any more. Not since—"

"Right." Charlotte nodded.

"How are you two doing?"

"Not great."

"Not since...?"

"Not since."

Leo fiddled with the register, which beeped and squawked and spat out a blank receipt at him. "I remember I worked the night of the car rally."

Charlotte poked at a lollipop tree standing beside the rows of chocolate bars.

"James Comeau and Delilah Cooke came and told me what happened and we went to the hospital together. I closed early. It didn't matter, it was pretty slow all night, except for people in and out buying stuff to get points. Will Douglas took out a pyramid of Red Bull. It was a mess."

"Jesus. Sean made me babysit for his friend that night. I barely missed being in that car, too."

Leo pulled his slushie back and took a sip. "Sean helped me clean up."

"What?"

"The Red Bull. He was in the store."

"Oh."

"Are you here to buy anything?" Leo asked. "Not that you need to be."

"No." She shook her head. "I'm just on my way to Max's. Left my car there."

"I didn't see him again after the dance floor fiasco. Was he okay?"

"Yeah," Charlotte said, "he was talking to his dad. Then he and I had a bunch to drink and sat in the bathtub."

"Is that code for something?"

Charlotte snorted.

"I didn't really think you two were friends," Leo commented lightly.

"Yeah, we're...working on it, I guess."

"No, I mean, I didn't think you *were*. Like before. Max talks about you a lot. I think he thinks you're friends now." He caught Charlotte's eye. "Don't tell him I told you that."

Charlotte bit down on the straw of the slushie to hide her smile.

"And," Leo continued, "I've never seen Max—or anyone, really—push someone into a chocolate fountain before. So he must like you a bit."

Yeah, she did kind of owe him one for the (second) Nick thing. Of course Nick had showed up. It was a good thing Sean decided not to come after all. He'd have lost it. For about twenty seconds this morning she had considered telling Sean what had happened at the party, until she envisioned Sean going to jail for murder.

"Wait, Sean?" she asked aloud.

"No, *Max*," Leo articulated. "I think, probably, your *brother* likes you, too, though."

"No, Sean helped you clean up?"

Leo stared at her blankly. "What?"

"The Red Bull," she clarified.

"Oh. Yeah."

"The night of the accident?"

Leo frowned. "Yes."

"My brother was out of town the weekend of the accident. With his friends." Charlotte was positive. She'd called him in Cape Breton. She didn't see him for three days.

"Oh. Uh." Leo unfolded and refolded the newspaper on the counter. "I could be...I'm probably remembering wrong, or something. There are lots of other guys in River John that I'm afraid of. Could have been one of them. Sorry."

"No, no, don't apologize." She waved him off and turned for the exit. "I should go get my car, though. I'll see you."

Did she love Sean? Sure. Did she trust him? The little bell at the Quik Mart door tinkled loudly above her head before she finished the thought.

• • •

Nick had her by the arm. "Sean knows," he growled.

Charlotte tried to wrestle away from him, but he grabbed her tighter, twisting her arm at an impossible angle until she screamed. Sophie swam in and out of focus; Charlotte was trying to run but all she could do was drag Nick along behind her.

"You're dead," Nick said. He shoved her, hard, and she fell back—off a cliff, into the dark, and she was dead, really.

Charlotte rolled over, pulling herself awake. The nightmare felt like a hand around her throat, down her back and under her skin. She shivered, pressing her eyes shut and willing the waves of panic shuddering through her to stop.

God, she hadn't had a nightmare like that since boarding school. She'd thought they were gone.

It was almost instinctual—she grabbed her phone from under her pillow and put it to the side of her face. Charlotte glanced at the clock as the line trilled. After 3 A.M. She shouldn't be calling. She needed something to fill her brain, something to cloud over the thoughts of Nick and the anxiety and everything else.

He answered after two rings.

"Mhello?" he mumbled from his end.

A different panic struck her—embarrassment, shame, white and hot—and she regretted her decision to call for help. What was she thinking? "Hi," she said, "sorry. I shouldn't have...go back to sleep."

"Charlie? No, what's up?"

She paused. "Sorry. I had a nightmare. And I...have no friends."

Four seconds of silence.

"I have nightmares too," he finally admitted.

"I'm sorry I woke you up," Charlotte said. She couldn't shake the images of Nick, of Sean, of everything that was burned in her brain. She thought of Max and his easy smile at the party and everything else dimmed a bit. Hearing his voice more clearly, she felt her heart slow a bit. Knowing he was on the other end of the line—feeling them tied together by some invisible string—stopped the spiralling. She was okay. "I just needed someone to talk to."

"No, no." Max groaned with what sounded like effort. "I'll come."

"What?"

The call ended.

She curled up, half sure she had dreamt the conversation. Ten minutes later, she saw headlights through her bedroom window. The engine stopped. Driver door slammed shut. She counted fifteen seconds, and she heard him at the back door. It was locked; she'd made sure of it before she went to sleep.

Charlotte threw the covers off of her and went to let him inside. Twisting the lock back, she pushed the door open. Max, in a hoodie and pyjama pants, looked back at her in the darkness, rumpled and still half-asleep. He had a sleeping bag tucked under his arm.

"Hey," she said sheepishly. She couldn't meet his eyes.

"Come on," he smiled a tiny bit, placing a hand on her shoulder and directing her back to her room. Charlotte slid between the sheets and pulled the covers back up over herself. She shivered again, from the cold and from the nightmare and from something else.

Max uncurled the sleeping bag and spread it out on the floor, a few metres from the bed.

"You—" she started, but stopped herself. She wanted to say she felt bad he was going to sleep on the floor, but the alternative was what? Sleeping in her bed?

She could see him smiling in the darkness as he unzipped the bag. "I used to do this for Sophie a lot," he said quietly. "When she didn't want to be alone. Are you okay?"

She could just see his silhouette, backlit by the moonlight drifting in through the window behind him.

She nodded against her pillow. "I'm..." *embarrassed*, she thought to herself, "I hadn't had one like that in a while."

"It wasn't real. It never is." He wiggled into the sleeping bag and zipped it up. "Not helpful, I know. It sucks because all it takes is one thing and you feel like all the progress you made is just... wiped."

"Thank you for coming over," she said quietly, "you didn't have to—"

"Shh," he cut her off. "Do you want to go to sleep?"

"I'd rather talk to you for a bit," she admitted, even though her brain felt foggy and heavy as it tried to drag her back to sleep.

He rolled onto his back and stared up at the ceiling. "Talk away," he said.

# nineteen

THE DAYS TUMBLED AROUND. They never talked about it, and it was never romantic. Sometimes they would spend the entire night talking, about boarding school, about things she had missed—he always called it "the missing year"—but they never talked about the fact that they were sharing a room, or that when he was asleep she would sometimes press her face to the edge of the mattress to look at him. Other times, they didn't talk at all. Max would come in through the back door that she left unlocked for him and silently slide into his sleeping bag, which he had started leaving in her room. She would roll over to face him in greeting but that was it. One night, she didn't wake up at all, so he'd touched her hand to let her know he was there. He'd apologized when she'd startled awake, but they never touched again.

Tonight, she couldn't sleep, even though he was there. The wind howled relentlessly, flying over the house and twisting itself inside the crevices where the shingles didn't quite meet. From the kitchen, she could hear water *splat splat splatting* from the leaky faucet. If she wasn't so lazy she'd go fix it, but her limbs felt heavy from the sleep that refused to creep up to her brain. Max was lying facing her, his mouth a bit open. She had to get that kid an air mattress.

A slamming car door snapped her attention from Max and to the window across the room. She frowned, glancing to the clock on her bedside table. It was just after two. Was Sean just getting home?

She could hear the low rumbling of voices. Two.

Charlotte propped herself onto her elbow. "Do you hear that?"

Max rolled away from her.

"Max!" she whispered sharply.

"Hear what?" he grumbled.

"I think there are people outside."

"A fact of life, I think."

Charlotte ignored him and sat up, straining to hear. She was right—it was definitely two voices. Loud enough that she knew they were yelling, but too muffled to make out any words.

She climbed clumsily over Max (judging by the sound he made, she'd kicked him in the face) and tiptoed out of her room and toward the back of the house.

Two bodies—disfigured by the condensation on the glass— were standing out by the workshop. She recognized her brother from the way he stood, though his back was to her. The second person was cornered between Sean and the side of his truck.

"What the *hell* are you hanging around here for?" she heard Sean demand.

"Waiting for you. I heard you got an order back from buddy in the city. I just wanted to check it out for myself...I'm sure he wouldn't even notice."

Charlotte recognized the voice. Nick. Also, she was going to kill Sean if he was dealing pot again.

"Are you joking? I should rip your head off for what Scotty says you pulled at that party."

"What? Your sis has grown up. I couldn't stay away."

Sean made a move and for a second Charlotte thought he was going to put his fist through the window of the truck, but he restrained himself.

Charlotte felt gentle hands at her back and had to stifle a yell.

"Sorry," Max murmured as she turned to him. "What's up?"

She motioned over her shoulder and out the door, raising a finger to her lips.

"I don't care if I have to go down with you," Sean said, "but I swear to god if you push me—"

"Sean, my friend, it might be time you ask yourself if your sister is worth all this trouble."

Charlotte threw the back door open as she watched Sean slam Nick back against the truck.

"Sean!" she cried. Her plan didn't go much past that. Sean twisted his head around, surprised to see her. Probably more surprised to see Max standing behind her.

Nick spoke before her brother could say anything. "Well, well, well. Look who decided to show up."

"Don't," Sean snapped at him, "talk to her. Charlie, go inside."

"I was only saying hi," Nick leered.

"You say one more word to her and I will literally kill you," Sean said. "Max, take Charlotte inside."

She felt Max's fingers at her wrist but yanked her arm away.

"Sean," Charlotte said firmly. "Come on. Come inside."

Sean looked back at Nick for a few seconds. "If I have to rot in jail, I will."

He released Nick, who stumbled away from the truck and down the driveway. He threw a venomous look over his shoulder. "You're done, Romer. You're both done."

Sean sighed and turned toward the porch. "I know."

Without a word, he moved past the two of them and went inside. Pulling away from Max, Charlotte followed him in disbelief.

"You know what would be, honestly, hilarious," Charlotte nearly shrieked, "if we could be one of those, like, chill families that didn't get almost murdered regularly. That didn't start fights with lunatics who have previously tried to kill us."

"Why didn't you tell me what happened at that party?" Sean spat, looking at Max as if he'd organized a party where inviting Charlotte's-would-be-murderer was on the agenda right next to musical chairs.

Charlotte intervened. "Because nothing even happened! Nick didn't touch me. And I knew you'd freak out!"

"I've heard you," Sean told her quietly. "At night. I know you're having nightmares again. Something must've happened to start that."

"It doesn't matter! I can't have you picking fights and getting yourself arrested. You know with your record you're *this* close to jail. Real jail, Sean. Not juvie."

"It *does* matter, Charlie! My priority always has been and always will be keeping you safe, all right?" Sean breathed. "I don't care about—"

"Don't act like you don't know," Charlotte interrupted, "how this is going to end. Nick won. It's over. If either of you take this any further—"

"Nick is *never* going to stop, Charlotte. I did the only thing I could think of when I sent you away." He looked at her closely, and she could see his expression soften a tiny bit. Underneath the anger and frustration, she knew what Sean really wanted was just to keep her safe. He wasn't angry—he was scared. "Has he tried anything else?"

"What?"

"Nick. Had you seen him before the party?"

Charlotte glanced at Max, who was leaning in the doorway. "No," she said.

Max raised his eyebrows.

Sean looked to him. Max stayed silent.

"Hold on," Sean said, as if he had just remembered Max was there. "Why are you even here?"

"Uh—" Max looked behind him, either scouting the exit or the imaginary person Sean was talking to.

"You think I don't hear you sneaking in at night?" Sean asked. His eyebrows were in danger of completely disappearing into his hairline. "Are you two like...a thing?"

"Just sleeping," Max said quickly. Charlotte could feel him looking to her for help, but she was preoccupied.

"Do not change the subject," Charlotte told Sean.

"You're *sleeping* together?"

"Just sleeping," Max said again.

"You should go," Charlotte said to Max. He met her eyes for half a second, then nodded.

"Yeah, I want to talk to Charlie, Max," Sean said.

Charlotte puffed out her cheeks and took Max's spot against the door frame as he disappeared down the hall. She was gripped momentarily with the anxiety of returning to an empty bedroom and spending the night alone. A quiet nervousness flared in her stomach.

"Was that really necessary?" she asked.

"What?"

"Telling Nick you're going to kill him. Go to jail."

Sean shrugged. "Because I am."

"Well, don't," Charlotte said.

There was a heavy pause, like Sean was considering this. "Mom left when I was, like...five years old. You were two, and I was in primary or first grade or whatever. You were so small—giant eyes, wild hair." He sounded almost like he was going to laugh at the memory, but it never reached his face. "And I still remember the day I came home to find Mom packed. She had the station wagon full of all her stuff, this idea about how she was gonna be with this guy from Halifax she was seeing, her suitcase, and...you."

Charlotte recoiled. "What?"

"You were just a baby. Mom might've been a shit person but she was still a person. You were her baby girl. Mom and Dad were out in the yard yelling at each other when I got home. Dad was crying. And it was because she was going to take you with her."

"Mom was going to take me?" The words weren't making sense in Charlotte's head. She'd lived her whole life under the impression that their mom wanted nothing to do with any of them. "I thought she left us."

"She left me and Dad. Not you. But Dad went on this huge spiel about how she couldn't break up the family, and how you were just gonna end up abandoned in some hotel room while she was out messing around."

"And she just gave up?"

Sean cleared his throat. "No. No, it was...it was a bad scene, Charlie. I was crying and Dad was screaming and Mom was raving. I ran over to her, was pulling on her, and on you. In all the chaos I guess you slipped and...she dropped you."

"Oh." Charlotte tilted her head. Stuff like that happened, she figured. "I was all right, then?"

"You didn't hit the ground. Not really." Sean nodded a couple of times. "I kind of caught you. We went down together. And that was it. Mom left."

"You've never told me any of that."

"Of course not," Sean said gruffly, "because it changes things, doesn't it? I wonder, still, if Dad made the right choice. Maybe if you went with Mom things would have been better. For you."

"Dad was right," Charlotte said without hesitation. "God knows where Mom is now. God knows where I would be. But I wouldn't be here. I wouldn't have been with Dad, and I wouldn't be with you."

"Maybe that wouldn't be the worst thing in the world."

"I...." Charlotte chose her words carefully. "I guess I've always resented, you know, not feeling like I had any say in my life. Like, not being able to choose what I want. I wish we'd never lost Dad. I wish we didn't have to struggle with money and I wish you could have gone to university." She pulled on the sleeve of the big T-shirt she'd been sleeping in. One of her dad's. "I know you sent me away to protect me, but I also wish I could have chosen to stay. I wish I could have had the option to stay with Sophie. But I would never resent, not for one second, that Dad chose to keep me." She paused, trying to catch his eye with her smile. "They say you can't choose your family, but you guys chose me."

Sean laughed at the floor. "Well, it was you or the station wagon, so."

"You can't protect me from everything. The only thing we can do is just...try to be okay."

He finally looked at her. "You should get some sleep. It's late."

She didn't question his change in subject. "Okay."

He moved to pass her, pausing to place a hand on her shoulder. "You're gonna be okay. All right?"

She nodded. "I know."

She padded down the hall back to her room. Max was sitting on her bed, waiting for her with the lights off. He'd stayed.

"Did you want me to go home?" He reached out for her in the semi-darkness, half like he was exhausted and half like he just wanted to show her that he was there. Her hand found his as she sat down beside him, the sagging of the mattress shifting them together.

"No," she said.

# twenty

CHARLOTTE HAD JUST CRAWLED INTO bed when she heard the crunch of footsteps on gravel outside. Max walked over sometimes. Shit. He was early—it wasn't even 1 A.M. yet. She prayed Sean had crashed early enough that he wouldn't hear them. He'd let it drop after he discovered Max sleeping over the first time, but she didn't think he'd be as forgiving if he realized Max was sneaking into her room every night.

She could hear Max fumbling with the door and bumping his way through the entry. His steps were heavier than usual. He fell right into bed beside her and buried his face in the pillow.

Charlotte wrinkled her nose. "You stink." Like beer, and cigarettes, and maybe puke.

He turned his face toward her. "Sorry," he said, his eyes fluttering open, "was at Delilah's."

Right, Charlotte had heard. Leo had tried to convince her to come. But a party at Delilah Cooke's was not something Charlotte wanted to be a part of. Or something she thought she'd be welcome at. Not after the last social gathering had left her covered in punch.

"I see. Why'd you leave?" Charlotte asked.

Max twisted his face like he was upset, his eyes avoiding hers. His hands curled around her hips and he pulled her closer to him across the mattress.

"Because," he said quietly, drunkenly, "I wanted to be with you."

Thrown off by his hands on her, she stilled for a few long seconds. She was surprised by how comfortable she felt with him so close. She felt warm. Safe. At home.

"Is everything all right?" she asked him.

"Sophie was there," Max managed. "It's hard...seeing her. Sometimes."

Charlotte nodded, feeling even more sure about her decision not to go to the party. "It's okay. I know what you mean."

"That's the first party I've really went to...in like a year." He sniffed.

"Because of Sophie?"

"Because of...everything." Max slid his hands up to settle around her waist. "Is this okay?" he asked.

She nodded again. Max dragged her to him, wrapping his arms around her body and holding on to her like it was the last chance he'd ever get. She pulled the bedsheet and comforter free from under him and laid it back carefully up around them.

"It's okay," she whispered against his shoulder, and she knew exactly what was wrong this time. She knew what it was like—the dread and the sadness that settled in your stomach, things you couldn't shake.

"It's my fault," he mumbled into her hair. "Sophie...that's what I dream about...it's my fault."

"It's not," she said quickly. She thought, briefly, about their fight when she came home. About guilt and blame and who carried the weight of everything. It felt like ages ago, now. In those first few days after the accident, Charlotte had heard the rumours that circled around town and back again. That Max had crashed. Emphasis on Max. People didn't say that anymore, because by now everyone knew that someone had hit them. But she knew people always made the point to mention that Max was driving before they said anything else. "You know it isn't."

He didn't say anything else for a very long time. She'd thought he had fallen asleep, but finally he shifted, his grip loosening on her slightly.

"Please don't leave again," he said to her.

"I won't," she replied.

When she woke up, it was light. Early. She could feel Max trying to untangle himself from her. Charlotte rolled over onto her stomach, grimacing against the sunlight. When she looked over, he was sitting on the edge of the bed, facing away.

"Hey," she murmured sleepily.

"Hi." He looked back at her over his shoulder. "Uh, I'm sorry, I didn't...." He motioned to the bed, to her. "I shouldn't have—"

She shook her head, pushing her face into her pillow. "It's fine." She was cold without him beside her, she realized. She wanted him to lie back down.

Max reached back like he was about to touch her but his hand froze in mid-air and he dropped it. "I'll see you later?"

"Mmm." She nodded and closed her eyes. Leo wanted them to all hang out. He'd actually used the words "family bonding." Whatever that meant. "See you."

She felt Max's weight lift off the mattress as a lazy sleep washed over her, but the rumble of low voices out in the main room dragged her back awake.

"Why are you here?" Sean.

"I just came to see Charlie. I'm leaving," Max said.

Silence. Charlotte imagined them just staring at each other uncomfortably.

"I hear her, at night," Sean said, "the nightmares. You stay over because of that, don't you?"

"Yes."

More silence.

"I don't want her to need you," Sean said. "Don't let her."

"It isn't like that," Max answered.

*Exactly*, she told herself. *It was never anything.*

"It's not," Max continued, "it's the other way around."

Charlotte sucked in a breath and rolled back over, facing the wall she knew Max and Sean were on the other side of.

When she woke up some time later, she told herself she wasn't remembering right, that she'd been dreaming.

"You," Max said dramatically, "are going to ruin my laptop."

Leo rolled his eyes. "Would you relax? I download from this site, like, every day. Your MacBook Pro Grand Supreme 2000 is gonna be fine."

Max slouched back into his seat, looking exasperated. "I saved all year for that laptop."

Charlotte sat between them in Max's living room. "By 'save' you mean you didn't spend your allowance until you had enough?" she said, arching an eyebrow.

Leo chuckled into the keyboard.

Max looked at her across Leo's shoulders. "That's what *saved* means. And I don't remember inviting you here."

"I invited her," Leo said, adding a few zeroes and other odds and ends to his search for a download of the latest episode of some HBO show. "She's only just returned to us, we must keep her entertained so she doesn't run off again."

Max laughed. "I see her enough," he said quietly.

Charlotte bit back a smile. She wondered if Leo knew just how much time they spent together. Probably. Leo knew everything. And to be fair, most of the time she spent with Max they were both unconscious. Didn't exactly count as hanging out.

"Does this usually take this long?" Max asked Leo.

"Your computer sucks," Leo said. "Too much junk on it. What are you hoarding on here? All your prom photos?"

"You know I would never delete those."

"Well, your date *was* exceptionally good-looking," Leo returned.

"Wait, Sophie?" Charlotte asked. "No. Who did you guys go with?"

"Max went to prom with the second best-looking person at school, next to Sophie," Leo said. "And I went with my second choice."

Charlotte frowned and Max shot Leo a look.

"We went together," Max explained.

Charlotte looked back and forth between them. "No one tells me anything! Am I third-wheeling right now?"

"It's a long story," Leo said, still talking to the laptop. "A statement. An uprising. A rage against the machine kinda thing. Anyone who didn't go to North Colchester had to be signed in and okayed by the school. They wouldn't let me sign Ben in because they said nineteen was too old."

"Which we know is bullshit because Delilah got her twenty-one-year-old hipster brewery boyfriend from Tatamagouche in," Max added.

"So, the next day at lunch Max told everyone in the cafeteria that I was the love of his life, yadda-yadda, asked me to be his prom date, I fake-cried a bit for the sake of theatrics, said yes, and obviously the school couldn't do anything."

Charlotte tilted her head and closed her eyes, trying to envision the scene in her head. "Why did I miss this?"

"Did you have prom at boarding school?" Leo asked.

"Yeah. I didn't go." Prom was something she and Sophie had talked about for years. She was either doing prom with Sophie or not at all.

"You didn't miss anything," Max said.

Leo threw himself back into the sofa cushions with a sigh. "There, it's done. Now we just need an HDMI cord so we can plug this into the TV."

"Shit. Hm." Max stood up. "I think there's one...somewhere."

Charlotte joined him as they poked around the living room, looking in baskets of other cords that weren't the right one, under the sofa, and in cabinets. She was digging through a trunk near the end of the room to no avail.

She poked her head into a smaller room off the living room, where Max had disappeared. "Any luck?"

It was Simon's office. Max was lifting and re-stacking huge towers of papers and files. He shook his head. "I thought there was one in here. Wait. What's that noise?"

She paused to listen. It was a distant, low buzz. Charlotte shifted a pile of papers on the top of the desk at her hip.

"Here," she said. "It's his phone." She held it up for him to see. Small, nondescript, old. Charlotte wasn't even sure it was one that could access the internet.

Max looked puzzled. "That isn't his phone."

"Oh." Charlotte looked back down at it as it began ringing again in her hand. The caller-ID just said "unknown."

"They've called five times."

Max squinted at the tiny screen.

"It's probably his work phone," she said.

"Maybe he's having an affair." Max smirked.

The phone quieted, but restarted immediately. Same number.

"Here," Max sighed, taking it from her. He pressed the green button with his thumb and held it to his ear. "Simon," he said, in a fake voice deeper than his own.

"Right," Max said after a few seconds, "and...so, what will?"

He pulled the phone back from his ear like he was offended. "They hung up."

"Who was it?" Charlotte asked.

Max shrugged. "No idea. Some guy."

"What did they say?"

"'It'll be next week.' Or something like that. Something about next week."

"Oh. Huh."

"It's probably just his work phone," Max agreed.

"I like your Simon voice. I didn't realize he was Batman."

Max dug through a couple drawers. "I wonder who my new mom is gonna be."

Charlotte rolled her eyes and joined him on the other side of the desk. "I don't think the cord is in here."

"What are you doing in my office?"

Charlotte's head snapped up. Simon stood in the doorway, his hand still on the knob.

"Hey, Dad," Max said without looking up. "Just doing some research for the exposé Charlotte is writing on our family. It's gonna be good. You ever see *Blackfish*?"

Charlotte held Simon's gaze as his eyes fell on her, almost looking like he thought his son was serious.

"Max," she said slowly, "we're just looking for that cord, right?"

Max finally looked up and glanced between them. "Um, yeah... you know you're not actually writing an exposé, right?"

"Get out of my office," Simon barked. "And stay out."

She felt Max's hand at her waist as he shuffled her out of the office. She didn't know why she felt so uncomfortable. They hadn't been doing anything. She didn't like the way Simon had looked at her. She could feel Simon's eyes raking over her like she was a bug. But like she was a whole infestation that would cause trouble down the line, and had to be eradicated.

The door shut behind them.

"He's just still mad about the chocolate fountain thing," Max explained. "We didn't get the deposit back."

"Yo, Hardy Boys," Leo called from the couch. "It's a good thing you're cute. But the cord is plugged in already. It's hanging off the back of the TV."

While the boys were engrossed in the show (there was a lot of nudity), Charlotte found herself watching the door to Simon's office. He left once, but returned, leaving the door just barely open. She thought maybe he wanted to be able to see them.

*Jesus. Pull it together.* Charlotte pulled her attention to the TV and tried to follow along for a few minutes. She was losing it. Maybe Simon was just a cranky weirdo who really was upset about the chocolate fountain's demise.

The show ended and Max and Leo took a few minutes to debate the significance of something the dragon girl said and what it meant for the overall plot. Leo suggested it meant she was going to die, which made Max very upset and start looking off sadly into the distance.

"Anyway," Leo said finally, "wanna go get Chinese?"

Max agreed and Charlotte thought her bout of paranoia might have just been brought on by her hunger. And maybe she needed to drink more water.

"Bye, Dad!" Max called in the direction of the office. "We're leaving, forever! I *love* you! Give my regards to your mistress!"

No answer.

"Where's Deirdre?" Leo asked.

"I think getting groceries," Max said. "But not sure. She doesn't cook. Last we talked she'd decided she wanted to be a sommelier. I think she cleared out the NSLC in town, for educational purposes."

"God, I love her," Leo said.

"Hey," Max said to Charlotte when they stood up, his hand catching her elbow. "You good?"

"Yeah." She nodded as they headed for the door. "I'm fine. Oh. Wait, I'm gonna use the washroom."

Leo was already on the deck and Max was stepping through the door, positioning an unlit cigarette between his teeth. "We'll wait in the car."

After she was done, she stood outside the bathroom door, kitty-corner to Simon's office. The door was still open a tiny bit. Charlotte could hear Simon talking. He must be back on the phone. She waved off everything she'd ever learned from Nancy Drew books and crept closer, his voice swirling into focus.

"It'll have to be sooner," Simon was saying.

And then as if he knew she was listening, the call ended, or at least she assumed it had. No more talking. Okay. She'd learned enough from Nancy to know better than to wait around for Simon to discover her. She left the house, sliding the door shut behind her.

# twenty-one

CHARLOTTE DIDN'T FEEL LIKE EATING, making some excuse about not feeling well once they got to the restaurant. She knew by Max's expression that he saw right through her, but he didn't press it. She worked tonight so she'd be back at May's later, anyway. Laurie had been so good to her. She was getting four shifts a week and could pick up more from the other girls if she wanted to. It felt good to finally be putting money away somewhere. It wasn't much, but it could be a foundation for more.

Charlotte left Max and Leo to their egg rolls and headed in town, toward the library. She didn't know what she wanted to do there; maybe it was the air conditioning and the Wi-Fi. (The River John library was the only place in town with free internet. It was on the town sign.)

The place was cool and quiet. She didn't think there was anyone else inside. Charlotte busied herself with a shelf that announced the new arrivals (which included *Twilight*, 2005). She picked a few up anyway, for nostalgia's sake.

"Charlotte?"

She turned around. At the table in the corner of the room behind her, Sophie was almost completely shrouded from view by the bookshelves.

"Ah, h-hi," Charlotte stammered, looking away quickly. She placed her books on the table and waited a few seconds. Her brain had been so wired the last few weeks toward convincing Sophie to forgive her that she had temporarily forgotten Sophie's reaction to her at Max's party. Taking a deep breath, she turned around again.

"What's up?" Sophie asked.

"Um, nothing, really." Charlotte practically tiptoed into the room toward her. Bookshelves lined the walls and stood back to back in the centre of the room, creating a few cubbies with tables. "How are you?"

"Oh, you know me." Sophie had a newspaper crossword before her. She could usually polish them off in less than twenty minutes. Sophie was smart—way smarter than Charlotte and probably Max, and way smarter than she ever let anyone give her credit for. "Same old, same old." Sophie was also really good at talking to you like you'd managed to annoy her, no matter what you said.

"Right." Charlotte nodded. "You come here a lot?"

"Yes. You'd be surprised how few people from school show up here."

"Not that surprised."

Sophie flipped her pencil around, erasing a few squares. "Listen. I'm sorry about what happened at the party. With Amy and Emma."

Charlotte slid into the seat across from her and rested her elbows on the table. "Don't worry about it."

"I was just...angry, because Emma kept going on about how she was sure you were trying to get with Max and I...I dunno, I was in a bad mood, I guess."

If she didn't know better, she'd swear she saw Sophie's lips curling at the corners as she doodled a flower in the margins. "I told Emma to piss off," Sophie continued. "That you would *never* do something like that to me. Even though Max was telling people at Delilah's last night that he was on his way to your place. But I know there's nothing going on with you two." She looked at Charlotte, a challenge in her eyes.

Charlotte felt like she was going to be sick. Max was such an idiot.

Sophie raised an eyebrow and looked at her out of the corner of her eye. "Right?"

Charlotte had known Sophie for ten years. And if there was one thing Charlotte Romer knew about Sophie Thompson, it was that Sophie rarely asked questions she didn't already know the answer to.

Charlotte twisted her hands in her lap. "There's nothing—"

"I *knew* it," she said, shaking her head and pursing her lips at her paper. "Amy owes me a quart. Considering you're grovelling at my feet every time I see you, you're not doing a very good job of winning me back."

"We're just friends," Charlotte insisted. And they were, really. They hadn't done anything wrong.

"Well, then, I wish you'd gotten something out of it. You should have slept with him while you had the chance." Sophie tossed her hair back behind her shoulders. "I don't really want you spending time with him."

Charlotte scrunched up her face. "All right, *Mom*."

Sophie frowned at the crossword. "Not that you'd know, though, right?"

*Ow.* Charlotte stood up. "God, Sophie. Go to hell."

"Okay, here it is." Sophie rubbed at the side of her face like she was tired. "You're not going to see Max, all right?"

"Why?"

"Because I don't want you to have anyone," Sophie said, suddenly much angrier than Charlotte had originally thought. "Not my ex-boyfriend. Not my ex-friends. I want you to know how it felt. You can't just come back here and work your way back in. You left River John and you don't get to come back."

Charlotte paused, and the realization clicked into place. Ten years hung in the balance. "You're never going to forgive me, are you?"

Sophie folded the newspaper in half. Charlotte could see that the crossword was complete. "No," Sophie said.

"When did you decide that?"

Charlotte could hear Sophie breathing.

"The day Sean told me you were gone," Sophie said blankly.

So, that was it. Charlotte knew defeat when she saw it. For a second she wondered why she'd even come back at all.

"Bye, Sophie," she said, turning to leave.

"And Charlie," Sophie sang after her, her anger once again shrouded by her usual gleeful malice. "I meant what I said. I don't want you hanging out with Max. I'm just saying...everyone was drinking so much the night of the car rally. Me, Delilah, Max."

Charlotte whipped back to look at her, nearly dropping her books. "Max wasn't drinking. He was driving. Everyone who was there...would know that."

Sophie tilted her head. "I'm pretty sure everyone there was pretty focused on themselves. And you weren't there, were you, Charlie?"

"He wasn't," was all Charlotte could think to say.

"Well." Sophie shrugged again and pushed back from the table. "If you're so sure then you have nothing to worry about."


Charlotte couldn't describe what she felt. The walk home from the library felt a lot longer than it should have. She was angry. As she stomped down the road toward her driveway, she hated Sophie. But she was sad. Sad that Sophie would ever even suggest doing something like this—to Max and to her. Sad that this was what they were now. And she was scared, because she either had to say goodbye to Max or he could end up...she didn't want to think about it. An optimistic part of her was trying to convince her that Sophie was bluffing, trying to scare her. That she wouldn't do anything. But Charlotte didn't trust optimism.

The driveway was empty when she got there; Sean wasn't home. She glanced toward the workshop and for a few seconds let herself miss her Dad. Most of the time she tried to ignore it, because it was too hard and it didn't do any good. Her eyes focused on the heavy door, and she noticed something new—something different than the last time she'd tried to go inside.

There was a shiny new padlock across the door. Charlotte pulled on it, confused. Locked. It must have been Sean, she guessed, to keep the animals out. Or her.

As Charlotte turned back to the house, her phone buzzed in her pocket. It was a text from Max: *I wanted to say I'm sorry about last night. I shouldn't have slept in your bed without asking you. Do you still want me to come over tonight?*

Charlotte stared down at the screen. She thought of Sophie.

Charlotte swiped her thumb on the screen and deleted the conversation.

# twenty-two

THERE WAS A KNOCK ON her bedroom door a few days later. Charlotte peeled her eyes away from her laptop, where she was streaming a shitty pirated version of *Gone Girl*. Sophie's favourite book/movie.

Sean stood in the doorway. "That guy is here."

"Are we just not using Max's name anymore?" she asked. She figured that's the only person it could be. He had sent her a few texts after the first one she deleted, but she hadn't answered any of them. Then he stopped trying.

"No. It's the other one. The small one."

"Charlotte!" Leo's face appeared over Sean's shoulder intermittently as he hopped up and down. "Hey! We're going to a party."

Charlotte pushed herself off of her stomach and sat back on her heels. "Thanks, Sean."

"Thanks, Sean," Leo repeated as Sean left them. Leo did a weird sort of half-bow in Sean's direction before he threw himself down on her bed. "Connor Hickey is having a party tonight."

"The tenth grader with the pool?"

"Well, he's in grade eleven now," Leo said, "keep up. But yes. We should go."

Charlotte groaned and leaned forward, folding her arms to use as a pillow. "I don't want to see anyone. I don't think I'm even allowed to be at things anymore."

"I need a wingman."

"You have a boyfriend."

"No, I mean at beer pong. And I can't take Max since he's been acting like it's the end of the world because you haven't talked to him for three days." Leo looked at her meaningfully. "You broke his heart."

"I did not," she said testily. "His heart is perfectly fine."

"He's been locked in his bedroom listening to The Smiths for the last three days. The *Smiths*, Charlotte. Jesus. I wasn't aware we were living in an indie film. And there was a documentary on called *The Red Scare and You* and he didn't even record it!"

She scoffed. "He's probably seen it."

"Why the Cold War, anyway?"

Charlotte picked at her quilt and didn't look at him. She'd been ignoring Max's texts since Sophie's warning, and the other night was the first time in what seemed like a very long time he hadn't slept on her floor. "I just don't think there's a point in us being friends."

"Okaaay," Leo sounded like he didn't believe her. "Well. I'm getting you out of the house. We're going to Connor Hickey's."

"Is Max going?" She remembered what he'd said about not going to things anymore.

Leo had already rolled off the bed and was out the door, and apparently hadn't heard her question.

She insisted she drive, so she could abandon ship whenever she wanted. Leo didn't seem to mind, because it meant he could drink. She picked him up at eight and drove the ten minutes to Connor's house. The majority of their high school was already there and drunk by the time they arrived.

Charlotte linked her arm through Leo's as they walked up the path to the door. "Ready to do this?" she asked him.

Leo knocked. "Born ready, baby."

The door swung open. "Hey—"

Max's expression fell comically fast, his arms draped across the shoulders of Delilah Cooke and Amy Chamberlain. "Oh," he said blankly. "Hi."

Charlotte felt the air rush out of her. Leo stiffened. She never thought she'd be so thankful for Delilah Cooke, but she was the one who broke the silence.

"Come on, Max, let them in," Delilah slurred in a singsong voice. "Let's go sit."

Max gave the two of them a look—mostly surprise and mostly aimed at Leo—but allowed himself to be dragged away by the girls.

Leo patted Charlotte's arm comfortingly. "See. It can't get any more awkward than that. So it's over. Like a Band-Aid. I'm the one who's going to get in trouble, anyway. Now we can enjoy ourselves."

Charlotte took a deep breath and steadied herself. "Let's go play beer pong."

Beer pong was shockingly hard when you weren't drinking, Charlotte reflected. After a while she was only hurting Leo's game. She was half-sitting on the back of the sofa, facing the game and serving as moral support. She didn't think Leo even noticed.

Charlotte found herself kind of enjoying the quiet in the middle of the party. No one was paying her any attention, which she liked. The novelty had worn off. The newest River John scandal was a rumour going around that eleventh-grader Wesley Walker had bought a secret engagement ring for his girlfriend.

She could see into the kitchen, where Max was sitting on the kitchen counter. Delilah Cooke stood between his legs, toying with his collar and nuzzling his neck and rubbing his chest. Charlotte was reconsidering her decision to stay sober. She could always walk home. She rather aggressively tore at a loose thread on the back of the sofa. Delilah's makeup was smudged under her eyes and she was looking dangerously close to Charlotte's memories of Martini Mondays back at boarding school. Max looked up, catching her staring. *Shit.* She had been staring. She met his gaze bravely, until Delilah noticed his lack of attention and pulled his face back toward hers with her fingers, brushing her lips against his. Charlotte shifted and looked away.

"Greetings. May I join you?"

She looked up. John O'Neil, whom she would have graduated with, stood before her with a red plastic cup in his hand. She'd spoken to him only a few times in all the years they went to school together.

"Um. Be my guest." She waved to the edge of sofa beside her.

He settled down next to her. "So, how've you been?"

"Um." She was trying to process what exactly John wanted from her. "Fine?"

"Come on." John adjusted his glasses. Were there even lenses in those? The kid was a mystery. "I heard things have been kind of hard for you since you got back."

She looked at him. She didn't really like that that was general knowledge. Or something everyone gossiped about.

"That's just what Sophie says, at least."

Charlotte sucked in a breath, suddenly bitter. "Well, thank god I have someone like you looking out for my feelings."

John squinted at her. "Is that sarcasm?"

"Would you be offended if it was?"

He cleared his throat. "Okay, well, anyway. I was thinking about driving into the city this weekend—do you like foreign films?"

"They aren't really my thing—"

"Can you read subtitles?"

"English subtitles?"

"Yeah."

"You're asking if I can read English subtitles?

"I know you can *read*, I was just wondering if you could, like, watch a movie and read subtitles." John rolled his eyes. "It might cheer you up a bit."

She wondered if she could throw herself off the back of the couch hard enough that it would give her a concussion and put her out of her misery. "I'm perfectly cheered, actually, but thanks."

"So, do you wanna hang out or not?"

"Can I have your drink?" Charlotte asked.

John frowned. "No."

"Then I gotta go. I need to be drunk after this." She jumped to her feet, but he stopped her.

Grabbing her forearm, John yanked on her so hard she fell back down into her seat.

"Ow. Let *go* of me, John," she said, wrenching her arm away.

She glanced back toward the kitchen, where she saw Delilah untangling herself from Max and stumbling out of Charlotte's line of sight.

"Where are you going? Listen, I just need like two grams. If you want, we can go back to my place and smoke and—"

"I, uh...." She peered past him. Max was gone from the kitchen. Charlotte snapped back to her senses. "I don't have anything."

"Doesn't your brother sell?"

"No. Not anymore."

"I got some from him a month ago."

Charlotte chose to ignore that.

"Well," John said slowly. She could feel his hand on her knee. "We can still go hang out if you want."

She shoved his hand off and twisted away from him. "No, thanks."

John looked offended and scoffed. "Sophie said you were easy."

"Yeah, but it looks like I'm still drawing the line at hooking up with you."

"Whore," John spat, louder than the rest of their conversation.

Charlotte's stomach was doing angry flips as she stalked away from him. She didn't get more than a few steps before a staggering crash had her whipping back around.

John had been thrown backward off the edge of the sofa, knocking a few glasses and bottles off the coffee table. His red cup bounced sadly onto the ground and his drink stained the carpet.

"Apologize to her."

Charlotte looked up to see Max standing behind the sofa. He was a whirlwind and the rest of the party was at a standstill. John looked startled and red was creeping into his face.

Charlotte made a mental promise to go with her gut from now on re: going to parties she didn't want to attend. *Shit*. If word got back to Sophie that Max was throwing people around to defend Charlotte's honour, Sophie would not be happy. She should leave—now. John and Max were both looking at her but she didn't wait to hear if any apology came. She didn't want one anyway.

She was glad, at least, that she had her car. She could be home and in bed in ten minutes. She checked in with Leo, who told her he had to stay until he was the resident beer pong champion and was okay to walk home. Slipping outside, Charlotte took a five-second pause on the porch. Sophie probably already knew by now.

The door opened behind her and Max sauntered onto the porch, his head swivelling around like he'd been looking for her.

"You're leaving?" he asked. He was holding a half-crushed box of cigarettes in one hand and digging around for his lighter in his pocket with the other.

"What's your problem?" she countered. "Why do you have to make a scene?"

"You never minded before," Max said. *With Nick*, she added silently for him.

"Bite me," she said, "I don't need you to fight my battles, all right? And I especially don't need you to act like I'm your property."

He swore under his breath and looked away, and she felt a sense of relief that he wasn't going to continue the conversation. But a shuffling in the dark gave her a half-a-second heart attack and the unmistakable sound of puking followed within a few seconds. Charlotte leaned forward, looking past a cluster of bushes beside the porch.

"Hello?" she called.

Delilah Cooke turned around, wiping her mouth on the back of her hand as she straightened up. "Ugh. It's always *pink*."

Charlotte frowned. "It's the hard lemonade."

Delilah spun around and puked again.

"Actually, it's probably because she kissed you," Charlotte told Max, who didn't seem to have heard. He blew some smoke toward the lawn and coughed a bit.

"I gotta go home," Delilah said when she was back upright.

"I'll drive you," Charlotte offered. "I was just leaving."

"I'll go too," Max announced.

Charlotte's car was parked a little ways down the road. Max was following after like she was forcing him to come. Charlotte considered telling him he was perfectly free to walk home, but couldn't find the energy. Delilah was holding on to Max's back belt loops for balance along the gravel shoulder.

"Charlotte, d'you have a light?" Delilah asked.

"No."

"'s dark," she mumbled.

"It's not too bad."

"Scary."

"Max'll protect you."

They reached the car and Charlotte helped Delilah into the back as Max climbed into the passenger seat. He thankfully remained silent as she gripped the steering wheel, her knuckles fading to white. She was angry. At herself? Definitely at Max. At Sophie, too.

"Sseat belt," he slurred as Charlotte started backing out of the spot. She glared at him.

"It's because I never checked," he explained messily, "if Sophie was wearing hers."

"I looove Sophie," Delilah said. "Where'd she go?"

They didn't speak again the entire drive. They reached Max's house first, Charlotte pressing on the brake just enough to make him lurch forward abruptly in his seat.

"Okay, ride's over," she barked when Max didn't immediately throw himself from the car. He groaned and shifted toward the door, pushing it open. She heard him make a retching noise toward the grass beside them. Charlotte rolled her eyes. Charming.

She hopped out of the driver's side and walked around the front of the car. Anything to help speed the process along. Charlotte drummed her fingers impatiently against the window. "Get out of my car, Max."

*"Charlie,"* he whined, leaning his head against the side of the door. "Can you please be nice for like, two seconds?"

"She *is* nice, Max." Delilah rolled down her window and popped her head out. "Jesus."

"Thanks, Delilah." Charlotte shot her a small smile. Delilah stuck out her tongue.

Max was falling asleep against the side of the car.

"Go sleep it off, Max." Charlotte huffed, reaching in to undo his seat belt.

He was faster than she'd thought he'd be. He reached out for her, looping a hand around her wrist. "Look—I'm sorry, all right?"

"You're not sorry, you're drunk."

"Yikes," Delilah said quietly.

Max scrubbed at his face in frustration, letting out a sigh. His eyes were bleary from the alcohol, his mouth opening and closing a few times. Finally, he seemed to collect himself and looked directly at her. "Whadid I do to you?"

"Nothing," Charlotte said quickly. She thought about the last time he'd slept over, when he'd held her and stayed in her bed.

"'sit because of the other night?" he asked, as if reading her mind.

"No, Max," she said quietly, her anger ebbing away the tiniest bit. "We...shouldn't be friends. We don't have anything in common," she lied.

Max laughed bitterly. "We have one very big thing in common. This's because of Sophie, isnit?"

Charlotte didn't say anything.

"You wanna know what I felt when Sophie broke up with me? Relief—"

Delilah shrieked, scandalized.

"—and I hate myself for it. She and I both knew we were over, but if I said that to her then I'd be the asshole who dumped his girlfriend who was in a wheelchair." Max gestured around the driveway in the dark, as if to help him explain. "So she did me a favour and did it for me. But I hate myself for feeling relieved that it happened, and also that I was too afraid to do it myself. That I cared too much about what other people would think of me that I forgot to treat the girl I loved like a human being, and respect her enough to be honest with her. I hated that I was treating her differently because of the accident, which is exactly what she didn't want." Max was stumbling over his words and sometimes circling back around, but he held a steady force behind them. "So I'm not doing that again. I don't care what people think anymore. I like you—"

Delilah gave a high-pitched squeal.

"—Things are better when I'm with you."

He stopped himself, and they both seemed surprised that he had managed his speech in his current drunken state. Delilah applauded. Charlotte felt like she'd dropped priceless china or blown a stop sign or been struck by lightning.

"Max, I—" Charlotte shook her head, searching his face. She thought of Sophie. Of everything. If it weren't for the accident, Sophie and Max would probably still be together. They might have a baby together. Charlotte and Max would barely be friends. If Max knew what she did, would he still feel the same?

"I know. You can't. I get it." He slid out of the seat and stood up on the grass. Leaning forward, he placed a messy but affectionate kiss on her forehead, nearly missing when he swayed off balance. The action sent a jolt, like lightning, through her body. "G'night. Night, Delilah." He saluted to her in the back seat.

Delilah turned her head and jerked the side of her face in his direction, tapping expectantly on her cheek with her pointer finger. Max kissed her cheek.

Charlotte watched him make his way unevenly toward the house.

"Can we go to May's?" Delilah asked.

Charlotte looked at her. May's was open until 2 A.M. on Saturdays. Egg rolls were scientifically proven to aid boy problems, friend problems, all problems.

"Yes, we can."

# twenty-three

september
eleven months earlier

**A PERSON RUNNING THROUGH** a hospital only ever meant one thing.

Charlotte was crying by the time she reached the elevator. The man in scrubs behind the desk had directed her to the third floor. It was fine, it was fine, she would know by now if Sophie wasn't okay. Charlotte closed her eyes and gripped the railing behind her as the elevator rose three levels painfully slowly. She would have taken the stairs but didn't know where they were. The doors finally rolled open with a resounding ding. The lobby before her was the opposite of the deserted first floor. A cluster of police officers stood at the far side, chatting quietly with solemn expressions. At a bench against the wall, she saw Delilah and Leo. Team number five. Delilah was crying.

A few other kids Charlotte recognized from school and from the car rally were sitting together, clutching paper cups of steaming coffee. Amy Chamberlain leaned against a wall, looking flustered as she furiously typed messages into her phone. Charlotte wondered how many people knew what had happened by then. Then she realized she didn't even know what had happened.

"Charlie." Max appeared out of nowhere. Charlotte gasped. His right arm was wrapped in a sling, cuts and bruises decorated his face and peeked out from under his T-shirt.

"Where's Sophie?" was all she could manage. "Are you okay?

"I'm fine. Stitches," Max told her, motioning to his side. He was shaking his head quickly. "Sophie...Sophie, she's—"

He looked away, pressing his fist against his lips, and Charlotte saw he was trying not to cry.

"She's hurt, Charlie. Bad," he managed to choke out, his voice breaking on the last word.

"Is she okay?" Charlotte breathed, grabbing onto his arms.

"I—I don't know. They don't know." Max's voice was raspy, and he wiped his nose on the back of his hand. "Someone hit us. They came out of nowhere. We flipped over, and when I woke up we were upside down...I found my phone and called 911 and the paramedics showed up but she wasn't moving and I don't...she's in surgery now."

His breathing was coming in short, frantic gasps and his gaze was focused on the tiles beneath her feet. She felt like she was drowning, like she was being suffocated, as if his words were too heavy to bear, pounding down on her from all angles.

She took a shaky breath. "It'll be okay, Max." Charlotte placed her hands on his shoulders to steady the both of them. "It has to be."

He wrapped his good hand around one of her wrists and leaned in toward her helplessly. "It was my fault. I was driving. It's my fault if she—"

"Don't." Charlotte cut him off. "Don't say it." Being mindful of his shoulder, she pulled him into a hug.

"It's Sophie," Charlotte murmured, "she'll be okay."

It had been four hours. Simon and Deirdre Hale had rushed home from some kind of function in Halifax and arrived about an hour after Charlotte had. There wasn't much for them to say. Simon's son was fine.

From what Charlotte gathered, the second car had come seemingly out of nowhere, as Max had said, T-boned them, and fled the scene after the crash. Max never saw the other car, so the police had nothing to go on.

Sophie's parents, Robert and Ellen Thompson, were the first people Max had called. Charlotte didn't like to think about how that conversation had gone. She had glimpsed Ellen once at the end of the lobby, on the phone. But after that, Sophie's parents waited elsewhere; Charlotte suspected this was to be separate from the teenagers whose stupid game had gotten their daughter hurt, and so they didn't have to sit across from the boy who had been driving.

Max was speaking to the police again in another room. He had already given a statement and didn't seem to know much else, so in the back of her mind Charlotte was trying to puzzle out what else they could be talking about. Charlotte somehow found herself sitting on the floor beside the chair Max had occupied before the police called for him. Delilah, Leo, and a handful of other kids were taking up several seats on the other side of the room, but Charlotte couldn't bring herself to join them. She felt too heavy.

She didn't know why but she wanted to call her brother. He was good at fixing things. Not the toaster oven that had been broken for a year, or the second step on the porch, but he had a knack for making situations better. She pulled out her phone and hit his number. It went directly to voicemail.

"Hey, Sean. It's Charlie. I'm at the hospital—I'm fine, but," her voice cracked. "There was an accident at the car rally. It's Sophie. I know you're out of town with the guys but if you could call me back...." It was harder, saying everything out loud. As if it made it more true. "Please call me back." The phone slipped out of her hand onto her lap.

She eventually picked herself up off the floor, wandering down the hall in search of a vending machine. Charlotte rounded a corner away from the rest of the group, nearly interrupting an intense talk Simon and Max were having. She ducked behind the Coca-Cola machine, out of sight.

"...you need to tell me *exactly*," Simon said in a low voice, "what happened."

"I did, I swear." Max was sobbing, and Simon had his hand on his son's shoulder but Charlotte didn't think he meant it in a comforting way. "I don't remember what happened."

"Try harder."

"Dad, I don't...there was another car...I don't remember," Max heaved.

"Then you were drinking?"

"God, no. I swear, I already told the police. I was sober, Dad, I promise, c'mon," Max's voice was wobbly and muffled.

"Maxwell, no, I need you to tell me exactly what you remember—" Simon said loudly.

"Dad, I did—"

"Sorry," Charlotte said, stepping forward before she could stop herself. She didn't know what she was sorry for. She moved between them, and she felt Max's hand on her arm like he was tethering himself to her. "I think—" she felt so uncomfortable, "—Leo's looking for you, Max."

She tried to lead him away but Simon stopped them. "Leo can wait," he said.

"No," Charlotte said more bravely than she felt, tugging Max toward her and back down the hall. "He can't."

"You should stay out of things that don't concern you, Charlotte," Simon said.

Charlotte pretended she hadn't heard, though the words sent a chill through her. She led Max down the hall back to Leo, settling him in an uncomfortable chair along the wall. Leo moved to sit beside him and didn't try and say anything either, which Charlotte felt Max probably appreciated. She slid to the ground beside his chair, and placed a comforting hand on Max's knee.

They sat in silence for what felt like another hour, before a doctor appeared suddenly, silencing any activity in the room and making Charlotte feel like the air had been sucked from her lungs.

"I'm looking for Sophie Thompson's family," the doctor said, holding a clipboard to her chest.

Charlotte jumped to her feet, Max doing the same beside her. By then, Delilah and her group had risen and clustered around behind the doctor.

"We're here." Sophie's parents raced forward from the back of the room.

The doctor motioned down the hallway with her head.

Max started forward, almost automatically, but was immediately stopped by the ferocious look Robert Thompson sent him.

"You've done enough," he spat venomously.

"Robert," Ellen scolded, linking her arm through his and pulling him toward the waiting doctor.

Max covered his face with his hand and remained standing, Leo placing a hand on his shoulder. Charlotte could feel her heartbeat in every inch of her body, as if she was hyper aware of every nerve ending. She moved and slid her hand around to the low of Max's back, brushing it in small circles. Max wrapped his arm around her shoulder, pulling her against him.

Ellen and Robert returned within a few minutes. Ellen was crying, and Charlotte knew immediately that it was not with relief. Robert looked like he had no idea what he wanted to say.

When they broke the news, the sound that left Max shuddered through Charlotte as if she had made it herself. He pulled away from her and Leo, sliding to the ground against the wall behind them. Delilah was crying again, and Leo crossed the room to pull her into a hug.

The only person who didn't seem to have any reaction was Charlotte. She wanted to burst out crying because Sophie was alive. She would see Sophie again, talk to her again, hug her again.

She was still Sophie. But she wasn't okay. Everything about their lives would be different. They were too young and this wasn't supposed to happen and Sophie should have been fine. There was nothing you could do when your best friend was hurt in a way that wouldn't get better.

"She's out of surgery," Ellen said, "she'll be awake soon."

*Maybe she'll wake up and be fine,* Charlotte thought wildly. The doctors would call it a miracle. Everything would fall right back into place, and they would all be fine.

Max peeled his hands from his face, his cheeks pale and eyes red. "Can I—"

"Don't you *dare*," Robert roared. "You did this. This is because of *you*—"

"Do not speak to my son that way." Simon was on his feet.

"Your son should be in jail—he could have killed my daughter!"

"Robert, that's enough!" Ellen's voice cut above the two men. "He's a boy. It was an accident."

Robert glared down at Max, who looked utterly broken and miserable from his place on the floor. "You will not see my daughter. Not in this hospital, not ever again. Because you know it as well as we do—this is your fault."

Ellen rubbed her hand across her face, choking on a sob as she dragged a path across her eyes, smudging her makeup down her cheek. Charlotte wondered if that was how she felt, too.

The weight of Robert's words kept the room hushed for several beats. It was Ellen who finally broke the silence.

"Charlotte." It was the first time anyone in the room had addressed her, other than Max. "We'd like you to come. Sophie would want you there."

Charlotte wasn't sure whether or not she was ready for that, but she didn't have much of a choice. Her chin jerked in a nod.

"Come this way." Ellen turned in the direction she and her husband had come. Robert followed after her without another word.

Charlotte felt every other eye in the room on her, and was about to follow the Thompsons when a voice drew her back.

"Charlie." Max wasn't even looking at her, his gaze focused on the disappearing figures. "Please. Just tell Sophie...make sure she knows...." He finally looked away and pressed his hand to the back of his neck, squeezing his eyes shut as his shoulders trembled. "God. Tell her I'm so sorry."

Charlotte didn't think she was particularly artistic or creative, but she felt like she could see the process behind it. A painter would look at a scene and think: how would I paint this? How would I capture the slopes and dips and the bend of the light? A writer would think: how would I describe this? How could I explain the way her voice sounded? How do I line up enough words in the right order to express the way the energy felt in the room? Charlotte wasn't artistic but when everything fell down at once she forced herself to think: how are we going to survive this? What are we going to do to get through this, and be okay? Sean did it too—she could see the way emergency back-up plans formed behind his eyes whenever something went wrong. Maybe that was the family craft, and she came from a long Romer dynasty of surviving and fixing.

But right now she didn't have any answers. She didn't know how they would fix this.

Leo moved again so he was sitting beside Max, slinging his arm across his friend's shoulders. Max's ragged sobs were the only sounds in the desolate white room as Charlotte backed away and stumbled after Sophie's parents.

She was crying again by the time she entered Sophie's room and saw Sophie laid out in a hospital bed, smudges of her car rally war paint left on her face. She cried during the interim moments between when Sophie woke up, and when she realized.

And then it was Sophie's turn to cry, and Charlotte's turn to cry less. At least for a while. At least for the few weeks they had before Sean sent Charlotte to boarding school.

# twenty-four

CHARLOTTE SHOULDERED THE QUIK MART door open. It was chilly for an August afternoon, way colder than it had been the last few weeks. For once, the clattering air-conditioning that blasted down on her from above the door was not a welcome relief.

Leo popped up from behind the counter. "Hi, babe."

"Do you work every day?" she asked him. Charlotte could see there was no one else in the store as she dragged a loaf of bread off one of the shelves.

"Pretty much. I don't mind, though," Leo said. "I'm saving up for a car."

"Oh. That's great," Charlotte answered, pushing around a few cans of beans on the shelf. She felt like she was barely awake. Delilah ended up not being able to stomach much more than a bit of chicken fried rice, but they'd still been up late at May's. And Charlotte had eaten way too many egg rolls.

"You sound pretty hungover for someone who wasn't drinking last night." Leo's voice was muffled—she looked over to see he had disappeared behind the counter again.

"What are you doing?" she asked.

"I have a pillow down here on the bottom shelf."

"Ah." Charlotte chuckled and carried the few groceries she could afford to the counter. "I can see why you're going into engineering. It's nice to know you'll be building our bridges one day."

Leo seemed upset that he was being forced to actually complete a transaction, pulling her items across the scanner without getting up from his knees.

"I'm tired," Leo explained before she could criticize his customer service.

Charlotte balanced an elbow on the glass that encased the cigarettes and put her head in her hand. "Me too."

"Max told me what happened." Leo was eying her from behind a litre of milk. "He sounded pretty upset."

Charlotte had been able to go a total of four whole minutes without replaying the tiny bits of Max's speech she could remember clearly. Not because she had been drunk, which she hadn't been, but because it had felt like it. His words jumbled together in her head. Especially the last part.

"Yeah." Charlotte couldn't look at Leo. "I was kind of hard on him when I shouldn't have been. Did he tell you...what he said?"

Leo nodded and pulled himself to his feet. "But he had told me a while ago."

She didn't answer that.

"How do you feel?" he asked.

"I don't know."

Leo finished scanning her groceries. The weather wasn't the only thing cooler than usual.

"I just feel like," she clarified, "he was drunk, or whatever...that he doesn't, really, you know...."

"You aren't giving either of yourselves enough credit." Leo smirked and Charlotte felt a surge of relief that he wasn't entirely angry at her. "Don't act so surprised. You really never thought that he was into you?"

Charlotte sputtered for a second like he had insulted her. "I just, I dunno, didn't consider it. He never...I've known him for years and he never...not before I left—"

"Charlie," Leo scolded, "the guy's been through hell. Maybe consider that people change. What you want from other people changes. Relationships change." He shrugged as he bagged up her things. "I thought you of all people might understand that."

Charlotte bit her lip. Things were clearly bad if Leo Hudson, angel of River John, was calling you on your bullshit.

"God," she said. "I'm sorry. You're right."

"I usually am," Leo replied with an easy smile. "Listen, the focus since that accident has always been Sophie. Like, duh. Obviously. But Max is my best friend and sometimes I feel like people forget that he was in the car, too. He's changed a lot. Like, do you even remember Max a year ago?" Leo shook his head. "Telling you how he feels was probably really hard for him. That night affected him just as bad as it affected Sophie."

"Yeah, I—"

"Don't just say you know," he cut her off, not unkindly. "You don't. Max literally spent this year in his house. He stopped going to things, stopped hanging out with us. He missed a lot of school. He kept telling people he was going to see his mom in Halifax for the weekend, but he wasn't. He just stayed in his room and I was the only one who knew."

Charlotte was quiet for a long time. She and Max had both spent the year hiding.

"I'm just saying," Leo continued finally.

Charlotte took a deep breath through her nose. "I know, I know. I need to hear it."

Leo chuckled. "Sometimes you gotta face the music. Speaking of, please go talk to him. He's moved on to Adele and I can't listen to her anymore. I'm gonna drown myself, seriously."

Charlotte handed him her cash. "So, I guess I'm not allowed to go over there and completely break his heart, then?"

Leo guffawed loudly as he hip-checked the register drawer shut. "Yeah, right. As if."

She was determined to go to Max's and neither cut him out of her life nor propose their engagement. But Charlotte figured if he could be honest with her, then the least she could do was reciprocate.

*Maybe he won't be home*, she hated herself for hoping as she knocked on the door. No, Max was always home—either that or he was with her, or he was with Leo. There was a dull feeling in her head.

The door finally opened and he was there. He was wearing his North Colchester High hoodie with jeans, his hair all wet and curly like he'd just showered. She didn't like the frightened little flips her stomach did when she looked at him.

"Hi," he said, more pleasantly than she'd expected.

"Hey," she began slowly, "I was hoping we could chat."

Max grimaced but stepped aside to let her in. "That sounds ominous."

Charlotte stuffed her hands into the pockets of her sweater, her eyes sweeping the room for inspiration. "No, sorry. Um. I wanted to explain why I was kind of ignoring you before. And why I was such a bitch last night."

Max laughed. "I was going to go with *difficult*, or *hard to get along with*."

She smiled back. "Are your dad and Deirdre here?"

"Dunno where my dad is. Deirdre's at Blomidon for the afternoon. She sent me a Snapchat."

"Oh, yeah, she's an aspiring sommelier, right?"

Max frowned like he didn't remember telling her that and led her into the living room. "No, I think that idea has passed and now she's just drinking in the middle of a Tuesday."

"Come on, don't say that like it's any worse than being wasted at an eleventh grader's party on a Monday night."

"Any*way*," he cut her off quickly. "You were here to talk about our misadventures at said eleventh grader's place last night?"

"Yeah." She sighed, sinking down onto the sofa and pulling one of the throw pillows from behind her around to her chest. "I ran into Sophie last week, and...she doesn't like that we hang out."

Max sat down beside her, resting his long legs on the coffee table. He thought about this for a moment, his face twisted at the ceiling like he was trying to hear music from far away.

"Why?" he asked eventually. "Is she jealous?"

A very loud JEALOUS OF WHAT!!! alarm rang through Charlotte's head. They weren't a couple—nowhere near it, she told herself. There was nothing to be jealous of.

"No. I think she just hates me."

"Sophie hates everybody."

"Yeah, but she hates me more," Charlotte said, cringing. "I think it's different when you used to love someone."

"So, you didn't want to hang out anymore?" he asked. He almost looked hurt.

"It was more than that," she explained, curling a loose thread on the pillow around her pinky. "Sophie kept talking about the night of the accident."

"What about it?"

*Spit it out, Charlie!* she wanted to scream at herself. Why, after all this, was she still trying to protect Sophie? Trying to make her seem like she hadn't threatened Max with a lie that could ruin his life? Sophie wouldn't even entertain the thought of protecting Charlotte if the roles were reversed. Not anymore.

"Sophie said everybody was drinking that night and that you probably were too, and I was scared she would tell people," Charlotte blurted out quickly, "if we didn't stop being friends."

Max was looking at a spot on the wall behind Charlotte's head and not completely at her. There was no mistaking Max looking hurt this time.

"And what did you say?" he asked finally.

"I don't really remember."

"Do you think she would really do that?"

A good question. A year ago, Charlotte would have said no, absolutely not. Sophie was bluffing. "I don't know," Charlotte answered truthfully.

"And that's why you stopped hanging out with me?"

"Yeah. I didn't know what else to do."

Max stretched back into the couch, readjusting his feet. "Part of me's a bit relieved," he admitted. "I thought it was because of the other night, when I slept over in your bed."

The jolt of the memory made her accidentally pull the thread free from the pillow. "It wasn't because of that."

Max took the pillow she was wrecking away from her and held it in his own lap. "We'll just...slow it down, I guess, then."

She stared at him. "What?"

"Us hanging out. Less public outings. More of this."

Charlotte raised her eyebrows. "But, Sophie—"

"She's bluffing. Or she's not, and I'll burn that bridge when I get to it," Max said shortly. He turned to her, more seriously. "And Charlie, think about it. There's no way that she could prove something like that."

"You don't know that."

"Yes, I do," Max said, reaching out to touch her arm. "Because I was there and I wasn't drinking. She just knows that would get to you. Sophie knows you, and knows exactly what she can prey on. That's just how she is."

"What if she can fake it, though, or—"

"Charlie, I promise. She can't. And besides, it doesn't matter. It's not like you and I can stop being friends."

"This sounds like a very, very bad plan. One that will result in jail time."

He ignored her. "Thanks for telling me this, though."

There was no point in arguing with him. "I thought you deserved honesty. You know, at least once. You're always honest with me."

"As far as you know."

She rolled her eyes. "Anyway. That's my good deed for the day. Feel free to resume nursing your hangover."

"I wasn't *that* drunk."

"Yes, you were." *That's why you said you had feelings for me, idiot.*

He shook his head.

"Do you remember everything that happened last night?" she asked, suddenly feeling brave.

He looked at her and she knew he understood what in particular she was referring to. He stood up, bristling slightly, like he was annoyed.

"Yes, I do," he said. "Don't bring it up again."

But he was smiling at the floor as he said it. Charlotte stood up and for a bursting moment was overwhelmed by an urge to hug him. Her body lurched forward for a second before she stopped herself, settling on a slightly awkward pat on the arm. When Max looked at her, she knew he knew what she meant by it. He chuckled quietly. She was relieved she wouldn't have to give him up after all.

"All right," she said to him. "I won't."

• • •

"What time is Leo coming over?" Max asked.

Charlotte glanced at the clock above the stove. "He said whenever he gets off work. A half-hour, maybe?"

True to what he'd said, Max didn't seem fazed by Sophie's threat. He and Charlotte were still friends, just more quietly.

"I miss him," Max said wistfully from the living room as Charlotte rolled her eyes into the pot of Kraft Dinner she was stirring. "Can I use your phone charger?"

"Mm." Charlotte ripped open the powdered cheese packet and dumped it into the pot. "It's in my work bag, by the door."

She licked a bit of fake cheese off her thumb.

"Why do you have Sophie's jacket?" she heard him call.

Charlotte frowned and poked her head out of the kitchen. "I don't."

Max held up an army green bomber jacket that had been hanging by the door.

"Oh," Charlotte said, crossing the room toward him. "Delilah left that in my car, the night I drove her home."

"She must've borrowed it from Sophie. I bought it for her for her birthday before we broke up."

Charlotte shrugged. "I guess."

"You should wear it in front of Sophie," Max said, "so that she'll call the police and say you stole it and have you thrown in prison."

"You aren't funny," Charlotte snapped as Max unzipped the pockets and jammed his hand inside. "What are you doing?"

"Looking for money. Here," Max handed her a wadded-up crumble of receipts, "trash from your arch-nemesis."

"Hilarious," Charlotte said as she uncurled the soft papers. They were debit receipts or something similar.

"Mail them back to her, one by one," Max suggested.

"What is wrong with you?"

It was a deposit slip, Charlotte guessed. It said Sophie's full name under the header. Deposit amount: two thousand dollars. Jeeze. The date at the top was October of last year. She thought the next receipt she unfolded was a duplicate...until she saw the date: November.

"What is it?" Max asked.

She handed the papers to him. "Sophie's banking stuff. Is there more?"

Max traded her the jacket for the receipts. Charlotte stuck her hand in the other pocket, her heart pounding like she was doing something wrong. Two more, for December and January. Both for two thousand dollars.

"Is this weird to you?" she asked Max. Looking at them, it was like she could almost, *almost* piece together what they meant. Like trying to remember the lyrics to a song.

"Yeah." Max nodded, looking right back at her.

Where would Sophie get this money? Who would regularly pay her an even two grand? What was worth that kind of money?

"Sophie was getting paid?" Max asked.

"For what? Something from the accident? Damages, or whatever?"

He frowned. "Pretty sure I would know about that," Max said.

"What about insurance?" Charlotte suggested.

"I don't...I'm not sure how insurance works. And this says cash deposits. So it can't be like a transfer or automatic deposit or anything like that," Max said, looking thoughtful. "Maybe it doesn't have anything to do with the accident."

"What else could it be, then? Does someone owe her money?" Charlotte asked him.

"I dunno." Max shrugged. "I can't see who would owe her that much. And the only money I can see Sophie acquiring for herself would be, like, revenge money."

Charlotte shook her head. "It can't be that."

"What did Sophie do?" Max asked finally.

That was the wrong question, Charlotte realized. She replayed what Max had said. Revenge. Who would Sophie be blackmailing?

"No, it's what did they do to Sophie," she breathed. She looked at him—he wasn't quite there yet. "Revenge money. You're right."

"Charlie, what?"

"What if Sophie knows who hit her?"

# twenty-five

CHARLOTTE FLICKED A SWITCH AND the hefty camera snapped to life in her hands.

"I'm surprised the battery isn't dead," Max said from beside her.

Charlotte folded her legs underneath her on the floor, straightening her back against the side of Max's bed. She flipped through the photos on the fancy camera Max had gotten as a gift for "graduating" grade ten. Max's words. Charlotte wasn't sure the jump from grade ten to eleven merited a graduation present.

She squinted at the bright screen, the daylight from the windows obscuring her view. She cupped her hand around the edge of it, trying to block out the sun.

"Hey," Max said, pulling her hand back to her lap with his. "I wanna see, too."

Charlotte had spent the last week or so since Connor Hickey's party making an extremely conscious effort not to flinch any time Max accidentally touched her. Not that she did it in a freaked-out way. Just, like, in a more-aware-of-him way. Like when you hear a familiar song on the radio and you weren't expecting it.

On top of that, on top of everything, was whatever they'd rid-dled out from the receipts in Sophie's jacket. It was just a theory with no real proof, but the way it fit together made Charlotte ner-vous. Could she and Max be right? Could Sophie know, and have known since right after the accident? The first receipt was for that same month. September 2016. He never said it, but she knew it was hurting Max. That Sophie may have hard evidence that he hadn't been at fault, when they all knew how hard on himself he had been since last year. That there might be someone else everyone would blame. They didn't really talk about it. Charlotte still had a feeling they were missing something.

"Haven't you looked at them?" Charlotte asked, thumbing back in time through the photos. They were of a party she didn't rec-ognize—it must have been from when she was gone. She almost never missed social events before she went away. Sophie wouldn't let her.

Charlotte flicked to a photo of Sophie and Delilah embracing in front of a beer pong table, Sophie tall and slender, red war paint on either cheek. The photos weren't from when she was gone; they were from before.

"I haven't looked at them," Max answered her question.

"These are from the party before the car rally."

Max, who mirrored her position on the floor, leaning back against the bed, stretched his legs out, and re-adjusted them for something to do. "You are correct."

Most of the pictures were of Sophie and their old friends. Charlotte could never get over how beautiful Sophie was—*is*, she thought—how, even in pictures, it looked like all the light in the room was refracted through her.

"I used to think seeing her in the chair was weird, but this"— Max nodded to the screen—"this is weirder."

Charlotte switched the camera off. "It's weird what you get used to."

"Also weird that Sophie now wants me to go to jail."

"You need to stop joking about that."

"She was just messing with you," Max said seriously. "You need to realize that."

Charlotte picked up the camera again. "What if we can use this? What if there's something on here that can prove it? That you didn't drink?"

Max screwed up his face and pulled the camera away from her. "Charlie, c'mon. You're looking for a photo of something not happening? And I don't think there'd be many pictures of me in there."

"Why?"

"I think I was with Amy most of the night."

"Why?" she said again.

Max looked to the ceiling, and then his dresser, but not at her. "Why do you think?"

"Oh."

"Sophie wouldn't have cared."

"Did you run it by her first?"

Max rolled his eyes. "Nothing happened. We were just hanging out. I just wanted Sophie to think something was happening. I only did it because I was mad at her. You'll remember, she had been pissed at me all week."

"Okay," Charlotte said shortly. It wasn't her business. But an uncomfortable sort of feeling settled in her stomach. Like she owed it to Sophie to tell her, which was stupid.

"It's not like I was supposed to be with *you*."

Charlotte felt her eyebrows shoot up. "Uh, yeah. I didn't say that. I didn't even say *anything*."

"You seem mad."

"It seems like a shitty thing to do to your girlfriend."

"This is also the girl you just told me was going to lie to the police to get me in trouble. Sophie deserved it."

Charlotte glared at him. "No, she didn't. That was a year ago. She didn't then." Sophie, who at that exact time had been pregnant with Max's baby.

Max laughed sarcastically. "Yeah, right. Sometimes I wonder if you and I are talking about the same person."

"And it sucks," Charlotte said, "that you would go after one of Sophie's friends the second you and Sophie get in a fight. I don't know who I feel worse for. Sophie, or those girls you use to get back at her."

"Well, at least you aren't sorry for yourself for a change," Max blurted out. He looked up at her once the words were out of his mouth and for a split second she thought he was going to take it back, but they were interrupted when the door opened.

"Charlotte," Deirdre drawled in a cheery voice, her entrance an ominous wave of expensive perfume and hair products. "I thought you were here."

"Hi, Deirdre," Charlotte said, pulling herself to her feet and thinking about how Max would had lots of time to contemplate the meaning of feeling sorry for oneself while he rotted in prison. "I'm just leaving, actually."

"No, no," Deirdre said, fluttering a hand at her. "I made dinner. I set you a place."

"Oh, no, really, I don't want to impose—"

"Well, to be honest, I thought you were Leo, you two sort of have a similar...tone," Deirdre trailed off. "Anyway. Please, stay. I made tetrazzini."

Max heaved himself into a standing position and Charlotte wasn't sure if he was going to forcefully escort her out. Their eyes met for a quick second and she could tell he was angry.

"Should be ready in about twenty minutes," Deirdre trilled, sauntering out of the room in what had to be a white-wine-embellished gait.

Charlotte raised a hand to her face.

"Twenty minutes," Max grunted and moved past her, following Deirdre out the door.

"This looks really great," Charlotte said honestly as they approached the table, even though it was closer to forty minutes of extremely painful non-conversation with Max later.

There were only four seats at the elegant-looking table; every-one forced to face each other. Charlotte slid into a leather-backed seat across from Max, who wouldn't look at her. Simon emerged from his office, eyes on the phone in his hand—a very normal, not-suspicious looking iPhone, Charlotte noted—when he reached the table. He looked up and his eyes fell on her.

"I thought you said Leo was staying for dinner," Simon said to Deirdre.

"Well, I said I *thought* Leo was staying." Deirdre pulled her-self into the table. "Leo is the only person Max has had here in forever—no offence, Max—so, I just assumed."

Simon didn't seem to have an answer to that, and sat down opposite Deirdre. "It's nice of you to join us, Charlotte," he said finally.

Charlotte had not forgotten the implications Simon had made at Max's birthday regarding her being a gold-digging floozy, but she aimed a vague smile in his direction anyway. Charlotte thought of her dad, who was never rude to anyone.

"Shall we say grace?" Max asked dryly.

Deirdre snorted into her drink.

The plus side was Deirdre's turkey-mushroom tetra-some-thing-or-other pasta turned out to be very good. It had been a while since Charlotte had eaten anything that didn't come out of a box.

"Charlotte, Max tells us you're taking next year off to work," Deirdre said delicately, as if Max had informed them she was tak-ing the year off to commit crime.

"Uh, yeah," Charlotte said slowly. "I just don't have the money right now, for school."

"I took a gap year," Deirdre said in an encouraging tone that surprised Charlotte.

"To work?" Max piped up.

Deirdre shot him a look, like he already knew the answer. "No."

"Ah, right." Max jammed a forkful of pasta into his face. "Forgot. Brewery heiress."

Deirdre took a long drink.

*Huh.* Charlotte twirled the noodles around her fork, watching Max fish what looked like a bit of green onion out of his teeth. So Deirdre hadn't married Simon for his money. She must really love him to move to River John. Like, head over heels. Max swiped the green onion on the edge of his plate. Charlotte wondered what love like that must be like.

"Max is going to Dalhousie," Deirdre said.

"I know," Charlotte replied. "That's where I'd like to go, eventually."

"How are you grades?" Simon asked.

"*Dad*," Max cautioned.

Charlotte felt her cheeks growing hot. "They're...average, I guess. Better in some things than others."

"You and Max can start a club, then," Simon said. "At least you have some time to improve, before you start. And there are scholarships to apply for—Max can tell you all about those. He certainly *applied* for a lot of them."

Charlotte half-smiled, half-grimaced. She knew Max didn't like relying on his dad for money, as much as he often had to, and as much as there was nothing he could do about it.

"Hey, but at least Charlie will actually work for her education," Max said, "whereas I am probably already beyond the point of valuing money and when I flunk out of my first year, you can make a generous donation to the computer science department and pop me back in there, right Dad?"

Charlotte covered her face with her hand to shield herself from Simon's expression, and wondered if Deirdre would give her some wine if she asked.


The rest of the evening continued much in the same way that dinner had. Simon made backhanded comments about his son, and sometimes about Charlotte, and Deirdre laughed harder each time—a direct correlation to the number of drinks she was throwing back. After approximately thirty-six minutes of painful living room talk, Max announced his offer to drive her home.

"Thanks again for having me," Charlotte said to Deirdre as Max helped her into her coat. Outside, it was just starting to rain. Max ushered her out the door and they walked to the truck without speaking. And she thought dinner had been awkward. She buckled her seat belt before he could remind her. They drove in silence.

Many times she considered saying something, but her brain didn't seem to want her to form the words. She was thankful for the rain, as it provided a distraction from the quiet.

"Are you cold?" Max asked, motioning to the dials beneath the radio.

"No." She shook her head.

She watched the windshield wipers fling left and right over and over again. They rumbled down the dark road as she mentally rehashed the evening's events. They approached the intersection in front of the Quik Mart. Charlotte sighed, folding her legs, and Max turned his head to look at her. The car in the oncoming lane was far enough back that they might have been able to beat it if Max hadn't stopped to think about it. Maybe he thought the other car was going to stop.

Max stepped on the gas, swinging through a left turn a split second before the light changed from yellow to red. The second car accelerated to beat them. The screech of tires, glaring headlights, and a blaring car horn was suddenly all around. Max swerved onto the shoulder and slammed on the brakes once he'd cleared the intersection. Over before she even knew what had happened. The car that had been cut off—a blue Honda driven by a middle-aged woman who gave them both the finger—sped off behind them and disappeared.

Charlotte took a few seconds to steady herself and twisted around to watch the other car disappear into the dark, the streaks of water on the road reflecting the red tail lights. She closed her eyes and took a single deep breath. They were fine. Charlotte made riskier moves all the time.

She turned back to Max. Hunched forward in his seat, his hands were curled around the steering wheel.

"Max?" Charlotte laid a hand on his shoulder. She could feel him shaking under her fingers.

"Are you okay?" he asked without looking at her.

"Yeah, yeah, I'm fine. Are you?"

"I'm s-sorry, I'm so sorry," he stammered, "I wasn't paying attention—"

"Max, hey," she said, scooting closer to him along the seat. "It's okay. We're okay. It was just an accident. People slip up all the time when they're driving."

"For a second I thought...it felt like—"

"I know, okay? But it wasn't."

Charlotte pressed her cheek to his shoulder as he bowed his head against the steering wheel. She traced her hand up and down his back for what felt like a long time, and eventually his breathing steadied.

"I'm sorry," Max said finally, "I just kinda...lost it, for a second."

Max pulled the truck back onto the road, continuing toward her house. Charlotte reached across the seat and slipped her hand inside his, pulling it back to hold in her lap. They were quiet again, but it was a softer quiet. The tension from the rest of the night had drained away and instead was replaced with something completely different. Charlotte felt worse.

When they got to her house, Max left the engine running.

"Are you okay?" she asked him again.

Max nodded toward the windshield, but didn't look at her. "I'm sorry about what I said earlier tonight," he said.

She shrugged and released his hand. "It doesn't matter."

"Things have just been...I feel like I'm going crazy. Over Sophie. Over everything."

Charlotte almost laughed. She could relate. Thinking about the accident had infected everything, every part of her and them. She could feel it everywhere, like heat. A year ago it had destroyed everything and it wasn't finished yet. Charlotte wondered if it would ever go away, really. If there would ever be a morning they might wake up and not relate every little thing back to the same summer night when they were seventeen.

"Come inside," she said quietly.

Max finally looked at her. He hadn't slept over since Sophie's ultimatum. They were taking things slow. Supposedly.

"Are you sure you want me to?"

"Please. I don't want you to be alone."

Max's face was unsure in the dark. "I don't know, Charlie."

She slid closer to him. "Do you remember the first night I called you?"

"Yeah. Of course."

"You came over right away. I'm just saying, you're allowed to hurt too, Max," she said, thinking of her talk with Leo the other day. "Just because you aren't the worst off, doesn't mean you have to ignore it."

Max swallowed hard, and she felt his arm slip around her waist, drawing her closer. "Thanks," he said.

Inside, they crept past Sean's room and she shut her bedroom door behind them, gently easing the doorknob into place. Max was stooped over, uncurling his sleeping bag in his usual spot beside her bed. While his back was turned, Charlotte pulled out a baggy T-shirt and sleep shorts from under her pillow.

"Don't turn around for a sec," she requested, shimmying into her pyjamas. She wasn't nervous—she knew Max would never look at her, even if she hadn't said anything. She felt silly being shy around him when they'd spent the entire summer showing each other parts of themselves. A different kind of exposed. "Okay, you're good," Charlotte said, freeing him. Max hadn't moved a muscle since she'd spoken.

Charlotte slid under the comforter, pulling it tight to the space beneath her chin. She was weirdly reminded of the first time he'd slept over; she felt the same kind of apprehension, like they were about to do something there was no going back from.

"Just sleep in here," she said.

"What?" Max asked. It was the first he'd spoken in ages.

"Sleep with me."

Wordlessly, Max moved into the space beside her, but was careful that they didn't touch. She laid on her stomach with her head turned toward him, and he was looking at her too. She felt him hook his fingers around her wrist, just for a moment before releasing her.

"Good night, Max," she said. She reached back out, pushing her fingers between his, tangling them together by a thin line. A thread in the dark.

"Good night," he answered.

# twenty-six

CHARLOTTE'S FIRST OFFICIAL PAYCHEQUE was presented to her after work on Friday with little fanfare. Laurie swirled the R in Romer in a tight curl and pulled the cheque free of the little book.

"Make sure this doesn't all go toward booze, hm?" Laurie said as she handed the cheque over.

Charlotte accepted the money gratefully, but figured she couldn't make any promises about the booze considering the way things were going.

At the top of her mind was Sophie, as per usual. Charlotte yanked open the door to her car and hopped inside. So, Sophie had some anonymous benefactor handing her buckets of money every month. If Charlotte was right and Sophie did know who had hit her and Max last year, then they were at the centre of some conspiracy that Charlotte wanted no part of. She felt like they were trapped in one of those teen TV dramas she and Sophie used to watch together.

She shook her head and buckled her seat belt. It couldn't be that.

The bank was just down the road, across from the library. Charlotte pulled over in front of it. She didn't realize she had to, like, physically deposit the paycheque to get the money. She'd only ever been paid for babysitting and other odd jobs. All cash. She envisioned herself stumbling into the bank waving around her cheque for one hundred and ninety-six dollars and asking for help—Simon in the background making a mental note to tell his son that the girl he spent all his time with was a moron. She put her best adult face on, re-reading the cheque to make sure it really did have her name on it before she went inside.

Charlotte was hardly ever at the bank—in her previous life, she had only ever come here to visit Sophie at work. There were a few potted plants strategically placed around the room, and the large reception desk was in the centre, with two tellers seated at either end. Hallways led to offices and whatever else.

The ATM she was looking for was just inside the front door. Charlotte was just tucking her beloved cheque into an envelope and pressing it closed when she heard someone behind her.

"Charlotte Romer, *hello*," the woman chirped.

She was Kathleen Langille, who had gone to North Colchester High with her dad way back when, and had sent a few casseroles when he'd died.

"You look so grown up," Kathleen said. "Beautiful, just like your mom."

Charlotte held back a cringe. She didn't like being talked at about her mom. No one ever did it to be rude, but Charlotte was only ever reminded that whoever was reminiscing about Eliza Montgomery actually knew her, while Charlotte did not.

"Thank you." Charlotte smiled anyway, not knowing what else she should say.

"Emma said she saw you at Max's big birthday party," Kathleen continued.

*Ah, yes, your daughter Emma who threw a drink on me*, Charlotte recalled, pressing her lips together. Kathleen's husband, Emma's dad, had left them when Charlotte and Emma were in elementary school. For a while Charlotte had wanted her dad and Kathleen to get married. She and Emma could have been sisters. Joy.

"Right, yeah, I saw Emma," Charlotte said, smiling vaguely.

"What's new with you?"

"Nothing really. I'm working for Laurie, at May's." Charlotte held out her envelope as proof.

"Oh, how wonderful," Kathleen cooed. "Good for you. How's your brother?"

*He threatens to murder people regularly but that's just a boy thing, isn't it?* "He's good. Busy."

Kathleen smiled at her. "He still mows my lawn every second Sunday."

"Yeah, he's...great." Charlotte fed her cheque into the machine, which croaked weakly.

"And how is Miss Sophie?"

"Oh." Charlotte swallowed. "Good, I think."

"Such a trooper. We miss her here. She really could have gone on to do anything, you know?"

Charlotte cleared her throat, annoyed at the weird twisting her stomach did whenever she had to talk about Sophie. "Well, I'm sure she still will."

Kathleen nodded and waved her hands. "Of course, of course."

They were silent for a few slow seconds. The ATM spat out Charlotte's receipt. Chequing account was resurrected, huzzah. There had been next to no money in there for god knows how long.

"Oh, you know what?" Kathleen exclaimed suddenly. "You can bring Soph her things."

"Huh?"

"We still have them," Kathleen explained. "Wait right here," she said, backing away from Charlotte and then disappearing.

Charlotte stood awkwardly by the ATM. Please don't let it be what she knew it was going to be. Sophie had always kept a ton of bric-a-brac shit and little succulents on her desk. What was Charlotte going to do with that?

Kathleen returned. She was carrying a box the size of a microwave and thrust it into Charlotte's hands. "This is perfect,"

Kathleen said. "Sophie never came back for them, poor thing. You don't mind dropping them off?"

"Uh...I shouldn't take this," Charlotte tried to say, nodding down at the box.

"Honey, it's just collecting dust here. I would give it to Emma but she says she doesn't even really see Sophie anymore, what a sin." Kathleen tsked. "But I know you must, and Sophie probably misses her things. And there are photos of you in there."

Charlotte grimaced and swallowed a painful lump in her throat. She was suddenly desperate to get out of there. "Okay. Thanks, Kathleen."

"Bye, sweetie. See ya around."

Charlotte kept her head down and swiftly exited the bank before some other distant friend could appear with a box of things for Charlotte's grade-ten boyfriend, Jude. *God*, Charlotte thought bitterly as she chucked Sophie's box into the passenger seat, *why does this feel like a never-ending break-up?*

Charlotte flipped one of the flaps open, her suspicions confirmed: there sat Sophie's brittle, brown, half-dead mini cactus that she'd gotten at Pete's Frootique in Halifax last summer. And, just as Kathleen had said, there was a framed photo of Charlotte and Sophie. Charlotte tried to place it...first day of grade ten, maybe?

Charlotte shifted a few things around. A few notebooks, an overpriced paperweight, and other miscellany from some stationery store Sophie always ordered from online. Charlotte pulled free a piece of paper sticking out from one of the notebooks: another of Sophie's mysterious deposit receipts. Charlotte recoiled and released it back into the box as if it were poisonous. Another reminder of the mass conspiracy. She almost pressed the box shut again, probably forever, when she cast one last glance on the receipt.

June 2016.

Months before the accident.

Same deposit slip, same amount. But it meant whatever Sophie was getting paid for, it wasn't to keep quiet about the accident.

There was a tapping on her windshield, making Charlotte jump.

Max waved merrily at her as she rolled down the window, Leo behind him.

"Whatcha doing?" Max asked. He was wearing a forest-green T-shirt and had a dart tucked behind one ear.

"Nothing," Charlotte said quickly, practically shoving the box onto the floor and out of sight. "What are *you* doing?"

"Looking for *ladies*," Leo explained.

"Ah, well, you'll have to keep looking," Charlotte answered.

"Can you please point us in the direction of the nearest gentleman's club?" Max asked, leaning against her door.

"Hah," Charlotte said, "are those still a thing? Use protection."

"Don't worry," Leo placed his hands on Max's shoulders and pulled him away. "Max is saving himself for marriage."

"What a golden boy," Charlotte hummed.

Max cast Leo a sour look.

"I'm kidding." Leo rolled his eyes. "No one wants to have sex with him. Same thing."

Charlotte laughed. "Are you exercising some born-again virgin thing or just suppressing the memory?"

Leo looked giddy at the suggestion. "Are you kidding? You think sweet, darling, Maxwell Jedidiah Hale slept with Sophie Thompson and *stopped* talking about it?"

Charlotte scrunched up her face. "What?"

"My middle name is not Jedidiah," Max said.

"No, but you and Sophie didn't—"

"We never quite got there, I guess." Max glared at Leo. "Glad we could *explicitly* clarify, though. Like, on the sidewalk in the middle of the day."

Charlotte's conversation with Sophie had been burned in Charlotte's brain since it happened. Charlotte had just assumed that Max and Sophie had slept together. Sophie had never said otherwise.

"I have to go. Work," Charlotte muttered, almost amputating Max's arm when she rolled up the window.

"Didn't you do the morning shift today?" Max asked.

She looked at him for half a second and didn't answer, leaving them on the sidewalk.


Charlotte rattled the beat-up knocker on the door. She felt a deep contrast to the last few times she'd found herself at Sophie's door, half-hoping she wouldn't answer. The door flung open within another few seconds.

Ellen Thompson leaned against the door frame, like she thought Charlotte would try and slip past her. "What can I do for you?" she said coldly.

Like her daughter, Ellen was very tall and blonde and very good at making it clear when you were annoying her. Right now, she almost looked like she was waiting for an explanation. *Hey, Charlie, remember that time you abandoned my daughter?* Ellen wore her hair swept back in a low bun, but the flyaways that framed her face made her look younger, drawing out her resemblance to Sophie. Charlotte didn't blame Ellen for the way she looked at her. It wasn't just dislike; it was firmly planted contempt toward someone who had hurt her daughter. Charlotte knew she was the villain here.

"I—" In all the excitement Charlotte had forgotten it was mid-afternoon and entirely likely Sophie's mother would be home. "Sorry, Ellen. I'm looking for Sophie."

Ellen cocked her head. "Hm."

"Is she home?"

"Yes." A year ago Charlotte would have waltzed in unannounced and chatted with Ellen for as long as it took Sophie to drag herself from her bedroom. She didn't think Ellen would be in the mood for a girl chat right now.

"She's in her room," Ellen continued in her flat tone. "I wish you luck."

She moved aside, allowing Charlotte to pass. Charlotte avoided looking at her and marched to the bedroom in the back of the house.

The door was closed. She knocked once.

"Yeah?" came Sophie's disinterested reply.

Charlotte figured an introduction probably wouldn't do either of them much good, so instead she pushed the door open.

Sophie was sitting in bed, her hair piled on top of her head in a giant blonde bun. The laptop open in front of her kept her attention for several seconds after Charlotte opened the door. Sophie's eyes left the episode of *Breaking Bad* and flickered to her. Denzel was curled up at the end of the bed and lifted his head.

"I didn't realize I had to give my mom an approved guest list," Sophie said.

"Honestly, Sophie," Charlotte said, shutting the door behind her. "I'm over this."

"Right. Have you come to murder me, then?"

"Why did you tell me you were pregnant with Max's baby?"

She'd cracked the glass expression on Sophie's face. "What?"

"Max just told me you never slept together," Charlotte said. She leaned back against the door, reluctant to get any closer to Sophie. She tilted her head back, so she was staring above Sophie at her faded green curtains. The door was steady; it held her in place.

"That must be the first time a guy's ever told a girl that to get her to sleep with him," Sophie said eventually.

Charlotte rolled her eyes. "I'm not here to fight. I just want to know the truth. He might be lying to me but I don't think he is." She squinted at Sophie. "What's going on?"

Sophie's expression was frozen, but Charlotte could practically see the gears working in her head.

"Did you make it up?" Charlotte continued.

Sophie threw her hands in the air. "Yep. That's just what I needed. Another reason for people to feel sorry for me."

"So it wasn't Max's."

Sophie let out an even breath. "No. And I never said it was. I just said he would hate me if he knew. You filled the rest in yourself."

Charlotte let a few seconds pass. "You don't owe me anything more than that, I guess. We don't owe each other anything anymore. I just...I know about the money."

"What?"

"Are you in trouble?" Charlotte asked. That was her worst fear, at the end of it. If Sophie was involved in something she shouldn't be. Like Charlotte had been, a year ago.

Sophie shook her head. "What money?"

"Sophie." Charlotte didn't realize she'd been pacing but stopped herself short.

"How do you know?" Sophie asked very slowly, her hands twisting around the edge of her bedspread.

"It doesn't matter."

Sophie pursed her lips. "I'm fine. Don't ever mention it again, please. Forget that you know about it."

"Did it have something to do with the baby? Who were you with?"

Sophie looked out her bedroom window, feigning disinterest. "It doesn't matter. Are you going to tell Max? That I cheated?"

An entirely new wave of anxiety washed over Charlotte. "I don't know."

"Please don't," Sophie whispered. Charlotte looked at her, caught off guard by Sophie's eyes, wide and pleading. "Like you said, we don't owe each other anything. But I'm asking you. It's just going to ruin his life even more. I'll never ask for anything again."

She was damn right. But while Sophie had no problem lying to Charlotte, Charlotte didn't want to make any promises she couldn't keep. "I have to go."

"Charlotte, *please.*" Sophie pulled herself from her pillows, sitting up straighter. "I don't want to hurt Max more."

Charlotte paused with her hand on the doorknob, facing away from her. "You're never gonna tell the police—or anyone—what you were gonna say about Max."

Sophie was quiet, and Charlotte looked back at her over her shoulder.

"I would have never done that to Max," Sophie said. "Ever. Of course I wouldn't have. Besides, Max isn't the one I hate."

Charlotte turned away again, pulling the door open. "I'm sorry, Sophie."

Sorry that this was where they were. Sorry that all they had become was ultimatums and lies and secrets. Sorry that every time they saw each other they took another step toward becoming strangers.

• • •

"I'm so *full*," Charlotte groaned as she slid out of the car. It was almost midnight, a few days since her confrontation with Sophie.

Sean glanced sideways at her. "You say that every time we go, and yet you always overdo it with the fried rice."

Charlotte shut the passenger side door. "They give us extra at the end of the night. You know I can't just leave it. It's basically *free*."

Sean followed her up the stairs of the porch. "Basically."

Charlotte felt a weird sense of calm these past few days. There was a small part of her, now, that didn't feel like she needed to fix things anymore. That she probably couldn't anyway. But she was also gripped with the reality that she was now lying to Max about Sophie's baby. Every time Charlotte wanted to tell him, she stopped herself. Not until she knew more. It was also clear that Sophie didn't know who had caused the accident. Sophie knew something else.

Charlotte fished her key out of her jacket pocket and jammed it in the door, but she realized she didn't need it.

"Did you forget to lock this?" she asked.

Sean frowned. "I don't remember."

"Hopefully no one came to steal any of the many priceless artifacts in this house. If we lose our backup cheese grater, that's the end of nachos for us."

Sean pressed his hand to his chest. "Don't joke about that. Not that I ever got to eat any of those nachos before you demolished them."

Charlotte shot him a look and swung the door open.

"Shit, left my phone in the car," Sean said, "one sec."

Charlotte wandered into the dark house, wiggling out of her jacket.

"Did you find it?" Charlotte asked as she crossed the room to turn the lights on, hearing Sean behind her. She flicked the switch and turned around. Not Sean.

Nick had her by the hair and wrenched her sideways. Her cheek caught the edge of the wood stove and the pain was blinding.

Everything, black.

The end, quick.

# twenty-seven

IT WAS BRIGHT. TOO BRIGHT to be hell, which was probably where she'd be, so Charlotte knew she wasn't dead. Not to mention that every inch of her hurt, so she was definitely still alive. A rhythmic, mechanical whirring; slow beeps. She knew where she was. She and Sean had spent a lot of time here before their dad died. While he was dying.

Sean.

Charlotte opened her eyes. Her face felt like it was split open. She tried to raise her hand to check, but it felt too heavy. She glanced down. Her arms and hands were still there, resting on top of blue hospital sheets. She just couldn't move yet.

What happened?

Max, she noticed with a vague feeling of affection, was asleep beside her, holding her right hand and hunched over in his seat. His head rested on her bed beside her hip. What time was it? Grey light pressed against the blinds, so morning?

Charlotte pulled her hand free from Max's and patted his head. He shifted and she watched his eyelids flutter and open. After the second where he remembered where he was, his head shot up.

"Hey," she managed. It hurt to talk.

"It's okay, you're going to be fine," Max said.

The panicked look stretched across his face conjured a memory, and between half-closed eyelids she remembered Sean's face swimming above her, wearing the same terrified expression.

Nick. Nick had been in their house.

"Sean," she croaked. "Where's Sean?"

"He's gone," Max said quietly.

"What?"

"Sorry," Max said quickly, shaking his head when he realized his word choice, "he's okay. He's just...gone."

"What do you mean?" she repeated. The words were clear in her head, but came out all garbled. She didn't know how Max understood her.

"He brought you in, called me," he elaborated. "He waited until we knew you were gonna be okay." Max took her hand back in his. "But he's gone."

"Gone where?"

Max shook his head. "I don't know, Charlie."

"What about Nick?"

A pause. Max grimaced, shifted his shoulders a bit. He looked around like what he was about to say was a secret. "I don't know, exactly," Max said, "it was an accident, but, Nick's dead. Sean killed him. I think...he just lost it."

Just like that, the one issue that had been twisting and smothering Charlotte's life for the last year was extinguished. She didn't want to think it had cost her her brother. She couldn't think about it. Nick was dead. Not just dead—killed. By Sean.

"I was so...." Max looked like he was struggling to string the words together. "They wouldn't let us see you, at first, and I've never seen Sean like that."

"What happened?" Charlotte asked. She couldn't look at him; he was so relieved and she felt the farthest thing from it.

"Nick got your face. They said nothing's broken. The doctor will explain it all to you, I guess." Max leaned far back in his chair like he needed a time out, covering his face with his hands.

She had stopped listening to him. All she could picture, over and over again, was Sean slamming Nick to the ground, off of her, or however else he'd done it. She didn't like knowing the memory was probably tucked away somewhere in her brain. She couldn't process it.

"Sean was...messed up, when he called," Max said, as if almost entirely reading her mind. "I think he thought you were.... It was bad." He took a breath. "It was like last time."

She turned her head away from him, trying to push herself farther into her pillows. She heard herself crying before she really registered it. He was talking about Sophie. It triggered the memory of Charlotte's last conversation with her. That Charlotte knew, for sure, that Sophie wasn't blackmailing whoever had hit her and Max, and that Sophie had been cheating on him. Charlotte didn't know why she didn't tell him then and there. Her head hurt but she didn't feel much else.

She was discharged later that day. The doctor had explained everything Max had tried to; that she was pretty bruised and her left wrist was sprained, and she'd have to come back in a few weeks to get the stitches in her face removed. She was lucky her cheek and jaw weren't broken.

The police talked to both Charlotte and Max before they left. They wanted to flesh out her version of events—she told the cops that Nick had broken in to rob her and Sean (half true), attacked her when she found him (true), and that was all she knew, really. She told them Sean had accidentally killed Nick in her defence, which is what Max had said too. She didn't say anything about her history with Nick. No need to get Sean in any more trouble. But she had a feeling he was in about as much trouble as you could be. The police asked if Charlotte had any idea where Sean might have gone. She said she didn't, and wished she were lying.

Max took her home, helping her into his truck and with her seat belt. They had to go to Max's, because the police weren't done searching her place. It was late into a grey summer afternoon when they got to his house. He kept looking at her like she could drop dead at any moment.

Thankfully, Simon and Deirdre weren't home—they'd gone to Wolfville overnight for a wine tour. Charlotte wandered inside and toward the bathroom, because all that she really wanted was to brush her teeth.

An unfamiliar face—her face, she realized—greeted her in the bathroom mirror. She hadn't gotten a good look until now. Max had been averting her attention away from any reflective surface. Underneath her eye was swollen, and the blue-black cut that slashed across her cheek was tied together with a dozen little black stitches. Her throat and collarbone looked like they'd been tattooed with dark shadows. She looked almost as bad as she felt.

Max appeared in the mirror behind her and she was reminded of the last time they were here like this.

"You can borrow anything you need. We have extra toothbrushes and stuff," Max said.

"I didn't realize I looked like this," Charlotte said, gazing at herself.

Max moved her hair away from her neck and the action sent a shiver dancing down her spine. He swiped his fingers just below her jaw. "It'll go away. It's still you."

She braced herself against the sink, disgusted by the person in the mirror. "I don't even look like me. He took that."

"Charlie—"

"He took *so* much."

Max reached around her waist and twisted the faucet on. He took a facecloth from the shelf beside the mirror and held it under the stream. "Here. For your face. I'll get you some ice. It might help. And here," Max opened the mirror cabinet and reached for a tube of antibiotic cream. It sat on the shelf next to a few skinny orange pill bottles with his name on them.

"What are those?" Charlotte asked.

"Uh." Max frowned and shut the mirror. "I got them after last year. For anxiety and stuff."

She leaned back against him, just barely, unable to tear her eyes from the mirror. She felt weak and miserable and defeated. Like even though he was gone, Nick had still won.

"I'm sorry," she said quietly to him through the glass.

"For what?"

"That it was so hard for you." She swallowed. "And that you were alone."

She watched his reflection, his face registering her words. He slid his hands to her shoulders, holding on to her protectively.

"It's still hard," he said without looking at her. "But I had Leo. And I have you now. Like you have me." He put two fingers under her chin and tilted her head to look at him through the mirror. "Nick can't hurt you again."

"Sometimes I wish he had just killed me the first time he tried." She felt dizzy with the realization of it. "None of this would have happened."

"Charlie," Max said, dropping the facecloth. "Don't say that—"

She couldn't catch her breath and felt like her chest was contracting around her lungs. She hugged her arms around herself. "I mean it," she cried.

She turned to face him, as if he had answers. Max placed his hands on either side of her face and kept repeating that it would all be okay. She hadn't cried like this in a long time—not before this morning, at least—and she felt like everything that had happened since she'd come back to River John was rushing out of her all at once.

"Sean can't ever come home," she cried. She was so angry at him. Why did he have to kill Nick? And why did he run, and make it so much worse? "He killed Nick but Nick killed him, too. He may as well be dead."

She felt Max's face against hers and his lips against her forehead. "It's okay, it's okay," he said again and again. "Baby, look at me."

Charlotte gripped him by the waist as she pushed backward, sliding herself up to sit on the edge of the sink. Without stopping to think, she moved her head and caught his lips with hers. She pulled him forward so he stood between her legs.

Max's body went rigid with surprise when she kissed him, but neither of them stopped. Charlotte's thoughts were moving so quickly she felt like she was drunk. She'd thought about this, sure, as their friendship had grown and teetered on the edge of more than that. When he slept beside her and she woke up with his arm across her shoulders, she would think about what it would be like if things were different.

"Charlie, wait. We shouldn't—"

"I want you," she said. "Please."

He pulled her off the sink and they stumbled to his bedroom, falling into bed a tangle of limbs and loose clothing. Charlotte worked on the buttons of his shirt, pushing it down off his shoulders and he pulled her sweater off her.

She could feel his eyes on her body, felt him stop moving. "I—we shouldn't. I don't want to hurt you. Your face."

Charlotte cut him off, dragging his face to hers and kissing him again. "I can't feel anything. Please."

"Christ, Charlie," Max whispered, his mouth trailing down her throat and chest delicately. He looked back at her. "What do you...?"

"I want to have sex." She cleared her throat. Max was the only one left. She wanted to show him how much it meant that he'd stayed. Because she didn't see the point anymore in hiding from him, or really, from herself. Max had become a part of her life and a part of her. "Do you?"

"God. Yeah." She felt him pull away from her and he fumbled for something in his side table. She heard him rip the foil open.

Max moved slowly at first; she could tell that he was nervous. He held her carefully, her body moving to meet him as they moved together. His weight held her in place against the mattress. His movements became harsher, his hands twisting around her and his mouth moving down across her. She pressed her face to his shoulder and clutched at him tightly, and they were all skin and tangled bedsheets instead of clothes, and at last they both fell silent.

Charlotte rolled away from him, facing the wall and pulling the sheets up around her. She felt his hand on her waist, but he didn't say anything either. What had she done? There was no going back now, no acting like whatever was between them just existed in their heads. What if she'd misunderstood how he felt? What if he didn't want this, or her? Thoughts of him and Sean and Nick swam in front of her and bled together, sinking beneath the surface as she tried to push them away. She was too scared to look back at Max. So she didn't.

Charlotte woke up much later. The moonlight cast his room and her body under the sheet in a smooth, pale glow. As soon as her senses collected, she realized Max wasn't there. Fear vibrated through her, both that he had left her and that she was now alone in the house. But as she lifted her head from the pillow, she could hear music playing quietly in the main room.

Charlotte found the nearest piece of clothing—his North Colchester hoodie—and pulled it on over her head, being careful of her face.

Max was sitting at the kitchen table, his back to her. His elbows rested on the table and he held his head in his hands. Music was drifting out of the stereo over on the armoire.

"Hey," she said quietly.

He jumped, surprised by her voice, but barely looked at her. She watched him press the heels of his hands into his eyes. "Hi," he answered.

"I love The Beach Boys," she said softly, nodding to the radio. "Reminds me of my dad."

Max looked in the music's direction, as if in agreement. "They always cheered me up," he said, his voice wobbling and uneven.

"Max," she said. Something was wrong. She stilled, worried it was about her, about them, and what they'd done.

He looked at her finally, the same light from his room pouring over his face, carving out his features in the dark. He looked at her like he knew her but also like he didn't. Like he recognized her but couldn't place her, or maybe like they'd met before in a past life and his current incarnation was trying to bridge the gap. He looked like he was remembering all their fighting with each other and for each other, and everything else they'd been through. Of all the universes where they might have met and didn't, he looked at her like he loved her in every single one. She met his gaze finally, and she realized she'd been stupid these last weeks to think that he didn't love her, and even stupider to think that she didn't feel the same about him.

Charlotte crossed the room because she could see his face shifting, unsure; just the way she felt. As soon as she was in range, he took her gently around the elbows and pulled her to him.

"It's my fault," he said. His voice was hoarse. He sounded like he had been crying.

"What? What is?" she asked, his hands finding hers in the darkness.

"This. All of it," he said. "You leave the door open for me, don't you?"

"Max, what?"

"At night," he said, twisting on the word, "you leave the back door open...so I can sleep over. That's how Nick got inside. That's why you're hurt. Why Sean's gone. Why he's dead."

He shoved the chair back and pulled her closer, wedging her between the table and him. She found herself in his lap, both legs over one side of his and her body turned to face him.

"It's not," she assured him. Her voice was rough, like her own body was protesting ever talking about this and Nick again. "Even if that door had been locked, he would've just broken in. It wouldn't have mattered."

Max's arm coiled around her waist, pressing them together and holding her steady. "I'm sorry. I'm so sorry, Charlie," he said, his fingers spreading out along the bruises that decorated her collarbone, acknowledging every one.

She raised her hand to his face, tracing the edge of his jaw and sliding her fingers up into his hair. His hair was so dark it looked almost blue in the moonlight.

"And, Christ," Max said, regaining his composure a little. "You're the one who was attacked and you're consoling me."

She sighed the tiniest bit. "It doesn't matter," she said seriously, "you can't help how you feel."

His hand mirrored hers on his face, his fingers settling just under her row of stitches.

"You still look like you," was all he said. "Your eyes." Max hooked his hand around the side of her head, their eyes and noses and lips aligned. Max slanted his face toward her and she curled her hand around the collar of his shirt when he kissed her—years from now if she thought about it, she knew she would think of this as their first real kiss. It meant more now. Max pressed his lips to hers gently, and she wasn't sure if it was because he was worried about hurting her, or because he was nervous, or both.

When they pulled away she just stared back at him in the dark. The dark made it easier. All they were was what they could barely see. The space between them as she held his gaze was full with the weight of them.

She curled against him, tucking her head into the crook of his neck. She held onto him and he held onto her, his hand tracing slow circles up and down her back. Max pressed his lips against her forehead and she listened to his breathing and the ocean outside. She could hear the wind and Max humming along softly to The Beach Boys.

"God only knows," Max said quietly, and it was the last thing she remembered before she slipped back to sleep.

# twenty-eight

THEY BOTH SLEPT UNTIL LATE into the morning. It was grey again today, Charlotte noticed when she pushed the corner of the comforter back from her face. The days of hot July sun seemed to have finally died off and they were left with August's purple mornings and dark blue nights. She moved to wipe the sleep out of her eyes but stopped herself. Oh, god. It was like it took the pain a second to wake up too, before it swam up and settled under the skin around her eyes.

Damnit.

Charlotte touched her fingertips gingerly to her cheek, which felt hot and puffy and a hell of a lot more sore than yesterday. She didn't even want to look. Easing herself onto her back, she turned her head to look at Max.

He was awake, reading something on his phone but she could tell he had been waiting for her to wake up. He looked up when he heard her stir. "Morning. How's your face?" Max asked.

"Bad," she said, realizing even moving her jaw to talk made it hurt. "How does it look?"

Max rolled onto his shoulder, closer to her, and placed his hand under her chin as if he was getting a better look. "Uh. Do you think it'll get worse before it gets better?"

She sighed and turned away from him, toward the window so he couldn't see her face. "I think most things do."

Max slipped his hand around her waist and slid himself closer to her. "How do you feel?"

Charlotte flip-flopped between what he could be referring to. About her missing brother? About the murder said brother had committed in their house? About the sex she'd initiated in Max's bathroom last night? She wasn't feeling too great about any of it.

"Um. I've been better," she mumbled without turning around. "You?"

She felt Max place a kiss on her shoulder. "I'm okay. Last night—"

"I shouldn't have done that," she said quickly. "I was a mess. I'm sorry."

Charlotte felt him shift like he was half sitting up. "No, don't be. I wanted it. I wanted you—I *want* you—and I don't...I don't want you to regret it." He paused. "Do you?"

Charlotte looked back at him over her shoulder. *Did* she regret it? "No," she said, assuring herself and him. "But I wish it had been under better circumstances."

Max put his hand alongside her head and tilted her face gently toward him. "Can I kiss you again?"

Charlotte tried for a weak laugh. "If you don't do it hard."

He kissed her and she felt his mouth twist into a tiny smile against her lips. It hurt, but she considered it collateral. He kissed her a bit more and they ended up pushing off each other's clothes again as the morning faded into a rainy afternoon. She felt more alive this time and when they were done she was smiling back at him. Smiling definitely hurt. Max eventually slipped out of bed to make coffee and she drifted back to half-sleep.

When she woke up again later, she got out of bed carefully and found him in the kitchen, poking at eggs in a frying pan.

"The police left a message," Max said. "I gave them my number at the hospital. You're free to get back into your house."

"I guess there wasn't much mystery to investigate," she said dryly as he handed her a mug. Her cellphone was on the counter. One message from Leo, checking in with about a dozen emojis: smiley wearing a sick mask, four blue question marks, kissing face, ocean wave, sparkles, and two green hearts.

"Anything?"

She knew he meant from Sean. "No."

She pushed the thoughts from her mind. She wasn't going to wait around for Sean to contact her. He left because he'd had to, she knew he would say if they ever met again.

Charlotte was suddenly hit with a wave of whatever Sophie must have felt a year ago. She shook her head, trying to focus on anything but Sophie. Her eye caught the letter stuck to Max's fridge with a magnet. His letter from Dalhousie.

"Oh," she said quietly and mostly to herself. "You leave in, like, two weeks."

Max glanced at the fridge. "Yeah," he said, almost sounding guilty.

"You must be excited." She stood on her tiptoes and eased herself onto the counter.

Max dumped the eggs onto a plate and looked at her. "I won't go."

Charlotte jerked her back straight. "What?"

"I'll defer," Max said, placing a hand on each of her knees.

"Why?"

"Charlie, I can't just leave you here."

"Max." She shook her head. "That's...crazy."

"What are you going to do? Who's going to look after you?"

Charlotte opened her mouth to respond and Max immediately recanted when he saw the look on her face. "Sorry," he said. "I didn't mean it like that."

"I think I would survive without you while you're at school."

"Yeah but what about without Sean? And Leo? And Sophie, even?"

Charlotte folded her arms. He was painting a pretty grim picture. "I'm not asking you to not go to university."

"Not forever." Max stepped closer. "And I know you're not asking. I'm saying. I don't want you to be alone and, if I'm being honest, I don't want to be away from you. Just until we...figure this out."

It wasn't that. Charlotte looked at him, and for a split second she saw Sean. Sean, who had miraculously gotten into Saint Mary's and was so looking forward to university before their dad died. Before he had gotten landed with her. Charlotte knew Sean loved her, but she also knew there had to be a small part of him that saw her as the reason he'd never made it out of River John.

"You can't stay here for me," Charlotte said, angling her head down so she was staring precisely at the centre of his T-shirt.

"You could come with me, you know."

Charlotte swallowed a shaky breath at the proposition. She could go to Halifax with Max. Leave everything behind. She could, she could, she could.

"He might come back," she said. "Sean," she clarified, her voice crackling over his name. "I have to stay."

Max softened. His hand took hers. "Then I'll be here with you," he promised.

"I just don't want you to have to wait for me," she said quietly. "To catch up."

"There's no catching. I'm right with you. Look at me." He lined his fingers under her chin, along the edge of her jaw. She looked at him. "Here."

Max kissed her. They didn't talk about it again.


"Are you sure you want to go home?" he asked as they pulled up to her house. "We can still stay at my place."

"Yes. I'm sure. As I've said four hundred times."

They got out and climbed the porch steps together. Max paused with his hand on the doorknob.

She caught his eye, reading his hesitation. "Max. I can handle it."

He looked like he didn't believe her but pushed the door open anyway.

Inside, everything was the exact same. Same couch and books and walls and floors, the same floor that Nick had died on and that she very well could have, too. She caught Max looking at her expectantly and snapped out of it.

"What? I'm fine."

"I know." Max nodded a few times.

There was noise in the kitchen. Someone else in the house.

Charlotte whipped around to look at Max and could feel her heart pounding in her ears. Retaliation? One of Nick's cronies come to finish the job?

Neither of them moved in the split second before Leo popped his head out of the kitchen.

"Hi," Leo said, not his usual chipper self. "I just put the kettle on. Thought you might want some tea."

"Oh my god," Max groaned, rubbing his face. "I asked you to make sure everything was okay at the house, not re-enact her home invasion."

Leo's expression faded quickly when he saw their faces. "Oh, shit, I thought—"

"It's okay, Leo," Charlotte said, trying to steady her shaking breathing and the heart that was thrashing inside her ribcage. "Tea would be nice."

Leo moved toward her and pulled her into a hug. "You okay?" he asked against her shoulder.

She pulled back and tried to smile, but avoided his eyes. "I'm still kicking."

"You really scared us."

"Leo was with me," Max explained. "When Sean called." His knuckles were pressed to his lips like he was nervous. Charlotte was trying to ignore him looking at her like she was a science experiment, waiting to see how she interacted with other members of the species.

"Ah," Charlotte said.

"Well, your face is gnarly," Leo said. "You're gonna look like a badass."

"Thanks. That's what I was going for."

"I think I'll leave you guys to it," Leo said. "You probably need to rest."

"Thanks for the tea, Leo," she said.

Leo patted Max on the shoulder as he passed him and left.

"I'll get you a mug," Max said once they were alone, starting toward the kitchen.

"It's okay." She shook her head. "I don't want it."

"Can I get you anything? Are you hungry?"

"I don't want anything."

She headed down the hall and made a point not to look toward Sean's bedroom.

• • •

Back at home, the days seemed to roll around. Charlotte didn't answer her phone—calls or texts. She always checked to see if it was Sean and it never was, and there was no one else she wanted to talk to. Not even Sophie. Not that Sophie had texted her in months. Charlotte wasn't scheduled at the restaurant this week, so that was one less thing to worry about, though she'd have to reach out to Laurie eventually. But now that Sean was gone, Charlotte wasn't sure how much time she could afford to take off work.

Max was always there. Almost overbearingly so. But sleeping was hard—her old nightmares about Nick were nothing compared to now. There was always a few seconds of panic between when she woke up and when she found Max in the dark. And sometimes when she came down the hall into the living room her mind sent her back to Nick waiting for her. Max's hovering made her feel anxious and fussed over, but she didn't want to think about what it would be like if he wasn't there. Sometimes when the panic over everything warped through her and left her shaking, telling her that everything was her fault and Sean was gone because of her, Max would hold her and at least it wouldn't get worse. She thought of him a year ago, navigating the worst year of his life, without

Sophie and certainly without her. Max was stronger than she ever gave him credit for.

It was a sunny afternoon, nearly a week after everything. Max was on the couch, reading the mythology book she'd given him for his birthday. Charlotte mostly busied herself with cleaning and sorting and reorganizing. Kept her mind occupied. She had spent the last hour dusting the photos hanging on the wall in their living room, even though some of them were hard to look at now.

Charlotte lifted down one of her and Sophie in the eighth grade. Charlotte was skinny and speckled with unflattering front bangs. Sophie was beautiful. She always was.

"We should talk to her," Max said. He must have seen what she was looking at.

"Huh?"

"We should talk to Sophie," he said. "She might tell us."

"What are you talking about?"

Max waved his book nonchalantly. "Remember? The money? The accident?"

Every time Max mentioned Sophie, Charlotte hated herself. Hated that she hadn't told him, after all this time, that Sophie didn't know what he thought she knew. Charlotte didn't know why she hadn't told him yet. It was something she thought she'd be okay lying to him about, but she wasn't. She told herself she was waiting for more information, or until things had settled down a bit. Every day she didn't tell him, she felt like too much time had passed and she felt sick over everything. And now every time she thought about Sophie, uneasiness bubbled in her stomach and she wondered if Max would hate her for keeping it from him.

"She didn't," Charlotte said quietly. She held her breath. "She doesn't."

"What?"

"Sophie doesn't know who hit you." Charlotte straightened the photo of the two of them. "It's something else."

Max set his book down. "Wait, what? How do you know that?"

Charlotte pulled the next photo, one of her and Sean as kids, off the wall and toward her chest. Her heart was beating in her ears, begging her to pick a different course for the conversation.

Max stood up. "How do you know that, Charlie?"

She looked at him, finally. "I found more receipts. Dated from before the accident. I asked Sophie about it. Whatever she knows, it isn't about the accident." Charlotte stared back at the wall and he was silent for a long time.

"Are you kidding?" Max said after a while.

"I'm sorry."

Silence again.

"I spent the last two weeks thinking that my ex-girlfriend knows who almost killed us and has been making money off of it," Max started. "That it's someone we know. You *know* I've been obsessing over it. I've been thinking about it constantly, but I haven't said anything. Because of you. Because...you're more important, you getting better is more important, but—"

"Max, I just wanted to wait until I knew more—" she tried.

"I have *never* lied to you, Charlie," Max said. "Not once."

"I know. I know that." Charlotte could feel tears clawing their way up her throat. She felt hot and dizzy, the same way she'd felt the last time they'd had a huge fight, right after she came home. When he told her he hated her.

"How could you let me think that?"

"I'm sorry," she said again. "I was just thinking—"

"Of what?" Max snapped. "This has a hell of a lot more to do with me than with you."

"You're right," she said, trying not to cry as she held the frame to her chest. "I wasn't thinking. I should've told you, I should've—"

"Is there anything else?"

"What?"

"Is there something else you're not telling me? Because I don't...I don't know how you could keep this from me." He was staring at her.

Charlotte felt like her heart hung suspended inside her ribs. Moment of truth, quite literally. Charlotte knew this was likely the nail in the coffin of whatever they had been.

"Sophie was pregnant and miscarried after the accident."

Max blinked.

"There. Now you know everything I know," she said.

"How," Max hissed. She could see the colour flush in his cheeks, and she knew what was coming. "*How* could you not tell me this? How could you spend all week...kissing me and sleeping with me? I was going to miss university for you."

She hated that he'd spun that around on her. "You were?" Past tense.

"I can't...look at you, right now, Charlie." His words hurt, and she flinched weakly. "I think I'm gonna go," Max said after several seconds.

"Max, wait." The familiar panic gripped her. He couldn't leave. She couldn't be alone. Not this soon. She hadn't realized how hard it would be, being in the house where it happened—in the house without Sean. "Please don't leave."

"I would never lie to you," Max said, in an almost backhanded voice, "so I'll tell you that I don't want to be around you right now."

"Max, please. You can be mad but don't leave." She was crying now. "I'm scared to be alone."

For a moment it looked like she may have swayed him; his body stilled and he looked at her the way he'd looked at her a million times. Really studying her.

"Who was—" he started, his voice shaky and jerky like he was trying to walk on uneven ground. "Who was Sophie with? The baby, I mean...who did she...?"

"I don't know," Charlotte said quickly. She hadn't really had time to speculate, but also didn't think she wanted to. What did it matter, now? Prying every last bit of truth from Sophie wouldn't help anyone. Charlotte didn't need to know. "Really. I don't."

"Right. I'll call you later, Charlie." He moved swiftly by her, towards the door. She tried to grab for him but he brushed her off. "I'll be back."

"When?"

The screen door clattered shut.

She couldn't even wipe her eyes, which made her angrier. She was angry at Sean and at Max and at Sophie and everyone else.

She hurled Sean's photo across the room; it crashed against the wood stove and shattered. *Poetic*, Charlotte thought during the silence that hung in the air after it hit the ground.

She moved to clean it, collecting the shards of glass in her hand, so at least they'd be off the floor. The frame had wedged between the corner of the stove and the woodpile. She yanked it free, revealing a dull silver item on the floor underneath it.

Charlotte reached down, pulling out the plastic object. A phone. Sean's?

No, this was prehistoric—even for Sean, who had a crappy old iPhone. This one flipped open. And the battery was charged and working, so it hadn't been there long. The only other person who'd been in their house recently was....

Nick.

She pressed the centre button and the recent calls sprang up. Just jumbled numbers—no names. She was reminded of the nondescript cellphone she and Max had found in his dad's office. That felt like years ago.

A weird feeling crept into her stomach. Suspense? Charlotte dialled the most recently called number. Nick had called this person six times.

The ringing stretched on for ages before someone answered.

"Simon," said the voice on the other side.

# twenty-nine

june
two years earlier

IT HAD BEEN TWO WEEKS since he died. The end had been quiet—she and Sean were the only ones there, though Sophie and her parents were just outside in the hallway.

"Sean," Charlotte called, her voice hoarse like she hadn't been using it. No answer. Their kitchen felt cold, grey, and haunted, even as the June sun shimmered and danced against the window.

Charlotte clattered a dish down onto the sink, jamming it sideways into the barely soapy water even though it didn't quite fit. "Sean," she repeated. Louder. Angrier. "Come and help me."

Sean was thumping around in his room supposedly cleaning, but she kept hearing the clink of glass bottles and wasn't so sure. Still no answer.

"God*damnit*," she was almost yelling then, spinning around to look at the rest of the kitchen like that was what was pissing her off. A mess, everywhere. Stained casserole dishes from meals donated by family friends and church ladies—they would have to soak forever before the crust even budged. They had so many they couldn't even eat them all, not before they went bad, because they couldn't fit any more dishes in the freezer. All they had now was a kitchen full of dishes that didn't belong to them and no dad and she couldn't think of what else.

"What's the problem?" Sean grumbled, finally appearing at the far door of the kitchen. His hair was cropped short and uneven like he had cut it himself, and the sweater he was wearing had food or beer strains down the front. He looked like shit. She wondered if she looked better or worse. She felt worse.

"You have to help me," she demanded. "We need to clean up."

"The hell we do," he said gruffly, but the words spilled out uneven and blurry. She was right. Drinking. "We don't need to do anything."

"Yes," she spat. "They're going to come check on us sooner or later and if this place is a pigsty—"

"No." Sean shook his head slowly, like he had to think through the action. "Not two goddamn weeks after, Charlotte. We get time to...adjust."

"He died two weeks ago. The funeral is over. Everything is over. This," she gestured around the tiny kitchen, "the stream of food and cards and everything—that's done. It's back to real life, Sean. And you know it's not just that." She fixed him with a hard stare. "I know you were out with Nick last week. And about the drinking, and the weed. If the social workers ask people about you, they're going to say that your friends are deadbeat drug dealers and you get busted by the cops every other month—"

"Watch it, Charlie," Sean barked. "Get off your high horse. You never cared before."

"You know it would *kill* dad if we got split up."

"Well, something might have beat it to the punch."

"God, Sean," she said, running hot water over dish one of eighty. "We're doing this now or we're never going to. Help me."

"Do it yourself."

"Wow, what a legal-guardian-like thing to say," Charlotte snapped.

"Bite me, Charlotte."

"Sorry Sean, why don't you call the social worker now and they can come take me away as soon as possible, then you won't have to clean up at all."

"I'm not that lucky," Sean snarled.

"Go to hell." Charlotte flicked the water off, stabbing a pan with a crusty metal scrubber. She'd clean this whole place herself and she'd make sure Sean ended up her legal guardian, just out of spite. She didn't realize that she was crying, thought it was water splatter and that her eyes were blurry from the sunshine. It took her longer to realize Sean was still standing there.

"I'm sorry," he said after a long time.

"Whatever," she levelled out. "Just help me clean up."

Sean joined her at the sink, shoving the sleeves of his hoodie up to his elbows. "I'd never let them take you. Never let you go anywhere."

She handed him a dry dish towel. "I know."


By the next morning they weren't speaking to each other, and the house settled into the same quiet of summer afternoons when their dad would still be at work. The not speaking was better than the yelling. It wasn't angry. Just sad. But a new day either way.

Charlotte had her legs curled under her on the couch the way their old cat used to, wedging down into a sunny spot. Planned to stay there reading all day. She was trying to get through *1984*—exams were this week.

It was almost noon, but Sean had only just pulled himself out of bed. He was stirring a bowl of cereal at the kitchen table when Charlotte heard quick, uneven steps and frustrated mumbling on the other side of the screen door. Charlotte looked up from her book. *Please not another casserole.*

Sophie burst through the door, a flurry of glitter and sunshine and hairspray. She had two long, flat garment bags over her shoulder and about four bulky-looking ones tangled in her arms. She was all limbs.

"Hey," Sophie said breathlessly, heaving all her stuff onto the coffee table beside Charlotte. Her eyes swept the room, like she could see the sad and the quiet, and sense how nothing seemed to be moving in the house anymore.

Charlotte shut her book and Sean looked up from his breakfast.

"Sophie, Jesus." Charlotte stood up and moved closer to her. "Shouldn't you be getting ready?"

"Just need makeup," Sophie explained, shaking her head a bit to show off her intricate hairdo. She must have driven to the salon in Pictou for it. "How're you doing?" Sophie asked quietly, gently laying her hand on Charlotte's cheek like she was checking for a fever. Sophie always made Charlotte feel better just by being around—like magnets that snapped together and made one tight piece. Meant to be together.

"I'm okay," Charlotte said softly, and it was the first time in two weeks she thought she might actually mean it.

"You doing all right, Sean?" Sophie asked once she had registered Charlotte's answer.

Sean was looking back down at his bowl but nodded a few times. "Yeah, thanks, Soph."

"Okay, so listen." Sophie's fingers slipped around Charlotte's wrists and held onto her—Sophie's go-to gossiping stance. "I can't go to this without you. Not when things are this sad."

Sophie was the only tenth grader to be asked to the senior prom. Jason Langille was on the football team and Charlotte knew Sophie was only going with him to say she did.

"Sophie," Charlotte half-laughed, rolling her eyes. "You're gonna have to. You can't just leave Jason hanging."

"I know. I'm not." Sophie smiled, and Charlotte recognized the diabolical grin that Sophie reserved for when she was up to something. "You're gonna go with Jason."

Charlotte opened her mouth but Sophie was ready for her—years of practice in talking Charlotte out of her comfort zone.

"Look." Sophie was holding one of the garment bags in front of her like she was a Roman soldier brandishing a shield. "I asked Delilah for her sister's dress. She graduated last year. Remember, it's, like, lavender? Totally your colour."

"What? Sophie, you can't just Parent Trap me into your prom with Jason." Charlotte waved her hand in front of Sophie's face. Clearly Sophie had inhaled too much hairspray.

Sophie scoffed and batted Charlotte's hand away. "Jason knows. He's fine with it."

"Yeah, *right*."

"I'll still make out with him," Sophie explained with a shrug. "Trust me, he's fine."

"I am not taking your spot at prom," Charlotte said, as if that was the end of it. She should know better by now.

"Duh," Sophie said, waving the second garment bag at her. "I'm still going. Sean is gonna take me."

Sean was mid-bite and looked at Sophie like he hadn't heard correctly. A long pause. Sean slid the spoon out from between his teeth.

"Nope," he said finally.

"But you can't take your *sister*," Sophie whined.

"I'm not taking anyone," Sean insisted. "I'm not going."

"Well, listen," Sophie began, "Charlie is gonna go with Jason whether we go or not—" Charlotte shook her head aggressively at this, "—so I guess it's up to you if you want to leave your baby sister with the captain of the football team...."

"I don't have tickets," Sean tried again. "I didn't register or sign up or whatever the hell else you have to do."

"I know. I called Crowell this morning."

Charlotte raised an eyebrow. "You have the principal's home number?"

"There was really nothing he could say when I gave him the whole 'newly orphaned Sean Romer changed his mind and wants to go to his senior prom after all, so can we please have two more tickets' story. Charlie, you'll take mine and Jason's."

"Sophie, I don't—"

"Charlie, relax. You're not going to prom with Jason. You're going with me. We just need the boys to get us in and then we don't. No offence, Sean," she added with a glance at him. "It'll be a dry-run for our grade twelve."

"You'll definitely get asked next year," Charlotte said.

"I know. But I mean, us together. Practice."

"I'm. Not. Going," Sean said slowly, like Sophie didn't speak English.

"Sean, come on." Sophie had begun unpacking her makeup and bobby pins and kept moving around pieces of Charlotte's hair like she was a sculptor staring down a giant block of marble. "Not to sound insensitive, but it's not like you don't have a suit."

"*Sophie,*" Charlotte scolded.

"What? He's gonna wear it one time and never again?"

Sean was scraping the bowl with his spoon, trying to clean out the last bits of sugary milk. "Well. Charlie, do you want to go?"

Charlotte looked between them, like it was some sort of trick. Sophie didn't look at all surprised—like she knew all along Sean would cave.

"Yeah," Charlotte conceded.

Sean shoved his chair back, rumbling along the wood. He stood and they waited.

"Guess I'll shower," he said.

Sean mostly ignored them while they got ready. Charlotte wondered when he was going to snap and announce he'd changed his mind.

"Okay, suck."

Charlotte tensed and pulled in every bit of her body that she could, imagining herself as an alien being absorbed into some zero-gravity space vacuum.

Sophie whipped the zipper up Charlotte's side, settling it under her armpit. "There. Ta-da. You look great."

"It feels too small."

"Nah," Sophie said, tugging down on the skirt a bit for her so it wasn't so bunched up at the top. "Delilah said her sister was doing some weird juice cleanse for the week before prom. Never works. I'm sure it has some stretch."

Sophie was already dressed—a royal blue A-line with little butterfly sleeves. Simple, by Sophie's standards. She said she was saving the extravagance for their own prom.

"Here, don't move." Sophie craned her neck, tilting Charlotte's head back into the light. "You have mascara." Sophie swiped her thumb at the space under Charlotte's eyebrow.

"Thanks for doing all this," Charlotte said once Sophie looked satisfied. "I'm really glad Sean's going."

"Me too. And that you are."

"I can't believe he agreed."

Sophie laughed and then stopped herself, like she was meditating on what Charlotte had said. "Really? I can. Sean would literally do anything for you."

Charlotte knew that. Really, she did. Sean just had a funny way of showing it.

"Probably doesn't hurt that I'm the trade-off." Sophie grinned. "Let's go get him. I want us to get some pictures."

Charlotte followed her. Sophie turned out to be right—the night of dancing and fun and trying to feel back to normal was a practice run, a rehearsal. For a senior prom they would never have.

# thirty

"CHARLIE. COME ON. I can hear you watching *The Office*."

Charlotte paused the TV and burrowed down further into the sofa. It was Leo at the door. He'd been by three times in two days. She never answered.

Max hadn't called like he said he would. It was better that way, Charlotte figured, after the second day passed in radio silence. For one, because she had no idea what she'd say to him if he did come back, after his dad had answered Nick's phone call. And for another, because she wasn't sure she wanted to see him anymore anyway.

She'd been an idiot, she thought, to think she and Max could ever be anything. If he and Sophie didn't work because they were too different, she and Max had crashed and burned because they were too similar. Oh yeah, and his dad was definitely involved with Nick, the sketchiest person in town. Or, he was.

It was like she could feel it in her bones, knew everything had to be connected—Sophie's money and Nick and Simon. Like it was on the tip of her tongue.

Charlotte heard Leo give up and shuffle back down the porch steps. The police had come by yesterday, as they had the day before, asking her if she'd heard from Sean and asking her (again) if she had any idea where he went. She (again) told them no. They told her, formally, that Sean was wanted for Nick's murder. She knew they didn't believe her when she said she didn't know where Sean was, and she wished Max had been there, sitting beside her, while they asked her to retell what had happened over and over.

So, now her days were filled with watching TV and barely eating. She couldn't keep anything down—nothing tasted good and if she did eat, she missed Sean so much she made herself sick. Charlotte missed her last two shifts at the restaurant, which she felt guilty about. Laurie had called and left a message, explaining that she'd heard what had happened—or at least sort of—and told Charlotte not to worry about work until she was feeling better. Charlotte didn't know when that would be. It was hard. Harder than expected, because every time she closed her eyes she saw Nick—or worse, Sean—and it wasn't getting any better. She'd barely slept last night. Didn't move from the couch. She always kept one eye on the door, just in case. Didn't look in the mirror, at her stitches. She knew she was supposed to go back to the hospital to get them removed, but she couldn't remember when.

Charlotte drifted into an uneasy sleep without un-pausing her show. It could have been minutes or hours later, but a noise through the screen eventually drew her back.

"Charlie! I know you're inside."

Leo again.

Charlotte groaned and rolled over to go back to sleep, planning to ignore him.

"I can't do the stairs."

Charlotte opened her eyes. That wasn't Leo's voice. She raised her head.

*"Charlie!"*

Charlotte rolled off the couch and tucked her sweater tighter around her. She caught her reflection in the mirror by the door.

Christ. She looked pale and gaunt and sick. She approached the screen carefully, although she knew there was only one person it could be.

Sophie was in her chair, on the driveway, looking impatient. "No ramp," she said.

Charlotte opened the door. "What do you want?"

"I heard what happened. Everyone has."

Charlotte teetered down the stairs and sank down on the bottom step. Charlotte's dark eyes on Sophie's light ones. If Charlotte was the ocean, dark and twisting, Sophie was all wildflowers, strong and beautiful, pink-grey like the colour of the sky the second before the sun disappears. She could feel Sophie's eyes burning into her face.

"Jesus," Sophie said quietly. "Did...he do that?"

"Nick. Yeah. And the wood stove."

"And he's...?" Sophie tried.

"Dead." Charlotte nodded.

"And Sean's...?"

"Gone," her voice tripped up on the word, like it was a different language.

"Where's Max?"

"Don't know." That last bit was the hardest to say.

Sophie didn't press it.

"I didn't know you could drive," Charlotte changed the subject, gesturing to the SUV.

"Yeah," Sophie said. "It's a custom car. I like driving. I always thought it was fun, good for clearing your head. I drive myself to sailing early in the morning when everything is still all foggy and it's just...peaceful."

Charlotte didn't answer her, instead looking over at the grey ocean, which surged and slid over the smooth rocks at the edge of the shore.

"Do you need something?" Charlotte asked finally. She didn't mean to sound rude. She wasn't even mad at Sophie. She just didn't care anymore.

"I wanted to check on you," Sophie said simply. The rumours must be pretty bad for Sophie to be concerned for Charlotte's well-being. "And on Max, actually," she continued. "I figured I owed you guys a talk. I thought he'd be here."

"Yeah, me too. A talk about what?"

"About everything."

The money, Charlotte guessed, though she still didn't know what it meant. And the cheating. "Max knows," Charlotte told her, "well, we kind of figured it out together, but he knows about the money."

"Ah."

"We thought maybe you were blackmailing the person who hit you."

Sophie's mouth fell open. "Oh, my god. I'm not a criminal mastermind, Charlie."

"I know it's not that. But I also know you've been getting paid since last summer."

Sophie readjusted in her seat and avoided Charlotte's eye. "Can you just trust me when I say you don't need to know what it is? I promise it doesn't have anything to do with you."

Charlotte leaned her head against the railing and nodded. "Yeah. I just...I've learned to stay out of things, I think." She motioned vaguely to her face. Meddling had almost killed her, had definitely cost her her brother, and probably Max, too. Time for a break.

"Charlie, I'm sorry, okay?"

Charlotte raised her eyes to look at her. "For what?"

"I shouldn't have cut you out of my life when you came back. Not after everything that happened and not after everything... that I did."

Charlotte shook her head. "We've all done horrible things, Sophie. And you had every right to cut me out."

"I was so angry at you, because you leaving hurt. And I think I just thought that the best way through that hurt was...around it. If I could ignore you then I could ignore how bad it messed me up. But...I couldn't just ignore it. I should've known that. And Leo told me that it...that this was really scary and—and that Max was terrified when he heard you were in the hospital and what if—" Sophie hiccupped, and Charlotte was surprised to see that she looked scared. "What if you weren't okay?"

"Sophie. I am, though."

"We would have left things," Sophie said, "with you hating me."

"I've never hated you," Charlotte told her. The truth, for real.

"I did hate you." Sophie sniffed. "But only because...boys aren't really the ones who break your heart, eh? Maybe we deserve each other."

Charlotte looked at her and waited.

"I'm just saying," Sophie continued after a moment, "it would have sucked to end it there."

Charlotte made a *hrmph* kind of noise in agreement. What felt like a significant amount of time passed, and eventually Sophie stretched her arms and started turning her chair.

"I guess I'll leave you to it, then," she said. "I just wanted to... say hi."

"Yeah, um." Charlotte stood up. "Thanks for coming by."

"Thanks for coming outside." Sophie turned back to Charlotte from the door of her SUV. "Why did Sean do it?"

No matter what they went through, there was a part of Charlotte that automatically trusted Sophie. Never lied to her.

"Nick was trying to kill me," she said simply. It was almost laughable, how casually she could say those words.

Sophie froze. "What? Why? Your face...I thought—I didn't know you were *attacked*."

"It's a long story."

"How do you even know Nick?"

Charlotte cleared her throat. It was weird, the things that didn't matter anymore. "Nick is the reason I left a year ago."

Sophie's expression was unreadable as Charlotte elaborated, telling her the story the same way she'd told it to Max a month ago. When she was done, Sophie's face was much more clear. Calculating. Like the gears in her head were working.

"Nick was going to kill you for what you saw?" Sophie asked.

"I guess so."

More silence.

"I...shouldn't be saying this," Sophie nearly whispered. "But I maybe was wrong, before, when I said the money didn't have anything to do with you."

Charlotte felt the hairs on her neck stand up.

"What?"

"Um." Sophie was clearly cycling through words, trying to figure the best way to string them along. "It's the bank."

"Huh?"

"The bank—Simon's bank—owns property."

Charlotte didn't follow. "Okay."

"It's off of West Branch, behind the old school. Way back in the woods. There's a trail. A house."

Charlotte frowned. "What does this have to do with you? Or me?"

"All the records—the contact information on the deed and stuff—the phone numbers and addresses, they're all for the bank. There's a fake name on the lease."

"I don't understand."

"That's all I can say, or all that I want to," Sophie said. "But that house is a secret for a reason."

"Sophie," Charlotte said, trying to piece together the fragments of what Sophie was telling her. "I don't understand."

"I know, I'm sorry." Sophie was opening the door. "I can't say more. I can't. I'm...I can't."

"Sophie, please—"

"Bye, Charlie. I'll see you soon, I promise."

Sophie left, and Charlotte didn't think she said anything back to her. Charlotte was looking at the ocean again, frustrated by how cryptic Sophie had been. She wished Max was there to talk it out with.

Something, at least, was clicking into place. Nick's connection to Charlotte had been what forced Sophie to be honest, and whatever Sophie was so nervous about explaining was connected to Simon. And really, Charlotte knew, there was only one person in town with enough money to be paying Sophie two grand every month.

Maybe her meddling days weren't quite over.

# thirty-one

**THE DAYS TRICKLED BY.** It had been officially a week since she'd heard from Max. She'd called him a dozen times in the first few days after he left, leaving pathetic voicemails that tasted sour as she spewed them out. He hadn't returned any of her calls. She didn't call again, and every day she didn't hear from him, she told herself that she thought about him less. Whatever. One more person to strike off her list of people she'd loved and lost. Her mom. Her dad. Sophie. Sean. Max. Everyone that mattered.

Well, and Leo. She was being a bitch not answering his texts or even his in-person visits. While the wound was still fresh, she saw him as an extension of Max, which she knew was unfair. She just hated the thought of letting Leo in and having him relay everything she was doing to Max. Maybe in a few more days she could talk to other people again.

Charlotte spent the days doing what she always did when she was stressed or angry or scared: cry and drink tea and reorganize her possessions. She'd torn apart the living room, ready to re-alphabetize their DVD collection and weed through literally every storage unit in the room.

At one point, she found herself in Sean's room. It was the first time she'd really gone in to investigate. Everything was the same.

Everything was a complete mess; stacks of dishes and laundry. She'd given up quickly—being in there was not only sad, but even thinking of cleaning it was nearly impossible.

A day later, she stood in the bathroom, glaring at herself in the mirror. Her face was beginning to heal, regular skin beginning to creep back over the black bruises. In the mirror, she was starting to look more like herself, but she was looking at a version she hadn't seen in a long time. This was early-boarding-school-era Charlotte, who'd been so devastated by the accident and leaving her hometown that she couldn't eat or sleep. At least at school food had been readily available, and a class schedule kept her preoccupied.

Charlotte's stomach hurt, and she didn't know if it was because she was starving or not, but either way it forced the appetite out of her. It was getting harder to get out of bed, to do much of anything. Charlotte braced her hands against the sink. It had been a long time since things had been this bad. But the familiarity of the feeling was what made her feel the worst.

She sighed. *Don't let this win. Get some groceries.* She figured it was time she broke into the family savings. She was running out of money, and the missed shifts didn't help.

She returned to Sean's room and gingerly edged to his bed on her hands and knees, carefully avoiding any old food and garbage. Reaching under the bed, she retrieved an old English biscuit tin and pried the top off. It had been their dad's—he always kept stray bills and leftover change in it and left it on top of the fridge. Their dad made her and Sean "sign out" the money whenever they took some. Taped inside the lid was a scrap of loose-leaf and a record of their transactions. Her latest: *four dollars, chips from Quik Mart.* Sean had scratched this out and corrected it to seven dollars. Which was true. She'd thought she could get away with buying her and Sophie ice cream too. This would have been...what? Five years ago? Before their dad was sick. Sean's latest entry was: *ten dollars, for not cigarettes.* Charlotte smiled. In the bottom of the tin was a wad of fives, tens, and twenties. Maybe a couple hundred bucks of Sean's savings.

Charlotte sat back on her heels. God, her head hurt. She needed food. Halfway to pulling herself to her feet, she caught sight of a long object jutting out from near the head of the bed. Pulling it out by the neck, she found a quart of rum. Dark. Dinner. Perfect. She straightened up, swiped a few twenties from the tin, and took the bottle with her to the kitchen.

Charlotte was trying to think about what it had really been like when her dad was alive and Sean wasn't on the run and they all lived together under one roof and things weren't a mess. Charlotte didn't realize she was shaking until she reached onto her tiptoes for a glass from one of the higher shelves. Her hand was trembling as it closed around the cup and it slipped through her fingers, bouncing off the counter and shattering against the floor. She jumped back on instinct, surprised by the noise and way the glass sprayed out in pieces.

Transfixed by the pattern, she removed the cap from the bottle and took a swig. It burned a bit and she nearly gagged, but it settled warmly in her stomach. She took another sip and reached for the identical glass beside the first, but tipped it off the shelf and sent it to the same fate.

It became a one-person drinking game.

Sean was gone. Drink. Break one of the pastel-coloured plates leaning in the drying rack.

Max was gone. Another drink. More plates.

Nick was dead but it felt like he had more control over her than ever (drink; cereal bowl). She had no money and no plan, everyone would go off to university and she'd be stuck in River John forever, destitute and alone. She threw a mug; it caught the corner of the oven and the sound rang in her ears.

She was crying but she didn't really care, and when she pulled the bottle to her mouth again, she missed the first few tries. Not eating had done her in quickly. She must have stumbled, because her hips bumped back against the counter and her knees gave up. Charlotte slid to the floor amid the rest of the broken things. On her left was the bigger chunk of the mug she'd just destroyed.

It was huge, way too big to be safe for coffee—more like a bowl with a handle. It was hand-painted yellow and red. Way back when they were little, she and Sean had convinced their dad to drive them all the way into the city so they could go to one of those pottery places. The places where you pick something out, like a plaque or a little statue of a kitten or a mug, and you would paint it and then the people there baked it for you and it came out all shiny. She and Sean painted their dad a mug for Father's Day. The base of the mug, the part Charlotte was looking at now, had the messy initials S.R. and C.R. written in blue paint.

"Cheers," she said to the mug and to no one. She didn't know how long she stayed there, only measuring time by how much of the rum was drained out of the bottle. The sun cut uneven across the front of the counters as it hung lower in the sky. Dark swam in and out of her vision as she drifted between sleeping and not. She didn't move until a knock on the door pulled her back through to consciousness.

Charlotte froze. Shit. It was probably Leo. The door was locked, like she made sure it always was, now. He would leave eventually.

"Charlotte?" She heard the voice and the person wrestling with the tricky lock as they clattered the door open. She snapped to attention. Only one person had a key.

"Sean?" she croaked, but the word strung out messy and slow. "Charlie?"

But it was Max who appeared in front of her. He stared at her and she stared right back. She didn't even bother thinking about how pathetic she must look, curled up on her kitchen floor with half a bottle of rum and a bunch of broken plates. Part of her was happy that he had come home to her. But the drunker, angrier, more present part of her found herself staring back at someone who had left her when he promised he wouldn't.

"How—" she started, trying to nod toward the door.

"I went and got Sophie's key from her. Leo told me you weren't answering the door."

Charlotte leaned her head back against the counter and closed her eyes, barely awake and very drunk.

"What happened here?" Max asked, crossing the kitchen.

Charlotte didn't answer and took another swig from the bottle, wiping her face with the corner of her sleeve.

He lowered himself to the floor, sitting with his back propped against the counter across from her. Max reached across the space between them toward her leg.

"Don't touch me," she snapped, surprised by how hard her voice sounded.

"No," he shook his head and reached farther, pulling the bottle away from her. He took a mouthful for himself before placing it behind his head, on the counter and out of reach.

"Are you okay?" he asked, looking at her closely.

Charlotte bent her legs back toward her, pressing them against her chest. "Yup. Best day of my damn life."

"You look awful. Sick," Max said.

She tilted her head so she didn't have to look at him. "Well," she rasped, "I don't have any food. And I haven't been working. And I've been," her voice was shaking, "too...afraid to get any sleep. So, yeah, that's probably fair."

"I'm sorry," he said.

She wanted to cry but choked on a laugh instead. "I don't care."

"I shouldn't have left you." Max shifted forward on his knees, closer to her. "I knew I shouldn't have as soon as I went. I was just...mad. And I didn't think."

"I begged you not to go," she bit out, "and you still did. You left me in the house where a lunatic tried to kill me a week ago."

He bowed his head. "I know. I hate what I did, all right? I should've called you that night like I said. But I was angry. So I didn't."

She sniffed and still wouldn't look at him, the sound of the breaking glass still echoing inside her head.

"It's not like I can be mad that you left," she said. "I did it first."

"But you came back," Max said.

She peeked at him from the corner of her eye. "So did you. And I didn't think you would." Her voice cracked on the second part, her face twisting to keep the tears back. Things weren't done falling apart, it seemed.

Max was closer to her than she'd thought, and he pushed the hair back from her face, taking her chin in his fingers. "Can we try again?"

Charlotte slipped her hand inside his. "I hope so."

They had to. Max had come back for her, and that was something worth trying for. She wanted to feel relief, comfort in Max's presence, but it was like she couldn't let herself. What if they couldn't find each other again; what if that thread that had connected them was too frayed now? She was scared Max had come back to her, and it would all be for nothing.

"It's gonna be okay," he said vaguely, his finger swiping along her cheek.

She cleared her throat and straightened her back, trying to push away the alcohol that was seeping into her brain, making her feel hot and shaky.

"I don't know," she managed.

"Charlie, it will."

"Do you remember when you told me that sometimes it doesn't matter how much you love someone? That sometimes it doesn't mean anything?"

He nodded like he knew where she was going and pulled her body toward him, as if in protest. He tucked her into a hug, holding on to her like he was trying to keep her.

"This feels like that," she said against his shoulder, her words intercepted by a sob that pushed past her lips. But she knew he'd heard. With his arms around her middle, Max lifted her carefully and helped her to the bathroom. She could barely walk—bunched his T-shirt in her fists as she clung to his sides, but Max was doing most of the work.

"Wait," she mumbled. Too much movement; her insides were sloshing. She pushed herself down onto her knees in front of the toilet and heaved. It was all acid and bile.

"Oh, Charlie," she heard Max say gently, and he said it almost like a sigh. He rubbed his hand up and down her back and pulled her hair behind her shoulders, out of the way.

Charlotte finished, her eyes watery and throat burning, throwing a hand up to flush. Max pushed a cup of water to her lips. Thank god for him, she thought through her humiliation. He guided her to the edge of the tub, reappearing with a cool, wet washcloth. She felt like she was only catching glimpses, specks or showers of what was happening.

Max held her face like she was art, fragile. He wiped the cloth over her cheeks, under her eyes that were streaked with old makeup and over her mouth. She just barely noticed that the cool water felt refreshing. Woke her up, almost. Made her think of the first swim of every summer. Charlotte always hoped for June but Sophie always made them go in May. Charlotte reached out and grasped Max's waist. A quiet thank you, the only one she could manage.

"Here, be careful." Max pulled her sweater off over her head, stained from liquor and sick and whatever else. He wiped her throat and chest and the tops of her shoulders before throwing the cloth back over to the sink.

She waited for him to say something about pulling herself together, tried to catch if he was annoyed by what a mess she was. Max stood up from between her legs.

"Let's go to sleep," he said quietly. He reached out and slipped his hand around to settle at the base of her neck. She teetered herself onto her feet and he didn't let go of her. It was almost like he was nervous to leave the bathroom. In the exact moment, at least, they were safe. They were together.

"Do you forgive me?" he whispered, close to her face. Eyes wide and waiting.

Charlotte nodded and closed the space between them. Of course she did.

"Do you hate me for not telling you?" she rasped. Words, finally.

Max pushed his fingers up into her hair and kissed her just beneath her eye, hovering just above the mark on her face. "I can't," he answered.

He led her to her room and to her bed. He stayed. She slept.

# thirty-two

A DULL THROBBING AT THE base of her skull pulled her awake. Charlotte didn't think she'd ever been so hungover. She didn't think anything could top spring formal at the end of grade eleven. But she'd woken up after that in Sophie's bed, with Sophie, fake eyelashes stuck to her cheek and glitter in her hair. And her brother hadn't just murdered someone and her life hadn't just fallen apart.

Pieces of memory from last night swam around her head and tried to string themselves together. She was drinking, obviously, right out of the bottle, because...right. The pang of realization burst in her stomach the same way the glassware shattered against the kitchen floor.

Max had come back, she remembered. Charlotte checked over her shoulder, the tiniest movement sending her head spinning. Not here. She knew he'd stayed at least some of the night. She had a blurry memory of her face in the toilet, heaving out an empty stomach while Max rubbed her back and held her hair. Charlotte pressed her teeth together and grimaced into her pillow.

She could hear Max—she assumed it was Max, at least—in the kitchen, the tinkling sound of glass drifting over to her bedroom. It sounded like he was cleaning up. She couldn't let him do that.

If she was going to have a hysterical breakdown and destroy her house, she would clean it up herself, goddamnit. Part of the healing process.

Charlotte uncoiled her body, stretching out her limbs as if to test that they still worked. All four were there. So far, so good. She stood up a bit too quickly, she realized, and of all her near-death experiences she figured this was the closest she'd ever come to actually dying. Jesus. Her head. Her stomach. For the first time in a few days, she wanted something in her body. Water.

She crept to the kitchen. Max was standing over a bag sitting on the counter, unloading groceries into the fridge and onto shelves. She noticed the remnants of her destructive rampage had been swept into a pile in the corner.

"What's that?" she croaked, nodding to the bag. Her voice sounded goopy and thick out loud.

Max looked up at the sound of her voice. "You're alive," he said, sounding half-surprised. "I went out for these this morning. You don't have any food. You literally only have mayonnaise."

She moved down the counter, closer to him, stopping when they were hip to hip. "There's definitely ketchup in there, too."

"Ah, the biting sarcasm," Max said. "Makes me think you're feeling a bit better."

Charlotte inspected the contents of the bag—bananas, eggs, cheese, bread, milk, peanut butter. "You didn't have to buy this stuff."

"Yes, I did," Max said. He lifted a carton of strawberries out of the bag. "You look like you're on the verge of death. Have you been eating?"

Charlotte popped one of the strawberries in her mouth defiantly. "I have."

Max shook his head and ignored her, putting the rest of the items away. When he'd finished, he leaned back against the opposite counter and looked at her, arms crossed against his chest.

"What?" she asked.

"You were...kind of scary last night. I mean, I was scared for you."

"It's been...hard," she sighed. She was tired of talking about it already. Talking about feeling sad and hopeless wasn't going to fix anything. "I just lost it."

"Do you not want to talk about it?" he asked, like he read her mind.

"No," she said. "Not yet."

"How do you feel right now?"

She bit her lip. She was still angry—no, she corrected herself, she was still hurt—by him leaving, and a small part of her was reluctant to let him back in. Behind Max's head, on the shelf, she spied a new, too-big bag of Reese's Pieces. They were her favourite, but the Quik Mart only had M&M's. You had to drive to the gas station in Tatamagouche to get Reese's Pieces.

"I'm just glad you're back," she admitted finally.

Max looked relieved, and he crossed the space between them in the tiny galley kitchen to wrap his arms around her.

"I'll pay you back for this," Charlotte told him when she finally pulled away, trying to do a mental calculation of what the bill would be.

"Stop," he said quickly. "It's not my money, anyway."

Simon. If Charlotte had been feeling somewhat better, that feeling went flying out the window and into the Atlantic Ocean. The phone call that Simon had answered and Sophie's cryptic visit pressed to the front of her mind.

"I need to tell you something," she said, sliding her hands around his waist. "More than something, actually. A lot." No more secrets.

She tried to recount everything Sophie had said—that the bank, so likely Simon, owned a property at the edge of town, and that nobody knew about it, and that there was a reason nobody knew about it. She explained how scared Sophie had been after she said it, like she had revealed something she shouldn't have.

"So, Sophie came over to tell you this?" Max asked. Charlotte could tell he was trying to steer the conversation away from his father, intentionally or not. It was one thing to not get along with your dad, it was another to agree that he was mixed up in something potentially illegal.

"No," Charlotte said, "she just came over to check on me."

"Then how did you start talking about my dad?"

"We didn't. She never said anything about your dad, really," she assured him, though she didn't think that meant Simon was innocent. "She brought it up when I mentioned Nick."

"What does Nick have to do with my dad? And with Sophie?"

*That's the question, isn't it?*

She paused, sucking in a breath. "I would think nothing. But then I found something, right after you left."

Charlotte told him about the phone and hitting redial and his dad picking up.

She could tell Max was getting more agitated. Not really at her; he kept touching her face and her arm and her waist like he was trying to distract himself. "You're sure it was my dad?"

Charlotte nodded. "He said his name when he answered."

"So you think Nick was working with my dad?"

"I think he worked *for* your dad," she said, wondering if that was too much of an accusation. "Max, we don't even know what this is. It could be...," she trailed off. There was no positive, innocent explanation she could come up with. Unless it was just nothing at all. Maybe Sophie was somehow wrong.

Max thought about it for a long time, and she guessed he must have been trying to do the same thing she was. "Okay," he said finally. "There's only one way to find out. Where did Sophie say the house was?"

They walked, because Charlotte was too nervous to go near the mystery house with a car that could identify them. Plus, she needed the fresh air.

Max was quiet the whole way. She repeated what Sophie had said, about the path snaking up from behind the farthest corner of the old elementary school. When they disappeared into the treeline, along the uneven and overgrown trail, she slipped her hand inside his and he squeezed it tightly.

Sophie didn't say anything about how far back it was—it occurred to Charlotte that Sophie likely didn't even know where the house was exactly, or if she'd even been to it. Sophie'd probably just looked it up on Google Maps.

It was about fifteen minutes of mud and wet leaves before they came to a clearing. There, tucked behind a chain-link fence to their right, was what looked like a dilapidated farmhouse. It looked abandoned, with shingles missing on the caved-in roof and boards over most of the windows. Signs zip-tied to the fence warned them to stay away: *No Trespassing*, *Do Not Enter*, *DANGER*. Around the front of the house, and across the porch, door, and windows, yellow caution tape fluttered in the breeze.

She chanced a look at Max. His face was hard set, but she couldn't quite read him. She looked back at the house, torn between being better off not knowing and finding out what Sophie was so afraid of.

"Let's go," he said.

She was scared of what they would find, but Max pulled on her hand and she followed him. Max boosted her up over the fence; she landed unevenly on the other side, head pounding on impact, as he climbed nimbly over. They crept up to the porch and Max ignored the tape, but was careful not to disturb it.

"Maybe you should wait out here," he said to her.

"Shh," Charlotte hissed, both in a don't-be-stupid and a don't-make-any-noise sort of way.

The house was, as it looked, abandoned. Some old furniture remained, but it was faded and gloomy and looked like it had been cut out of an old-fashioned photograph. Dust and cobwebs seemed to hang in the air out of nothing. From the entryway,

Charlotte stepped into the room to the left. It looked like it had been a living room. Mostly empty, and overall not suspicious. As she turned to leave, a dark object against the wall beside the door made her stop. It was a sleeping bag.

She moved closer, spotting something lying on top of it. A box of cigarettes. A black lighter with yellow smiley faces. Charlotte picked it up.

*To me, from me* said Sean's voice in her head.

*Shit.*

"You okay?" Max asked, poking his head into the room.

She dropped the lighter back onto the sleeping bag. "Yup," she said quickly, her head swimming in a silent panic.

*Shit, shit. Please, don't let him be involved.*

"Let's go upstairs, there's nothing down here," Max said.

Like a zombie, Charlotte followed him up the stairs and through the first door on the landing. It looked like the walls that divided all the upstairs rooms had been knocked out, creating one wide-open space.

And there was everything.

Stacks and stacks—grouped into piles and piles—of thick, fat packages, wrapped over and over in plastic. They looked like flattened bags of sugar. But Charlotte had seen enough *CSI* to know it wasn't sugar.

"Oh, my god," she choked. This was worse than she thought. They had to leave. Now. Right now. "Max."

Max looked like he was glitching. His mouth kept opening and closing. "What is that?"

It couldn't be drugs. This was River John, the quietest most boring town in Nova Scotia.

"Max, we gotta go."

As if in agreement, a car door slammed outside. It snapped Max back to reality. She grabbed his hand and they raced back down the stairs. They had to beat whoever it was to the door. Charlotte's heart was pounding in her head, adrenaline neutralizing her hangover. If they were caught, they were dead.

Max pulled Charlotte around the stairs, away from the front door. He seemed confident there was a back exit. The kitchen. They stopped short—the floors were rotted out, and a fallen beam blocked their path.

They were trapped. Finished.

Max pressed her back against the wall, wedging her as close to the stairs as they could get. She could feel his heartbeat.

Max hooked a hand around the side of her face, holding her close as they waited.

Footsteps.

The creaking of old wood on the porch.

Max was shaking and Charlotte couldn't tell if she was afraid, or too scared to be.

Whoever it was went directly upstairs. As they crossed to the first step, Charlotte saw his face. Simon Hale, unmistakably. He was on the phone. She knew Max saw him too.

"No, we have two for Halifax tonight" were the only words she made out.

As Simon's face faded, Max moved for both of them, dragging her back down the hall and out the front door. They stumbled over the fence. They ran until they hit the trees.

• • •

"Maybe it wasn't drugs," Charlotte tried.

Max eyed her. "Then what was it?"

"Counterfeit money?"

"Is that better?"

Charlotte puffed out her cheeks. "I don't know."

It was the next day. They had hardly spoken once they got home. They went straight to bed, but she didn't think either of them slept.

Max was sitting cross-legged on her kitchen floor. "Shit. That piece does not go there," he muttered. He was working on a large yellow dinner plate.

Charlotte ran the glue across the jagged edge of a china saucer. The cleaning was helping, keeping them thinking about something else. "Sophie must have known," she said.

"About the house?"

"About the drugs"—she avoided his look—"or whatever it is. About everything. She knew. She found out when she was working at the bank. And your dad was the one paying her. To be quiet." Charlotte sighed, pressing the delicate pieces of the saucer together. "It all fits."

"I know," Max said. "I just...don't want it to."

"And Nick must have been involved," she continued, thinking aloud. "He was probably a dealer or something." *And Sean probably was too*, Charlotte reminded herself, thinking of the lighter.

"Probably good money in it," Max reasoned. She'd told him what she found, thinking it meant Sean might still in town. "I mean, *if*"—he was treating Sean with the same eggshell attitude as she was his dad—"Sean was dealing too, it was probably just for that."

"Yeah, money doesn't always justify being a criminal. That's kinda the whole point."

"But," Max slid together two halves of a blue pasta bowl, "the money was for you guys, you know. He would have done it for you."

"That doesn't make me feel better."

"Did he leave you any money?"

"Some. Enough for a few months. Probably all he had." She reached for three pieces of a teacup. "I don't think he was dealing, honestly."

"Or maybe he did, and then stopped. Do you think that's how he paid for your boarding school?"

"I—"

"Damn," Max said, interrupting her. He showed her his finger, which had a small gash leaking the tiniest bit of blood. "Dangerous work."

"I'll grab the first-aid kit."

She was referring to a dusty old tin on the top shelf of the cabinet that was filled with bandages and gauze.

"I think we have Dora the Explorer Band-Aids," she told him as she reached onto her tiptoes and her hand closed around the tin. Max half-heartedly pumped his fist while she pulled the tin free. With it, a folded piece of paper fluttered down and landed on the counter. Frowning, she placed the tin on the counter and reached for the yellowed paper. She had a sneaking suspicion of what it was before she unfolded it.

*Sean,*

*I've been writing you letters since before you were born, but I haven't written you one in a while. Today, your mom left. But also today, you kept your baby sister from getting hurt. And I hope that's what you think of first when you think of this day. I'm so proud of you. It's just the three of us now, and looking out for each other has to be the most important thing. When your mother stormed out of the house this afternoon, I panicked at the thought of taking care of a kid and a baby by myself. But now I know that you know how to be a big brother. In life you two are going to need to protect each other. There will never be anything more important than family.*

*Hell or high water,*

*Dad*

Charlotte felt her stomach flip-flop, like the feeling you got when you drove down a steep hill. She folded the letter in half, using her nail to emphasize the crease.

"What is it?" Max asked.

"Uh, it's a letter." Charlotte waved the paper. "From my dad. He used to write them to us when we were kids. It's to Sean, on the day our mom left."

Max placed his hand comfortingly on the space behind her knee and placed a light kiss halfway up her thigh. She managed to smile down at him and placed the letter on the counter. "I'll get you your Band-Aid."

She pried the lid off the tin. A crumbled piece of receipt paper bounced out. Charlotte tore off a pink Dora the Explorer Band-Aid and passed it down to Max.

He peeled it open carefully. "I think this glows in the dark," he said.

"I really don't know how you're ever going to repay me," she said, un-crumbling the receipt. It was from the Quik Mart, for a Powerade and twenty dollars worth of gas. She looked at the date stamp at the top.

"September ninth, 2016," she read aloud.

Max looked up quickly. "What?"

"That's the day of the car rally."

"Yes."

"9:41 P.M. The night of the accident."

"What is it?" Max asked.

"A receipt from the Quik Mart. It's not mine. Must be Sean's, I guess, but...Sean was out of town that weekend." She scanned the receipt over and over. What the hell? She had had the only car that night for her babysitting gig. Sean hadn't even been home. What car was he putting gas in? Charlotte looked back down at her dad's letter.

A thought struck her.

She blew out of the kitchen and out the back door, crossed the porch, and ended up in front of the workshop. Max had followed her.

"Sean put a new lock on this when I got home," she breathed. "Because he thought I'd been in here."

Max looked at her nervously.

"We need to get in there," she told him.

At the other edge of their yard, Sean kept an axe for when he was sometimes inclined to chop firewood for the wood stove. Max retrieved it for her.

The big barn doors gave way easily; they could have probably kicked them in. Charlotte pushed inside and flicked the overhead light on. In the back corner, the shape of her dad's old truck loomed, as it had for as long as she remembered.

A huge drop cloth covered the truck. She picked up a handful of the paint-splattered fabric. Moment of truth. It would be worse than ripping off any glow-in-the-dark Dora the Explorer Band-Aid. She tore the cloth back.

Both the headlights were smashed; the hood twisted, the windshield cracked like a spider-web.

"Holy shit." Max joined her beside the car.

"No." Charlotte shook her head. "No."

The driver-side door was unlocked; the keys were still dangling from the ignition. She climbed inside while Max seemed to be transfixed by the front of the car. The bottle of blue Powerade in the cup holder wasn't even half empty.

"What did you find?" Max asked finally.

"I...someone was driving this the night of the accident, and obviously—" she couldn't say it out loud.

"Sean hit us," Max finished for her.

No. No way. Charlotte would know. Sean wouldn't have been able to hide something like that. Sean had a conscience. She would have noticed if her brother had almost killed her best friend and her boyfriend and tried to cover it up.

*But,* said a voice in her head, *you were gone for a year.*

"It doesn't make sense—he, he would have helped you, he wouldn't have just left you there, he would have done *something.* He wouldn't have hidden it, not from me—"

"But, what if he was trying to protect you from...to protect you—"

"He wouldn't, I know him—"

"Charlotte." Max had come around to the driver side and grabbed onto her suddenly by both arms. "Sean needed to get you away from Nick. What if he did it to protect you? To get you away?"

"What, hid it from me?"

Max shook his head and looked her in the eye. "No. What if Sean wasn't dealing for my dad? What if it was something else? What if my dad got tired of paying Sophie to be quiet about the property? What if he paid Sean instead? To—"

Charlotte recoiled. "What are you saying?"

"I'm saying I think I know where Sean got your boarding school money."

# thirty-three

IT HAD BEEN A ROUGH NIGHT. Charlotte piled up theories and explanations and excuses and twist-endings, because there was no way Sean could have done it. Max shook his head at every one. It was his turn to be delicate, to be careful as they unravelled what her brother had done. There was a lot of crying. A lot more denial, mostly on her end. But the more she fell apart, the more the pieces of what happened a year ago seemed to fall right into place. Turned out she hadn't been that far off when she had accused Sean of being a hit man at the start of the summer.

Simon had paid Sean the money he'd needed to send Charlotte away; all Sean needed to do was get rid of Sophie, who knew all about the drugs and the property. Sophie, who'd been extorting Simon and was a liability. That's why Sean had banned her from the car rally, because otherwise Charlotte would have been in that car with Sophie and Max. That's why Sean hated when Max was around. That's why Sean wanted to keep her out of the workshop. That's why Charlotte had been kept safe, away from Nick—because Sean was desperate for the money and Simon was desperate for something else.

She lay in bed with Max, the night deteriorating into a cold, rainy morning. It had been storming for days; the only break had arced over their excursion to the abandoned house. The river must be high by now, Charlotte thought. It overflowed almost every summer, near the end of August.

Max was facing away from her, his shoulders an effective barrier against conversation. She didn't know if he was mad. She knew, even less, how she felt. She was mad at Sean and mad at herself for not figuring it out, but like a song playing in the distance, there was a faint feeling that they still had to be wrong. There was no way.

Charlotte reached out and placed her hands at the low of Max's back, sliding them over his sides to rest against his stomach.

"Are you all right?" he asked.

She wondered if Max was thinking about his dad not caring that his son would be in the car too, when Sean hit Sophie. Charlotte pressed her forehead to the space between his shoulder blades. "I feel like I'm dreaming."

Max rolled over to face her, untangling her hands to hold them himself. "We might be wrong."

She looked at his eyes, the silhouette of his head and hair backlit by the grey sunlight from the window. They were the only things that felt real—the sun and his eyes—that hazy morning. The world outside seemed like it was standing still.

"I don't think we are," she admitted, feeling like she had betrayed Sean just by thinking it.

"Then we should tell someone," he whispered, dragging her closer to him. "The police."

Charlotte bobbed her head against the pillow, nodding, sealing Sean's fate. She wished they didn't know where Sean was, so they couldn't tell the police. She didn't know if she'd reveal him, if they asked, but she couldn't ask Max not to. Max didn't owe Sean anything.

"We can wait," Max said, noticing her silence. "A few days."

Charlotte shook her head, tucking her face against his shoulder. "No. We shouldn't. We'll go when the rain stops."

Her hand skimmed down his front to the bottom of his T-shirt, slipping under the edge and up. She stopped on a jagged line along his rib cage that she could feel beneath her hand.

"This is from the accident, right?" she hadn't wanted to ask before.

"Yeah. Stitches."

"How many?"

"Twelve."

"I only had eight." She shifted a bit and tightened her hold on him, feeling his lips against her hairline. Charlotte closed her eyes. She could have lost Max, too, she thought. Not just Sophie. The world felt bigger and smaller all at once. The accident had brought them together, but it could have just as easily dragged all three of them apart. For good.

When she woke up again, there was still an orchestra of drumming against the tin roof. Still pouring rain. She grabbed Max's wrist to check his watch. Past six. Charlotte was restless; she didn't want any more time to think, she wanted answers.

She wanted to talk to Sean.

Charlotte pulled herself out of bed, carefully edging out from under the comforter. Max was sprawled on his back, asleep. Kneeling on the corner of the mattress, she leaned forward and pressed a kiss to his forehead.

"Back soon," she promised.

Charlotte knew this was a bad idea. Really bad. You never confront the villain at the end. That's how people die. But the villain was never supposed to be Sean. Charlotte twisted her hands nervously around the steering wheel as she headed in the direction of the elementary school.

She parked in the school lot, as close to the edge of the woods as she could get. The rain pounded the windshield as she steadied her breathing. She tried to rehearse what she was going to say, what she was going to demand answers to, but the thoughts dissipated as quickly as her breath.

Charlotte flipped her hood up over her head and trudged towards the trees and the path. The walk felt quicker this time; she pushed through the trees like she was following a trail to a familiar spot. Mud splattered in all directions as she went, spraying her boots and knees. Charlotte could feel her heartbeat rattling in all her bones, sometimes fast and sometimes slow, like it was trying to synchronize with the way the rain was hitting the ground.

She found the farmhouse. It was quiet—no armed bodyguards outside, and no sign of anyone else. No cars. No Simon Hale. Charlotte nearly ripped her pant leg climbing over the fence without Max to boost her, landing on the wet ground on the other side with a thud. She ducked under the caution tape and crept inside, only pushing the door open enough to get in, and still half-terrified the entire structure was going to collapse. The house seemed to be sagging with the weight of all the water from the last few days. The murky earth holding the foundation was probably sliding and uneven by now. The inside of the house was dry, though. Some old houses were just built to withstand the rain.

Charlotte checked the living room. It was cold, and the sleeping bag was still there, beside some cigarettes and empty can of corn. There was a pyramid of empty beer cans beside the makeshift bed. But no Sean.

She listened for someone upstairs, or anywhere, but the rain made it impossible. She reached out for the sleeping bag, in case there was something under it. Lifting up one edge, she must have disturbed a mouse hiding underneath. It writhed and scurried away as Charlotte jumped back, but the mouse careened into the empty cans, and her quick movement knocked them to the ground.

If anyone was in the house, they had definitely heard that.

She heard movement in the other room, confirming her fears. Charlotte spent more time than she should have debating whether she could make it to the door, out of the house—the answer was no. There was a smaller door at her right, and she slipped into the tiny closet and pulled it shut, leaving just enough of a crack for her to see.

It was Sean.

He looked wet and exhausted. He checked his watch—their dad's watch—and stood completely still. Waiting. Charlotte could hear her own breathing, and she tried to force her brain to reveal herself. It was just Sean. She could burst out and scream at him and accuse him of everything. But she couldn't move. She knew she couldn't do it. She wasn't ready to look right at him, and have him confirm that he was the one who tried to kill Sophie.

The front door slammed and she almost gave herself away with a yelp of surprise. Sean didn't look at all fazed.

"If you're going to be squatting here, the least you could do is clean up after yourself," rang a vaguely familiar female voice from the hallway; Charlotte couldn't quite place it.

Sean looked over his shoulder and scoffed. "Right. It was *really* the Four Seasons before I got here. You said you'd be here an hour ago."

High heels clicked across the floor as the woman walked in the centre of the room before looking back to face him.

Charlotte's brain whirred with alarm signals, like a siren in her head.

"I'm sorry, you must have *so* many places to be," Deirdre snapped, folding her arms across her chest.

"What do you want?" Sean asked.

"I need four to Sydney by tomorrow morning," Deirdre said, looking over her shoulder and around the room like she was envisioning how to redecorate the place.

"Short notice," Sean grunted.

Deirdre's head flicked back to look at him so fast she must have gotten whiplash. "Well. It was Nick's run, but you, uh, *killed him*, if I'm remembering correctly."

Sean grimaced. "He deserved it. Went after Charlie."

"Yes, I know all about your Nancy Drew sister. You know Simon doesn't like her sniffing around."

Sean glowered. Charlotte felt her stomach stirring uneasily. Nick worked for Simon. Simon wanted her to stop meddling.

"And don't give me that," Deirdre said to Sean. "Your sister wouldn't be butting in where she doesn't belong—and my husband wouldn't have to hire people to try and kill her regularly—if you had just done what you were supposed to last summer."

Sean whipped back around. The most energy and life Charlotte had seen in him in a while. He was angry. He stepped toward Deirdre, who stepped back and drew her hand out of her purse.

She was holding a gun. A small one, but a real gun. Charlotte couldn't help it; she yelped, clapping a hand to her mouth.

The noise distracted Deirdre and Sean recoiled.

"Just don't," Deirdre said, lowering the gun but waving it at him like she was asking a child not to misbehave. "What was that sound?"

"I didn't hear anything," Sean said.

"Is there someone here?" Deirdre began circling the room, poking her head into the doorway of the adjacent room.

"Oh, yeah, I forgot," Sean said, "all my friends are over. We're just about to get the Xbox set up."

"Check," Deirdre commanded, as she stalked to the hall and toward the kitchen.

"There is no one here." Sean shook his head and paced the length of the room. He pulled open a closet door across from Charlotte's and her heart sank. Sean turned and approached her hiding place. *Shit, shit, shit.*

"I would know if someone was—" Sean yanked her door open, still facing the direction that Deirdre had disappeared. He looked back—directly at Charlotte—and she watched him flinch in surprise. "—here," he finished quietly.

Charlotte could hear her heart beating so loudly it felt like it was suspended between her ears. Her hands gripped her own shoulders in an effort to make herself smaller and to keep her breathing under control.

"Did you find anything?" Deirdre called from the other room.

Sean looked at Charlotte warningly. "No," he said, shutting the door.

Deirdre click-clacked her way back to the living room. "You should leave now if you want to get there in time. Nick's car is out back." Deirdre slid the gun back into her purse like it was an iPhone. "And don't get all worked up on me again. Simon might not have had it in him to get rid of that bitch, but I did. And I might have been the one who paid for it, but you're the one who did it." She smiled sweetly. "So I think that makes us partners."

Deirdre strode out of the room without another word. Charlotte listened to the front door slam behind her. She stood in her closet for a few more seconds before she hesitantly pushed open the door. Sean was standing by the wall, his hands on his hips. He took a deep breath and turned to look at her. He looked like their dad when he was thinking.

"Stay right there and I'll tell you everything," he said. "The truth, from start to finish."

# thirty-four

CHARLOTTE BURST OUT OF THE house, ducked under the caution tape, and down the rickety steps. She pulled out her phone. Eight missed calls from Max. She slammed the phone to her ear, stumbling over the muddy ground and trying to find her way back to the elementary school parking lot.

"Charlotte!" Max barked when he picked up.

"Max, we were wrong, I'm at the house—"

"I knew you were there as soon as I woke up. I'm on the path now."

Charlotte tugged her hood around her face. She was disoriented and couldn't find the opening at the trees that led to the path.

"It was Deirdre. We were wrong."

"What?" Max's voice was crackly, like the service was breaking up in the storm.

Charlotte circled back to get her bearings, and she spotted a car around the corner of the house. There must be a back road, and that must be how Deirdre and Simon got there. She squinted at the car. A Buick. A nice one. Deirdre.

"*Shit*," Charlotte breathed.

"Charlie?" Max asked over the phone.

She heard the rustling of trees behind her. That had to be him. She pivoted, but it was Deirdre, her normally perfect hair slicked down the sides of her head.

"I knew I heard someone!" Deirdre shouted over the wind and rain. She raised the gun before Charlotte could move.

The bullet missed her by some miracle, probably lodging into the porch behind her. Without thinking, Charlotte spun, scrambling for the trees closest to the house. She thought she heard Deirdre fire a second time. The sun was starting to set on what had been a gloomy day anyway. The dark would be to her advantage.

Charlotte wound herself through the trees, trying to put as much space between her and the house as possible. She didn't know if Deirdre was following her into the woods. She heard the snapping of branches on her left—Deirdre or an animal or the wind.

Charlotte stopped. Or Max, who was almost to the house, looking for her. She glanced down at her phone; the call she'd forgotten about had disconnected.

"Charlie?"

Through slivers of trees, she could just make out a figure in the clearing by the house. Max.

"Max!" Charlotte cried, but she didn't even know if any sound came out. She weaved back toward him. She must have yelled his name again, because as soon as she cleared the trees he saw her.

"Charlie," Max bellowed, his face breaking with relief. His back was to the house, to Deirdre.

There was another crack that might have been thunder, if Charlotte didn't know Deirdre had a gun. Max rippled like he was surprised, his upper body lurching. She watched his hand fly to his side, pressing against his shirt, a dark pool blooming under his fingers. He looked back at her and it was like all of River John was holding its breath before he crumpled.

It was Deirdre's screaming that finally made Charlotte move.

Charlotte must have choked over his name a hundred times in just a few seconds, half-wailing, and once she reached him in the dark her hands flew over him like she knew what she could do to help. The blood spilled over her hands as she tried to stop the bleeding, but it just leaked between her fingers the same way it did his. He was still on his knees, half upright, hinged at the hip and his hands dug into the mud. He looked at her, his eyes holding a mutual agreement of how much trouble they were in.

Deirdre was at his other side, and for a second Charlotte wondered if she was going to help them. Deirdre looked wild, like a trapped animal—surprised and scared, and something else she couldn't quite recognize. Charlotte was reminded then, as she looked at her, that Deirdre was barely older than them.

"Help," Charlotte managed. "Help him. Do you have your phone?"

She knew it was naive to cling to the tiny shred of hope that Deirdre was going to help them. Deirdre stared back at her, and as the rain splattered down on them Charlotte realized the look on Deirdre's face was anger.

"I thought he was you," Deirdre sputtered. Her mouth was opening and closing, like she couldn't process what she'd accidentally done.

Charlotte could see Deirdre's hands scrambling around in the wet leaves and dirt. Searching. The gun. Charlotte snapped her eyes back to the clearing where they'd been moments earlier. Deirdre must have dropped it, and Charlotte watched her realize the same thing.

She and Max would have a head start, if Deirdre wanted to kill them.

As if someone had blared an air horn, Deirdre leapt backwards and scrambled towards the farmhouse, while Charlotte heaved all her weight against Max.

"We gotta go, Max, c'mon," she begged, pulling his arm across her shoulder and pushing his legs back beneath him. "We have to get back to the road."

"It hurts," Max bit out, the words slipping through gritted teeth. "Charlie."

She was glad he was talking. Good. No one died mid-sentence. Not in real life. "I know, I know, come on."

She had to get them away from Deirdre. Max kept his free hand pressed to his side. She was half-dragging him over the uneven ground and between the trees, trying to keep him upright and make sense of where they were in the rain.

Charlotte could see lights in the distance, filtering through branches. A road. Maybe houses. She could get help. They might actually make it. He would be okay. She thought of her favourite things—Sean laughing and Max playing with her hair and the look Sophie used to give her when she knew exactly what she was thinking. Adrenaline pumped through her, and she was shaking all over as she pushed them both forward.

They broke through the treeline and Charlotte realized where they were. They must have gotten turned around in the confusion and in the dark. The river. The road was dim, the streetlights barely working, and the bridge that ran over the churning water led into town, to the library and the bank. Nowhere to run to in the little time they had.

Max made a quiet sound and she made the decision to hide, to re-evaluate. She clumsily navigated a path for them down the muddy bank beside the bridge. She and Sean, and every other kid in town, used to spend summers here, hurling themselves into the water. She pulled Max down toward shelter from the wind and rain, forcing him to sit so he would be at least half-hidden by the guardrail.

"Okay, it's gonna be fine." Charlotte sniffed, kneeling beside him and touching his face, mostly to see if he still noticed it. "Do you have your phone?"

Max looked like he tried to answer but all that came out was a shrug that used his whole body. "Left it in my car," he finally said.

Hers was long gone; she must have dropped it when she ran back to the house. Damnit. Charlotte tried to think of every movie and detective show she'd ever watched, wracking her brain for everything she knew about getting shot. The bullet had hit him low, just below his ribcage, but more in the centre. What organ was there? His appendix? Liver? Kidney? She had no idea.

She watched Max's face, watched him squirm and twist his hand against his bloody side. Nothing. She knew nothing about getting shot.

"I have to go," she said quickly, "I can find help."

Would he be safe here? It would be a risk, but the alternative was—

"No," Max rasped. He circled a bloody hand around her wrist. "Don't go."

"Max," she cried. Her hand grazed his side, where eighteen years of life was steadily pouring out of him. "I don't know what to do."

He didn't say anything, and his head was rolling like he was falling asleep. But for a split second his eyes settled on her face, and she was reminded of when he'd looked at her through the passenger window of his truck. The night he found her walking on the side of the road, and they saw each other for the first time in a year. She'd come home then, and they were home now.

She moved closer to him. Charlotte spotted movement in the trees, from the direction they'd come. It could only be one person. Deirdre, miraculously still in heels, stumbled toward them. Charlotte counted her options: none. She held Max tighter.

"You done?" Deirdre spat. She had her gun again.

Charlotte just cried and prayed and didn't answer.

"Never rely on anyone," Deirdre said vaguely, and Charlotte didn't know if she was talking to Charlotte or to herself. Deirdre shook her head quickly, like she was trying clear it. "But yourself. That's how you lose. Simon thought she'd be quiet...that the money would be enough...didn't realize she was a liability, you know? I did it for him."

Charlotte closed her eyes.

Another earth-shattering crack, and a few beats of silence.

No pain.

Nothing.

"Charlie." A new voice, or an old one.

Sean, who had gotten them into this, would get them out. In the dark, Charlotte could see his eyes focused on her from behind Deirdre's shoulder. She had never thought that she and Sean looked very much alike, but they did now. They did when they were desperate.

Deirdre had her arm circled around her own shoulders, trying to reach onto her back. Charlotte could see a stain of blood, and it was spreading.

"Shit," Deirdre croaked. Her gun fell to the ground.

Sean took a step to the left, and Charlotte could see what he was holding in his right hand. Where had *he* gotten a gun? Deirdre stumbled sideways to the bank and Sean stepped around her.

"Are you hurt?" Sean asked, dropping to his knees. He looked unsure of what to do with Max, who was still clinging to her, quiet. "I called 911."

"I'm okay. You have to help him," Charlotte said, her hands flying over Max as if to explain. "She shot him."

"I...." Sean trailed off. "I don't know what—"

"Charlie," Max groaned and it almost sounded like a warning.

"Sean, do something," she sobbed, "fix this."

Sean wasn't able to manage a response before time seemed to stop. The faint whirring of sirens in the distance sounded over and replaced Max's breathing. There was the slamming of car doors and the rotation of pale lights against the dark wood beams of the bridge. Shouting grew louder as the police jumped the barrier onto the bridge, a few minutes too late.

"Max, they're here, the police are here," Charlotte said gently, mostly to herself. This couldn't be happening. They didn't get this far to only get this far.

She looked up. Sean was standing now, dangerously close to the railing. The water underneath them folded over itself over and over, dark and cold and unforgiving.

She knew there had to be several armed police officers right behind her.

"Hands on your head!"

Her brother glanced down at her for a second.

"Like dad used to say, right?" he asked, slowly lifting his hands toward the black sky.

But she knew him too well. Sean wasn't the type for quiet surrender. Sean jumped, clearing the guardrail, and disappeared from view.

Hell or high water. She realized her dad had never left them any advice for what happened when you got both.

# thirty-five

one week later
september

CHARLOTTE ROMER MUST HAVE WALKED the path up to Sophie Thompson's house more than a thousand times. Some she couldn't remember and some she could, but Charlotte didn't think there were any that she had shown up to say goodbye. The only time they'd left each other, she hadn't said it—which they both knew too well.

The back window of Sophie's SUV in the driveway was blocked with Rubbermaid containers of what Charlotte guessed to be Sophie's university stuff. Sophie was the one leaving this time. Charlotte crossed the lawn, climbed the porch steps, and knocked on the door. It was the first time in a long while she didn't pray no one answered. The day was warm and bright and the air was soft, an ocean breeze without an edge. It would have been a nice beach day.

"It's open!"

Charlotte cracked the door. Stuff was scattered all over the living room—very Sophie. A mess until the last minute and then completely pulled together in a split second. Sophie emerged from down the hall, a stack of folded laundry on her lap. It was hard to gauge her reaction.

"Hi," Sophie said. "I wondered if you'd come."

Charlotte studied her feet and lined them up with the tile in the entryway. "Well, last time I didn't say goodbye it didn't go over too well."

Sophie smiled.

"How are you?"

"Um." Sophie dropped her laundry into a larger pile on the floor. Charlotte wasn't sure which pile meant what. "I'm fine, I guess. Busy. You?"

Charlotte shifted to sit in one of the dining chairs near Sophie, but stopped herself. Maybe it was easier from here.

"I'm still,"—what, kicking?—"here."

Sophie didn't ask what she meant by it.

"Any news?" Sophie didn't look at her when she asked, instead focusing on flipping through a different pile of clothing.

"No. I was just there. No change." Charlotte said it robotically, automatically, quickly. She didn't like thinking of Max lying in a hospital bed where machines were keeping him alive. She watched Sophie's face contort for half a second.

"I begged my mom to let me stay," Sophie explained. "But she and my dad want me to move in when everyone else does. So it'll feel normal. At least I get the best dorm room on campus," she said with a small smile.

"It's okay." Charlotte waved her hand dismissively. "I'll be here. I'll call you when he wakes up."

If Sophie thought *if* and *when* were interchangeable in this scenario, she didn't say anything.

Charlotte glanced down the hall. "Is your mom home?"

"No, she went to get emergency Advil. Apparently they don't sell it in Halifax."

Charlotte focused on the boxes, full and empty. "You're the one leaving this time. Did you consider sneaking off without saying goodbye?"

Sophie raised an eyebrow. "I'm actually just waiting for nightfall."

Charlotte snorted.

"Too soon?" Sophie asked.

"I think we'll both lose it if we don't start to joke about things."

"Can I ask you about something not so funny?"

Charlotte leaned back against the dining room table in preparation. "Shoot."

"Simon must be, like, going to prison."

"Uh, yeah," Charlotte said, studying the floor. "I'm not sure of the details. They let him visit Max, but otherwise I don't really know."

"And I heard she's awake."

Charlotte raised her eyes from the ground. "Yeah. I think they said she'll be fine, but...she's guilty of a lot, too. They said she'd go into custody as soon as she's released from the hospital."

"Huh." Sophie drummed her fingers along her cheek. "I bet Deirdre'll take her time recovering, then."

There was weight in the air, and she could almost feel Sophie debating whether or not to bring up the one thing they hadn't talked about.

"Any news about...." Sophie trailed off, like she couldn't say Sean's name. "Did they find his—*him*?" Sophie corrected herself quickly.

"No," Charlotte levelled out. Investigators from Halifax had searched the river and area the next day, but the storm, when it finally ended, washed away any evidence and washed away Sean.

"I'm sorry," Sophie said.

Charlotte shook her head. "You don't have to be."

"Do you think there's a chance he's—"

"No," Charlotte blurted almost immediately. "I would have heard from him, if he was. He's gone."

"I *am* sorry," Sophie said gently. "He was your family."

Charlotte cleared her throat. There was only one thing that had been consoling her this week. "I wanted you to tell you: Sean didn't know. He told me the last time I saw him. Deirdre only told him the car he would be hitting was someone Simon needed to get rid of so they wouldn't expose him. That doesn't make it better, but...."

"Do you think Sean wouldn't have gone through with it, if he'd known?"

It was a question Charlotte had asked herself a hundred times this week. She wanted to say no. Wanted to. But she knew if she asked anyone what Sean would do if it came down to protecting her, they would say Sean would do anything, no matter what.

Charlotte let her thoughts pull her back to a week earlier, after the night on the bridge. She remembered seeing Sophie, a distance down the hospital hallway, for the first time since they had pieced everything together. There had been a few seconds of silence: would Sophie be angry? If so, at her? That shouldn't have been Charlotte's first concern, and she knew that.

Charlotte remembered thinking about the last time they had been at that hospital together. She still wasn't sure who had told Sophie the full story the first time. Charlotte assumed a police officer? A regurgitated, facts-only version that didn't even begin to scrape the surface. Charlotte had been sitting down in one of the hard plastic chairs that lined the hallway when Sophie showed up. More silence.

"Did we do this?" Sophie had asked eventually.

Charlotte couldn't answer. They were alone. They sat in silence for a few hours, waiting for news. Sophie's parents showed up. Leo, too. Sophie started crying and Charlotte did, too. When the sun came up, they had looked at each other and Charlotte felt reassured for the first time in a long time that things might be okay.

"Charlie?"

Sophie had said something.

Charlotte snapped herself back to reality. "Sorry."

"I think things will be okay. Max will get better. You'll be all right. Do you remember when we'd used to lay in my bed after school and watch *Friends* and talk about if we thought we'd still be friends when we were thirty?"

Charlotte half smiled. "Yeah. You were always skeptical."

The far side of Sophie's face curled into a smile. "Only about the living in Manhattan part. Not the rest. I've never really doubted it, until now."

Charlotte met Sophie's eyes, a grey-blue that leaned green in certain light. She knew Sophie was right.

"And it's not you, you know," Sophie continued. "Just...both of us. Where we are. Circumstance."

Charlotte nodded. "I know. Sometimes it doesn't matter how much you love someone."

"And it's not Sean," Sophie said, saying Charlotte's brother's name like he was someone Sophie didn't know, "because...I don't even blame him that much. It was Simon and it was Deirdre and it was me." She sighed. "If I hadn't waved it in Simon's face that I knew about everything—if I hadn't thought I could get something out of it—Sean would still be here, and Max would be fine, and I would be...."

Charlotte was quiet. She didn't blame Sophie—it hadn't even crossed her mind. But Charlotte knew if she were in Sophie's position, she'd blame herself too. You were always the hardest on yourself.

"My mom's selling this house," Sophie said finally, looking around. "She's moving to the city, to be close to me. I'm never coming back here. I just—this is life, you know? Not *our* life...my life. I want to go to university and then I want to go to law school. I want to live in New York City and have a rich husband, but one who's not quite as rich as me. Maybe I'll write a book. Maybe I'll open a restaurant. Point is, my life goes beyond this town." She looked pointedly at Charlotte. "Yours should, too, CBR."

When Charlotte stood here two months ago, she hadn't been able to imagine them not working things out. It would be hard, sure, an uneven retreat to what they were so used to being. She never thought that working things out could end with them not together. Not friends or even enemies, but being nothing in between was worst of all.

"I might not see you for a long time." Sophie's voice crackled like water in the heat. "But, when we do, I hope we're grown up and happy, and we bump into each other in a big city far away from here and we can start again."

A promise—a far-off one. The kind of what-will-be-will-be pact that Charlotte usually hated.

"I feel like we're breaking up," Charlotte said. She didn't feel the sadness she thought she would. It felt natural. Simple.

"No, no." Sophie shook her head, her hair catching the sunlight and Charlotte glimpsing her tiny smile. "We're on a break."

Charlotte looked at the clock hanging above the TV. Past eleven. Sophie would have to leave soon if they were going to get to Halifax and get everything moved in by this evening. Frosh Week stuff would probably start tomorrow. Sophie would excel—she was one exemplary drinker and an even better conversationalist. On the mantle beside the TV was the card Charlotte had sent Sophie for her birthday.

"I still can't decide if I regret coming home," Charlotte said.

Sophie raised her eyebrows and studied her for a second. "Well, I'm glad you did. All this wouldn't have happened, but who knows what would have. And now there's nowhere to go but...on."

Charlotte almost smiled. "I'll see you around, Sophie. Soon, I hope."

"Doesn't matter." Sophie propped her chin in her hand and looked at her. "Moon and tide, you know. We don't need to see each other—it's always there."

# epilogue

december
four months later

IN RIVER JOHN, WINTER COMES racing over the hills without much
of a warning. It gets the air first, and then the trees, and then
settles deep into the ground like it's burrowing down to stay. One
day Charlotte is clinging to the last colours of fall, and the next
she's cursing over having to scrape out her car windshield from
under a shell of ice.

But once winter arrives, it lingers everywhere, filling up the
cracks in houses, the nooks behind bathroom doors, and, most
noticeably, a third empty bedroom in a house that once held a
family.

Charlotte checks her watch—her dad's watch, Sean's watch. She
had found it at the house after the night under the bridge. It's just
after eight in the morning.

In a lot of ways, winter is good for her. Winter hides away the
sunshine that blooms freckles on Sophie's cheeks and streaks
lines of copper through her hair. It pulls grey against the sparkling water, which will too often crash against the shore a certain

way and sound like Max's even breathing, face tucked against her pillow. The snow covers the grass that reminds her of summer, reminds her of coming home, and reminds her of Sean. By the time winter blows into River John, things are very different. And the winter helps her forget where and what she used to be.

The snow is just beginning to fall as she steps away from the mailbox, six by six little community lockers outside the Quik Mart, which is, as always, open. She thinks of Leo, behind that counter almost every day all summer. He's isn't there now—he's with his family in Orlando for Christmas. Of everyone who has left River John, he's the one who checks in with her the most—and uses the most emojis. He loves university, loves being in the city. Charlotte misses Leo every day.

The walk home is slower in the snow, but it's not cold. The snow flares up against the sides of houses and trees and filters down from the sky slowly, like it's not even real. This version of winter seems optimistic, and makes her think of Max shaking snow from his coat and of baking shortbread with Sophie and wrestling a Christmas tree upright with Sean.

The snowflakes swirl in front of her face like tiny ballerinas as she lifts her gaze to the sky, where the snow twists down in cylinders and between breaks in the high clouds she can see more trickling down from higher still.

When they were kids, it used to be a Christmas morning tradition to walk to the Quik Mart, where their dad would buy her and Sean each a pack of scratch cards. Their dad would get himself a coffee and a copy of the *Globe* and they'd do the cards over breakfast, before they opened any presents. *If either of you win big*, their dad would say, *we drop everything and we're going straight to Disney. Been packed for a week.* The destination changed year to year, and Charlotte was never sure if he really did have them all packed and ready to go. They never did win.

After their dad died, Charlotte put her foot down against their routine gambling, but she and Sean would still walk to get coffee and a copy of the *Globe*, even though Sean hated buying coffee when he could make it at home, and neither of them read the paper.

When she finally gets home, Charlotte is careful not to let the front door slam. A skinny tree stands in the corner of the living room, illuminated by a tangle of white string lights. It makes the house smell good, and every time Charlotte sees it she's reminded of why she used to love Christmas so much. Out of the corner of her eye, she notices the arrangement on the table—two plates, two mugs.

She sighs and throws the mail onto the coffee table. "You aren't supposed to be up," she scolds, wandering toward the kitchen. She leans her shoulder against the doorway. He glances up from the stove and looks at her with an expression he's given her a thousand times.

"I can't stay in bed forever." He shifts his weight onto his right leg and winces a bit as he turns back to the stove. She knows it still hurts.

Max woke up the day Charlotte went to say goodbye to Sophie, on the afternoon Sophie left for Halifax. Poetic, maybe. Charlotte can't riddle out the metaphor there. Since the night on the bridge, the doctors had never been sure. Said it could go either way. Charlotte took that to mean it was up to Max. And just like he had promised he would, he'd stayed.

"Forgive me?" he asks brightly, in a way that sways her immediately, because she still thinks about how close she came to not hearing it again.

Her eyes give her away and she grumbles some type of agreement. Max skims a hand affectionately over her cheek before he releases her, shuffling the eggs frying on the stove with a flipper.

He will go to Dalhousie in January, when the winter semester starts. He'd missed the fall, recovering from being shot and then recovering from a lot more than that. Maybe he'll run into Sophie there. Charlotte likes to think of them seeing each other in a Halifax coffee shop, that flash of a face from home. They could share the feeling of leaving River John behind, whether that was happy or sad or maybe something in between. Charlotte hopes, if everything comes together, she'll be there, too. Eventually. Maybe not with Sophie, but with Max.

Charlotte goes back into the living room, picking up the mail. Bills, bills, and more bills, as she had guessed.

The last item in the pile is an envelope, thin but more square than the rest. She digs her pinky under the flap and tears it open. It's a card, generic and nondescript, with a golden Christmas tree on the front. She checks the envelope again—no return address. An old photo slides out from between the folds, and she recognizes it as that old one of the three of them from a million years ago. The one that hung on their fridge forever, until—she looks up to check—now, apparently. It would have been easy to get back at the house in all the confusion afterward, when Charlotte was spending all her time at the hospital.

On the back of the photo, *merry christmas* is scrawled in handwriting that looks like hers but messier, and slanted the other way. Their dad had been left-handed; Sean got that from him. The card is blank.

Sometimes you have to die first. Tear everything down and start over, just for the hope that you could build something anew. She watches the snow falling past the window and wonders if it's snowing in Halifax or wherever else the people she loves are.

She can just barely make out the ocean beyond the snow and the grey light and she thinks of the sea hitting back against the shore no matter what, no matter the winds or the storms. Thunder could crack and lighting could flare and the waves could roll and crash and break over and over, but the only thing as certain as a storm coming was the promise that it would end.

Charlotte hears Max move into the living room, hears the sliding of a chair against the floor.

"Anything in the mail?" Max asks.

She tucks the photo and the card back inside the envelope and places it face down on the coffee table, just for now. Friendships and stories and lives ended, but so did everything else.

Charlotte finally looks at Max over her shoulder. "Nothing. Bills and stuff."

High water would settle and still. She hears the kettle sing from the kitchen. They would make it.

# acknowledgements

THERE WERE SO MANY PEOPLE involved in this book/journey and I am so thankful to all of them. Thank you to my family for encouraging me to write, and especially to my mom, who is a writer, too. Mom, thanks for putting up with me and for everything you did to help me along the way.

To the writing group—you guys made this book what it is. I am so thankful for our Thursday nights, and my writing is so much better for your company.

Thank you to Sarah for being my most trusted advisor—you basically deserve an author credit on this one; I feel like we wrote half this book together over text message.

Thank you to Olivia for your constant support, encouragement, and for rooting for this book probably even more than I did. Having you in my corner has meant so much to me.

Thank you to Patrick, Morgan, and Heather for reading this book way back when it was barely anything (and a whole lot worse). You guys are the very best.

And of course, thank you to the whole team at Nimbus Publishing for everything you do for Atlantic Canadian writers. Thank you to Whitney Moran for taking a chance on a first book by a twenty-three-year-old unpublished author. To my editor,

Emily MacKinnon, you are unreal. You made this book so much stronger and I am grateful for all the laughs we had along the way. Thank you to April Hubbard for taking the time to read and review this book before it was officially published. Your invaluable insight as a wheelchair user and disability advocate has meant more to me than anything.

**ALEXANDRA HARRINGTON** is a writer living in Halifax, Nova Scotia, where she has worked as a restaurant manager, fiction editor, and server. She has a degree in journalism from the University of King's College in Halifax. *The Last Time I Saw Her* is her first novel.